'I'm not thinking about your twin or the game or the money, Shannen.'

He cupped her cheek with his hand.

Reflexively Shannen closed her eyes and leaned into his hand, letting the warmth of his palm envelop her. If she intended to tell him to leave, this was the time to do it, a small voice inside her head counselled.

'How can I think of anything else but you?' His voice was a low, seductive growl. He curved his other hand over her hip in a firm, possessive grasp.

Shannen's eyes stayed closed. She didn't want him to go, she achingly admitted to herself.

'Everything is so…unfinished between us, Ty,' she whispered.

'I think it's time we altered that, don't you?' Ty trailed kisses along the curve of her jaw. When his mouth finally, lightly brushed hers, she exhaled with a hushed whimper. It was all the invitation he needed to deepen the kiss. Shannen felt desire and urgency erupt inside her with breathtaking speed…

Do You Take This Enemy?
by Sara Orwig

🔊 ⚭ 🔊

'Mr Brant, get off my ranch.'

Ashley didn't bother to hide the fury in her voice. 'You can get right back in your truck and go.'

'Hear me out, and I think you'll let me stay. Give me ten minutes.'

Her eyes narrowed. Gabe was facing a beautiful woman who was poised and determined. And she was going to be trouble.

'Ten minutes is all you have,' Ashley said. 'You've already wasted the first minute. Now what do you want?'

Crossing his arms over his chest, Gabe took a deep breath. 'I'm building up our ranch, and I want more land and more cattle. I can get the cattle, but I can't get land in this neck of the woods.'

'If you think we would ever sell you one inch of this land, you're very wrong.'

'I know you don't want to sell. I didn't come to buy.'

Gabe realised he could gaze into her blue eyes indefinitely.

'What *do* you want, Mr Brant?'

'I came to offer you a marriage of convenience.'

Available in September 2003 from Silhouette Desire

Searching for Her Prince
by Karen Rose Smith
(Crown and Glory)
and
The Royal Treatment
by Maureen Child
(Crown and Glory)

All in the Game
by Barbara Boswell
and
Do You Take This Enemy?
by Sara Orwig
(Stallion Pass)

The Sheriff & the Amnesiac
by Ryanne Corey
and
Comanche Vow
by Sheri WhiteFeather

All in the Game
BARBARA BOSWELL

Do You Take This Enemy?
SARA ORWIG

SILHOUETTE®
DESIRE™

*Silhouette, Silhouette Desire and Colophon
are registered trademarks of Harlequin Books S.A.,
used under licence.*

*First published in Great Britain 2003
Silhouette Books, Eton House, 18-24 Paradise Road,
Richmond, Surrey TW9 1SR*

The publisher acknowledges the copyright holders of the
individual works as follows:

All in the Game © Barbara Boswell 2002
Do You Take This Enemy? © Sara Orwig 2002

ISBN 0 373 04877 7

51-0903

*Printed and bound in Spain
by Litografía Rosés S.A., Barcelona*

ALL IN THE GAME

by

Barbara Boswell

BARBARA BOSWELL

loves writing about families. 'I guess family has been a big influence on my writing,' she says. 'I particularly enjoy writing about how my characters' family relationships affect them.'

When Barbara isn't writing or reading, she's spending time with her *own* family—her husband, three daughters and three cats, whom she concedes are the true bosses of their home! She has lived in Europe, but now makes her home in Pennsylvania, USA. She collects miniatures and holiday ornaments, tries to avoid exercise and has somehow found the time to write over twenty romances.

To Irene Goodman and Joan Marlow Golan,
whom I'd never vote off the island.

One

"**E**verybody ready to shoot another day in paradise?"

Tynan Hale, chief cameraman for the reality game show *Victorious,* assembled his crew for their daily briefing before heading from their camp across the island to the contestants' camp.

"Paradise? Come on, Ty, no need to sugarcoat things for us. We all know what we're really shooting is the seventh circle of hell," kidded Reggie Ellis, a junior cameraman.

The crew snickered appreciatively. Ty grinned, too, though he guessed he probably shouldn't encourage such irreverence toward the show and its contestants.

The Powers That Be—the network suits, the show's creator, the sponsors, virtually everybody connected with *Victorious*—viewed their project with a seriousness usually reserved for nuclear weapons. No jokes or humor there.

Ty found the job of trailing around contestants on an island, hour after hour, filming their every word and action, to be sometimes interesting and/or irritating and/or dull, but hardly a matter of the gravest concern.

No wonder he would never be a member of The Powers That Be. Not only was his attitude all wrong, his family already had been there, done that.

And failed spectacularly. The family downfall had been such a public sensation that not a day went by without Ty Hale pausing to relish his current anonymity.

He paused to relish it now, while he and the crew loaded their equipment onto the boat to take them to the *Victorious* contestants' camp. Here he was, Ty Hale, chief cameraman, good at his job but essentially a nonentity. It wasn't the standard dream come true, especially in the entertainment industry, but it was certainly his.

And it was the name Hale that made it all possible. Changing his surname seven years ago—unofficially, though not legally, because *that* would've drawn attention to it—was the smartest move he'd ever made.

If anyone in the media were to know that he was actually Tynan Howe, son of the notorious former congressman Addison Howe, a member of the infamous Howe clan…

It wouldn't happen, Ty assured himself, for possibly the millionth time. The contestants were the attraction and sole focus of fan and media attention. Nobody knew the names of the camera and editing crews, nobody was interested enough to learn who they were. Why should they? To the fans of *Victorious,* he was as invisible as his camera.

And he wouldn't have it any other way.

Every morning, as close to dawn as possible, the *Victorious* crew arrived by boat on the side of the island where the contestants dwelled in their makeshift camp. There was a shorter, more direct route through the jungle forest, but it was never used by the crew. That might've tipped off the contestants, who weren't permitted to know how close they really were to the amenities of civilization in the crew's camp. Plus, lugging all the equipment on foot via jungle pathways was impractical.

Ty eyed the contestants' camp, a familiar sight to him after filming it all this time. It would've been considered a squalid setting if it weren't located on a gorgeous island in the Pacific—and if the inhabitants weren't in a voluntary contest to win a million dollars.

Those factors turned "squalid" into something else entirely, Ty had remarked—innocuously enough, he'd thought—to the show's executive producer, Clark Garrett, who had coldly ordered him to "can the laughter."

So much for small talk with the brass, Ty told his crew later. He hadn't even been trying for laughs.

But though he mocked it, Ty did understand the network obsession with *Victorious*. After all, when the number of reality shows had proliferated on all the networks a few years ago, the TV-viewing public had tired of them. Audiences began tuning out in droves and ratings plummeted. Companies would no longer pay the exorbitant rates charged for advertising spots throughout the shows.

No advertising revenue meant no profits, the networks' worst nightmare.

Eventually all the shows were canceled, no new ones were developed and the reality-TV craze was officially pronounced dead.

And then, one of the networks decided to resurrect the concept to schedule in the moribund Saturday-evening time slot. Ty knew that television executives assumed that nobody under ninety was actually at home watching network TV on Saturday night, but airing a test pattern was not acceptable, and even the worst sitcoms or dramas were expensive to produce.

So the new show *Victorious* was born. With a few variations, it was still pretty much a shameless clone of the original reality game show that had started it all. And with no star salaries and writers to pay, even the million-dollar prize money was deemed cheap.

Just right for Saturday-night television.

When Ty landed the job, he'd learned that *Victorious* was to be filmed and edited on location, a deserted island in the Pacific, for sixty-three days. Within the same week of shooting, the footage would be edited into a one-hour episode and then broadcast.

"It's 'truly live television,'" proclaimed executive producer Clark Garrett. "Or fairly close to it." Clark hyped the fact that nobody, not even he, would know who won the million-dollar prize until just before the last show aired.

The sixteen participants, divided into two tribes of eight each and flown to the gorgeous tropical island, were all telegenic in their own way, some more than others. Currently, the cast was trimmed to six, after combining the survivors of the original two tribes into a single one.

Ty and the crew assembled their equipment while waiting for the remaining six contestants to straggle out of the mosquito netting and bamboo posts that served as their sleeping quarters. The contestants called it a tent, though Ty thought it looked more like a shredded parachute that had fallen out of the sky and landed on some random sticks of bamboo. He wisely declined to share this observation with the ever-testy Clark Garrett.

As usual, the crew filmed each contestant emerging from the tent, from earliest risers to sleep-in slackers. The order never varied from day to day. The Cullen twins, Shannen and Lauren, were always the first up and out; Jed was always last. Rico, Cortnee and Konrad, in varying order, appeared sometime after the twins and well before Jed.

The six had all been members of the same tribe initially and formed an unlikely but ultimately unbeatable alliance, always voting as a block and never against each other. They'd survived while everybody else was voted off the island.

With the crew's camp Internet access, satellite dish and daily newspaper drops, Ty knew that the Final Six had become subjects for water-cooler discussions in offices on Monday morning all over the country. Watching *Victorious* before going out on Saturday night had become the newest fad in the coveted eighteen-to-thirty-four demographic age group, and the network execs were giddy with joy.

He was also aware that the contestants had no clue that ratings for the show had skyrocketed, and the media buzz about each participant was in high gear. The six were isolated from any contact with the outside world and unaware of their new fame.

Ty wondered how much the exposure would affect them, how they would change when back in the real world. He'd wager that it would and they would. He'd learned that lesson only too well from the glare of the Howes' media coverage.

He pointed his camera at the twin sisters splashing water on their faces in their morning wake-up ritual at the small freshwater spring, an idyllic spot where the beach blended into the jungle opening. He was well aware that the twins had found the spring themselves while exploring the island in the first few hours after their arrival, making them heroines to their tribe. Fans speculated that the game-winning alliance had begun then and there.

''Who's your favorite contestant?'' asked Heidi, the young production assistant, who stood beside Ty as he was filming.

She asked that question every day or two, more to alleviate boredom than from any real desire to know, Ty suspected. Still, he wasn't about to give out that information, not to anyone.

He said what he always said, remaining scrupulously neutral. ''They all have their good and bad days.''

''Well, my favorites are the twins,'' said Heidi.

"You and a lot of others." Ty remained noncommittal, as usual.

"Identical twins are a novelty on any show," Heidi pointed out, not for the first time. "And according to *TV Guide Online,* these two are *incredibly* identical. Wow, like, how true! We've been filming them for weeks, and nobody here can tell them apart yet. Naturally, the viewers can't, either."

"Naturally," Ty echoed dryly. It was true, though. Twenty-six-year-old Shannen and Lauren Cullen were virtual mirror images.

"What would it be like to look like that? *And* be in duplicate?" Heidi wondered aloud. "They're so pretty," she added matter-of-factly.

What could he do but nod in agreement?

The Cullen twins were pretty. Very pretty. Striking brunettes with thick, shoulder-length dark hair and big blue eyes fringed with black lashes. With their youth, their fair skin and delicate bone structure, they had no need for makeup. An application of sunscreen, a quick swipe of the brush through their hair, and the twins were ready to face the day—and the camera crew and the challenges to stay on the island till the end and win the million-dollar prize.

That only one person could win, and that perhaps one twin might have to vote against the other, was an observation made frequently by the program's host, Bobby Dixon, often referred to as Slick Bobby by the *Victorious* contestants. To his face. But while on camera, Bobby's deep-dimpled smile never faltered.

Ty filmed the next contestant who crawled out from the tent. It was Cortnee, a self-described "aspiring superstar," who was using her stint on *Victorious* as a showcase for her singing and dancing talents. At twenty-two, blond, curvaceous Cortnee was the youngest contestant on the island.

Next came Rico, charismatic, energetic and twenty-five, who also aspired to stardom. His singing and dancing talents equaled Cortnee's. Often the pair entertained their fellow contestants with impromptu duets and dances.

And for those viewers not enthralled by the performances, there was always Shannen's stare of irritable impatience to look forward to. Ty always turned his camera on her during a spontaneous Rico and Cortnee number and lingered on her scowl.

Her exasperated mutter, "On no, not again!" was on its way to becoming as much of a highlight as the act itself.

The "evil twin," "the cranky one," Shannen was dubbed on the Web sites devoted to dissecting each episode and each person on the island. Lauren was the "good twin," the nice, sweet one. Not that anybody could tell the sisters apart physically. But "Spitfire Shannen" distinguished herself from "Lady Lauren" every time she raised one dark brow, enhancing the power of her steely signature glare.

Then there was muscular, handsome Jed, twenty-eight, who boasted a résumé including adventure guide, which he proved by excelling in every physical challenge. He spent most of the time in a minimum of clothing, keeping his sculpted body well oiled with the bottle of emollient he'd chosen to bring as his luxury item.

And finally there was Konrad, the oldest of the group at thirty, a former convicted felon who'd arrived on the island sporting a shaved head with a tattoo of a snarling wolf spanning his back. He had other tattoos, on his chest and both arms, all of vicious animals or birds of prey. Konrad spoke in a growl and had never smiled once during the episodes filmed.

His first remark in the first episode—"I paid my debt to society and I want to go straight. If I win, I will. But if I lose, well, I learned plenty in prison to become a world-class burglar. Good skills to fall back on"—had been widely quoted on the Internet discussion boards, drawing both disapproving and admiring responses.

Ty withheld judgment, wondering if Konrad was actually serious. Was the burglary remark a threat? Or was he merely playing to the audience like Rico and Cortnee, though in a very different way?

Everyone, including the crew, agreed that these contestants shared a definite chemistry. Viewers speculated endlessly about the off-camera goings-on based on the contestants' on-screen behavior.

Had the twins and/or Cortnee slept with Rico and/or Jed? Had Rico and Jed slept together? It was unanimously concluded that no one would get physical with Konrad.

The crew did their own speculating about such matters, Ty sometimes joining in, striving for an air of nonchalance about the whole thing. His name was enough of a secret to keep around here; there was certainly no need to introduce his other secret, which would be even more significant to the *Victorious* crew.

However, there was one person right here on the island who knew both his secrets.

One word while the cameras rolled—while *he* made them roll!—and the horrible media circus that had propelled the Howes into the worst kind of fame could start all over again.

And one word about his previous relationship with Shannen Cullen could probably get him fired.

But Shannen didn't give him away, and Ty began to think that perhaps she didn't remember him, after all. It was a definite blow, particularly since he'd admitted to himself long ago that he would never forget her. Seeing her again after long years apart only affirmed her visceral imprint on him.

It would be a fitting irony that she'd forgotten him, a Howe's just desserts, Ty decided wryly. So he came to accept that when Shannen Cullen glared at him, raising that dark eyebrow of hers as he pointed the camera at her, it was nothing personal. Shannen glared at everybody behind the cameras. He wouldn't delude himself that she was singling out him for any special animosity.

But he couldn't help singling *her* out. He couldn't keep his eyes off her—nor could he keep his camera away from her for long. Luckily, she had a twin sister, which seemed to make the film time equal, since nobody else could tell the twins apart.

Tynan had no trouble differentiating Shannen from Lauren. He knew "his" twin instantly, at first glance every time, whether the sisters were alone or together. There was no way to explain how, he just *knew*.

Despite his determination to be different from the other members of his family, it seemed that he was as foolish and dysfunctional as any other Howe, Ty mocked himself. How like a Howe to develop an unhealthy fascination with the very person who could wreck the normal, productive life he'd worked so hard to create.

But his unhealthy fascination with Shannen was not new. Worse, it was as urgent and powerful as it had been nine years ago. More so because now she had become the woman he'd thought she was, back when she had been just a girl.

He'd wanted her then, but he wanted her more now.

And he couldn't have her. Not then and not now.

Being chief cameraman had its perks, one of them being his own private tent in the camp. It was not as large as Bobby Dixon's or Clark Garrett's abodes, of course, but definitely more spacious than the tents that the assistant camera crew had to share. The editing team were likewise housed according to their positions, while the production assistants shared the most cramped quarters, befitting their slavelike status.

The crew had knocked off filming early at eight o'clock tonight, on Clark's orders. By the time Ty returned to his tent from the dinner provided by the catering service, it was almost dark.

The sunsets in the region were nothing less than spectacular, and during his first days on the island, Ty had been dazzled as he filmed them. Now he scarcely glanced at the colorful sky as he called good-night to Reggie and the others.

He'd passed on the invitation to play cards, to monitor the Internet, to watch TV from the satellite dish and all other group activities. He wanted to get to bed early; he was tired and hadn't been sleeping well.

Too many nights in a row he'd awakened from particularly vivid dreams of Shannen Cullen, dreams that left him frustrated when, technically, he should've been replete. It was humiliating to be betrayed by his own body this way. He was thirty-four, not seventeen!

Spending hour after hour filming Shannen, watching her every move yet being unable to approach her, was taking its toll on him, Ty decided grimly. He was on his way to becoming unhinged....

He spied the note on his pillow as soon as he entered his tent. It was written on stationery with the network logo imprinted on the top, and he reached for it, more than a little bemused.

Nobody left notes for others in their tents; that was just too summer camp. Which undoubtedly explained its origins. It had to be one of the crew's practical jokes, probably hatched by the production assistants, Ty surmised. Despite being run ragged by everyone involved with the production, those kids never seemed to run out of energy. And they were into playing pranks, though until now, the gags were directed at one another. Now it seemed that they'd moved up to the senior ranks, Ty thought wryly.

His eyes widened at the sight of the unmistakably feminine handwriting. Then he read the note....

It was a joke—it had to be!

He thought of his brief conversation with Heidi today about the Cullen twins. Was that the beginning of the setup? How else to explain this note, signed "Shannen," ordering him to meet her tonight at a very specific location?

Ty couldn't even summon a laugh at the jest. To him, it wasn't funny—it was appalling! Had he given himself away? He thought he'd remained impeccably indifferent to Shannen Cullen while filming her, but had some of the staffers seen through him?

He wouldn't go, of course. The best way to react to such a practical joke was to blow it off.

But what if this note actually *was* from Shannen?

The renegade thought leaped into his head and took hold. He tried to dislodge it with logic. How would Shannen get hold of network stationery, for starters?

Perversely, he was able to answer what should have been an unanswerable question. If she'd found her way to the crew's camp—to his tent!—swiping a piece of official stationery would be a piece of cake.

Should he go to the trysting place tonight?

Of course he shouldn't!

Ty spent the next two hours debating what to do and finally decided that he *would* go. And he decided, as well, that when he saw one of the PAs—Heidi or Debbie or Adam or Kevin—he would laugh heartily and then accuse whomever, girl or guy, of having a fervid crush on Jed. Or Rico or Cortnee. Or even Konrad. Then he would write the PA in question notes every night, allegedly from the "crush." He'd let Reggie and the rest of the camera crew in on the joke.

He would make the lives of those bratty production assistants a living hell for daring to notice his attraction—okay, maybe it was closer to an obsession!—with Shannen Cullen.

"So you actually showed up."

It sounded more like an accusation than an observation.

Shannen was glowering at him. The brilliance of the full moon illuminated her face as clearly as studio lighting. The air was thick with the exotic scents of tropical plants and the piercing calls of nocturnal birds.

Ty wondered if his eyes were popping out of his skull. Was it possible for his heartbeat to skyrocket this high and still sustain life?

But Shannen was the epitome of cool, just as she was during the days of filming. No eyes popping or thundering pulses for *her* at the sight of *him,* so Ty carefully maintained an imperturbable facade of his own.

He shrugged. "I have to admit I was surprised to find your note requesting me to meet you here," he replied, his voice equally casual. "I'm curious. How did you manage to—"

"I managed to, okay?" Her blue eyes flashed.

"Okay." He waited for her to tell him the reason why she'd demanded this meeting.

And though he had tactfully rephrased it as a "request," it was not. It had been a demand, and they both knew it. The demanding tenor of the note was one of the main reasons he'd decided it had to be a practical joke. Shannen Cullen wouldn't order him to meet her.

And yet it appeared that she'd done exactly that, because here she was.

Here they both were.

Shannen said nothing.

Silence stretched between them. It occurred to Ty that she was waiting for him to speak first. And that no matter how long the silence lasted, she was prepared to outwait him.

Ty heaved a sigh. "You're strategizing, aren't you? Can you stop playing the infernal game for just a few minutes and—"

"Play the game or be played. Isn't that how it goes?"

she challenged, her tone mocking. "Well, since you see me as a master strategist, can you guess what my alleged strategy is?"

"Time to check your ego, honey. I didn't say I saw you as a master strategist."

She shot him a fierce look of contempt, a look that would've sent a more cautious man running. But Ty had never been particularly cautious, so he stayed where he was.

"Definitely not a master," he reiterated. He was pleased he'd gotten under her skin, at least a little. "Your ploy is right out of Strategy 101, the course for beginners. You believe you'll gain an advantage if I have to ask why you *demanded* this meeting."

This time he not only used the correct word, he emphasized it. Just a bit of his own simple strategy. Plus, he was certain it would annoy her.

It did. "Don't call me honey! And it was a request, not a demand. A polite request," she added loftily.

"Not going to concede an inch, hmm?" He laughed, a peculiar lightheartedness flooding him. "Just like old times."

"Are you trying to be ironic?" She fairly spat the words at him. "If you are, it's not working. Oh, just forget it! Forget that I wrote that stupid note and—"

"Suppose I willingly and knowingly succumb to your masterful strategy instead. Why did you *politely request* to meet me here tonight?"

Shannen took a deep breath and averted her eyes. "I…I want you to stop following me around," she said sternly.

It was a jaw-dropping moment that left him totally nonplussed. "You're joking," he murmured uncertainly, for neither her tone nor her expression held even the hint of a joke. "Or maybe *you're* trying to be ironic? Given the circumstances of—"

"You know exactly what I mean," she snapped.

"I certainly don't. And let's not forget that *you* demanded to see *me* tonight. It'll be interesting to hear you rationalize how I followed you when you set up this meeting yourself."

Her eyes narrowed into slits. She was furious.

He grinned, unable to resist baiting her further. "Would it be gameworthy of me to point out that I have a job to do, and you have a role, so to speak, which makes—"

"This goes beyond any job or any role, and you know it," she said. "I've seen the way you watch me. You're always staring at me, always filming me. Don't bother to deny it."

"Ah, in addition to your many other charms, you're also paranoid...little girl," he added pointedly.

She picked up his point instantly. "I am not a little girl, you...you—"

"Condescending, self-righteous jerk?" he suggested. "Oh yes, I remember that, Shannen. I remember everything. But I wasn't sure that you did, not until I got your note tonight."

He didn't bother to add how he'd decided the note was bogus. He was too elated that it was real.

"You thought I didn't remember you?" For a moment Shannen looked genuinely surprised, but she quickly resumed hostilities. "Well, I do—and it's obvious that the description still fits you. You're still condescending, you're still self-righteous and you're still a jerk!"

"How would you know? This is the first time we've spoken since—"

"A tiger never changes its stripes," she said. "Or is it a leopard who doesn't change its spots? Oh, who cares! I know I can—"

She abruptly stopped speaking when he advanced toward her.

"You can what?" He stood directly in front of her, towering over her.

The aroma of saltwater and sunscreen, mixed with an alluring scent all her own, filled his nostrils. "You can what?" he repeated huskily.

She swallowed. "I...I forget."

"How about this, then? You can prove you're not a little girl anymore?"

Her eyes widened as he slowly lowered his head toward her. His hands were at his sides and he made no attempt to hold her in place or restrain her in any way.

She could easily have stepped aside or pushed him away; she could've ordered him to go back from her or made a threat that would have sent him on his way.

But she did none of those things. Slowly Shannen raised her arms to encircle his neck. Their gazes locked and held for a long moment. He watched her eyelids flutter shut as he touched his mouth to hers.

What began as a light, tentative caress of his lips against hers quickly turned into something else entirely. There was nothing light or tentative about the hot, hungry coupling of their mouths.

Ty murmured something unintelligible as her lips parted to welcome his tongue inside.

Shannen pressed closer, twisting restlessly against him, opening her mouth wider in sensual invitation. He accepted, deepening the kiss, thrusting his knee between her thighs and molding her to him, his hands smoothing over her, possessively, eagerly learning every curve.

The kiss went on and on, desire building, passion burning. Ty slowly lowered her to the ground, pulling her on top of him. His fingers nimbly opened the clasp of her halter top, freeing her breasts. His hand cupped one soft milky-white breast, and he groaned with pleasure.

A split second later, he was lying on the sand alone. Shannen had pulled away from him and jumped to her feet with disorienting speed.

"No!" she exclaimed, fumbling to close the clasp he had

so effortlessly undone. Her dexterity didn't equal his and she gave up, holding the halter together with one hand.

Ty rose slowly, almost painfully, to his feet. "Let me help you with that."

She backed away from him as if he were radioactive. "Go away! I...I told you to keep away from me."

"Yes, you did." His lips twisted into a wry smile. "But your message was—hmm, how can I put this tactfully?—mixed."

She flushed scarlet, the bright moonlight highlighting her color. "You're a snake!"

"I've been called worse." He ran his hand through his dark hair. "Anything else?"

"I don't know what you're doing here or who you're pretending to be or why, but I don't trust you!"

"Thanks." Ty chuckled softly. "And let me return the compliment. I don't trust you, either."

Shannen turned and stomped away from him, still clutching her top with one hand, using her other hand to smack away the hanging vines and lush foliage that dared get in her way.

Ty stood watching until she disappeared from view.

Two

"Do you think we'll get mail-in-the-tree today? Or a visit from Slick Bobby with some kind of instructions?" Cortnee asked during her rigorous aerobic workout, which she performed daily on the beach. Today she wore her tiniest bikini, the neon-pink one. "We haven't had a victory contest or a food contest this week."

Konrad, Rico and Jed gathered on the beach in various positions of repose, watching Cortnee. The twins were there, too, Lauren braiding her hair into a thick plait, Shannen tying strings to three makeshift bamboo fishing poles.

"I checked the tree for mail earlier and there wasn't anything," Shannen reported. "Why don't one of you guys go check it now?"

"Later," said Jed.

"And we're almost out of bait," continued Shannen. "Somebody should go to that place farther down the beach and see if more clams have washed up. That's the best bait on the island."

"Later," murmured Rico.

"We can check for tree mail and then swing down for clams after we fish, Shannen," Lauren suggested.

"I just thought maybe someone else would like a chance to do the daily errands around here," murmured Shannen, adding tersely, "for a change."

"Remember how those idiots in the other tribe ate some bad raw clams instead of cutting them up for bait?" Konrad sniggered. "Man, were they sick! When they tried to hang on to the rope in that tug-of-war between the tribes, they fell flat on their faces." Clearly, it was a fond memory for him.

"Our tribe won every single contest, forcing the other tribe to keep voting off their own till they were all gone," observed Jed. He began idly doodling in the sand with a stick.

"We won all the contests, so our tribe was able to stay intact a long time, and it's mainly thanks to you, Jed," Lauren said, her voice filled with admiration.

Jed nodded his head. "True."

"Partially true," corrected Shannen. "You forgot to add that you couldn't have done it alone, Jed. I didn't hear you say that all of us did our part to win, either. Did you forget that we're a team?"

"Jed isn't a team player—he doesn't want to share credit for anything," Cortnee called between deep breaths. "He really believes he does *everything* better than anybody else."

Jed opened his mouth to speak, but Rico beat him to it by sighing heavily, gaining the attention of the cameramen. "I just want to say that I don't miss the other tribe because I barely knew them, but I do miss Keri and Lucy from our tribe." Rico sighed again. "I really bonded with them. They were probably some of the best friends I ever had in my life."

"You voted them off the island without blinking an eye, Rico," Shannen pointed out.

"Untrue!" protested Rico. "Maybe it looked that way because I hid my pain so well, but I've been torturing myself for getting involved in this unholy alliance with you guys. You made me turn against my friends!"

His face a portrait of agony, Rico stared soulfully into the camera that had been turned on him the moment he began to speak. He pouted when the camera abruptly shifted to Shannen, who was now baiting the hooks, frowning in concentration.

"Cut to the evil twin. Nice move, Ty," junior cameraman Reggie Ellis whispered to Ty, who was filming Shannen. "Makes for good TV. She looks distinctly unmoved by Rico's brooding torment. Like she's remembering how Rico was the first to suggest that they 'vote off those schemers Keri and Lucy because they're allied against us.' The viewers will remember, that's for sure."

"Rico wants to show the talent agents who'll be watching that he has range," Ty said dryly. "That he's not just a song-and-dance man."

"Yeah, he's good at brooding and backstabbing," Reggie observed. "The kid does have that slightly sleazy manner about him, too. A handy survival trait in showbiz."

"I can see Rico winning an Oscar someday. Unless he decides to run for political office instead," murmured Ty. "He'd do well in that arena, too."

Having completed her task of baiting the hooks, Shannen looked up and saw Ty filming her. She shot him a withering glare before looking away.

"Looks like she'd enjoy baiting those hooks with pieces of you, Ty." Reggie guffawed. "Y'know, for somebody who volunteered to be on this show, she sure hates having the camera on her. I think I'm starting to be able to tell which twin is which, just from that. Lauren doesn't pay any attention to the camera, but Shannen looks as if she'd like to shove it down your throat.''

"You noticed that, too?'' Ty was casual.

Reggie nodded. "We're not the only ones to wonder. I logged onto the Internet last night, and there's a debate going on as to why the twins auditioned to be on this show in the first place. Especially since Shannen looks eternally ticked off because she's here.''

"Remember their interview tapes? Both twins said they did it as a lark,'' said Ty.

He didn't add that he wondered himself why the Cullen twins had auditioned for the show. The "for a lark" reason didn't ring true to him. Nine years ago Shannen's behavior had been quite purposeful. Filming her every day here on the island didn't contradict his impression that she was a person who rarely made an unplanned move.

But there had been nothing calculated about that hot kiss they'd shared last night. It had been as impetuous as it was passionate. Ty tried to tamp down his nascent arousal.

"Maybe Lauren did it as a lark, but Shannen doesn't strike me as the lark type.'' Reggie chuckled. "If we're talking birds, she's more of a shrike. You know, the one that impales its prey on a stake. Oh, Ty, quick, pan over to Cortnee. She has her back to us and is touching her toes. Every red-blooded male in the audience is gonna love that. And she's wearing that pink thong bikini that almost caused a meltdown on the Internet the first time she put it on.''

"You can have the pleasure of filming her, Reg. I know you're one of Cortnee's top fans. I'll keep my camera on the twins and Konrad. Looks like they're going fishing.''

Each carrying a primitive bamboo fishing pole, Shannen, Lauren and Konrad walked briskly into the ocean. Ty followed close behind, camera whirling.

"Do you think we should go out in the rowboat?'' asked Lauren as the surf broke around their knees. "We might have better luck catching fish in deeper water.''

"Yeah, but then we'd have the fun of swimming with the sharks when that leaky old tub sinks," growled Konrad. "Remember when those two idiots in the other tribe took the boat out and it went down like a stone with them in it? Had that big dramatic rescue 'cause they couldn't swim. You know Slick Bobby and Clark Garrett woulda rather seen them drown. And now they claim the boat's fixed, but I don't buy it. They're still hoping to get lucky with a fatal accident."

"That's entertainment for those two human piranhas," Shannen pointed out.

"Never mind the boat, then, let's try our luck right here," suggested Lauren, casting her pole. "Oh, don't look now, but we're on camera again. I was sure the whole crew would stay on the beach filming Cortnee. Doesn't she do her jumping jacks after touching her toes? None of the guys want to miss that."

"Gets old when you see the same stuff day after day." Konrad shrugged. "Me, I'd rather hang out with you two, even though I don't know which the hell is which."

"Konrad, how gallant!" Lauren smiled sweetly.

Shannen turned her head to see Ty standing less than a foot behind them. She swung her fishing line at him, clipping him with the clam bait.

"Oops." She snickered. "So sorry."

"You're only sorry that your aim was off." Ty turned off the camera. "You meant to smack me in the face with the clam guts. But you missed, Shannen," he added, saying her name with alacrity.

"You're sure I'm Shannen?" She looked ready to whip the pole at him again. "How do you know I'm not Lauren?"

"Could be, you know," Lauren chimed in. "We're dressed exactly alike. Denim cutoffs, red bandanna triangle tops. The only difference is that one of us has a braid and the other has a ponytail. Can you be sure who styled her hair which way?''

''You two play that twin stuff for all it's worth,'' said Konrad, with respect. ''No wonder. Two people looking exactly the same...talk about messing with minds! If I had a twin in the lineup with me, nobody could ID me. Because it might be my twin, y'know? I could've beat the rap every time.''

''We'll keep that in mind if we decide to go in for a life of crime, Konrad,'' said Shannen.

''I don't have a problem telling them apart.'' Ty moved closer to Shannen. ''This is Shannen. Unquestionably.''

When she took a step backward, he advanced, knowing she would force herself not to retreat again. She would view that as a tactical error.

He was right. She stayed put.

''Remember the rules? The crew isn't supposed to interact with us in any way.'' Shannen's fingers clenched the pole tightly, and she stayed as still as she could, despite the unsteadying waves rising and breaking around her. ''You're supposed to be invisible. So shut up and film, Tynan.''

''Who's to know I'm not? From on shore, it looks like I'm filming the three of you out here.''

''How do you know his name, Shan?'' Lauren was puzzled. ''We weren't introduced to any of the crew. Clark and Bobby said to think of them as part of the camera equipment and forget they're human.''

''Which isn't hard to do, in his case,'' Shannen sneered.

''You dodged the question, babe.'' Konrad studied her curiously. ''How come you know his name?''

''Maybe she made a good guess. Am I right, Shannen?'' Ty's bland tone contrasted sharply to his baiting smile.

''As a matter of fact, you are. I read a book about names, and Tynan means 'condescending, self-righteous jerk,' so I immediately guessed he must be a Tynan.'' Shannen met and held his gaze. "An obvious fit."

"If Cortnee was out here, she'd say, 'What did the book say that Cortnee means?'" Konrad laughed.

It was a startling moment. Shannen recovered first.

"The first time Konrad laughs, and you aren't filming, Tynan," she scolded. "You're not doing your job. I ought to tell Slick Bobby next time he oozes by so he can pass it on to Clark. Then you'll get fired."

"But you won't tell, will you, Shannen?" Ty leaned down to wash off the bits of clam that clung to his bare shoulder. Like the other cameramen, he rarely wore a shirt during the long days of filming in the sun. He was bronzed and muscular.

Shannen quickly looked away from him, staring instead into the sparkling clear water.

"How do you know my sister won't tell on you?" demanded Lauren, her eyes darting from Shannen to Ty and back again.

"Because I read the same name book that she did, and Shannen means 'not a snitch,'" said Ty.

"A bitch but not a snitch," amended Konrad.

Lauren stamped her foot. "My sister is not a bitch! You should apologize to Shannen right now, Konrad."

"He doesn't have to, I've been called worse names than that." Shannen stole a glance at Ty. When she found him staring at her, she looked away again. "It doesn't bother me."

"I'm sure whoever called you…worse names, regrets doing so, Shannen," Tynan said quietly.

"I'm sure I don't care, Tynan," she retorted. "Sticks and stones and all that."

"Y'know, that's just crap," Konrad said vehemently. "Some of the names I got called as a kid made me a helluva lot madder than getting whacked with any stick. And in the joint, you better watch your mouth—you get what

I'm saying? You diss somebody there and you're dead meat. It's worse than punching him out.''

"That's an interesting point." Ty raised his camera. "Would you say that again when I turn the camera back on?"

"Sure." Konrad looked pleased. "Uh, should she say the bit about sticks and stones before I say it?"

"Yeah, that's good." Ty nodded. "Shannen?"

"I'm not saying anything," Shannen said crossly. "You aren't directing a movie, and we're not supposed to rehearse our lines. Get out of here, Tynan. Go back and film Cortnee."

"Hey, I made an interesting point," argued Konrad. "It should be on TV."

"I'll give you a lead-in, Konrad," Lauren volunteered. "Okay, Tynan, 'Camera, action, take one,' or however that drill goes." She tilted her head, her expression suddenly wistful. "Shannen, remember how the kids at school used to call us freaky clones? And Gramma told us to say, 'Sticks and stones may break our bones but names will never hurt us.'"

"Who called you freaky clones?" demanded Konrad. "Just tell me who and when I get back *I'll* break every bone in *their*—"

"Nobody ever called us that." Shannen heaved an exasperated sigh. "It was just Lauren's cue for you to say your—oh, turn off that camera, Ty. This is ridiculous."

Ty turned off the camera. "Makes you really respect directors, doesn't it? Imagine doing take after take after take of the same botched scene."

"Acting is harder than I thought," admitted Konrad. "Care to try it over again?"

"No!" Tynan and the twins chorused.

The four of them looked at each other and laughed. They immediately lapsed into silence, nonplussed by the unexpected moment of camaraderie.

"I got a fish!" Lauren suddenly shrieked, hanging on to her bamboo pole, which was waving and twitching. "I bet it's big, it's really strong! Help!"

Tynan turned on his camera to film Lauren clutching her fishing pole as it swayed precariously, back and forth and around. Konrad reached over and took hold of the string, swinging it out of the water. The fish on the primitively fashioned hook went flying into the air.

"Get it! Get it!" cried Lauren.

Konrad did, catching the impressive-size fish with his bare hands.

"That was so quick!" marveled Shannen. "Like watching Gramma's cat reach up and nab the bird who'd made the fatal mistake of flying onto the porch while he was napping there."

"Except we can eat the fish," said Lauren. "That bird incident—yuck, it was so gross!"

Ty's lips quirked. He caught Shannen's eye and found her looking at him. Both immediately turned their attention back to Konrad and the fish.

"I think I'll turn off the camera until that fish is officially pronounced dead," said Ty.

"Feeling queasy, Ty?" taunted Shannen. "You didn't seem to have any qualms filming us drinking snake blood in that over-the-top victory contest a couple weeks ago."

"The snake blood scene was sexy in a vampire-ish sort of way, to quote a TV critic," said Ty. "But nobody is going to find strangling a fish sexy in any sort of way."

"That's disgusting!" scolded Shannen.

Ty wondered if she was referring to him, snake blood or fish strangulation.

"The fish is dead," announced Konrad.

Ty resumed filming.

"This fish would make a decent-size meal for two people, maybe even three, but we'll only have a few mouthfuls each if we split it six ways," said Konrad. "So let's not."

"It's only fair to share it with everybody," insisted Lauren.

"We could outvote her." Konrad turned to Shannen. "Two against one not to share."

"My stomach wants to go along with you, but my better instincts tell me that Lauren is right." Shannen sighed.

"Better instincts? More like idiotic instincts," Konrad muttered, then added a few unintelligible growls as they trooped back to shore.

Cortnee was so delighted to see the fish, she squealed with joy and hugged Konrad and the twins in turn.

Rico and Jed tried to look happy but weren't altogether convincing.

"Their smiles are so fake, I'm surprised their faces haven't cracked," observed Shannen to no one in particular. "They want to be the heroes, but you can't catch anything, lounging around on the beach all day."

"Told you it was stupid to share," Konrad needled her.

Ty noticed that Reggie had moved closer to film the group, and he turned off his own camera. "Shannen." His voice was lower than a whisper, but Shannen heard.

"Don't talk to me," she warned, her voice even quieter than his.

It was a warning Ty didn't heed. "Meet me tonight. Same time and place as last night."

"No!" She looked alarmed. "I can't! I...I—" She was truly rattled.

"Be there," said Ty, and moved away from her.

"Shannen, what's wrong?" Lauren called out to her.

Shannen looked up to see Reggie, a few feet away, filming her.

Lauren was staring at her, confused. "You look—you don't look happy, Shan."

"Maybe she's jealous because she wasn't the one to catch the fish," mocked Jed.

"Maybe I'm not happy because I expect you'll try to

grab yourself some glory and insist on cooking the fish yourself,'' Shannen countered. ''Thereby rendering it inedible.''

Jed took instant umbrage. ''I'm a damn good cook. I even contributed a recipe that I invented myself to the *Living off the Land* cookbook.''

''What was it, how to barbecue roadkill?'' Konrad snickered. ''Step one, you pick it off the side of the road. Step two—''

''It was how to make elk stew,'' Jed inserted disdainfully. ''And—''

''Whatever,'' snapped Cortnee. ''Just don't get anywhere near this fish!''

''He's only had a few cooking…mishaps here on the island.'' Lauren tried to make peace.

''You mean disasters, not mishaps,'' corrected Rico.

''I've never cooked a bad meal,'' Jed said huffily. ''You're all just a bunch of picky eaters.''

''Jed's already proved that he doesn't know the difference between cooking something or cremating it,'' Shannen said flatly. ''I vote that he *not* cook the fish.''

''I'm with you, twin,'' said Rico.

''Me, too,'' said Konrad.

''You've got my vote,'' said Cortnee.

''Are we seeing cracks in what has previously been a staunch and solid alliance?'' Bobby Dixon asked in his smiling, smooth soliloquy, filmed a mile down the beach.

A light breeze ruffled his thick hair and he smoothed it down with his hand, dimpling deeply.

''Tonight, after the victory contest, these six survivors, who have stuck together from the very beginning, will have to vote out one of their own.'' His voice took on a note of urgency and suspense. ''What shifts of allegiance will occur to form new alliances as we count down to five and then to the Final Four? Who has what it takes to be *Victorious?*''

Later the six contestants gathered around the fire, eating the fish cooked by the twins.

''That was great,'' Rico said expansively, patting his washboard stomach. ''If the food is as good at that diner your family owns, I'm heading there as soon as we're off this island.''

''Shannen and I have been short-order cooks since we were in junior high,'' said Lauren. ''Of course, it's much easier at home, because we don't have to catch the food ourselves.''

''Well, no matter what you hear, the food in prison isn't bad,'' Konrad interjected. ''And you get more of it than one lousy fish split six ways.''

''I'm still hungry,'' wailed Cortnee. ''Having only a couple bites of fish and a blob of wretched rice is like being on a starvation diet.''

''I cooked the rice and it wasn't wretched, it was fine,'' snarled Jed.

''It really wasn't wretched at all,'' Lauren hastily agreed.

''Uh-oh, look what's headed our way.'' Shannen was the first to spy Bobby Dixon strolling down the beach toward them, wearing his immaculately pressed khaki slacks and matching safari shirt.

''He looks so neat and clean all the time, I can't stand it.'' Cortnee groaned. ''It's been how long since we had a hot shower? And washing your hair in the ocean is really bad. There's a reason why saltwater shampoo was never invented.''

''Wouldn't it be thrilling to see Slick Bobby look less...dapper?'' Shannen flashed a naughty smile. ''It might even take my mind off being hungry out here all the time.''

''Yeah, but it'll never happen.'' Rico heaved a disgruntled sigh. "We'll stay hungry as long as we're on the island, and Bobby will stay clean. You just know he has his clothes cleaned and pressed every day over in the crew's camp. And somehow he never sweats, no matter how hot it is."

"Makes you wonder if the guy's human," murmured Shannen. "I've had my doubts. Those dimples of his look like computer animation."

"I bet Slick B would sweat if we poured fish guts over him," said Konrad, staring moodily into the bean can holding the fish remains. They'd saved the can from their first days on the island, to use as a container.

"Anybody want to try it and see?" Rico asked eagerly. "Cortnee? Twins?"

Shannen laughed. "You're evil, Rico."

"Hello, all." Bobby joined them, dimpling at the camera. "No mail-in-the-tree today. I brought the contest requirements to you in person."

"Watch out, Bobby. They've hatched this juvenile plan to drench you in fish guts," Jed called out.

Konrad scowled. "Anybody know what that stoolie is talking about?"

The others shrugged and shook their heads.

"I do know that Jed is a rat." Cortnee sniffed. "And if he didn't win every contest and get himself immunity, I'd gladly vote him off."

"You can dream, but it's never going to happen, babycakes." Jed positioned himself so his sculpted body had full camera advantage. "And keep in mind that we're no longer a team anymore. Now it's everyone for himself—or herself, as the case may be."

"Jed is right," agreed Bobby. "It's everyone for him- or herself, and the contest today is a rowboat race. All six of you will take turns rowing out to the crew's boat and back."

He pointed to the large boat anchored about a hundred

yards out in the sea. "The one with the fastest time, of course, wins immunity in the council vote tonight."

"Have I ever mentioned that I crewed in college?" Jed began his warmup exercises. "And kayaked down the Colorado River when the white water was at its highest and fastest?"

"Kayaks are for sissies," scoffed Shannen. "Lauren and I rode the white water at its highest and fastest using rubber duck floatees."

Shannen glanced up to see Tynan and Reggie chuckling behind their cameras. She pretended not to notice them, turning her attention to Rico and Cortnee, who were also laughing at her joke. But when she looked over at her sister, Lauren wasn't even smiling.

"Are you okay, Lauren?" asked Shannen, concerned. Lauren looked so…cross? Shannen almost did a double take. Was Lauren angry about something? But what?

"Sure." Lauren smiled slightly, shrugging. "I'm fine, Shannen."

"Hey, Jed, my man, since you're so sure you're going to win, would you mind letting us five losers go before you?" Konrad asked with unusual servility. "You know, to build up the suspense and all?"

"I don't mind going last," said Jed. "Although I can't guarantee suspense, because the outcome will never be in doubt. I'm going to win."

"Yeah?" With mercurial speed, Konrad's expression turned to disgust, and he suddenly picked up the can of fish guts and tossed it at Bobby.

But Bobby was on the alert, thanks to Jed, and deftly jumped aside. "That was uncalled for, Konrad!" Bobby was peeved. His clothes, however, remained pristine, as if he'd just picked them up from the dry cleaner's. "You could be disciplined for—"

"Disciplined for a little food-fight fun?" Shannen cut in.

"Where's your sense of humor, Slick B? Anyway, this isn't high school, and you can't 'discipline' anybody."

The crew snickered. Bobby Dixon's off-camera behavior as a prima donna had earned him no friends among them.

"That chick has a righteous attitude," said Heidi. "She doesn't put up with anything from anybody."

"She never has," murmured Ty wryly. "Since she arrived on the island," he was quick to add.

Ty and two others remained on the beach filming, while cameramen Reggie and Paul were stationed on the crew boat, to film the contestants racing to it. Bobby Dixon was also on the boat with a large stopwatch to record the times. The production assistants were scattered in both locations.

Cortnee went first and threw herself down on the sand on her return. "I'm so tired I could faint. That awful rowing took more energy than playing the lead in my senior-class musical." She wiped away tears with the back of her hand.

Rico went next, then Lauren and then Shannen.

"Well, that was hellacious," Shannen groaned, sitting down between Lauren and Rico after her own long row. "My arms feel like they're going to fall off, my hands are getting blistered and I'm exhausted. Not to mention hungrier than ever."

She looked into the camera and met Tynan's eyes. "I'm going to bed right after the council meeting, no matter what."

Slowly Ty turned his head from one side to the other. He mouthed the word "tonight" and watched her jaw drop. Clearly, she was not expecting such obvious interaction with him.

But nobody noticed except her. The others were ignoring the camera and cameraman to watch Konrad push the rowboat into the water.

"I said I'm going straight to bed tonight," Shannen repeated, giving Ty her most forbidding grimace. "Nowhere but my own bed."

"You girls should've done what Konrad is doing," said Jed, who was standing nearby, watching Konrad in the rowboat heading out to sea. "You should've saved your strength and taken your own sweet time, like him. He knows I'm going to win, and since every other score is irrelevant, why wear yourself out?"

He swaggered off toward the water to wait for Konrad to return with the rowboat.

"I hate Jed," Cortnee said fiercely, watching him walk off. "He thinks he's so hot. Did you know he slept with both Keri and Lucy? They each tried to get him to switch his alliance from us to them, and he let them think he would. I wanted to tell you all, but I didn't think the time was right. Till now."

"He slept with both of them?" Lauren gasped. "Cortnee, are you sure?"

"I heard them, I heard everything." Cortnee shuddered. "They were right outside the tent on my side and I'm a light sleeper. I wake up at the slightest noise."

"Do you hear people get up during the night to, um, well—you know?" Shannen was not her usual frank self.

"Uh-huh. I heard you or your sister get up last night to—" Cortnee laughed. "No need to be shy, we're among friends—to use the facilities."

"I can't believe Jed would use Keri and Lucy for sex," said Lauren. "If he did, he would've switched his allegiance from us to them, and he didn't. He was loyal and he stuck with us all this time. You…you must've misinterpreted what you were hearing, Cortnee."

"I know exactly what I heard," insisted Cortnee. "Believe me, I didn't misinterpret a thing."

"The man is slime." Shannen scowled.

"And the reason why Jed didn't switch from us to them is because we five were the stronger choice," Rico pointed out. "Loyalty had nothing to do with it. Too bad we're stuck with him now. He'll keep winning every contest for immunity, and we'll get kicked off, one by one."

"We made our version of a deal with the devil. Now it's time to pay." Shannen looked over at Ty. "Gramma always says, 'If you let the devil into the cart, you'll have to drive him home.' And she wasn't talking about hitchhiking in biblical times."

Ty grinned broadly. Shannen lifted her chin and turned away.

Konrad joined the group after his long, slow turn in the boat race. He looked downright cheerful. "So, tonight we vote out Jed. Everybody cool with that?"

"If only!" Shannen gingerly moved her aching arms and flexed her fingers again. "But Jed'll have the fastest time and win immunity so we *can't* vote against him. We five will have to vote out one of us. Jed is going to be the winner in this game, I think that's screamingly obvious."

"Speaking of screaming." Konrad cocked his head. "Do I hear some?"

"I don't hear anything." Lauren looked around. "Even those screeching monkeys are quiet for a change."

Seconds after she'd uttered that declaration, a scream pierced the tranquil air. All heads turned in the direction of the ocean.

Jed was standing in the boat, yelling at the top of his lungs.

"That was definitely a scream," Shannen said dryly, turning toward Konrad. "A primal one. Is there a scorpion in the boat with Jed or something?"

"It looks like Jed is trying to throw handfuls of water out of the boat." Cortnee looked confused. "Why isn't he rowing?"

"Too bad he doesn't have a bucket," said Konrad. "Lots easier to bail with a bucket than with your hands." He surprised everybody by roaring with laughter.

"The boat's sinking!" exclaimed Rico. "Look, it really is! In another couple minutes, Jed is going to be in the ocean."

"Oh, poor Jed!" cried Lauren.

"Yeah, poor poor Jed." Konrad laughed harder. "Good thing Mister Wilderness Guide is such a strong swimmer, huh?"

"Good thing," agreed Shannen. "Because the rowboat is history. All that's left is an oar. Well, Konrad did say it was a leaky old tub." She shot a quizzical glance at him.

They all stared out at the lone floating oar and at Jed, two far-off blurs in the sea.

"Everybody!" Cortnee cried. "I just thought of something. Since the rowboat sank, Jed won't be able to complete the contest. He won't get immunity. One of us will have the fastest time and one of us will win immunity!"

"It won't be me," predicted Konrad. "I was really slow out there."

"We noticed." Shannen said dryly. "There were times when we couldn't see you at all, you were slouched down so far in the boat. You have an interesting way of rowing, Konrad. And you're good at predictions, too, it seems," she added, raising an eyebrow in his direction.

"Thank you, ma'am." Konrad bowed from the waist.

For a few more minutes they all watched Jed swimming toward the crew's boat as the waves broke over him. There wasn't a trace of the sunken rowboat.

Later, a soaking-wet Jed was returned to shore in the dinghy from the crew boat. He stomped into camp with accusations of sabotage and demanded another chance in another rowboat.

As the cameras continued to roll, he threatened to sue the show and the network and everybody on the island, especially Konrad, if he ultimately won the game.

Bobby Dixon was unmoved. "Sorry, Jed. The rules of the game plainly state that do-overs are never allowed.

There's no proof of any wrongdoing, and the cameras were on the rowboat at all times.''

"On the rowboat, but not on Konrad!'' argued Jed. "He got himself out of sight and did something to make it sink, I know he did. He cheated!''

"Not winning is obviously difficult for you, Jed, but you must accept it and move on like everybody else,'' Bobby said unctuously. "In today's contest, the fastest time was Rico's, and he wins the immunity statue.''

Bobby handed Rico the foot-high painted wooden totem pole that looked as if it had been purchased at a roadside souvenir shop.

"This is the first time in the game that anybody but Jed has won that thing,'' said Shannen. "No one can vote against Rico tonight. Gee, I wonder who everybody will vote off the island?''

Three

———

The full moon had waned only slightly, so the bright path through the tangle of vines and low-hanging branches was as easy to follow as it had been last night. Shannen slowly, carefully made her way, as familiar with it by night as by day.

She had thoroughly explored this island during the long daylight hours, looking for food and anything else that might be useful to their group. She'd easily slipped off alone, when the cameras were fixed on groups of the others.

With Lauren unwittingly serving as a decoy, Shannen's absences went unnoticed. Since the twins weren't always side by side, as long as one of them was in view, who was to say which sister it was? That sort of fungibility sometimes bugged Shannen, but not on this island, not in this game.

Especially since her solo wanderings had provided her with quite a bit of useful information, some of which she didn't share with anybody. Like the undiscovered shortcut to the crew's camp on the other side of the island and the secluded palm grove where she was now headed.

Shannen's heart began to thud heavily.

She'd slipped away from camp tonight, wondering if Cortnee had heard her leave. But there was nothing questionable about someone getting up and heading off "to use the facilities," Shannen reminded herself.

Cortnee hadn't been suspicious last night; plus, she wouldn't know whether it was Lauren or Shannen who'd left on either night.

Certainly the last thing anybody would suspect was that practical, logical, no-nonsense Shannen Cullen was sneaking off to meet the chief cameraman. Not even Lauren, the person who knew her best in the world, would ever fathom that.

But then, there were some things that not even Lauren knew about her twin.

Nine years ago, in the throes of rebellion and intense first love—she'd often wondered how much one had fueled the other—Shannen had stopped sharing every single thought and feeling with Lauren. Her wild passion for Tynan Howe had been the biggest secret she'd ever kept. Deliberately, she hadn't even mentioned his name to her twin.

And though she'd gloried in her secret love, when it was over—after *he'd* ended it—the price she had paid was enduring her heartbreak alone. For the first time in her young life, Shannen hadn't had loyal Lauren to share her pain, thereby halfing it. Another grudge to hold against Tynan Howe, and she'd held fast to it.

Yet now, though supposedly older and wiser, here she was repeating her mistakes—the rebellion against the rules, the secrecy from her sister—and with the same man!

What was happening to that practical, logical and nononsense character she'd spent years honing? Why was she sneaking out at midnight, like the recalcitrant teenager she'd once been, to meet Tynan Howe? *Again!*

Nine years ago he had insisted he was too old for her. In her calmer moments back then—and since—she might even have seen his point and agreed. She might've dreamed of a day when she was out of high school, out of her teens, and had reached whatever age Ty deemed "old enough."

But her age wasn't the sole reason cited by Tynan as to why they couldn't be together. It was those other, far more hurtful reasons he had supplied—the reasons she came to believe were his true reasons—that still resonated within her.

Well, she was of legal age now, and thanks to the multiple Howe scandals, Tynan was not quite the "catch" he once had been. Not that she wanted to catch him, Shannen quickly assured herself.

She didn't for many reasons—the current, main one being this game they were playing, on opposite sides of the camera, making Tynan Howe off-limits to her.

It was déjà-vu all over again, as the saying went.

If their clandestine meetings were discovered, she would undoubtedly be kicked out of the game, in full camera view, of course. Clark Garrett and Slick Bobby would want to milk every dramatic possibility.

Lauren would feel so betrayed by her twin's secrecy, both past and present, and the cameras would record her reaction to it all. Shannen flinched at the thought of wounding her sister.

Furthermore, if she were eliminated now, how long would Lauren last without her in the game? From the time they were little, Shannen had felt compelled to protect Lauren, to make sure no one took advantage of her more naive twin.

Would Konrad, Rico and Cortnee gang up on Lauren if her more formidable sister were gone? Being legitimately voted off the island was one thing, but foolishly getting herself kicked out of the game was unacceptable.

Unexpectedly she and Lauren had come this far. Why throw away a possible chance to win?

Though it would be wonderful to win the top prize, just making the final four would be okay, too, Shannen told herself. Being one of the final four meant a cash prize, with each runner-up—the third, the second and, finally, the first—making more in turn.

Were she and Lauren *both* to make the final four, the payoff would be considerable. That was not something to be lightly dismissed.

The Cullen twins hadn't turned over their lives to a prime-time game show for the hell of it. They needed the money—the family was counting on them.

As for the risk Tynan was taking meeting her...

Well, keeping his job because he needed his salary wouldn't be a concern for *him*. Whatever their transgressions, the Howes must still be rich. After all, during the entire time the Howe family had been under the full glare of the media spotlight, one story that had never appeared was their plunge into poverty.

Ty probably wouldn't even lose his job. Wasn't it a universal truth that men rarely paid the same price for breaking the rules that women did? And, of course, Tynan was a Howe, whose family knew a thing or two thousand about rule breaking.

Victorious concerns aside, Tynan Howe was emotionally dangerous to her. Any man who could effortlessly turn back the clock nine years and transform her into her impetuous young-girl self was a must to avoid.

Unfortunately, Shannen couldn't seem to stay focused on all the practical, logical no-nonsense reasons why she should keep away from him. She kept getting distracted by other thoughts.

Like his name. He wasn't even using the name Howe.

She'd realized that the first day they had all arrived on the island. There were no introductions to the crew, but when she'd seen Ty among them—after getting over the initial stunning shock—she had paid close attention. And heard him called Ty Hale.

Hale, not Howe. Scrapping Howe for Hale didn't surprise her nearly as much as the fact that he was working as a television cameraman. After all, the Howe name was no longer a proud symbol of wealth, achievement and privilege. The family had dragged it through so much mud, it had become a stigma.

But Tynan had gone to law school. He'd been a senior law student at West Falls University Law School when they'd met. She knew he'd taken and passed the state bar exam. The names of graduates passing the various state professional examinations always were proudly published in the university newspaper.

Since when did a lawyer work as a cameramen on a network game show? Tynan Hale, attorney at law, made more sense than Tynan Hale, working-stiff cameraman, didn't it?

She wanted to know; she wondered every time she looked at him behind that camera. Which was nearly sixteen hours a day. The omnipresence of the camera crew was annoying enough, but having Ty always there had re-awakened feelings she thought—she'd hoped!—had died.

Not so. Never had she been so aware of anyone in her life—except during their last go-round nine long years ago.

So why didn't you ask him all those pertinent questions last night, Shannen? she silently chided herself. Instead, she'd ended up in his arms within minutes, after making that pathetically lame excuse of why she had risked meeting him.

Why *had* she risked meeting him in the first place?

No use pretending she didn't know the answer to that

one. Seeing him every day, all day... Having him so near yet so totally out of reach...

The tension built and burned inside her. Unaccustomed to passivity, she couldn't stop herself from taking action.

Oh, who was she kidding? Shannen exhaled an impatient sigh, unable to talk herself into the convenient self-deception. Taking action and losing control were too very different responses, and she knew which one had prevailed last night.

Memories of last night whirled through her head, making her wince. Tynan had accused her of strategizing by using silence. Thankfully, he hadn't known she'd been struck dumb by the sight of him, by the tantalizing prospect of being alone with him. On a tropical island late at night, *both* of them legal, consenting adults.

Her imagination raced to places that made her blush.

It was definitely to her advantage that he believed she was cool enough to plot and plan and play a game. Now all she had to do was keep up the pretense.

It wouldn't be very hard to do, Shannen pep-talked herself, as she slowed her pace. She wasn't a giddy schoolgirl anymore, she was a mature woman known for her competence and self-control.

All she had to do was be herself—her *current* self. To tell Tynan Howe that this was the last time she would sneak around the island to meet him, and nothing he could say or do could change her mind.

That was all she had to do.

The moment Shannen spied Tynan Howe/Hale standing in the secluded grove of palm trees, the confidence-boosting tape she was playing in her head became a jumble of blather.

Fortunately, she had a moment or two to regain her composure before he sensed her presence. She knew he couldn't hear her approaching. The wind and the sounds of the nocturnal birds and animals provided ideal cover.

That secret moment or two also provided her with time to study him, and helplessly Shannen made a thorough mental inventory.

He was tall and tanned and muscular, and his *Victorious* crew T-shirt and loose khaki shorts emphasized his build to perfection. His face was all arresting masculine features: the coffee-colored brown eyes alert with intensity and intelligence, the strong jaw and sharp blade of a nose, the mouth well shaped and sensual.

His dark-brown hair was cut short, perhaps in concession to the island heat? She remembered he'd worn it longer nine years ago, when at twenty-five, he'd been a legal adult and she, only seventeen, was not.

Unbidden came a visceral pang of memory, that hungry yearning she'd felt back then every time she'd looked at him.

It was remarkably similar to what she was feeling right now.

Shannen was aghast. This was a mature woman known for her competence and self-control? She had to get out of here, and fast!

"Shannen," he called to her quietly.

Too late she realized she had accidentally moved into his line of vision. Okay, let's get this over with! She took a deep breath. "Hello, *Mr. Hale.*"

Her deep breathing had the unfortunate effect of making her sound throaty and breathless. That was certainly unintended. Shannen frowned.

"Do you disapprove of my alias?" Ty walked forward to meet her, his hands in his pockets, looking relaxed and cool and calm, everything she knew she was not.

She resented his composure mightily. "You can call yourself anything you want, it doesn't matter to me."

"I wonder who voted to oust Cortnee tonight?" Ty

stopped in front of her and attempted another conversational sally. "It seems obvious that Jed cast the vote against Konrad, but the vote against Cortnee came as a surprise."

Diverted, Shannen nodded her agreement. "I thought the five of us would unanimously vote against Jed, but there were only four votes against him. Enough to send him away, thank heavens. Maybe either Konrad or Rico decided they'd had enough of Cortnee?"

"Or you or your sister did," suggested Ty.

"We both voted against Jed. Bad enough he's an insufferable braggart, but hearing he's such a user totally clinched it."

"It's a secret ballot, so who knows? Unless you and Lauren discussed your votes?"

"We didn't have to. We can't stand Jed. And what a poor loser he was, throwing that big tantrum. It was pretty funny when Konrad couldn't stop laughing, though." Shannen smiled at the memory. "Konrad's been absolutely giddy today."

"The Internet discussion boards will be lit up over this," said Ty. "Jed does have a loyal following, who will be furious that he's out of the game. That vote against Cortnee will be dissected, too. She has her own fan base. And you and your sister have an even bigger one."

"We do?"

"Absolutely. Clark Garrett said you two are even being discussed on twins.com, which is normally used for parenting tips on multiple-born kids. He's elated with the scope of the show. Watch him try to find quadruplets for *Victorious II.*"

Shannen stared at him, completely nonplussed. "I haven't thought about public reaction to the show since the first few days after we arrived here. You're…keeping up with it?"

"You can't escape it in the crew's camp. Viewer response to *Victorious* is in the air we breathe there. Clark

Garrett is obsessed with the ratings, and he and Bobby monitor the show's Internet activity like overanxious mothers.''

She twisted her hands. "It's strange how life in this game seems to be more real than real life back home right now."

And it was downright unnerving how she had managed to fixate on him to the exclusion of real life back home! Shannen gulped.

"What is your real life like back at home, Shannen?" He sounded genuinely interested.

She didn't want him to be. "Haven't you read my *Victorious* bio? The basic facts are all there," she said glibly.

"The basic facts are pretty minimal. You and your sister graduated from West Falls University. You're a nutritionist at West Falls Hospital, and Lauren teaches home ec at West Falls High. You both were granted leaves of absence from your jobs to do this show—which you claim you tried out for as a lark. There isn't any real personal information."

"Such as?"

"Mention of a boyfriend or fiancé." He cleared his throat. "A child or ex-husband. That sort of thing."

"Because there aren't any. Lauren and I are both happily single and free."

Their eyes met. Ty was the first to look away. "It's your turn to ask me," he said in a peculiar tone.

Shannen guessed he'd been trying to be wry but had ended up sounding sheepish instead. Best of all, he knew it. His discomfiture delighted her.

"I'm supposed to ask if you have a girlfriend or fiancée or wife and kids? No, I'll pass. I really don't care."

"Don't you?"

He met her gaze again, and Shannen's pulses jumped. Sexual awareness crashed over her like a wave breaking on the shore. They were standing way too close, she realized with a start.

How had that happened? She had no recollection of either of them moving, yet they must have, because now they were in each other's personal space, within easy touching distance.

"I don't mind volunteering that I don't have a girlfriend, fiancée or wife and kids. No ex-wives, either," Ty said, breaking the brief charged silence.

"You Howes are so dedicated to honesty," she said sarcastically. "Such role models for morality! Oh wait, I forgot—you're a *Hale* now, you're keeping your true identity a secret. Which is just more Howe deception, if you ask me."

"You could look at it that way, I suppose. But my sister Jessie Lee and I see it from a different angle. She gladly and permanently dropped Howe for her married name. Jessie Lee says nobody in their right mind wants to carry the burden of the name Howe at this point in time. Well, I'm of sound mind, Shannen."

"Jessie Lee isn't the sister who embezzled the money from the flood relief fund, is she?"

"No, that would be Janice. Who is still serving time. She would disagree with Konrad about the tastiness of prison food, by the way."

"She had a trusted position with a respected charity organization, and she stole from the very victims she was supposed to be helping," Shannen said sternly. "She deserves to be in jail!"

"You won't get any argument about that from me." Tynan held up his hands in a gesture of truce. "My brother, Trent, took his rightful place there, too, after he almost singlehandedly brought down the biggest accounting firm in the country with his auditing schemes. Meanwhile, it's disturbing to consider what he might be cooking up in prison now, with all that time on his hands."

"There was a dreadful cousin, too," Shannen blurted out before she could stop herself. The Howe family's fall was not unlike a train wreck that you tried to avert your eyes from but couldn't help staring at anyway. "What finally happened to him?"

"Cousin Davis is locked up for a very long time. Between the postal service investigation and what they found on his computer, they nailed him cold, thank God." Ty sighed. "Being a Howe means serving as a target for numerous well-deserved potshots. Blame comes with the name, which is why I decided to use Hale."

"Because you're such a paragon of virtue?" she asked, baiting him.

"Because I didn't enjoy being a pariah by proxy. There are lots of people who believe that an uncorrupt Howe is an oxymoron, like a good terrorist."

"Are you going to be a Hale permanently?" Shannen was curious.

"I don't know. I do know that it's a great relief to be anonymous, something you've given up by being on this show. After the game is over and you're back home enduring the media attention, you'll—"

"Want to change my name to escape my notoriety? I seriously doubt it."

"Your name won't matter. Since you're visually known through TV exposure, you'll be identified on sight."

"Oh, well, how bad can that be?" Shannen gave a dismissive shrug. "As twins, Lauren and I have always been stared at. After this, a few more people will stare at us. Then we'll go back to work, interest in us will quickly fade and everything will return to normal."

"Maybe. Or maybe you'll win this game and be a millionaire, Shannen. That will surely change your life."

"Surely," she echoed mockingly. "Should I ask you in advance how to fend off fortune hunters? After all, you've been hounded by scheming gold diggers your entire privileged life, haven't you?"

He had the grace to look ashamed. "I knew it was too much to hope you'd forgotten…that."

"Being called a conniving gold digger and white-trash jailbait is rather memorable, Tynan."

He groaned. "Shannen, I never thought you were a—"

"Calculating fortune hunter? Of course you did. And to tell the truth, you were right about the appeal your money held for me. I liked the idea that you were very rich. I don't mind being called conniving, either. That's a compliment in some circles, and in this game it's crucial. But the jailbait, white-trash part—ouch!"

She hoped she'd pulled off the breezy insouciance she was aiming for. She certainly wasn't feeling that way. His invective had seared her brain and remained engraved there ever since he'd hurled it at her the fateful night he'd broken her heart.

Shannen gave her head a quick shake. No, she wasn't going to stir up all those old feelings, not here, not now!

"I didn't mean it, Shannen." Ty's voice was low and urgent. "I was desperate that night, and I didn't trust myself around you. Remember, I'd just found out a few hours earlier that you were only seventeen years old."

He paused and shook his head ruefully. "From the first time I met you, your effect on me was nothing less than explosive and exciting, and the more we saw each other, the deeper my feelings grew. But then I saw you getting off that school bus. A school bus, Shannen! I couldn't believe it. I did some checking around and finally found out the truth. You were way too young for me. It was wrong for us to be together, and I knew I had to say something to make you... You were too young to understand what you..."

His voice trailed off.

Shannen found hers. "That's ancient history. I don't want to talk about it."

She was both fascinated and repelled by his unsteady pronouncement. Was it the truth, or was he indulging in some self-serving revisionist history?

Not that it mattered. Not that she cared at all.

He was a condescending, self-righteous jerk, she reminded herself, recalling how she'd hurled the epithet at him that same night. It was the most insulting thing her seventeen-year-old self could come up with while grappling with the pain of what he'd called her.

And it was lame compared to his pernicious insult. She had a far better verbal arsenal now.

"I suppose it would be boorish of me to point out that you were the one who brought it up in the first place with your fortune-hunter crack?" Ty's lips quirked.

"You were boorish to say it back then," she shot back. "But when faced with packs of fortune-hunting vixens, all's fair, I suppose. Still being relentlessly plagued by them?" she added caustically.

"Not anymore. Fortune-hunting vixens don't bother us fortuneless guys."

"Do you mean—did you— You lost all your money?" The notion was staggering.

Ty looked uncomfortable. "The family legal bills and penalty fines equaled the national budget of a small country. And let's not forget all those civil suits filed against us."

"But don't the rich have trust funds and all, that can't be touched?"

"When you have an enterprising auditing genius like Trent in the family, nothing is safe," Ty replied.

"Your brother stole from his own family, too? My brother has done the same thing." Shannen lowered her voice, as she always did when talking about her brother. As Gramma said, There were some things that didn't need to be shouted from the rooftops. Big brother, Evan, was one of them, even here, alone with Ty in the middle of the island.

"From the time Lauren and I first learned what money was, we learned that Evan would swipe it from us—pennies, nickels, dimes. He didn't care how small the amount—Evan would take it.''

"Who would've expected we'd share a bonding moment over our thieving brothers?'' Ty gave a hollow laugh before turning serious once again. "Shannen, there is no justifying what I said to you that night. At the time, I believed I was doing the right thing to keep you away from me, but since then—''

"Oh, spare me the tired old 'cruel to be kind' excuse.'' Shannen's temper flared. Their bonding moment, such as it was, was over. "It's phony and self-righteous and I don't buy it. Motives can be either cruel or kind but not both.''

"Motives can definitely be mixed, Shannen.''

Fast as a heartbeat, he backed her against the thick column of a palm tree. He slipped his arms around her, trapping her between himself and the tree.

"I'd like to know your motives in renewing our relationship.'' His voice was husky. "I'd be willing to bet my camera equipment that they're…mixed. Would I be right?''

With a soft gasp Shannen tilted her head back and looked up at him. The hot gleam in his dark eyes challenged her; his smoldering sexuality fueled hers. She felt her nipples tighten as sharp coils of desire spiraled deep inside her.

"I'm not trying to renew our relationship, because we don't have one,'' she said huskily. "We never did. I had a one-sided crush on you when you were a hotshot law student and I was a teenage idiot. End of story.''

"It was more than that and you know it.'' Tynan nuzzled her neck, drawing her closer. "I was crazy about you, Shannen. When I found out you were just a kid, I felt like I'd been kicked in the gut.''

Sensual hunger was swiftly infusing her body with hot, syrupy warmth. Shannen knew she should fight it, and she tried to bolster her resistance against it.

"I was still the same person you claimed to be so crazy about.''

''Not even close, Shannen. I thought you were a twenty-two-year-old graduate student—because that's what you'd claimed to be. Quite a difference between that and a lying little teenager who was using me to rebel.''

''I wasn't! Using you to rebel, that is,'' she specified, because she couldn't deny she had been a teenager or that she'd purposely lied about her age.

Right now she was feeling much the way she'd felt back then when he'd taken her in his arms. The same pounding excitement, the same fierce arousal.

Almost a decade later he still evoked a hormonal hurricane within her. It should have been a sobering realization, not a thrilling one.

But thrilling it was. She was aching to touch him, and finally, nervously she allowed herself to. Just a little, Shannen vowed, just this one last time before she returned to camp and never did this again.

She reached up to curve her hand around his jaw. He'd been clean shaven this morning—she had noticed, just as she did every day—but now a light stubble covered his jaw. It felt sensuous and scratchy and very erotic.

Her fingers slid to his mouth and traced his lips.

He caught her thumb with his teeth and gently pulled on it at the same time his big hand closed over her breast.

A moan escaped from her throat, and she felt herself slipping under his spell. *Again.* Ty was the first man ever to make her feel weak with wanting. Who would've guessed that in the nine years that followed their parting, he would remain the only man to elicit that response?

All those years her icy control had never wavered, and then along came Tynan, and once again she melted like a Popsicle in tropical sun. He held such power over her!

Sudden alarm bells began to sound in her head. With power went control, and all her adult life Shannen made sure that she was the one with both.

She hadn't been that way at seventeen, though. She'd

been all too willing to cede everything to Ty, "white-trash jailbait" that she'd been. Shannen winced.

He brushed his mouth over hers in a tempting, tentative caress. "We've been down this road before, Shannen."

Yes, they had. Shannen's alarm turned into panic. Was she nuts? Or maybe just "white-trash jailbait-all-grown-up," out for a midnight romp on the beach with the man who'd coldly dumped her when she was utterly vulnerable.

Ty lifted his head and gazed down at her. "But we never got far enough, did we, sweetheart? Tonight—"

"Nothing is going to happen tonight, either!"

He wasn't expecting it, so when she pushed at his chest with both hands, Shannen successfully shoved him away from her. He had to make momentary use of his arms to maintain his balance, and she took the opportunity to make her escape.

"I'm out of here. And don't try to…to contact me again," she ordered, gulping for breath. "I won't meet you again, no matter what."

Ty snaked out his arm in time to catch the tail of her cotton T-shirt. She kept walking, but he held firm. The shirt began to pull and stretch.

Shannen struggled and the material grew thinner. "Let me go!"

"No."

"You'll rip my shirt!" Her voice rose.

"Then you'd better stand still, hadn't you?"

The amusement in his voice struck an incendiary chord in her. "If you don't let go of my shirt right now, I'll sue you for…for sexual harassment. I'm not bluffing, Tynan *Howe!* Jed's threats to sue might have no basis, but mine will be—"

"Based on my name? Is that what your emphasis on Howe means, Shannen?" The coldness in his tone was reflected in his eyes. "'Your Honor, this man is a Howe, which makes him a sexual predator by blood.' Case closed.''

Ty let go of her shirt. Shannen meticulously smoothed out the material.

All she had to do was to agree with him, and he would leave her alone. It was easy enough, and she would get what she wanted, right?

She opened her mouth to speak, but no words came out.

Because she knew a thing or two about the pain and rage caused by an accusation that hit way too close to home. Like being called white trash when certain family members acted in a—well, what might be deemed a white-trashy way.

Shannen thought of her mother and brother and their never-ending bad behavior—the drinking and fighting at seedy bars, jumping from one rotten relationship to the next, bouncing checks while running up exorbitant credit-card debts. You could make a case that they were the low-rent version of the Howes, though Shannen wasn't interested in making it.

She and Lauren and their older sister, Jordan, had worked all their lives to be different from Mom and Evan, the Cullen reprobates.

Surprisingly, Ty's situation was much like her own, since he was a Howe by blood, though in behavior unlike them. He was certainly no sexual predator like his odious father and cousin. She couldn't accuse him of that.

And worse than any false accusation was her sinking realization that she wasn't sure she wanted him to leave her alone. She might not wish to have sex on the beach with him tonight, but that didn't mean she wanted to give up his attention.

It was enough to make anyone edgy!

Shannen crossed her arms in front of her chest and glowered. ''Playing the martyr doesn't suit you, Tynan.''

His lips curved into a slow smile. As if he knew why

she hadn't said what was guaranteed to send him on his way. "Is that what I was doing, Shannen?"

"Yes!"

"I guess it must've worked, though, because we're both still here."

"Only because—only until—" She spluttered, gave up and tried again. "Tynan, you can't demand that I meet you and expect me to—"

"It was a request," Tynan said, his voice deepening. "A polite one." They were close enough for him to rest both his hands on her shoulders. "And you came tonight because you wanted to, Shannen."

"No." She ducked out of his grasp. "I'm only here because—"

"You kissed me last night and you loved it?"

"*You* kissed *me!* And I…and you—" She broke off, her cheeks aflame. "Look, the only reason I'm here is to tell you to forget about last night. I admit I shouldn't have contacted you in the first place. That was a big mistake on my part. I…I wasn't thinking straight. We haven't been getting the proper nutrition here on this island, and it's affecting my brain."

"Nice try." Ty nodded his approval. "More original than the overused 'not guilty for reasons of insanity.' Not guilty for reasons of malnutrition, with you being a nutritionist, sounds downright credible. So, help me out, Shannen—what's *my* excuse for being here? I've been eating three square meals a day."

"Go ahead and brag about all the great food you get every day," she grumbled. "Describe every meal in detail. Torture me with tales of every bite."

"Now who's playing the martyr?" Ty grinned.

"Good night, Tynan. I'm going back to camp now. Hopefully, everybody is still sound asleep, or I'll have to pretend I've been, uh, using the facilities an awfully long time."

"Wait! Before you go." Ty caught her hand. "I brought you something." His thumb glided over her palm, then he lifted it and stared at the blisters. "From the rowing?" he asked, frowning with concern.

She nodded and disentangled her hand from his. "They hurt, and when the salt water touches them, I want to scream."

Ty examined her other hand. "I have some antibiotic salve I'll give you. It speeds up the healing and has a pain ingredient in it, too. Wait here and I'll go get it. I'll be back in less then ten minutes."

"But I can't—you can't—"

"While you're waiting, eat this." Ty handed her a plastic plate, removing the cover to reveal a sandwich made with thick Italian bread.

"It's turkey, cheese, lettuce and tomato," he said. "I brought you some cookies, too." He handed her a paper bag with two peanut butter cookies in it. "And a bottle of iced tea."

Shannen stared at the food—unexciting everyday items on the family dinner menu, but here, on the island, where acquiring food was part of the game, a priceless bounty.

And illicit.

"Isn't this cheating?" she whispered nervously, sitting down on the sand and eyeing the food with longing. Her stomach was growling noisily now.

"I'll get the ointment." Ty disappeared into the night, leaving Shannen alone with the meal.

Four

***

Shannen stared at the unexpected treasure he'd given her. She'd actually dreamed of food while on this island, and now here it was, literally, a dream come true.

She picked up the sandwich and sniffed it. Who would've thought that deli turkey, swiss cheese, tomato and lettuce could have such a heavenly aroma? And was that honey mustard spread on the bread? Oh, happy day!

Who would've believed that this sandwich could smell more wonderful than one of Gramma's freshly baked apple pies?

But it did—because it was here in her hand, and she could eat it right now if she wanted.

If she wanted? Oh, yes, she wanted to eat that sandwich! And the peanut butter cookies, too. Shannen put down the sandwich to sniff each cookie. She felt almost dizzy with pleasure, and she wasn't even a particular fan of peanut butter in any form.

There was the bottle of iced tea, too. Lemon-flavored,

and one of her favorite brands. She'd had nothing to drink on this island but the bottled water supplied by the crew for health reasons and some terrible coffee they'd won in a food contest early on. Jed had insisted on brewing it and had ruined it, much to the bitterness of the tribe.

That is, she and Cortnee, Rico and Konrad had been bitter and quite vocal about the ruined coffee. Lauren and the two earlier departees from the tribe, Lucy and Keri, had come to Jed's defense and all claimed the undrinkable swill was actually delicious.

"Are you Jed's groupies or something?" Rico had groused at the time, and Shannen, resenting the aspersion cast at Lauren, had glowered at Rico for the remainder of the day.

Now Shannen frowned again, thinking about that unexpected alliance. Lauren had claimed she'd sided with *them* to keep the numbers even, which meant keeping the peace. Shannen didn't understand Lauren's reasoning then, and she still didn't.

She gazed longingly at the food as she thought of her twin. She couldn't eat this food without sharing it with Lauren, she just couldn't. Her sister was just as hungry as she was.

She could take the food back and hide it near the spring, then wake up Lauren and share it with her. It was as if a little cartoon imp had perched on her shoulder, to whisper in her ear. There would be no cameras around to film them at this late hour. She and Lauren could enjoy their treat and no one would be the wiser.

But just as in a cartoon, another little voice—that of the angel who'd just arrived to perch on her other shoulder?— also had something to say. Something completely different from the devilish imp.

Eating this food would be cheating. Sharing it with Lauren would be dragging her sister into a conspiracy of dishonesty. And she would also have to add lying to Lauren to the list of her wrongdoings, because where could she say that this food had come from? A sandwich shop in the jungle?

If she were to truthfully tell Lauren that Ty had given it to her, Lauren would want to know why. Which would mean either confessing her past fling to her twin or making up some reason why chief cameraman Tynan Hale had decided to slip the Cullen sisters some food on the sly.

Shannen suddenly glanced around her, half expecting to see the cameras filming her. What if this was some sort of setup?

But she was all alone, and her stomach was churning in hungry anticipation.

To eat or not to eat. What a dilemma!

No, it wasn't a dilemma at all, lectured Shannen's invisible but vocal Little Angel. It was something far simpler—and way more dangerous.

This was temptation.

Shannen heaved a groan. Gramma had a lot to say about temptation down through the years and never hesitated to say it.

"If you keep off the ice, you won't slip through."

"You can't be caught in places you don't visit."

"If you don't touch the rope, you won't ring the bell."

Those three sprang instantly to mind; if she were to think another minute or two, she could come up with at least ten more in a similar vein.

And, of course, there was the unnerving one about giving the devil a ride. Shannen shuddered. Maybe it was because Mom and Evan had completely ignored Gramma's warnings and messed up their lives, that Shannen, Lauren and Jordan—sometimes called "the third twin" since she was only a year older—paid Gramma such careful heed.

Except for that brief, dizzying period in her life when Shannen had thrown out Gramma's wisdom and sneaked around to meet Ty. No happy ending there. She hadn't strayed from the straight and narrow since.

She wasn't about to do it now. Shannen stared out at the dark ocean, leaving the food untouched. "If you don't take a bite of the forbidden food, you won't be cheating."

She could pass down that one, her own personal version of temptation shunned, to her own grandchildren...if she ever had any.

Ty returned shortly afterward.

"Here's the ointment." Before she could say a word, he knelt down beside her and smeared it on her right hand, then her left.

The salve was thick and warm and soothed her blisters on contact. Shannen immediately felt guilty.

"This isn't fair." She bit her lower lip. "The others—"

"I don't care about the others." Ty slipped his arm around her shoulder. "Keep the ointment. Take it back to the camp with you."

Shannen resisted laying her head against him. It would be so easy to do that. Too easy. Instead, she shook off his arm and struggled to her feet.

"You had that sandwich and cookies and tea with you before I got here tonight. Is that why you told me to come here, so you could give me food?" She was floored by the sudden realization.

"And you thought I was just out for sex," Ty said wryly, rising, too. "Of course, if you're willing, I'm—" He paused, glancing at the uneaten food for the first time.

"You didn't eat it." He sounded disappointed.

"Gramma would say I'd be letting the devil in the cart if I were to take one bite," mused Shannen.

"Relax. I promise you won't be held to the riding him home part."

She resisted the urge to smile. "You heard me quoting Gramma, hmm?"

"I filmed you quoting her, remember? I've heard a different version of the same theme—'Needs must when the devil drives.' I suppose that could be the Howe family credo, the true one. My mother should needlepoint it on one of those canvases she's forever working on. She's filled every room of the house with them made into pillows and pictures and foot stools and is still going strong.''

Shannen swallowed, unsure how to respond but feeling the need to say something. ''I saw your mother on the news when your father resigned from Congress after the, uh, um, final incident. She looked incredibly calm. Maybe the needlepoint helps,'' she added quickly.

''No, it's the tranquilizers around the clock that keep her comfortably numb.'' Ty heaved a sigh. ''Shannen, I'm not a devil and I don't want to lead you astray. It's just that I know you're hungry and I wanted you to have something to eat.''

''Why?''

He turned his back to her to stare out at the sea. The white caps from the waves were the only breaks in the vast stretch of blackness. ''Why wouldn't I?''

''No fair answering a question with a question. I'd like a straight answer. Why do you want to help me to cheat?''

''Not cheating, Shannen,'' he countered quickly. ''It's more like—''

''Of course it's cheating, Ty. Don't go all Howe on me and get weaselly with words.''

''Weaselly with words?'' he repeated, as if unfamiliar with the concept.

''You know exactly what I mean, Ty. After all, your father's classic line, 'It depends on what is meant by a call girl ring,' is still quoted by politicians *and* comedians when—''

''Can we skip the quotes and the commentary, Shannen? If you don't want my help, just say so.''

''I don't want your help, Tynan.''

''Okay. I won't offer any more, then.''

"And if you expect me to say 'thank you' for tonight, well, you can just—" She clenched her fists in frustration. "Would you kindly turn around when I'm speaking? I don't like addressing a person's back."

"I wasn't being intentionally rude, I was being... prudent." Ty slowly turned around. "But here we go again, anyway."

"What do you mean?"

"I mean we're doing it again. Picking an argument over nothing. Quarreling about anything. It's all an excuse to prolong our time together. And while fighting ought to keep us from touching each other, of course it won't. I predict we're moments away from another hot clinch."

"You are so far wrong, you're—" She had to catch her breath; his bluntness had physically winded her "—wrong!"

Very articulate, Shannen, she mocked herself. Why not call him a condescending, self-righteous jerk, too? Where are your allegedly superior verbal skills when you really need them?

"When you've filmed as many episodes of daytime television as I have, you know exactly what's going on here. Frustrated sexual tension. It's a staple on the soaps." He tilted her chin with his thumb and forefinger. "Unfortunately, we're caught in that same maddening trap."

Shannen gaped at him, uncertain what to address first. "You worked on a soap opera?"

"Three of them. It's where I got my start as a cameraman. I moved from daytime TV to primetime news magazines and the reality game shows. I've learned things on every job, and along with how to shoot close-ups of a person's best angle, I also picked up some true life lessons on the soaps."

"And you think we're like a soap opera couple?" Shannen laughed at that preposterous notion.

"Honey, we could *be* one. We even have the obligatory

conflict in our past." His fingers lazily stroked the slender column of her neck.

Shannen shivered, though it was pure heat streaking through her. She quickly stepped away from him, out of touching range.

"And don't you dare say I expect you to come after me and...and grab me. Because I don't!"

"So adamant." He laughed. "I'm tempted to see what would happen if I did."

"There's been enough temptation here tonight," scolded Shannen. "And I'm ashamed of myself for even *considering* a bite of that food."

She started walking back to the path. He followed her, placing his hand on the small of her back.

"It was extremely ethical of you not to eat that food, Shannen." His voice was thoughtful. "I bet any of the others would've bolted it down without a single qualm."

"Lauren wouldn't've touched it." Shannen stopped in her tracks so quickly he almost crashed into her. "You'd better not go any farther. If someone sees you—"

"I'll turn around when we see the camp. And here, Shannen, don't forget this." He pressed the tube of ointment into her hand.

"This is cheating, too, Tynan." She dropped it, and it would've hit the sand if Ty, anticipating her reaction, hadn't caught it first.

"Share it with Lauren and Cortnee. I'm sure they have blisters," said Ty. "Then you won't have any unfair advantage. Medicine falls into a different category than food. And I'm not using subterfuge—or weaselly words."

"They do have blisters, their hands are as bad as mine," Shannen admitted. "I think Cortnee's are even worse."

"Be sure that the three of you hold your hands up tomorrow so we can film them. We'll go in for some vivid close-ups." He smiled slightly. "The viewing audience loves stuff like that, the ever-popular gross-out scenes."

"Then they would've loved seeing Konrad barehandedly massacre that fish, but you didn't film it," she reminded him.

"True. I decided that Konrad and the murdered fish would be ideal for a show like *The World's Truly Disgusting Videos* but not for *Victorious.*"

"Clark Garrett would disagree. But I won't tell him about the fabulously nauseating footage he missed because you played censor."

"I felt I must. After all, we Howes are certainly the arbiters of good taste, among other things, are we not?" Ty was droll.

Or cynical. Or ashamed and quick to make a joke about his family's wretched reputation before anyone else did?

"Did you think I was going to toss off some Howe-related barb?" Shannen blurted her thought aloud.

She felt a pang of guilt. After all, she'd been quick to throw in the now-legendary statement made by his father when the news broke about the call girl ring being run out of Congressman Howe's office. As if that weren't scandalous enough, the congressman couldn't even plead ignorance to it all because he was getting a piece of the action himself, both financially and physically.

"I wouldn't blame you, I make them myself," Ty said laconically. "My family's antics were so outrageous, they turned themselves into cartoons who can only be comprehended by lampooning them. I wouldn't be surprised if the pope himself has told a Howe joke or two."

Shannen remembered how proudly Tynan had talked about his family nine years ago, before the Howes' infamous fall from grace. His father, the venerable congressman; his brother, the brilliant accounting executive who'd made his company stock a Wall Street darling. And the other Howes, seemingly equally gifted and talented, who'd turned out to be equally conniving and corrupt.

But back then the Howes had sounded like superbeings

to her, so very far removed from the Cullens, who eked out a livelihood from their West Falls diner. She had been so sure that Ty's true reason for breaking up with her had been based on class and status, not on her age. That it wasn't that she was too young for him, but not good enough for him, a wealthy, worthy Howe.

"It must've been—" she paused, searching for a tactful word but could do no better than "—strange for you, when everything…happened."

"It was strange when everything happened." He repeated her tortured attempt at diplomacy with a low rumble of laughter. "What's also strange is hearing you—Straight-Shooting Spitfire Shannen—suddenly go 'weaselly' with words."

He'd turned her own gibe back on her. He was deliberately provoking her. She should stalk off without a backward glance, after throwing the tube of ointment in his face.

But empathy for what had befallen him through no fault of his own kept her still. And standing there, she felt the heat emanating from his body, smelled his clean male scent.

She resisted a powerful urge to take the one step needed to close the small gap between them. To put her arms around him and lean against his solid warmth. To offer him comfort. And more…

She knew she couldn't, she shouldn't.

And she didn't. Frustration surged through her. She felt bone tired and suddenly hostile enough to start swearing.

Shannen looked down at the tube of ointment in her hand. "How am I supposed to explain where this came from? An all-night drugstore I found in the jungle?"

She heard the edge in her voice. That baiting, quarrelsome edge. As if she were trying to pick a fight with him.

To prolong their time together, to keep from touching him? Shannen jerked her head up and saw Ty watching her. The way he did when he was behind the camera. Always watching her.

He arched his brows.

She guessed what he was thinking. "We are *not* like a soap opera couple!" she snapped.

"If you say so." He gave her ponytail a quick tug. "Tell them you brought the ointment with you from home. Smuggled it in with your personal hygiene stuff."

"Lauren will know that I didn't."

"Say that you don't tell her everything. We both know that's the truth." He leaned down and lightly kissed her forehead. "Good night, Shannen. Sleep well."

"I will," she whispered after him.

"Lucky you. I know I won't."

"And remember, no more contact between us." Shannen's whisper, as adamant as it was soft, followed him as she walked away from him. "None at all. This is over, Tynan. You stay on your side of the camera and I'll stay on mine. Do you hear me? I mean it."

"I hear you, Shannen." His soft laughter echoed in the tropical night.

His laughter was long gone by the time he reached his tent. Ty clutched the rejected bottle of iced tea in his hand; he'd left behind the sandwich and cookies for whatever jungle scavenger should happen to find them. Unlike Shannen, the gulls or animals wouldn't turn down free food.

He'd begun to ruminate over her refusal to accept the meal during his late-night walk across the island. How she had resisted the temptation to eat, though he knew how hungry she was.

Why do you want to help me to cheat? Her words kept replaying in his head like the maddening hook of an advertising jingle.

Worse, he faced the fact that until she'd refused the food and made her pointed reproach, he hadn't considered what he'd done to be cheating at all. What he'd wanted to do was to help her. Period.

She was hungry and he wanted to feed her was the way he'd seen it from the moment he issued his decree for her to meet him tonight. If she should end up in his arms, so much the better, but his primary motive had been to give her food and drink.

To help her cheat.

Ty grimaced. Was this how it started for the others in his family? Doing something that seemed perfectly reasonable—even good!—when it was obvious to others from the start that it wasn't?

Did the Howes possess a defect in the ethics gene? Or was it an insidious element absorbed from growing up a Howe. His honesty gene could be afflicted, too.

Maybe that would explain why he had lied to Shannen about losing all his money. He and his mother and sister Jessie Lee all remained independently wealthy despite the rest of the family's travails, thanks to their own irrevocable trust funds.

Or had his reply been a self-protective response after hearing Shannen admit she'd liked the idea that he was very rich? Her words resounded in his head and he still wasn't sure if she'd been serious or sardonic when she uttered them.

From the time he had first learned that some people were nice to you only because they wanted what your money could buy—be it candy or baseball cards or jewelry or a luxurious life as a pampered wife—Ty had been on the alert.

Who knew if he'd been dishonest or cautious when he told Shannen that whopper tonight? Certainly he didn't.

Nature versus nurture. Had that conundrum ever been solved? He should offer himself up to be studied, Ty thought grimly. For the past seven years—since the first family scandal broke, bringing down the others in turn like a crashing line of dominoes—he had seen himself as a good Howe. The one too good to be saddled with the perfidious

Howe name, so he'd become a Hale, determined to make it a name to be proud of.

He wasn't feeling proud of himself now. Shannen wanted to win *Victorious* fairly, and though it had been unintentional, he'd tried to sabotage her.

But had it been unintentional? The question rocked him. Had he deliberately tempted her because he didn't want her to win? And was he also testing her by pretending he'd lost his portion of the Howe fortune? After all, she was in this game to win a million dollars. He'd been filming what she was willing to go through to get it.

He did want Shannen to win, Ty insisted to himself. Or more precisely, he didn't want to see her hurt, and it surely would be hurtful for her to be voted out of the game.

But if she were to win…

He could envision the aftermath of a win easily, simply by recalling past winners in the early popularity days of the reality game shows. The winner would be whisked between New York and Los Angeles for appearances on TV talk and radio shows. There might be offers from companies to star in commercials. If the winner was a girl, a plethora of men's magazines would dangle plenty of cash as an incentive to pose nude.

Ty's blood chilled at that thought. Cortnee could accept a nude centerfold offer and he wouldn't blink an eye; he wouldn't even buy the issue. But if Shannen were to pose nude…

He pulled off his clothes and threw them on the ground, cursing as he swung himself down on his hammock to lie inside his sleeping bag.

For the past nine years Shannen had been lost to him, and now that he'd found her again, now that he knew she felt something for him—and her responses to him definitely told him that—he was not going to share her with zillions of slavering males who pinned a nude layout of her on their walls.

He closed his eyes, picturing her naked. A sweet torture that guaranteed he wouldn't be falling asleep anytime soon.

As he lay there, common sense eventually reasserted itself. Shannen wouldn't pose nude for any magazine. She wouldn't take a nibble of a sandwich when she was hungry and she wouldn't strip naked for a centerfold layout.

But if she won the game, her life would definitely change from her current one as a hospital nutritionist in the small town of West Falls. She claimed it wouldn't, but he knew otherwise.

Money changed everything. And why would a beautiful young woman, enjoying a taste of fun-filled celebrity, want to make room in her life for *him?*

He might use the name Hale, but Shannen knew the disreputable truth about his family. Jessie Lee had been right on target when she'd said that nobody in their right mind would want to carry the burden inflicted by the scandal-ridden, joke-provoking name Howe.

Not only was Shannen in her right mind, she had done quite well without him since they'd parted.

And now, just as their relationship was heating up, the game was ending. Their time together on the island was drawing to a close.

Would she agree to even see him, when the game was over?

Possibly…if she lost. Fame was fleeting and fickle when it came to winners and losers. If she were merely one of the losers, instead of The Winner, he would at least have an opportunity to convince her that she wanted him— Tynan *Hale*—in her life.

If she won…

Ty thought of all the new people she would meet, the new *men* she would meet. Men who hadn't called her "white-trash jailbait"—a slur she clearly couldn't forget; men who didn't come saddled with a name and family eponymous with corruption and public disgust.

If Shannen won *Victorious,* she would be lost to him again, this time forever. The more he considered it, the more Ty was convinced that was true.

No more contact between us. This is over. I mean it, she'd said tonight, and though he'd glibly replied that he heard her, Ty knew he hadn't, not really, not until right now.

Now the impact of her words reverberated within him. She was ending their relationship before it had a chance to evolve into intimacy, exactly what he had done nine years ago. He hadn't relented then; he couldn't have. Didn't she understand that?

He mentally argued his case against making love to a seventeen-year-old girl. Maybe if he'd been a seventeen-year-old boy, the playing field would've been even, but he had been a responsible adult....

So he'd stuck to his decision back then.

Suppose that Shannen stuck to hers, whether winning or losing this game. And just in case that wasn't torment enough, he could also ponder the timing of her "no more contact" edict.

She had issued her decree after he'd informed her that he was no longer rich. Suppose he had said yes, his inheritance remained intact, and that due to savvy investing, he was even richer today than he had been nine years ago? That he worked as a cameraman because it was interesting and challenging, not because he needed the job to pay his bills?

Would she have been open to "more contact" if she'd known that?

Five

"Ty, what'd you think about that shocker revelation last night? You know, that Jed secretly slept with both Keri and Lucy and then voted against them, like it meant nothing to him? Which it probably didn't, the rat!'' By the sound of her voice, production assistant Heidi was highly indignant.

Ty was testing camera angles, adjusting light filters while waiting for the twins to emerge from their tent. Heidi flitted around him like a manic mosquito, talking nonstop, holding his coffee for him.

He said nothing, hoping she would take the hint and keep quiet. It was barely dawn—he'd slept about a total of an hour last night, and he hadn't given a single thought to the "shocker revelation" about Jed, Keri and Lucy.

With a long-suffering sigh, he reached for his coffee. Heidi handed it to him, chatting all the while. He'd obviously been too subtle with his hint; she hadn't picked it up.

"The other PAs, Kevin, Adam and Debbie—think it's possible that Cortnee made it all up, to turn the others against Jed,'' continued Heidi. ''I mean, the fact she's still in the game when she's never been able to do anything to help win a single contest, and that she seemed like such an airhead at the beginning—well, I guess this proves that she's not, doesn't it?''

Heidi waited expectantly for Ty to answer. Since he hadn't been paying attention to a thing she'd said, all he could offer was, ''Huh?''

''Cortnee turned out to be shrewd,'' explained Heidi. ''She figured that Jed would talk the others into voting her out, so she had to strike first. Saying Jed had sex with Keri and Lucy guaranteed that the twins would turn on him. Did you see the looks on their faces when Cortnee dropped her bombshell? Shannen looked ready to puke in disgust, and Lauren—well, she was devastated, poor thing.''

The mention of the twins immediately caught Ty's attention. He well knew Shannen's ''ready-to-puke-in-disgust'' look but, ''Lauren was devastated?'' he echoed. He'd definitely missed that.

''Well, yeah. It's obvious Lauren has this big crush on Jed, and to hear that he—''

''You're sure it's not Shannen with the crush?'' Ty cut in, feeling his face flame with horror. He sounded like an insecure eighth-grader!

He was truly drowning in the rocky seas of lovesickness with that inane question. He knew Shannen didn't have a crush on Jed, yet he couldn't stop himself from seeking reassurance that she didn't. Oh, he was a lovesick fool, all right!

But Heidi thought he was making a joke, and she laughed obligingly. ''Some crush that would be! Shannen usually looked at Jed like she wished she could dismember him.''

''She looks at a lot of people that way,'' murmured Ty. Himself included, at times.

''Yeah, she does. But Lauren's so sweet, and remember

how she'd just gaze at Jed and praise him and stand up for him when the others dumped on him? There was no mistaking which twin was which when it came to Jed."

"Do you think Shannen knows her sister has this crush on Jed?" asked Ty, his interest so piqued that he didn't bother to ponder what would've previously been unfathomable to him—that he would ever stand around eagerly gossiping with a production assistant.

"That's what we'd all like to know!" cried Heidi. "If you stop and think about it, we've never heard a personal conversation between the twins in the whole time we've been filming. We know all kinds of things about the others because they talk about themselves all the time. But the twins—zip, nada, nothing."

"Aside from mentioning the diner their family owns and occasionally quoting their grandmother, neither one has revealed anything about herself or her sister," Ty agreed. Though he was glad Shannen didn't feel the need to bare her soul in front of the cameras, it was driving him crazy that she didn't feel the need to bare her soul to him away from the cameras, either. She remained a closed book, one he wanted to open.

"The twins just stick to making comments on what's happening on the island," said Heidi. "Do you think they're hiding something?"

"Um, hard to say," he mumbled. Shannen was already keeping a lot of secrets—their past relationship, his true identity, their clandestine meetings in the island grove. But was she hiding something *else?*

"Kevin says the twins are masters of deception," Heidi reported.

"Maybe not deception." Ty's tone was thoughtful. "But certainly discreet. Their personal conversations obviously take place when the cameras aren't around."

"Wouldn't it be cool to shoot a scene of Shannen asking Lauren about Jed?" enthused Heidi. "I wish there was a way for us to interact with them and suggest it, but then we'd be accused of interference and get fired. Oh, look, here comes—'' A twin emerged from the tent. ''—one of them, although I can't guess which.''

Ty knew exactly who it was. Lauren. He filmed her going to the spring for her morning ablutions, all the while anticipating the pleasure and pain of seeing Shannen again. The two feelings had become so intertwined, he could hardly separate them.

But as an endlessly long hour passed, his anticipation was supplanted by mind-numbing boredom.

The contestants noticed Shannen's absence, too.

''I can't believe your sister is still sleeping,'' said Konrad.

He, Rico and Cortnee sat around the fire with Lauren, their cups filled with the morning brew of boiled water flavored with two used tea bags shared among them. Breakfast was always the leanest meal of the day.

''You don't think she's, like, dead, do you?'' Rico sounded only half-jesting. ''Maybe someone ought to check on her.''

''She's sick,'' declared Cortnee. ''She was gone a really, really, really long time last night. When she came back, she sounded like she was gagging or sobbing or something. I asked her if she was okay and she said yes, but I didn't believe her.''

Ty almost dropped his camera. Shannen had been sobbing—as in crying? He watched the entire production crew come alive with curiosity and felt the protective urge to drive them away. So he could go to Shannen inside that pitiful tent and...

Shannen crawled out of the tent at that moment.

''Shannen!'' Lauren jumped to her feet and rushed over to her twin. ''Cortnee said you were sick last night. Why didn't you wake me up?''

Quick as lightning, Reggie Ellis moved in with his camera for a super close-up.

Shannen's actions were just as swift and instinctive. She put her hand over the camera lens. "Get that thing away from me," she ordered, "and don't ever shove it in my face again."

A stunned Reggie stopped filming and stared mutely at the equally amazed contestants and crew.

"Cut!" ordered Ty, who was the senior crew member at the camp at this early hour. It was an unnecessary command, since both Reggie and Paul, the only two with cameras besides himself, weren't shooting anyway.

Ty walked over to Shannen. "Are you all right?" he asked quietly, restraining the urge to touch her arm, her face, her hair, just to have some physical contact with her, however slight.

But he knew how much she wouldn't welcome that, not with all the onlookers.

"I'm fine, thank you for asking." Purposefully she stepped away from him and turned to Reggie. "I'm sorry. I, um, I guess I lost it for a minute there. You can start the cameras rolling again."

Reggie and Paul looked uncertainly at Ty.

"You better do what she says," Konrad interjected, a trifle gleefully. "It's cool the way she bosses you camera guys around like she's Clark Garrett herself."

For the first time Ty considered the implications of Konrad being part of their unfilmed interaction in the ocean the other day. Would Konrad use it to somehow discredit Shannen? And if so, would Shannen blame Ty for it all? He frowned.

"What do you think, Ty?" asked Reggie, rousing him from his troubling reverie.

"Go ahead." Ty nodded to the two other cameramen, and they all resumed shooting.

There was an awkward silence before Rico's acting experience came to the fore, picking up the scene where they'd left off.

"So, you were sick last night, but you didn't wake up your sister for help?" Rico cued Shannen. Her outburst could be seamlessly edited out if The Powers That Be so decided.

"I was accosted by a germ last night." Shannen spit out the words as if she had contempt for them, glaring directly at Ty, whose camera, of course, was on her. "But that's over with—I got it all out of my system. No need to drag anybody else into it."

Shannen met his eyes, sending him a not-so-subtle message. That he was the "germ" she'd gotten out of her system. She looked, she sounded, like she meant every word.

But Cortnee had said she'd heard Shannen crying last night. And by the looks of her this morning, by her uncharacteristically late awakening, Ty guessed that Shannen had spent a hellish, sleepless night, similar to his own. The notion pleased him. He was still very much in her system.

He smiled at her.

She stiffened. "I found this." She tossed the tube of antibiotic ointment to Cortnee. "You and Lauren should put it on your blisters."

"Can I use it?" Rico piped up. "I have blisters, too."

Blister-free Konrad cast him a scornful glance, then turned to Shannen. "Where did you find it?" he asked suspiciously.

"At the spring. Somebody must've dropped it. My guess is a member of the crew." Shannen's tone was challenging, as if daring someone to come up with another explanation. "I used it last night and it did help." She held up her hands to Ty's camera to show the partially healed blisters. "See?"

Did anybody detect the taunting note in her voice? Ty wondered. On the other hand, how could anyone miss it?

He saw the production assistants exchange inquiring glances.

Reggie and Paul dutifully shot the others rubbing the ointment on their painfully blistered hands. Shannen went to the spring to wash up, followed by Ty and his camera.

And Heidi. Her presence prevented any private conversation between Ty and Shannen.

It was frustrating, it was maddening. Shannen followed the rules of the game, ignoring the crew as if they were invisible. As if they weren't human beings. She washed her face and brushed her teeth and braided her hair into one thick plait, all at an interminably slow pace.

Ty felt Heidi shifting restlessly beside him and knew she was bursting to ask Shannen something about Lauren's crush on Jed. He shook his head forbiddingly at her.

Shannen intercepted the look.

"It looks like he's trying to incinerate you with that glare of his. What did you do to make him mad?" Shannen asked Heidi. "Or is he one of those bad-tempered bosses who gets ticked off for no reason at all?"

Ty noted that her friendly tone was at odds with the demonic glint in her eyes.

Heidi was dumbstruck at being addressed by a contestant. "I...I can't talk to you!" she gasped. "I could lose my job."

"You'd fire her?" Shannen addressed Ty this time. "Or rat her out to somebody else who would?"

"Don't worry, Heidi, I've turned off my camera," said Ty, but his eyes were holding Shannen's. "You aren't going to be fired."

"Thanks, Ty." Heidi gulped.

"You're a real prince, *Ty,*" said Shannen. "So thoughtful, so concerned."

"I think I'd better go back to the camp and see if anybody needs me," Heidi said nervously. "Bobby should be arriving at any time now, and if it's okay with you, Ty, I'll just—''

"Sure. Go on back, Heidi." Ty was magnanimous. "I'll hold down the fort here."

Heidi left, giving him a look of gratitude mixed with sympathy, presumably for having to stay behind.

Shannen noticed. "Seems like your lackey feels sorry for you being stuck here with the Wicked Witch of the Island."

"You've terrified the poor girl," Ty said dryly. He set his camera down on the flat rock, giving up even the pretense of filming. "No fair dragging innocent bystanders into our own private war, Shannen."

"We're not at war," she snapped. "We're not anything."

"I'm merely the 'germ' you've gotten out of your system?" Ty laughed softly. "Liar."

Shannen clenched her fists at her sides. "You'd better pick up that camera and turn it on, or I'll get you fired."

"A smooth liar, too. Look how you handled the questions about the tube of ointment. You were so believable that the PAs will be in a frenzy wondering which one of them dropped it and if they'll be in trouble for it."

"I'm not a liar. Lying doesn't come naturally to me," she retorted.

"I see. Unlike the Howes, who have an inborn talent for lying, you've had to work to acquire the skill. But from your flawless impersonation of an over-twenty-one grad student to your ointment tale nine years later, it's obvious that you've mastered the art."

Shannen stalked off, only to return as if she were attached to some invisible string that Ty could pull as he pleased. It was almost too true; she'd wanted to get away from him, yet here she was, right back at his side. Making excuses as to why.

"After I deliberately didn't say anything about the Howes and their multitude of lies, you—"

"I understand. Howes and lying…too easy a target. Why bother?"

In spite of herself, she laughed. And quickly caught herself. "It's not funny, Ty. You don't always have to make the first joke about your family to fend off—"

"—the inevitable joke to be made by someone else? It's become a defensive habit, I guess."

"And it's not fair to keep referring to…what I did nine years ago. I was young and immature back then. I shouldn't have lied about my age and all, I know that."

"Then do you forgive me for doing the only thing I could back then, given those circumstances, Shannen?" he pressed, his dark gaze intense.

She averted her eyes. "Yes, but it doesn't matter anymore. We can't go back to the past. It's been too long, and we're different people now. I meant what I said last night, Tynan. We can't—"

"Cortnee said she heard you crying last night," Ty interrupted her again. "Were you?"

"No! And even if I was crying, it doesn't mean that it would have anything to do with you!" Shannen countered crossly. "Don't flatter yourself into thinking otherwise."

Ty stared at her. "I just had a thought."

She opened her mouth to speak, then shook her head. "Too easy a target. Why bother?"

They both grinned spontaneously.

Then Ty became intent. "Shannen, was it you Cortnee heard crying last night? She never mentioned you by name, and she can't tell you and Lauren apart. Did she actually hear Lauren crying? Is that why you're so upset this morning, Shannen?"

His face softened, and this time he gave in to the need to touch her. He laid his hand on her forearm, his fingers stroking lightly.

"Did you get back to camp last night, still hungry after staving off temptation, only to find Lauren crying her eyes out over Jed? That's more than enough to cause a sleepless night and to make you wake up in a ferocious mood."

"What?" Shannen's voice rose to a squeak. "What are you talking about? Why would Lauren cry over *Jed?* That jerk? *Please!*"

"Oh."

It occurred to Shannen that he was still stroking her arm. And that she was enjoying it way too much. She swatted his hand away. "What do you mean 'Oh'?" she demanded.

"Nothing." He shrugged. "Just 'Oh.'"

"You stand there looking totally clueless after making accusations about my sister and that narcissistic creep Jed but you—"

"I wasn't making an accusation. The production assistants all claim Lauren has a crush on Jed and that she looked devastated when Cortnee said he'd slept with those two other girls. I didn't see any devastation, so I thought I'd missed the crush, as well." His eyes narrowed perceptively. "Did you miss it all, too, Shannen?"

"Lauren wouldn't like a preening, self-absorbed twit like Jed," she insisted.

But a note of doubt had crept into her voice.

"Lauren could've been the one to cast the vote against Cortnee," said Ty. "In fact, she *must* have been the one. There was no reason for Rico or Konrad to vote against her, and you said that you didn't."

"Maybe Jed voted against Cortnee. She's been really bitchy toward him lately."

"But then who voted against Konrad?" countered Ty. "It had to be Jed. He was convinced Konrad did something to make the boat sink. I agree, but there's no proof—"

"It's irrelevant who voted against Cortnee, Ty." It was Shannen's turn to interrupt. "All that matters is that Jed was voted off. But I'll prove you're wrong about Lauren's supposed crush. I'll ask her about it. When we're alone and the cameras aren't around,'' she added pointedly.

"I wouldn't expect it to be any other way, especially given your penchant for secrecy—I mean, privacy.''

"By the snarky way you said 'privacy,' I know you really did mean secrecy. In a negative way,'' she added tersely.

"Not negative. Curious. You and Lauren never share any personal information about yourselves. We can recite Cortnee's musical triumphs from grade school on, we've heard all about Konrad's prison adventures and Jed's wilderness adventures and Rico's—''

"Is that how the crew spends their off time?'' Shannen interrupted. "Gossiping about the contestants?''

"Pretty much,'' he admitted. "But I didn't listen until they mentioned you and your sister. You're the only one on this island I'm interested in, Shannen. Now go ahead and throw it back in my face.'' Ty laughed ruefully. "I've set it up for you.''

"When you put it that way, any retaliatory zinger I might make loses its—'' Shannen paused, grimacing "—zing.''

"With that kind of encouragement, I may as well bare my soul,'' Ty said wryly. "Well, why not? At this point I have nothing to lose.''

Shannen felt her stomach do a Flying Wallenda-type somersault. And then Ty reached for her hand and gently tugged her toward him. She went, unresisting, squinting against the sun. Trying to stay immune to the urgency, the desire in his eyes.

"I know we can't go back to the past and that we're different people now, but that's a good thing, Shannen. I want to move ahead, not backward.'' Ty's voice was deep and low.

"I was actually glad to hear Cortnee say you were crying last night, because maybe it meant that you didn't really mean what you said when you left me. That you didn't want it to be over between us—to be over before anything had really begun," he added, as if expecting her to jump in to correct him.

He slipped behind her, brushing her body with his, in slow, sensual motion.

Shannen knew she was incapable of any kind of verbal gymnastics at this point. He was hypnotizing her with his tone, with his big hand that had begun to caress the bare skin of her back, between the end of her halter and the low waistband of her shorts.

"I hoped that what you really meant was that we should call some kind of moratorium until the game is over." The heels of his palms massaged her shoulder blades, and she tried to stifle a small moan of sheer pleasure.

Tried and failed. Her eyelids fluttered shut.

"We'll make plans to see each other after the game, to continue what we've begun. To be together." He lowered his mouth to her neck, flicked his tongue against her skin. "I want us to be together, Shannen. I want you to want that, too."

She didn't reply. Talking required too much thought, too much effort, and she didn't want to break the spell. Instead she inclined her neck to give him better access, shivering in pleasure at the feel of his lips, his breath against her hair. Didn't actions speak louder than words, anyway?

He whispered her name again and glided his hands around to the front of her, cupping her breasts with sensual care. He teased her nipples through the cotton of her halter, and she felt them tighten almost immediately. She pressed against his palms, encouraging, demanding.

This was what she wanted, what she needed. Ty, his touch, his voice murmuring what he wanted to do, what they would do together. Her defenses, already weak against him, crumbled. And she didn't care.

Suddenly, being caressed wasn't enough—she had to touch him, too. To kiss him the way she'd been dying to.

Shannen turned quickly and grasped his shirt, pulling him even closer, lifting her head as he lowered his to hers.

Their kiss was explosive, devouring. He held her head, burying his fingers in her hair as she clutched him, their tongues caressing, mating in erotic simulation.

They kissed long and hard, their bodies locked together, passion running hot and unrestrained. Shannen felt her knees buckle and she let Ty fully support her, knowing if he were to let her go, she'd fall. She was heady with sensual weakness and gave in to it, savoring it.

When Ty began to slowly, carefully lower them both to the ground, she clung to him, trembling with anticipation.

"Is there a hidden camera filming all this?" The voice, sounding exactly like Shannen's, filled the air. "Because the only camera I see is on a rock, and it's definitely not being used."

The sweet illusion of intimacy surrounding the lovers abruptly shattered.

Shannen pulled away first, and for a moment Ty stood there befuddled. He swore he'd heard Shannen's voice, but that couldn't be. His lips had been covering hers, his tongue deep in her mouth.

"Lauren." Shannen inhaled a breathless gulp of air.

Ty's head cleared and he opened his eyes. "Busted," he muttered.

"And then some," agreed Lauren. Ty blinked. She didn't sound as sweet as she usually did; her tone had an edge that was definitely Shannen-esque.

"What the hell is going on here, Shannen?" Lauren demanded, an auditory dead ringer for Shannen, as well as a visual one.

Shannen cast a covert glance at Ty. He nodded his head, giving her the go-ahead to tell all. In fact, he wanted Shannen's twin sister, the person closest to her, to know the whole truth about their relationship. Past, present and future.

Shannen bit her lip and looked down at the sand, seemingly disinclined to say anything. She needed time to regain her composure, Ty thought tenderly. Well, she could count on him to step in and explain everything.

"Shannen and I know each other," he began, giving Lauren his warmest we're-going-to-be-friends smile.

"Duh!" Lauren snapped. "I figured that out in the ocean yesterday, but I didn't know just how well you two 'know each other.'" She turned to her twin. "He gave you that ointment, didn't he, Shannen?"

Shannen nodded. "It's not truly cheating, I shared it with everybody," she said in a plaintive tone Ty had never before heard her use. "And he hasn't given me anything else, honest!"

"Not for lack of trying, obviously." Lauren was sarcastic.

"Look, let me—" Ty interjected, but both sisters ignored him.

"Shannen, we've come this far, we're almost down to the Final Four. One of us could actually win the whole game," cried Lauren. "We could win the million dollars! Why would you risk screwing things up like this?"

Shannen heaved a sigh. "I wasn't thinking, Lauren."

"Tell me something I don't know, Shannen," Lauren retorted acidly.

"You could plead not guilty by reason of malnutrition, Shannen," suggested Ty in an attempt to lighten the tension.

A mistake, he realized as the twins both glowered at him.

"Stay out of this, Tynan." Shannen's tone was sharp, dismissive.

"Sweetie, I'm in as deep as you are." He meant to sound cajoling and was surprised to hear the mockery in his tone.

Well, not too surprised. He was getting impatient, not to mention all that raging sexual frustration surging through him. Why wouldn't Shannen simply tell her sister the truth?

They hadn't committed a crime; they were two people in love....

That rogue flash of insight struck him with the precision of a stun gun. He knew he wanted Shannen, that she intrigued and attracted him as much as she had nine years ago. More. But he hadn't thought of himself as in love with her. When was the last time he'd been in love?

For that matter, when was the *first* time?

Howes didn't fall in love; they had relationships that invariably soured, whether those involved were married or not.

This time Ty felt as if he'd been hit over the head with a shovel. He'd followed the standard Howe emotional blueprint by lying to Shannen about his financial status because he didn't fully trust her not to want him for his money.

And yet he thought he was in love?

Ty remembered that long-ago "coming of age" talk his father had given him and Trent.

"You'll be hearing all sorts of nonsense about love from girls." Dear old Dad had snickered, not bothering even to try to keep a straight face. "Don't be chumps and fall for it. The only kind of genuine love that can exist between opposite sexes is the mother and son and father and daughter kind. Possibly sister and brother. But so-called romantic love is pure fiction and don't forget it. Men and women get together for either sex or convenience, and don't be duped into thinking otherwise."

Ty winced at the memory. Well, when it came to his feelings for Shannen, he could safely rule out convenience. But sex was an integral part of their relationship. Was that all it was between them? A hot sexual infatuation fueled by the lush tropical setting, plus the enticing element of the forbidden?

Shannen must think so; she certainly wasn't pouring out her abiding love for him to her sister.

"Pick up that camera and start filming us," one of the twins said.

Ty blinked. Which one had spoken, Shannen or Lauren? For the first time he was unsure.

"I'll start talking about how hungry I am for the fabulous silver dollar pancakes at the diner," said Shannen. "We might as well get in a little free advertising for Gramma."

One telltale sign clued Ty that it was Shannen who was speaking; her lips were still moist and swollen from their kisses. But that startling moment when he couldn't tell one sister from the other jarred him. It seemed symbolic. Of exactly what, he wasn't sure. Right now he was sure of nothing at all.

"Okay," agreed Lauren. She picked up the camera and handed it to Ty.

He didn't turn it on. "You're one superb actress, Lauren," he said lightly. "After all those hours of filming, this is the first and only time I've ever seen you lose your temper or even display a hint of aggravation. Who knew that beneath that sweet serene exterior is—"

"Lauren *is* sweet and serene," Shannen jumped to her twin's defense. "She only gets upset when she's with me."

"You mean she'll only allow you to see how she *really* feels," corrected Ty. "Everybody else gets the Lady Lauren facade. As a control freak, your sister beats you hands down, Shannen." He laughed. "I feel privileged to see the true inner Lauren. Makes me feel like family."

Lauren look at him, aghast. "Shannen, what have you done?" she wailed. "I can tell that we can't trust this guy. He could make us lose the game. And we're so close, I can almost feel that money!"

"Ah, the sweet feel of cold hard cash." Ty's dark eyes glittered. "I can relate. You, too, hmm, Shannen?"

Shannen shot him a glare and caught Lauren's hand, dragging her away to join the others back at camp. Ty followed them, his camera rolling.

Six

Bobby Dixon showed up later in the day with food, money and another contest.

"Today we're going to have an auction. I'm going to give each of you five one-hundred-dollar bills. You can bid on all of these savory delights and spend as much as you want on anything you want—until your money runs out."

With a flourish, he unveiled an array of food: a cheeseburger with choice of condiments, a piece of chocolate cake topped with whipped cream and hot fudge, an enormous fresh fruit salad and a turkey sandwich on thick fresh bread.

Shannen's eyes connected with Ty's over that one. She felt her stomach rumble because she knew exactly how that sandwich smelled and could imagine how it tasted. Ty merely smiled, and she looked away, scowling.

Bobby was offering more food to be auctioned. A large bag of potato chips and a cold beer, a liter bottle of cola, a plate of nachos, a barbecued chicken, a tub of potato salad. A movie theater counter's assortment of candy. A container of fruit-flavored yogurt, a container of frozen yogurt. A quart of designer ice cream packed on dry ice so it wouldn't melt before the bidding concluded.

"If we have any cash left over after bidding, can we keep it?" asked Konrad, fondling the stiff new hundred-dollar bills.

"Sure," Bobby assured him smoothly. "But I sincerely doubt anybody will have any money left. Did I tell you I also have a steak dinner, complete with baked potato and salad with the dressing of your choice? And I'll throw in whatever you want as a beverage to go with it."

Rico gasped. "I bid three hundred dollars on the steak dinner."

"I bid three-hundred-fifty," said Konrad.

The twins exchanged glances.

"Red meat, ick!' exclaimed Cortnee. "I'll bid one hundred for the fruit salad. And fifty for the frozen yogurt."

The auction unfolded at a lively pace, with the cameras filming each contestant avidly devouring what they'd won.

Except for the Cullen twins. Neither bid on anything. Both stared resolutely at the five one-hundred dollar bills they held in their hands.

Ty noticed right away, of course. Amid the auction hoopla, it took the others a while longer.

"Shannen, Lauren, you haven't bid on anything yet," Bobby Dixon exclaimed at last, his dimples deeper than ever. "Let me tempt you with this—a monster BLT, with a pile of crisp bacon, fresh lettuce and tomato on the bread of your choice."

"No, thanks. Gramma makes the world's ultimate BLT at the diner," Shannen said blithely. "I wouldn't want to settle for anything less."

"N-not even here, when you're starving on an island?" Bobby's dazzling smile faltered a bit, but he quickly recovered. "All right, then, here is something you won't be able to resist…a made-to-order pizza. And whatever you want to drink. And fresh garlic bread. *And* dessert—which you'll get to choose. Wow, I'm making myself hungry!''

"We're not bidding on anything," Lauren said sweetly. "We've decided to keep the money instead."

The other contestants gasped.

Bobby Dixon paled. "Surely you don't mean that."

"Yes." Shannen nodded. "We do."

Beside him, Ty heard Reggie Ellis chortle.

"Bobby'll be called on the carpet for this. He was supposed to get all the cash back. Guess nobody thought it was possible for any of them to hold out against all this food after what they haven't been eating. But now there's *two* holding out with a cool grand."

"Guess nobody thought the twins would love the feel of that cash in their little hands so very much," muttered Ty.

Reggie nodded, guffawing. "Think the network will deduct the twins' thousand bucks from Bobby's paycheck?"

Bobby must have thought so, because he went into an auctioneering frenzy, offering every kind of food and drink imaginable to entice the twins to bid. Long after Konrad, Rico and Cortnee had spend every cent of their five hundred dollars and proclaimed themselves stuffed to the point of nausea, Bobby kept it up.

And Shannen and Lauren refused to bid on anything.

"Give it up, Slick B," Konrad said at last. "They ain't buyin' whatever you're sellin'."

"I guess not." Bobby managed a tight-lipped smile. "Color me amazed at the strength of your willpower, girls."

Color me unfazed, Ty thought grimly. He'd already seen Shannen's willpower in action, and Lauren had given him a hint as to how much they wanted money. Given a choice of a thousand dollars between them and a chance to eat, it was no contest at all.

Bobby was visibly displeased. This outcome was obviously not what he and The Powers That Be had intended.

"Okay, listen up, everybody! After bidding and eating all that food, are you ready for a surprise?" Bobby asked robotically, following the script as previously written without noting the twins' unexpected lack of participation.

"This auction is also an immunity contest." Bobby's flat tone failed to convey excitement. "The person with the most money left is the one who wins immunity at the tribal council vote-out tonight."

"Hardly the moment of suspense you were hoping for, huh, Slick Bob?" Rico cackled. "We all know right off the bat who gets immunity. The twins. Too bad they aren't one person."

"Funny, that's what our mother said when we were born," Lauren piped up. "And many many times after."

Shannen gave her sister a censorial nudge that only Ty recorded with his camera. Everybody else was watching Bobby trying to smile deeply enough to get his dimples back in place.

The twins' mother was not entranced with the prospect of twins? Ty pondered that as he studied the sisters' identical looks of chagrin. Both appeared to regret Lauren's impulsive revelation.

"Does this mean both Shannen and Lauren get immunity?" Cortnee asked.

"No!" Bobby was quick to reply. "Only one can have immunity. Shannen and Lauren, one of you gets the totem pole and one of you goes to the meeting tonight without its protection."

"I can almost read your mind, so why don't you go ahead and say it, Bobby?" Shannen challenged him. "One of us goes to the meeting tonight to be voted off, am I right?"

Bobby went into a soliloquy that he'd obviously rehearsed, about one twin facing the prospect of leaving her twin sister on the island. Which one would it be? He gestured to the twins, directorially calling to the cameras to focus on them.

"You girls will have to make the decision yourselves, to choose which one of you gets the immunity totem," Bobby added dramatically.

Ty zeroed in on Shannen. Her expression was priceless, and he came close to laughing out loud.

"Do you expect us to have a catfight or something?" Shannen glowered at Bobby. "Not a chance! Lauren, you take the immunity totem. I'll brave the council on my own."

Shannen waited expectantly for Lauren to make the same offer back to her. She would insist that Lauren keep the totem pole, of course, but she fully expected Lauren to refuse at least once.

"Thanks, Shannen!" Lauren was all smiles as she threw her arms around Shannen's neck. "You're the best sister in the world!"

"I'll say she is!" seconded an admiring Konrad. "Because you know we're going to vote you off tonight, Shannen. Nothing personal, but we can't keep two of you around anymore."

"I understand. Two of a kind is one too many," Shannen murmured.

She managed to smile, though she felt sick with disappointment. It surprised her; she didn't think being out of the game would bother her so much.

Shannen kept her eyes away from Ty and clutched her money, smiling till her face hurt.

She wanted a little time alone with Lauren, but the cameras constantly stayed on them both. Hoping for some sort of sisterly tiff?

It didn't happen. The twins didn't mention the immunity issue. They recounted their hundred-dollar bills, all ten of them.

For a change, Ty wasn't filming them, Shannen noted.

He'd staked out a place on the beach by Konrad and Cortnee.

Cortnee was trying to teach Konrad some dance steps, and they both laughed uproariously at his failed attempts to match hers. Rico lay on the sand, clutching his stomach and groaning about the too-rich meal he'd eaten.

"Do you think Shannen will get voted off tonight?" Heidi asked Ty as they set up for filming at the tribal council area later that night.

"I didn't hear Rico or Cortnee jump in to refute Konrad when he said they'd vote her off, but who knows?" Ty shrugged.

"After experiencing Shannen's PMS moments today, I have to say that I like Lauren better," admitted Heidi. "She's always so sweet."

"PMS moments?" echoed Ty. "I believe Shannen blamed her bout of temper this morning on being accosted by a germ last night."

The germ being him, of course. And he hadn't accosted her! He frowned. Why had he prolonged this stupid conversation with Heidi, anyway? Because he wanted to talk about Shannen at every opportunity with anyone? He was bordering on pathetic!

"A germ is just a euphemism for PMS, of course," scoffed Heidi. "Like I used to call my ex-fiancé a germ because he made me sick."

Now that was definitely a discussion to avoid. Ty pretended to be completely absorbed in adjusting the angle of the standing camera.

The contestants filed into the meeting place, and Bobby launched into a long monologue about the Final Four and Destiny.

Shannen barely tuned in to listen. She was too preoccupied to pay attention and kept looking around, trying to prepare herself for the voting to come.

She knew she was going to be voted off and so did everybody else. She wouldn't throw a tantrum over it as some others had, Shannen vowed. She wouldn't tear up and babble something insipidly sentimental, either. She was going to make a graceful exit, smiling, saying it had been fun and wishing the others good luck.

Reflexively she located Ty behind his camera. He wasn't looking at her; he was filming Cortnee, who was chatting quietly with Konrad while Bobby droned on. It was strange not to have Ty's full attention, not to have him watching her through his lens.

Shannen realized just how accustomed she'd become to having him focus on her. But from the time the auction had ended this afternoon, he had ignored her, filming everyone else *but* her.

She thought back to the passionate kiss Lauren had interrupted this morning. No use kidding herself—that had been a kiss meant to lead to much more. And it was her last private interaction with Tynan and had ended on a sour note, with her snapping at him, glaring as she left him.

But that was how most of their encounters on this island ended, and it had never altered his behavior toward her. Invariably, the next time she saw him, he would be watching her, that intense look in his eye as his camera rolled.

But now…he didn't even glance her way when he thought she might not be looking. She knew because she watched him covertly but constantly.

She felt anxiety begin a slow, steady build inside her. Ty was acting as though he was completely uninterested in her.

Because he was? Shannen fought against the sinking of her heart.

We'll make plans to see each other after the game, to continue what we've begun. To be together. She closed her eyes and could hear his voice as she relived their brief time together this morning at the spring. *I want us to be together, Shannen. I want you to want that, too.*

She felt Lauren's hand squeeze hers.

"Shannen, don't fall asleep during Bobby's big talk," she whispered. "Though it's tempting 'cause he's such a windbag." Lauren giggled.

Shannen opened her eyes. Cameraman Reggie was filming her and Lauren, and Ty still wasn't looking their way. If—when!—she was voted out of the game tonight, she knew she would go to a nearby island to stay with the last seven contestants who'd been voted off the island.

There was a hotel there where they all stayed until it was time for "jury duty," when the ten rejected contestants would appear at the final tribal council to vote for a winner, choosing between the Final Two.

She would be over there, and Ty would be here on this island, filming the surviving contestants all day and spending the nights in the crew's camp. She wouldn't see him anymore!

Shannen inhaled a sharp breath of dismay. Though she'd told Ty repeatedly that she didn't want to see him, that whatever was growing between them was over, at last she faced the truth.

She wanted what Ty had said he wanted. *We'll make plans to see each other after the game, to continue what we've begun. To be together.*

But how could she tell him so, if she were on some other island? She knew the procedure: the rejects gathered their belongings immediately after the vote and were whisked away in a boat, not to be seen again.

The departure was never filmed. A pair of production assistants accompanied the loser until the boat left shore. She wouldn't have the chance to say anything to Ty.

When would she see him again? When the jury of contestants were brought back to the island to cast their votes for the winner? There would be no chance to be alone with Ty then.

The anxiety swirling through her was awful; she hadn't felt this nervous about a man since she'd been back in high school, wondering if Ty would call her.

In the midst of her unbridled emotional storm, the voting came as a distinct anti-climax. Shannen cast her vote against Rico.

"Nothing personal," she said, as the cameraman—who was not Ty—filmed her slipping her vote into the box.

Konrad, Rico and Cortnee voted against Shannen, as she'd expected. No, it wasn't personal, and she didn't take it that way. If she'd kept the immunity totem herself, they would have voted off Lauren. The alliance had included both twins until now, when one had to go.

What surprised her most was Lauren's vote against Cortnee. Was this the second time she'd done so? Ty would think so.

Ty. He was filming Rico, Cortnee and Konrad, who were trying to look somber over Shannen's dismissal and not quite pulling it off. She knew the relief they were feeling at having survived another round. Until tonight she'd felt that same way after each vote.

"Shannen, your light has been extinguished." Bobby took Shannen's flashlight, a symbol of her banishment. A torch would've been more dramatic, but *Victorious* had opted not to be totally derivative.

"It's better this way, Shan," Lauren whispered into her ear. "I'll be able to play Konrad and Rico against Cortnee. I know you wouldn't do it that way, but it's going to work, you'll see. They like me better than Cortnee."

"Ready to go, Shannen?" The two male production assistants, Kevin and Adam, came to Shannen's side.

"Let's get your stuff and put you on the boat," said one.

"You're going to love the hotel," enthused the other.

"It's a first-class resort with all the amenities. You can do anything you want and eat as much as you want. Think of it as a free vacation!''

She knew they were being kind, trying to ease the sting of being voted off. She smiled at them as she slipped an arm through each of theirs. "Thanks, guys."

She cast a final look back. If she were on camera, it would appear that she was taking a last glance at the familiar setting, or maybe checking on her twin.

But she wasn't on camera. Filming had stopped, and the crew was packing up the equipment. Ty chatted with the female production assistants, one of them Heidi.

For the first time, Shannen felt a stab of jealousy at the sight of Ty talking to another woman. He and Heidi would certainly have a lot in common, working in the same industry, on the same show. Did Heidi know his last name was Howe, not Hale? Shannen doubted it. Ty made it clear that his new life—

His new life. *His life without money!* Suddenly all the pieces began to fit, creating the most dismal picture. Shannen wanted to cry out with pain.

Suddenly she understood it all.

Ty's blatant loss of interest in her occurred right after she'd given the immunity totem to Lauren. *The moment it became clear that she wasn't going to win the game and the prize money.*

In fact, she wouldn't win a cent, since she hadn't made it to the Final Four. The auction money she'd held on to wouldn't interest him, not when he'd been hoping to rekindle a flame with the million-dollar winner.

It was weirdly cosmic that Ty, having been plagued by fortune hunters until the fall of the House of Howe, should seek to become a fortune hunter himself.

And now that she had no prospects for a fortune, he had abruptly given her up.

Shannen stoically held back her tears. She hadn't felt this hopeless since she was back in high school and Ty had ended it between them.

The hotel on the island lived up to the PA's promise. It was a first-class resort with all the amenities, including two swimming pools, one indoors and one outdoors connected by a tunnel one swam through, two bars, one small and dark and quiet, one noisy and raucous with a live band and dance floor. There were three dining rooms, each differently themed, and—perhaps to counteract all those gourmet meals—a fully equipped gym and steam room.

An enthusiastic young staffer, Miles, who worked for *Victorious* and was "in charge of the contestants here" gave Shannen the grand tour of the facilities.

"Tonight everybody's in the Parrot Room dancing," said Miles. "By everybody, I mean the contestants and the *Victorious* staff who are assigned here. We all hang out together. It's like one big spring break around here."

She'd arrived in the lowest spirits, but Shannen felt herself respond to the resort's allure. She'd seen places like this on *Lifestyles of the Rich and Famous* but had never expected to set foot in one.

"Seems like you have a better job being stationed here than the crew stuck filming on the island," she remarked.

"My uncle is Clark Garrett," confided Miles. "You'd better believe I decided to stay in this place instead of that bug-ridden crew camp."

He led her to her room and opened the door. "Order anything you want from room service, the network is picking up the tab." Miles was expansive. "And come down to the Parrot Room and join us later. They have a great band."

"Thanks, but I'm tired." Shannen gazed around her room, at the king-size bed, which had already been turned down invitingly.

The clean white sheets and big pillows piled high against

the bamboo headboard beckoned. She glanced at the screen door, opening onto a balcony that held a chaise longue and a round table with two chairs. The ocean breezes wafted through the curtains, filling the room with the cool refreshing scent of the sea.

"This looks like heaven." She sighed. "After I take a shower, I'm going to bed and sleep for the next three days."

Miles laughed. "Everybody says that when they first arrive here. But by tomorrow afternoon, I predict you'll be at the swimming pool and making plans to join us for dinner and dancing." He handed her the room key. "Your bag is in the closet—you remember, the one you packed in case you made it here."

Shannen remembered when she and Lauren had packed their bags according to the show's directive, bringing basics for a short stay at the hotel, should they survive long enough to be among the jury. How excited and nervous they'd been!

Now Lauren had made it to the Final Four and would definitely receive some prize money. Plus, she still had a chance to go all the way and win the million dollars.

That thought put a spring into her step as Shannen said goodbye to Miles. After carefully placing the thousand dollars' auction money in the small room safe, she headed straight for the spacious bathroom, bypassing the whirlpool for the shower stall.

There was plenty of water, soap and shampoo—things she'd taken for granted until she'd been deprived of them during her *Victorious* stint. It was sheer bliss!

After taking the longest shower of her life, she wrapped herself in a thick terry robe monogrammed with the hotel's name and smoothed coconut-scented lotion all over herself. As she dried her hair, she debated whether to go right to bed or to call room service and order something to eat. Could she stay awake that long?

She turned off the dryer and brushed her hair until it hung straight and sleek around her shoulders. After the lack of mirrors on the island, being able to see what she was doing was a luxury in itself.

Shannen heard the knock at the door and padded over to it, expecting to see Miles through the peephole, knowing she was going to turn down any other invitation to join the *Victorious* gang tonight.

Her heart slammed against her ribs, and she took another long look, wondering if she were hallucinating. Because it wasn't the young staffer standing outside in the hallway.

It was Tynan.

The rush of adrenaline that surged through her nearly knocked her off her feet.

He rapped again. "Open up, Shannen. I just heard you turn off the hair dryer, so I know you can hear me."

Shannen opened the door and stared at him, stupefied. "How...how did you—"

"I have my ways. Aren't you going to invite me in?"

She couldn't seem to breathe, let alone speak. Shannen could only gape at him, as if he were an apparition from some astral plane. An apparition wearing the same baggy khaki shorts and white T-shirt with the network's logo imprinted on the front, the clothes that he had worn all day today.

She'd certainly spent enough hours looking at him today to remember his clothing down to the exact detail. Equally unforgettable was the fact that he'd ignored her from the moment it was clear that she was no longer a million-dollar contender.

But now he was here. Shannen folded her arms in front of her chest in classic defense mode, blocking his way.

"Luckily I'm not a vampire, so I don't have to wait for an invite before entering," Ty said lightly and walked into the room.

He stepped around her, but only because she stepped out

of his way. If she hadn't moved, he seemed ready and willing to move her himself.

He looked around the room. "Nice. Bet you're not a bit nostalgic for the crowded old tent back on the island, hmm?"

Shannen finally found her voice. "Since being in the crowded old tent would mean I was still in the running to win the game, I'd rather be there than here. Though they've spared no expense to make us feel less like losers and more like tourists, I guess."

Ty had stooped to open the door of the small refrigerator in the corner of the room. "Plenty of snacks in here. Hawaiian macadamia nuts, cheeses, crackers. Cookies, fruit and yogurt. Miniature bottles of every kind of alcohol you can think of. A few full-size bottles of beer and wine, too."

"Miles would tell you to help yourself, it's on the network's tab," said Shannen, striving for a tone of nonchalance. By the tremor in her voice, she was fairly certain she hadn't pulled it off.

"Who's Miles?" Ty continued to peruse the fridge.

"Clark Garrett's nephew. He stays here and baby-sits us *Victorious* rejects."

"Oh, yes, the nephew." Ty chuckled. "I've heard about him from Heidi and the other PAs. They think he's a fool to be stuck over here while they get the on-location experience with the crew. They're sure his TV career won't last long, uncle or not, but I told them never to underestimate the power of nepotism in the industry."

He stood up, his hands filled with bottles and food packages. "The food isn't up for auction, and you don't have to worry about cheating anymore. Come on out here and enjoy it with a clear conscience, Shannen."

Without waiting for her to reply, he carried the food and drink outside to the balcony and placed them on the table.

Shannen was nonplussed to the point of inaction. Silently she watched Ty settle back on the chaise longue, one leg stretched out, his other foot on the ground. He opened a bottle of beer and took a swallow.

It occurred to her that she was clad only in the hotel robe. "I...have to get dressed," she called weakly, and snatched a bright red-and-yellow-flowered sundress and underwear from her suitcase.

She dressed in the bathroom and, taking a deep breath, joined Ty on the balcony.

"You clean up well." He gave her a slow, thorough appraisal as she stood beside the door.

"Are you going to tell me why you're here, or am I supposed to guess?" Shannen wanted to recall the words the moment she'd uttered them.

"Oh, definitely, go ahead and guess," Ty invited, laughter gleaming in his eyes. "I can't wait to hear what you'll come up with."

"I knew you'd say something like that," muttered Shannen.

"So why am I here, Shannen?"

"I'm too tired to play games," she said tersely, knowing it was a lie. She might've been tired before, but she was wide awake now. Every nerve in her body felt wired. "How did you get here, anyway? And find my room?"

"A couple of network honchos are here to discuss plans for the *Victorious* reunion show. I know, you're probably thinking—the game isn't over and they're already talking about a reunion?" Ty took another swig of the beer. "But our far-thinking executives like to plan ahead. Or more likely, they saw the chance for a company-paid vacation and grabbed it. I volunteered to bring the past few days' footage over for their viewing pleasure."

"So you took the boat here," Shannen concluded.

"As you know, it's a short ride. I was accompanied by Kevin and Adam, who went straight to the Parrot Room. Since I'm officially with the program, all I had to do to get your room number was to ask the desk clerk. Are we finished with the Q and A?''

Shannen concentrated on opening a package of crackers and tried to keep her voice steady. "I'm surprised to see you."

"I could tell." He leaned forward, his hands resting on his thighs. "What I can't tell is if you're glad or totally indifferent or smoldering with anger. You can be pretty hard to read sometimes, Shannen."

"As if you're an open book!" Shannen dropped the crackers and headed inside.

"Ah, a clue." Ty followed her into the room. "The answer is C—smoldering with anger. Next question. Are you mad at me or your sister or the other contestants—or just ticked off with life in general?"

She turned to him, startled. "Why would I be mad at Lauren?"

"Maybe because she hung on to that immunity totem pole and didn't even make you a token offer? Which you would've nobly declined, of course."

It was unnerving that he had voiced exactly what she had thought at the time. A disloyal pang of guilt surged through her.

"I wanted Lauren to have it." Shannen was defensive. "She knew that."

Ty shrugged. "Sure, but still—it would've been nice if she'd at least made the gesture."

Shannen saw the glint in his eye. "You're trying to be an instigator!"

"No, a detective. If you won't tell me why you're upset, I'm going to have to figure it out for myself. Unless you're not upset at all…just nervous. Just stalling." It took him only two steps to be standing directly in front of her. "If that's the case, let me assuage your jitters."

Shannen sucked in a breath. "If you're thinking that because Lauren is still in the game and could win the money—''

''I'm not thinking about Lauren or the game or the money, Shannen.'' He cupped her cheek with his hand.

Reflexively Shannen closed her eyes and leaned into his hand, letting the warmth of his palm envelop her. If she intended to tell him to leave, this was the time to do it, a small voice inside her head counseled.

''How can I think of anything else but you?'' His voice was a low, seductive growl. He curved his other hand over her hip in a firm possessive grasp.

Shannen's eyes stayed closed. She didn't want him to go, she achingly admitted to herself. But...

''Everything is so...unfinished between us, Ty,'' she whispered.

''I think it's time we altered that, don't you?'' Ty nibbled on her earlobe, his voice husky.

He trailed kisses along the curve of her jaw. When his mouth finally, lightly brushed hers, she exhaled with a hushed whimper. Raising her arms slowly, she laid her hands against his chest, feeling his body heat through the well-washed cotton material of his shirt.

It was all the invitation Ty needed to deepen the kiss. He opened his mouth over hers, luring her tongue into an erotic duel with his. Shannen felt desire and urgency erupt inside her with breathtaking speed, as though this morning's interrupted passion had been simmering deep within her, just waiting for the spark to ignite into a full blaze.

Ty sank down onto the edge of the bed, pulling her down on his lap. ''I want you so much, Shannen,'' he groaned, nuzzling her neck while his busy fingers pulled down the long zipper of her sundress.

His fingertips stroked her bare back and she shivered with response. Her sundress had a built-in bra, baring her breasts as it lay open around her waist. Ty caressed the nape of her neck and the smooth line of her shoulders before slipping in front to take possession of her breasts, which were swollen and sensitive with arousal.

Shannen felt lost in a sensual dream. She tangled her fingers in the dark thickness of his hair, holding his head to hers and kissing him hungrily. How many times had she fantasized being alone with him like this? For the past nine years, he'd been her fantasy lover.

And now, at last...

All rational thought fled, taking her self-control along with it. Shannen was only too willing to cede command to the voluptuous emotions surging through her body.

Ty lay back on the bed, his arms tightly around her, taking her with him. Her dress tangled around her legs, and he pulled it off in one deft sweep, tossing it to the floor. He eased her onto her back, his eyes dark and intense, drinking in the sight of her.

Instead of the self-consciousness she might've expected under such careful scrutiny, Shannen basked in the heat of his admiring stare.

"I need you, Shannen. I've wanted you for so long," he murmured hoarsely.

She lifted her hand and traced the fine shape of his mouth, her voice throaty with enticement and challenge.

"Show me, Tynan."

Seven

The need to feel his skin against hers was overpowering. Shannen slid her hands under his shirt and tugged at it. Responding to her demand, he yanked the T-shirt off, giving her access to the smooth, muscled expanse of his torso. Her hands and lips roamed his chest, feeling every smooth inch of his skin and the contrasting wiry hair.

He was equally thorough with her, learning the shape of her breasts with his hands, tasting the taut buds with his lips. At long last one of his hands traveled lower, pausing to trace her navel, to caress the pale hollow of her stomach. He found her center, his slow sultry strokes into her liquid heat rendering her mindless with pleasure.

The rest of their clothing was shed with mutual haste and sent flying in different directions. They kissed again and again, their kisses deep and passionate and growing more urgent.

Shannen clung to Ty, drunk on the taste and the smell and the feel of him. He touched her intimately again and she moaned, arching to him. Blindly, she scored her fingernails along his belly, to wrap her hand around the hard pulsing length of his arousal.

Their eyes met.

"I bought condoms at the shop here in the hotel," Ty said bluntly. "They're in the pocket of my shorts somewhere on the floor."

"You bought them before you came to my room tonight?" Shannen felt herself blushing, not sure what embarrassed her more—his frankness or his confidence. "You were that sure of me?"

It was his confidence, she decided. And it didn't embarrass her as much as irritate her. Immensely.

She sat up, averting her eyes from the sight of Ty retrieving the foil packets from the pocket of his khaki shorts.

"Let's just say I was hopeful." His ardor was undiminished by this break in their foreplay and appeared likewise immune from accusation in her voice.

She knew because she kept stealing glances at him, in spite of her resolve not to. "Do you think I'm that easy?" she snapped. "So easy that all you have to do is to show up at my door and I'll go to bed with you?"

It didn't help that she'd proved that statement to be true. The self-incrimination increased her agitation.

"Shannen, one thing you definitely are not is easy," Ty said, his tone heartfelt.

A bit too heartfelt. Her brows narrowed. "What do you mean by that?"

"It's taken us nine years to get to this point, which is so far beyond easy that—"

"Don't try to tell me you've been pining for me for the past nine years, because I won't believe you, Tynan." Shannen grabbed the edge of the quilt comforter and pulled it over her, covering herself. "And…and don't give me that oh-so-noble 'you were too young' speech again."

"You told me this afternoon that you understood, Shannen.'' Ty groaned. ''But if you're determined to hold a grudge because I couldn't take advantage of—''

''I turned twenty-one five years ago, Ty,'' Shannen said crossly. ''Legal age. But you didn't bother to look me up then. No, you forgot all about me until you saw me on this island.''

And realized I had a chance to win a million dollars, she added to herself. No use bringing that up now, when she was out of the running.

''I know when you turned twenty-one, Shannen. It was two years after the Howes had spent months on the front pages of every paper in the country and became joke fodder for comedians, morality sermons for the clergy and all the rest that goes with being a notorious media staple. I truly didn't think you would welcome a national pariah on your doorstep.''

''All of that was about the other Howes. *You* didn't do anything wrong. At least do me the favor of being honest with me, Tynan. Admit that you never once considered coming back to West Falls to see me.''

''I did, Shannen.''

''Of course you'd say that *now!* You're wearing a con-dom—and…and keeping it on while I'm yelling at you!''

His lips quirked. ''Not as difficult as it seems since you're naked in bed and I want you more than I've ever wanted a woman in my life, Shannen.''

''Which proves my point. You'd say anything to—''

''I want to make love with you, Shannen. I've been hon-est about it, I haven't tried to trick you into anything.'' He sat down on the bed and carefully lifted the quilt from her. ''You want me, too. We aren't playing a game of easy or hard to get. And thanks to tonight's vote, we're free from the *Victorious* game, too.''

He leaned over her, and as his head descended, Shannen was fully aware of what was coming next. And welcomed it, she allowed herself to admit. She was weary of putting up roadblocks between them. This wasn't a game. This was Tynan, whom she'd longed for since she was seventeen.

Never mind that in her girlish daydreams they had been in love when they made love. She was all grown up now; she knew lovemaking didn't have to include true love.

A small wistful sigh escaped from her throat as his mouth touched hers. Being with Ty tonight would be enough. It would have to be enough.

She held him tight as he gently yet inexorably pressed into her.

"Sweetheart," he whispered hoarsely, dropping his head to her breast. He had stopped moving, allowing her body time to adjust before fully sheathing himself in her liquid heat.

Shannen caressed him, her hands gliding over the full length of his back from his shoulders to his hips, savoring the feel of him in her arms, in her body. Her fingers tightened around him, pressing him down as she arched her hips upward, inching him even deeper inside her.

"More, Ty." She pressed again.

He resisted. "Shannen, you're so small, so tight. Let's take it slowly. I don't want to hurt you."

She shook her head. "You won't, you can't. I want all of you inside me now, Ty. I'm tired of waiting. We've already waited too long."

"Way too long," he agreed fervently. He filled her with one long thrust, then began to move, teasing her by withdrawing almost completely, waiting for her to moan his name before moving forward again.

He kept up the slow steady rhythm until she squirmed beneath him, locking her limbs around him in a silent plea. Ty wasn't one to settle for silence.

"Tell me what you want." He chuckled softly. "Faster, like this?" He moved faster, just as she wanted him to and then stopped, as if awaiting further instructions.

"Deeper?" he suggested, proceeding while she gasped

with pleasure. He stopped to propose, "Harder?" and to demonstrate exactly how that felt, too.

Shannen's breath caught. His teasing was sexy and arousing and maddening, all at the same time. "Yes," she panted. "Faster, deeper, harder. Please, oh, please!"

Every sensual nerve ending had caught fire and burned as their movements created a blaze that threatened to consume her. No, not *threaten,* she dizzily corrected. There was nothing threatening about this union with Ty.

Promise was the correct description. Their sexual conflagration promised to consume her and she wanted that—she wanted all barriers between them melted away forever.

And they were. The wild, intense pleasure finally overwhelmed them at the same moment. Shannen cried his name as she shattered into a thousand pieces. Through the firestorm she heard Ty call out for her as he pulsed inside her, their essences joined as they became truly one.

She was only vaguely aware of his weight collapsing upon her. It was the heat of his body covering her that penetrated her sensuous daze. It complemented the inner warmth that filled her with a sense of utter completeness.

Slowly she resurfaced, opening her eyes to find him smiling down at her. Their bodies were still joined, and she had no intention of moving. He stirred above her, but she tightened her legs and arms around him.

"Don't move." She purred the command into his ear.

"I'm too heavy for you," he protested, but he didn't move away from her. He trailed a string of gossamer-light kisses along her neck, licking and nipping her skin. "I can't get enough of you, Shannen."

His hands found hers, his fingers intertwining with hers. He felt satiated; he felt a kind of peace he'd never known. This sweet, languid time—with Shannen in his arms, defenseless and utterly trusting, no walls or barriers between them—was like nothing he'd ever known.

He raised his head and smiled into her eyes. "I'm trying

to come up with something profound to say that doesn't sound like a cheesy line,'' he admitted quietly. ''Because being with you…''

His voice trailed off. There really were no words to describe how he was feeling right now.

I love you sprang to mind, and he dismissed it just as quickly. No, that was beyond cheesy, it was more like fraud. According to the Book of Howe, love had nothing to do with what he felt for Shannen right now. It was the pleasurable afterglow of sex.

But to say *that* would be tactless—and then some.

''I'd love to know what you're really thinking.'' Shannen was staring deeply into his eyes. ''Your expression keeps changing, like there's a civil war going on in your head.''

''An astute observation.'' Ty slowly disengaged his body from hers and sat up. She was scarily close to the mark. He drew her into the circle of his arms and leaned back against the pillows.

''I'd like to know what *you're* really thinking, Shannen.'' He brushed his lips lightly over her hair, the clean, fresh scent of coconut shampoo filling his nostrils.

He wasn't simply trying to divert her from gaining access to his own conflicted thoughts, he assured himself; he was genuinely interested in her take on this development in their ever-evolving relationship.

''I already told you.'' She cast him a glance beneath her lashes. ''That I'd love to know what you're really thinking.''

''A winning combination of flirtatious and evasive.'' He was glad she was playing it this way, Ty decided. Keeping it light instead of getting all carried away with deep talk of love and promises.

Shannen studied him and had no trouble reading the relief that crossed his face. It was fortunate that she'd snuffed her afterglow impulse to rhapsodize about their love-making.

She wanted to tell him that being with him not only lived up to her long-held fantasies but exceeded them, that she not only loved having sex with him, she loved *him*, Ty Hale, the ex-Howe who worked for a living.

She supposed she could've at least told him that she'd never known making love could be this way, that with him she'd had her very first climax, but then he might feel encouraged to share his sexual history with her. Which she didn't want to hear.

Nor did she care to go into detail about her own lack of experience, which consisted only of Ben Salton, her college boyfriend and first lover. She'd been Ben's first lover, too, and their fumbling clumsy sex had been so awkward and miserable for them both that a year after they'd broken up and Ben had found someone new, he'd actually called Shannen to tell her that sex could be good, not awful, and she shouldn't let their unskilled forays keep her from trying it again—with someone else, of course.

Shannen had thanked good old Ben and wished him luck with his new love but declined to venture back into the sexual arena. From what she could tell, there were too many negatives and not a single positive, especially since she'd firmly suppressed any hopes of ever being with Tynan Howe. He was a closed chapter in her life.

Which had been now reopened.

Or had it?

That she had satisfied him, Shannen had no doubt, but he'd made a point of holding back the words that would elevate tonight from hot one-night stand to something more.

Something involving love and trust and commitment.

So she would follow his lead. No opening her heart to him, the way she had as a naive schoolgirl in love. He'd *crushed* her back then, and it wasn't going to happen again. She was a gameworthy opponent now.

A loud and unexpected knock sounded at the door, jolting them both from the thoughtful silence enshrouding them.

"Probably a maid," said Ty. "Tell her to—"

"Lauren, baby, are you still awake?" an urgent male voice called from the hall. "Lauren, open up. It's Jed."

Shannen sprang from the bed, her actions sheer reflex. *Jed?* she mouthed to Ty, who looked as startled as she did.

"He thinks I'm Lauren," she said in a whisper. "He called her 'baby'!"

"Lauren, come on! Let me in!" Jed's voice rose, the words slurring.

"Do you think he's been drinking?" whispered Shannen, still trying to process Jed's appearance at what he thought was Lauren's hotel room door—and demanding to be let in!

"I'd count on it," Ty muttered back. "Tell him to get lost, Shannen."

"Why would he think I'm Lauren?" She still looked confused.

"I'm going to hazard a guess. The resort has no TV access, and even if it did, nobody would know you'd been voted off the island yet. Someone would've had to tell the *Victorious* jury pool down in the Parrot Room which contestant arrived at the hotel tonight."

"And somebody said it was a twin and Jed assumed it was Lauren?" Shannen surmised with a scowl. "Why would he assume that my sister would get voted off before me?"

"Just making a guess here." Ty made a sound halfway between a groan and a chuckle. "But I think Kevin and Adam, the PAs who came to the hotel with me tonight, told Jed that Lauren was here."

"Lauren!" Jed was pounding on the door now. "Baby!"

"Kevin and Adam know that Cortnee told Lauren—and everybody else on the island the other day—that Jed had slept with Keri and Lucy," Ty continued. "And since the crew thinks Lauren has a, um, thing for Jed—"

"She does not!" protested Shannen.

"Whether she does or doesn't, I'm betting those merry pranksters decided to see what would happen when they sent Mr. Adventure Guide to *your* door."

"Jed couldn't have used my sister. I'd have known somehow, I know I would. But that 'baby' garbage of his is making me sick." Shannen was seething. "He has the unmitigated gall to think that Lauren would let him into her room and—"

"He seems *convinced* Lauren would let him in," Ty amended. "Otherwise, he wouldn't have come up here in the first place, would he?"

"I'm going to find out right now. Jed!" Her voice went velvety smooth, the anger magically disappearing from her tone but not from her glittering blue eyes. "Give me a minute. I have to get dressed."

"No need for that, babe," Jed called back.

A murderous expression crossed her face. Shannen whipped on her dress.

"Shannen, no! Whatever you're thinking of doing, don't do it." Ty pulled on his khaki shorts and T-shirt, dressing as swiftly as Shannen.

"Hide," Shannen ordered. "In the closet or the shower. Or out on the balcony. I'll close the curtains so he can't see you out there."

"Hide?" Ty was appalled. "You're joking, right?"

"No. I'm going to have a little talk with Jed and—"

"You don't want any witnesses?" Ty grimaced. "As for me hiding, forget it. I am not going to hide anywhere. People only do that in soap operas or wacky sitcoms. We're doing a reality show here."

"This is not any show at all, it's our life," Shannen said darkly. "And if Jed, that lawsuit-happy creep, sees you here, you could very well find yourself getting sued by him.

Or even fired by Clark Garrett for getting sued. You can't lose your job, Ty. You're no longer rich, remember? You work for a living, and take it from someone who always has, that means staying employed. Now, hide!''

She gave him a push toward the balcony and stalked to the door to the hall, flinging it open.

''Hello, Jed.''

''Hi, baby.'' A tousled, wrinkled Jed leaned against the doorjamb. ''Surprised to see me?''

''More than you'll ever know.'' Shannen extended her arm. ''Come in.''

''Oh, yeah, babe.'' Jed ambled into the room. ''Let's just—''

There was a loud rattle, and the door to the balcony was opened and shut with a bang. Shannen and Jed simultaneously turned to see Ty rushing toward them.

''Thank God I made it in time.'' Ty pretended to pant, as if he were out of breath from running and catapulting onto the balcony and bursting into the room. ''The guys told me what they'd done. Jed, this isn't Lauren, it's Shannen, and she isn't very pleased with what's been going on.''

Jed's jaw dropped. His eyes flew to Shannen's face, which was a mask of sheer rage. ''Ah, man!'' he gasped, and headed for the door.

''You're not going anywhere until you tell me why you came skulking up here looking for my sister!'' Shannen caught a handful of Jed's shirt.

He was drunk and off guard and she was pumped with rage, which rendered her surprisingly strong. She gave his shirt a forceful pull, and he stumbled and hit his head on the door frame.

''Ow! You hit me! I didn't do anything wrong!'' Jed wailed. ''Your sister said she—''

''I didn't hit you, you tripped, you clod! And don't you dare say my sister's name!'' Shannen grabbed the knob and swung it back, almost clipping him with it.

"He didn't say it, Shannen," Ty pointed out calmly. Swiftly, he caught her around the waist with one arm and pried her hand from the knob.

"You'd better get out of here now," he warned Jed. "Can't you tell just by looking at her that she has homicide in her heart?"

"I-I'm going. I'm gone!" Jed ran down the hall, disappearing from sight as he turned a corner.

Shannen was so furious, she kicked the door shut. "That jerk, that creep, that—"

"Calm down," ordered Ty, "or else I'll put you in the shower and turn on the cold water. That'll cool you off."

"Oh, just try it!" cried Shannen. "I dare you to try it."

Her eyes were flashing, her face flushed with fury. Ty started to laugh; he couldn't help himself. "You're a fierce one, Shannen. No wonder Jed ran out of here like a spooked horse. You scared him silly."

"You did your part, pretending to crash onto the balcony like…like Zorro. And telling him I had 'homicide in my heart'? Where did that come from?" Shannen gulped back a giggle. Her anger was fast morphing into pure giddiness.

"It was a line from one of the soaps I worked on. I stored it away for future use, but this was the first time I ever thought it might apply." A slow grin crossed Ty's face. "It's a line that requires a certain kind of overblown situation like, uh, this one."

"It's true, scenes like this don't come along every day," agreed Shannen.

"For that, we can only be thankful," Ty said dryly.

Shannen smiled with satisfaction. "I really did scare the rat, didn't I?"

"You scared him." There was a teasing glint in Ty's dark eyes. "I'm curious as to what you planned to do with him, though."

She shrugged. "I didn't have any real plan—I thought I'd improvise as I went along. I just wanted him to know he'd made a major mistake trying to…to seduce my sister, and to make sure he wouldn't try it again.''

"Shannen, what if Jed had every reason to believe that Lauren would welcome him?''

"I just don't believe that, Tynan. Obviously, Jed thinks he's irresistible, and after a few drinks he decided to try his charm on my sister, the newcomer to the hotel. Except he had the bad luck of finding me here instead.''

"He'd probably agree with you on the bad luck part, Shannen. But keep in mind, you had the element of surprise going for you at first. It wouldn't have been long before he recovered himself, and even with him drunk, you would've been in big trouble.''

"I guess so. I know how strong he is from all those stupid contests.''

"I'd like to hear you admit that my appearance was most timely, Shannen. Even if my entrance was…shall we say Zorroesque?'' Ty wrapped her in his arms.

"I admit it. Your appearance was most timely, Tynan.'' She put her arms around him and leaned into him. "And if you'd rather, I could liken it to Batman instead of Zorro.''

"You're still not taking the risk seriously, and I can't stand the thought of you getting hurt. If Jed had tried, I would've—'' Ty paused, considering.

"Beaten him up?'' Shannen suggested, cuddling closer. "You're so strong, you could take him easily.''

"Appealing to my inner Neanderthal?'' He kissed the top of her head. "I didn't know I had one until tonight.''

They stood together for a few quiet moments, holding each other as the tension from the encounter with Jed drained away. And then, a distinct rumble came from the vicinity of her abdomen.

Her stomach was growling! "Ohhhh!'' Embarrassed, Shannen tried to draw back. "Sorry.''

Ty held her firm. "Nothing to be sorry about. When was

the last time you had a decent meal, anyway? Call room service right now and order something.''

''On the network's tab,'' they chorused together, laughing.

''I know exactly what I want.'' She headed for the phone beside the bed. ''A turkey sandwich with cheese, lettuce and tomato with honey mustard. I've been dying for one of those.''

The food arrived shortly after she called, and Shannen carried it to the table on the balcony. Ty joined her out there while she ate.

''Did I tell you how much I admire your ethics in turning down the food that night on the beach?'' he asked, watching her enjoy every bite of the sandwich.

''Sort of. You sounded more like you were questioning my sanity than admiring my ethics, though,'' she teased.

He shook his head. ''No, I was awestruck. I truly admire your sense of fair play and your willpower, too, Shannen. Keep in mind that I come from a family that's severely deficient in both those qualities.''

''But those qualities aren't deficient in you, Ty,'' Shannen said softly. ''Every family has somebody who's deficient in something. It doesn't mean the whole gene pool is tainted. You have to give yourself a break. You're different from...the others,'' she summarized, because to individually cite his father, brother, sister, cousin and uncle seemed rather excessive.

Ty said nothing.

''I can tell by your expression that you don't think I understand what you've faced, but I do, Ty. I have. In a less public way, of course.'' Shannen finished her sandwich and sipped her iced tea. ''When you called me white trash—''

''Shannen, please believe me when I tell you that I didn't mean it. They were just words I used to drive you away from me because I had to make sure you'd go." Ty was emphatic.

"They were words that hit home because there was truth in them," Shannen continued calmly. "My mother was a wild teen herself and had my older brother, Evan, when she was just sixteen. His father was ten years older than she was, and they'd kept their relationship a secret. When you said what you did, it made me face that I was on the verge of repeating her mistakes. My grandmother had tried so hard to keep my sisters and me from turning out like Mom, and there I was, headed down the same road, anyway."

"I didn't know, Shannen. If I had—"

"You would've found some other words to drive me away?" she suggested with a ghost of a smile. "They probably wouldn't have been as effective. I'd seen how my mother had messed up her life—she's still doing it—and what you said was exactly what I needed to knock some sense into me, as Gramma would say."

"Your grandmother has a lot to say," said Ty, covering her hand with his.

"She raised our sister, Jordan, and Lauren and me. My mother married our father—he was her age and in the army—and had Jordan when they were both just twenty-one. Thirteen months later Lauren and I were born. Obviously, she wasn't thrilled to have twins at that time. Or at any time, really."

Ty winced. "It's too bad she kept telling you so. How did you end up being raised by your grandmother?"

"When Lauren and I were three, our dad was killed in a military training accident and Mom brought us back to West Falls to live with Gramma. Our brother bounced between us and his father. Mom came and went as she pleased."

Shannen paused, thinking back on that less-than-idyllic time. "Poor Gramma! She'd worked hard her whole life running the diner and raising a family, and then we descended on her and stayed till we were all grown up. How someone like Mom and someone like Gramma can be mother and daughter is a mystery, but then I wonder how Mom and my sisters and I can be…'' Her voice trailed off.

"Seems like your mother is the 'mystery.' There are a number of those in the Howe family, too.'' Ty laced his fingers with hers.

"Mom's been married three times and has had so many boyfriends not even *she* can remember them all. She goes to bars and gets drunk and into fights. She's written bad checks and shoplifted and has been in and out of jail. Evan is exactly like her. Gramma ended up using the money saved for improvements to the diner to bail Mom and Evan out of jail.''

"So that's why you and Lauren decided to try out for *Victorious?* For the prize money?'' He appraised her thoughtfully. "I never did believe your cast bio claiming you tried out for the show as a lark.''

"I don't do anything for a lark,'' Shannen said flatly. "I didn't even use those words—the show's publicist came up with them. She said it sounded 'more fun' than admitting we were in the game strictly to win money.''

"The truth is rarely fun for media spinners.''

"But needing money is the only reason why we tried to *win* once we were in the game. If we hadn't thought it was our best shot at staying on the island, we never would've forged an alliance with Jed and Keri and Lucy, who we didn't like from the beginning. Or with Konrad, who made us kind of uneasy.''

"I think you can drop the 'we' and use 'I,' Shannen. Lauren's feelings toward Jed, at least, are different from yours,'' Ty reminded her.

"That's only crew gossip,'' she reminded him.

"Oh, yeah? Then what do you call his arrival at what he thought was Lauren's door tonight? And him calling her baby and—''

"That was all Jed's gargantuan ego." Shannen shuddered. "What would Lauren—or Lucy or Keri for that matter—see in a jerk like Jed?"

"Aside from his boyish good looks? And what about his
brawny biceps and polished pecs and the rest of his manly
physique? Don't forget his adventure-guide résumé, either.
Just quoting from the Internet discussion boards, Shannen,"
Ty added, laughing at her expression of disgust.

"Oh, ugh! As if he isn't already vain enough!"

"He's also already rich enough not to need the million-
dollar prize money," Ty remarked, watching her. "Remember him mentioning his family's winter and summer
vacation homes, his beloved silver Lexus and all the other
things? You asked what a woman would see in Jed—well,
at the very least, there is his money. Wealth can make even
a toad appealing."

"You know, you're actually lucky you lost all your
money, Ty," Shannen said bluntly. "Because having it
made you doubt your own appeal."

"It's not uncommon to wonder if you're valued for yourself or your fortune, Shannen."

"Jed obviously doesn't have such doubts," retorted
Shannen. "And now that you're desperate for money like
most of us in the world, you're free to feel valued for yourself. Lucky man!"

"Are you so very desperate for money, Shannen?" he
probed.

"Not sell-an-organ desperate, but our family definitely
can use some extra cash. The bank wouldn't give Gramma
as big a loan as she needs for the diner, and her house
needs work, too. Major structural stuff. Plus our sister, Jordan, is married to Josh, and they have two little kids. Josh
is a really nice guy who's been trying to start his own
landscaping business but can't get enough money together
to buy the necessary equipment. The bank won't give them

a loan, either. Jordan buys powerball lottery tickets, but you know the odds of winning that.''

"About the same as being chosen as a contestant on a show like *Victorious*," Ty said wryly. "But you tried out for it, anyway.''

Shannen rolled her eyes. "Lauren was the one who wanted to try out. She's been bored in West Falls lately and said she just had to do something different for a change. She begged me to come with her. I went along mainly because I thought we didn't have a chance.''

"You were just humoring her, hmm?''

"I never dreamed we'd be chosen," Shannen said with feeling.

"Sweetie, you underestimate *your* appeal.''

"We were only picked because we're twins. I didn't think the producers would go for that gimmick, although Gramma said she wasn't surprised.''

"It seems that Gramma is savvy in the ways of network shows. Beautiful identical twin sisters are—''

"No more quotes from the Internet discussion boards!" Shannen ordered with mock severity. "Wouldn't the rumormongers have a field day if word ever got out about us? They'd claim it was a fix. Who would ever believe it was strictly coincidence that I came to the island, and there you were behind the camera?''

"What were those odds?" murmured Ty.

"Sometimes the odds are incredibly odd. I'll be sure to tell Jordan to keep buying those powerball tickets." Shannen drew back, suddenly aware of how long she'd been talking, of how much she'd revealed.

She gave a self-conscious laugh. "Now, why was I boring you with the history of the Cullens? Oh yes, so you wouldn't feel like the only one out here on this balcony whose family wasn't filled with paragons.''

"You're incapable of boring me, Shannen. You were being kind to me, wage slave though I may be." His voice held a challenging note that Shannen immediately mistook for something else.

"I like you better without all your money issues, Ty." She slipped from her chair onto his lap. "That fortune-hunter paranoia of yours was beginning to rub off on me. For a while today I thought you were pretending to be interested in me because I had a chance to win the million-dollar prize."

"What?" His arms clamped around her. "Is that the nonsense you were spouting when I first arrived here? I vaguely remember you saying something about the game and the money. Where did you come up with such a hare-brained idea?"

Beneath her, she could feel the flexing of his muscles as he held her. The warmth of his body heat began to penetrate her.

"After I gave the immunity totem to Lauren and it was clear I was going to be kicked out of the game, you stopped filming me. For the first time since we arrived on the is-land," she added softly.

"You thought my plans of helping myself to your prize money were finished, so I could stop *pretending* to be in-terested in you?" Ty was incredulous. He throbbed hard and insistent against her, and he took her hand and placed it against himself. "Does that feel like pretense to you, Shannen?"

"No." Shannen gazed into his eyes.

The sound of his low voice was as intoxicating as his masculine strength. Her breasts were crushed against his chest, and the sensual pressure felt so good.

"Are you still wondering why I turned my camera on the others?" He brushed his lips against hers.

When his tongue flicked to trace the fullness of her lower lip, she quivered. Her head was spinning too much to won-der about anything except the wonder of this moment they shared.

"You were disappointed with your sister and trying hard not to show it." He nibbled at her lips, between words. "It wasn't obvious, but I knew. I hated seeing you in pain, Shannen. I sure as hell didn't want to film it."

"A cameraman giving me some privacy from the camera," whispered Shannen. She kissed his cheek. "Thank you, Ty."

He glided his hands along the length of her spine until he reached her bottom. Provocatively, he traced the line of her panties beneath the silky material of her dress, then kneaded the rounded softness with his strong fingers.

"I want you again, Shannen."

"Yes, Ty." A fast-flowing torrent of desire swept her. The heat of it made her go weak and soft. She couldn't do anything but cling to Ty, to meet and match his demands, kiss for kiss, caress for caress.

He gave a low growl as he slid his hand under her skirt. Her breath caught on a moan as sensual currents eddied through her. His body was taut under her hands, and their mingled murmurs and sighs of passion joined the night sounds in the air.

A burgeoning ache radiated from the tips of her breasts to the liquid heat pooling between her thighs.

"Right here. Right now, Shannen," he demanded huskily.

In one of those sudden moves he executed so well, he scooped her up and carried her to the chaise longue a few feet away.

He came down on top of her, his legs between hers, opening her thighs wider as he settled himself against her. The weight of his body pressed her deeper into the soft cushion of the chaise. Acute pleasure shot through her, and instinctively she thrust her hips in counterpoint.

"That's it, baby!" he groaned. He shifted a little to push up her skirt.

All at once, Shannen felt as if she'd been catapulted out

of a sensuous dream. She tried to sit up but only managed to raise herself a little, using her arms as leverage. "Ty, stop."

He froze. "What's wrong, sweetheart?"

"You called me 'baby.'" Shannen stared up at him.

Ty groaned. "Did you hate it?"

She raised her brows. "I haven't decided. I'll let you know. Meanwhile we have to go inside."

"To bed." Ty sounded hopeful. He slowly eased himself off her and rose to stand. He extended his hand, and she placed hers in his. "You're right, of course." He pulled her to her feet. "The bed is much more comfortable than being out here."

"Out here was fine," she assured him dryly. "It's just that all of a sudden I felt like I'd been shot in the head."

He draped an arm around her and walked her inside the room. "Remind me *never* to call you baby again."

"It was a good thing you did, because it conjured up— well, a baby. A cute little consequence I don't think either of us is ready for at this point." Shannen handed him a foil packet. "We didn't have this with us out there."

A visibly startled Ty gaped at the sight of the condom she'd placed in his hand. "I can't believe I forgot."

"No harm done." Her voice became soft and sultry. "Shall we carry on?"

"I completely forgot." Ty was astounded. "That's never happened before. Not ever, Shannen! You go to my head like a double shot of old Granddaddy's 110 proof whiskey."

"Thank you." Shannen felt pleased with herself. It was thrilling to know that Ty had wanted her so much she'd affected his thought processes. He'd certainly obliterated hers! "Maybe you aren't as vigilant without your fortune to guard," she added thoughtfully.

"Believe me, you can take full credit for blowing my mind. Baby."

They both laughed, a bit uncertainly.

Shannen watched as he tore open the packet and sheathed himself.

His mouth took hers with breathtaking impact, and their interrupted passion instantly flared to flashpoint. Neither could wait. They fell to the bed, her body pliant and supple beneath him. She loved being filled by him and sighed her pleasure.

As they joined together, her body moved with him and for him, exerting sensual demands of her own. Abruptly a tidal wave of ecstasy carried them both to the heights of rapture that went on and on until they both lay sated and spent in each other's arms.

Time seemed to stop. Neither felt the need to move or speak or even think. They lay together, languorous and drowsy, their bodies still joined.

Ty was the first to break the idyllic silence. "I'm falling asleep," he murmured.

"That's okay." She stroked him lovingly, her eyes closed. "So am I."

"Good." He carefully withdrew himself from her and reached down to pull the top sheet over her.

Shannen turned to snuggle close to him again, but he wasn't there. Her eyes flew open.

He had gotten out of bed and was standing beside it. "I have to go."

She watched him hastily pull on his clothes. It occurred to her that this was the second time she'd seen him get dressed tonight, and he was donning his clothes this time as speedily as he had when Jed was caterwauling outside the door. She frowned, not liking the similarity.

Now fully dressed, Ty looked down at her. She looked away, holding the sheet to her chin, suddenly grateful for its protection against his gaze.

Ty heaved a sigh. "Shannen, as much as I want to stay with you, I have to round up the PAs and get back to the island. Filming starts at dawn, as usual.'' His lips curved into a smile. ''I'll miss not seeing you stagger out of the tent first thing in the morning.''

Shannen wished he would say that he'd miss *her*. Period. But she didn't tell him so. She'd already done too much talking tonight. Now he was ready to leave…because he'd gotten what he came for?

If it was her total capitulation and surrender to him, the answer was yes, she mocked herself. And now he was leaving her. She steeled herself against the hurt tearing through her. She was being unreasonable, and she knew it. Of course he had to go back to the island.

Anyway, what had she expected from him, a pledge of true love?

''Good night, Shannen.''

Their eyes met and held, and she could do nothing but gaze at him as his mouth lowered to hers. His lips touched hers, and her lips parted reflexively in response. The doubt and anxiety that gripped her for the past few moments dissolved as he kissed her deeply.

She responded passionately, feeling the hard heat of him, physical proof that he wanted her as much as she wanted him. At least there could be no anxious doubts about that.

Then Ty lifted his lips and cupped her face with his big hands, staring down at her flushed cheeks and kiss-swollen lips. ''If I don't leave now…''

He shook his head and straightened.

Shannen watched him walk toward the door and vowed not to ask that Dreadfully Desperate Question: When will I see you again?

''Don't forget your condoms,'' she called after him, clutching the sheet even tighter. She'd meant to sound playful, and surprised herself with her baiting tone.

Ty stopped in his tracks.

Shannen was mortified. How unsubtle could she be! She

may as well have gone ahead and asked him the Dreadfully Desperate Question itself. She didn't dare look at Ty.

"I thought I'd leave them here."

She didn't have to look at him—the droll note in his voice gave her a clear enough picture.

So he found her insecurities amusing? Shannen glowered. "Don't bother. I won't be needing them."

"Yes, you will. Tomorrow night when I come over," he added, quietly closing the door behind him as he left the room.

Eight

It's like one big spring break around here. Miles, the show's production assistant stationed at the hotel, had jovially proclaimed last night.

His words rang in Shannen's head as she stood beside the lagoon-like pool, watching the *Victorious* losers swimming and sunning themselves and consuming tray after tray of brilliant-colored exotic drinks.

During her four years at West Falls University, she had never experienced the fun-in-the-sun revelry of spring break. There hadn't been enough money. Time off from class meant extra time to work for pay.

So shouldn't she join the others and indulge herself in this belated, all-expenses-paid spring break? Instead Shannen sank listlessly onto a cushioned lounge chair.

She was bored. *Bored!* What was the matter with her? Who could be bored in a free tropical paradise?

She could. She was.

All she could think about was Ty. Instead of enjoying

the indoor-outdoor pool with its water slide and tunnel maze, she was sitting here daydreaming about him. She pictured his dark eyes, alternately cool and intense, depending on his mood. Of the passion glittering in them as he looked into her eyes while poised to enter her.

Her pulse began to race, and she tried to banish the provocative images from her mind. But how could she succeed when her body still bore the traces of last night's passionate lovemaking? She was hypersensitive in certain intimate places, tender and achy in others.

And she was all too certain that only Tynan's touch could soothe her—by arousing and satisfying her all over again. And again.

Her whole body flushed. Shannen snatched a drink menu from the table and began to fan herself with it. If merely thinking of him had this effect on her, how would she react to his presence?

And when, exactly, would that be? Would he come to her room tonight? And if he did, what then? He would expect to go to bed with her, and heaven help her, she badly wanted that, too. But after that...

He would head back to the island to film the contestants and she would spend another endless day like this one. Wanting him while wondering what, apart from their sexual chemistry, she meant to him. Waiting for him to say things he may never say.

"Hey, there, you! I'm not sure which one you are, but I remember you said you didn't like to be called 'Twin.'"

Shannen looked up at the sound of the friendly enough voice. She tried not to groan at the sight of Lucy, one of the girls who'd been in her tribe from the beginning of the game, until her recent rejection from the island.

According to Cortnee, Lucy was also one of the girls who'd slept with Jed in hopes of winning his alliance.

"It's Shannen," she supplied her name, hoping she

sounded friendly enough. But not feeling very friendly at all.

"Mind if I sit down?" Lucy dropped into the chair beside Shannen's without waiting for an answer. She was carrying a blue drink in a huge glass shaped like a hurricane lamp. Her words were slurred, her movements awkward, no doubt from the effects of that neutron-blue liquid.

"I want you to know I don't hold it against you for voting me off," Lucy announced.

"Thanks," murmured Shannen. "I guess we all have to go sometime—except for the winner, of course."

"The winner," repeated Lucy. "Wonder who that's gonna be?"

"I don't know. I wish it would be my sister."

"Oh, yeah, the other twin." Lucy took a long gulp of her drink. "Hey, are you the one Jed's been messing around with?" She looked confused. "Or is it that other one?"

"It's neither of us," Shannen said coldly. "We heard he'd been *messing around* with you and Keri."

"Among others, as we found out. Our boy Jed is a real player." Lucy smirked.

Shannen stared at her, nonplussed. "You don't mind that you've been, uh, played?"

"Why should guys have all the fun? We girls can, too, you know. Being here is like a vacation fling, we may as well enjoy ourselves." Lucy followed a hiccup with a giggle. "It's all in the game, you know?"

No, it was worse than "the game" of *Victorious,* Shannen mused bleakly. Lucy was describing a game of men and women sleeping together, using each other and openly not caring about the lack of…well, caring.

As if that weren't bad enough, it sounded like the perfidious Jed was not only boasting about his conquests, he was making them up and including Lauren in his tally. The gossip about her twin and Jed just *had* to be unfounded. Surely the only game Lauren was playing was *Victorious*.

Listening to Lucy's breezy assessment of the casual bed hopping sent Shannen's anxiety level soaring higher. She'd hopped into bed with Ty last night—twice!—without a single word of commitment, before or afterward, from either of them. As if it were nothing more than a vacation fling.

Maybe that's all it was for Ty? He wanted her, sure. But Jed wanted Lucy and Keri, and they weren't even pretending it went any deeper than that. Shannen thought of what she felt for Ty both before and after making love with him, of the words she'd wanted to say but hadn't. She had muzzled herself, and deep in her heart had believed that Ty was doing and feeling the same.

What if he wasn't? She flinched at that heartbreaking possibility.

"I came to ask you to have dinner and go to the Parrot Room with the gang tonight." Lucy's voice broke into Shannen's troubled reverie.

"Thanks, but I think I'll—" Shannen paused, trying to come up with an excuse that at least sounded viable. "I'm still tired, and I'll just eat in my room and go to bed early," she added lamely.

"Oh, come with us, you'll have fun," urged Lucy. "We all feel sorry for you, sitting here by yourself looking so glum. We know how much you miss your twin."

Shannen stiffened. "You feel sorry for me?"

"It's so sad! You and your sister are like together all the time for your whole life, and now you're here and she's over there and you—"

"We're not Siamese twins, we can exist apart from each other," Shannen interjected, stung.

The idea of the group feeling sorry for her because she and Lauren had been apart for less than twenty-four hours offended her greatly.

Part of her wanted to blurt out that she was sitting here

by herself looking so glum because she didn't know if the man she loved was in love with her or simply in lust.

Being Shannen, she would never make such a heartfelt confession.

"I'll hang out with the gang tonight," she said instead. "Thanks for including me."

Ty glanced at his watch for perhaps the tenth time in the past half hour. It must not be working; perhaps the sand and/or salt air had taken its toll.

But a check with Heidi confirmed his watch was up-to-the-second correct, and Ty faced facts. Time had not slowed to a halt, but his tolerance for his job had.

He did not want to be here; he wanted to be with Shannen. In her room in the hotel making love or sitting on the balcony with her chatting while they ate. Just being with her, doing anything at all, was preferable to being apart from her, especially after last night.

Instead he was here, trapped in a time warp of tedium, filming the Final Four contestants, Lauren, Cortnee, Konrad and Rico. Each one was posed, sitting or standing in a different setting while reciting a soliloquy about his or her feelings on making it this far in the game.

"Clark Garrett and the network can kiss their dreams of a *Victorious* franchise goodbye after broadcasting the banal blatherings of the Final Four," Ty muttered as Rico droned on. "This isn't merely dull, it's coma inducing."

"Maybe editing will help?" Heidi offered hopefully. "Why doesn't Clark or Bobby have them do something besides sit around and talk?"

"Cortnee's not even wearing her bikini," lamented Reggie. "And it's a shame the evil twin isn't the one who's still here. Wouldn't she have snarled at having to do these inane monologues! That would've been fun to see. Instead, we have the bland twin, who just simpers."

Ty thought how much Shannen would hate to hear aspersions cast against Lauren, who in reality wasn't bland at all. Just as Shannen was no evil twin. So much for reality shows being real.

But he agreed with Reggie on one point. Shannen's fire would've definitely livened up the glacial pace of the soliloquies. Shannen could never be boring.

He'd told her so last night, on the balcony.

You're incapable of boring me, Shannen. He was glad he'd at least said that, because there was much more he had kept from her. Things she deserved to hear, like his feelings for her. Things she ought to know, like his true financial status.

Last night she'd told him candidly that she preferred him without wealth. Without his "money issues," as she'd phrased it. Well, thanks to wise investing, he had more money now than when they had first met.

He could undoubtedly write a check covering what her family needed from his personal bank account. The diner repairs, the grandmother's house and the older sister's fledgling lawn business might seem insurmountably high to the Cullens, but not to him. He wouldn't even have to tap into his money-market funds or touch his major liquid assets for such a minor sum.

Suppose he were to offer to do it? He could make it an outright gift or a loan with no interest and no deadline to pay it back. Such a sum wouldn't even make a dent in his portfolio.

Ty tried to imagine Shannen's reaction if he were to make such an offer. And found that he couldn't.

Would she be delirious with joy, and then proceed to show him just how happy she was with him and his money? Or would she be angry at him for lying to her—and then make him work mightily to convince her to accept his generosity?

Shannen had said having money made him paranoid about being valued for himself. She certainly had a point there, Ty conceded. And when the notorious Howe scandals had hit, one after the other, he'd bailed on the name.

Had that been a mistake, a step into the world of denial instead of the smart self-defensive move he'd considered it to be? Until this minute he'd never even thought to question it.

Yet it helped immensely that Shannen already knew him as a Howe and didn't judge him as one. He'd kept his distance from everyone in his new life, not trusting anyone to accept him for who and what he really was.

Now he was playing his Trust No One game with Shannen herself by not being truthful about his "money issues."

Bobby arrived to announce another immunity contest. "You might be familiar with this one." He beamed at the camera.

Four wooden beams were being placed upright in the water—one for each of the contestants to stand on. It was an endurance test, and the last one left standing won immunity from being voted off the island.

"Familiar with it?" Ty muttered. "This stunt was a staple of the earliest game shows, and it was tired even back then. Not to mention about as interesting as watching paint dry."

"No, watching paint dry is way more interesting," Heidi countered snidely.

"These kids are young and strong. It'll be hours before one of them feels the need to move a limb." Reggie groaned. "They'll time-lapse the footage for the show, but we're stuck filming in real time."

"What am I doing here?" Ty asked himself. "I'm thirty-four years old. Why am I living in a bug-ridden camp with kids years younger than me, filming wannabe celebs who will do anything for a buck?"

"I hear you." Reggie was sympathetic. "Hang in there, friend. Better gigs are on the horizon—they have to be."

Ty was disconcerted to realize he'd spoken his thoughts

aloud. Truly a sign of how agitated he really was. He angled his camera to zoom in on a close-up of Konrad, who looked completely relaxed standing on the pole in the ocean.

He was a lawyer, Ty admonished himself, though silently this time. He should be practicing law, not holding a camera on a contestant in a game show. It was the first time he'd questioned his choice of a new career since leaving behind the world of Howe.

All lawyers didn't have to be corrupt and unethical like his father and uncle, just as all accountants weren't scheming thieves like his brother. He could choose to put his law degree and his talents toward a good cause.

With his personal fortune, he wouldn't have to take on cases for the money they would bring, which meant eliminating the criminal element and concentrating on those truly in need of legal assistance.

He could open his own practice or work for a nonprofit legal aid organization. He could buy a house and settle down instead of traipsing from efficiency apartments and rented rooms while chasing camerawork on random shows.

It seemed like an appealing alternative to what he was doing now. Why hadn't he thought of this before?

Ty fixed his camera on Lauren and wished she were Shannen, puzzling over why people had such a difficult time telling the sisters apart. Shannen was unique, remarkable, unmistakably herself.

What was she doing right now? he wondered. Was she looking forward to seeing him tonight? He allowed himself to anticipate their reunion, his mind blissfully detached from the Final Four as his camera rolled on.

Six hours of standing out in the sun on the post finally reduced Cortnee to tears. All four contestants had consistently refused Bobby's serpent-in-the-garden-like temptations to quit the contest and be rewarded with food and drink.

Ty didn't admire their stamina so much as question their sanity. He began to feel guilty filming them, as if he were aiding and abetting torture. They weren't even allowed a sip of water unless they abandoned their stance, thus forfeiting a chance to win the contest.

For six endless hours, none of them would yield. If one of the contestants were to drop dead, he could help the bereaved kin file a wrongful death suit, Ty decided, not entirely facetiously. And he wouldn't charge a penny for it.

Lauren and Cortnee continued to wilt before the camera lens, and Rico looked increasingly uncomfortable. Only Konrad was stoic, his demeanor unchanged from when he first climbed atop the post.

"I can't do this anymore!" Cortnee cried at last. "If I get down, can I have some water and that avocado salad you offered me a while ago, Bobby?"

"You certainly can!" Bobby assured her unctuously. "Plus, I'll throw in any kind of sandwich and dessert that you want, too. As much as you want of everything. Have I made you an offer you can't refuse?"

Sobbing, Cortnee jumped off and swam the short distance to the shore.

The roar of a high-powered speedboat engine was a jarring invasion into the quiet of the waning afternoon. Ty stopped his camera even before the shouted order, "Cut!"

All filming ceased.

"Say, that's one of the hotel's boats!" exclaimed Bobby, rising from his shaded deck chair. "It must be Clark bringing the network suits over for a look-see. I guess they want to meet us." He smoothed an imaginary wrinkle from his impeccably pressed shirt and ordered Heidi to bring him a mirror and comb.

Everybody watched as Clark Garrett and two older men

dressed untropically in business-casual wear disembarked from the boat, which had retractable wheels to drive it right onto the shore. The driver of the boat, a hotel employee, tied the boat to a stake, something of a primitive makeshift dock.

"As if this day weren't long enough," growled Ty. "Now it's going to be truly interminable."

There were groans of assent from the production assistants.

A far worse thought struck Ty. If the network executives were here on the island to watch the filming, there would be no need to take the day's footage to the hotel for them to view tonight. No reason to leave the crew camp for the resort. And no opportunity to see Shannen.

If he couldn't see Shannen tonight...

Ty resisted the urge to quit on the spot. He could buy that stupid boat and take it to the hotel right now. Neither his father nor his brother would hesitate to make such a flamboyant scene. They would even suggest a cameraman record the drama. It was that horrific flash of insight that kept Ty from acting it out.

And then...

"Lauren!"

Shannen? Ty was glad he'd put down his camera, because he probably would've dropped it at the sound of Shannen's voice. He wasn't delusional—it was really her!

She'd come out of the boat's cabin and stood on the small deck to wave at her sister, a few yards out in the water.

"Shannen! I can't believe it! You're here!" Lauren cried from her post.

Ty couldn't have said it better himself.

"These guys were nice enough to let me hitch a ride over with them." Shannen grinned as she hopped off the boat onto the sand.

She was wearing a blue paisley sundress, and it looked

as clean and crisp as one of Bobby Dixon's ensembles. Her hair swung loose around her shoulders and was ruffled by the breeze.

At the sight of her, Ty's blood grew hot. Every muscle in his body tightened as a surge of erotically charged memories flooded him. And then she removed her sunglasses, revealing eyes alert and shining with intelligence and—when she spotted him—something more.

Warmth. Humor. Tenderness. Was it possible to see such things in someone's gaze or was he projecting what he wanted, what he *needed,* to be there?

Ty walked toward her. Everybody was milling around; the production assistants bringing food and water to Cortnee, the rest of the crew taking a break with snacks or cigarettes while Bobby, Clark Garrett and the network execs toured the area.

Ty didn't care if everybody on the island was watching as he came to stand by Shannen's side. "You must know how glad I am to see you."

"Must I?" She shot him a quick smile before turning to look out at Lauren, Rico and Konrad standing on the posts. "How long have they been out there?"

"Over six hours. Cortnee just gave it up. Poor kid."

They both glanced at Cortnee, who was draining a bottle of cold water. Adam was fanning her with a large palm frond.

"Poor kid is right," agreed Shannen. "And if she gets voted off today, she won't even have the fun of living it up at the resort till the end of the game."

Ty wanted to take her hand and pull her into his arms. The hell with keeping secrets! There was no reason to pretend there was nothing between them, no reason for the pretense of a casual conversation between cameraman and ineligible contestant.

But he resisted the urge and didn't make his move. Shannen was standing beside him, not close enough for their shoulders to touch or their hands to brush. She was looking around at the Final Four, not up at him, sending clear non-verbal messages to keep up the pretense.

"Why won't Cortnee have fun at the resort?" Ty quizzed instead.

Maybe he couldn't touch her, but at least she was here to talk to. Her presence brought an end to the teeth-gnashing frustration he'd been suffering all day. With Shannen at his side, not even watching paint dry would be intolerable.

"What's not fun about an all-expense-paid stay in tropical luxury?" he prompted.

"Well, it's still tropical but not so luxurious now," said Shannen. "Lucy and the others say the network bosses turned the resort into a gulag."

"How is that possible? Last night—"

"—was the end of the good times. Apparently, the network bosses wigged out at the size of the bill the group has been running up at the resort."

"So that's why they look so grim." Ty glanced at the unsmiling network execs tramping around the camp. "Hmm, maybe *grim* is too upbeat a word to describe them."

"True. Clark Garrett called everybody together after lunch and screamed at us for almost an hour," said Shannen. "He claimed he'd been screamed at even longer by the network brass. They were *not* happy that the contestants and staffers at the hotel have all been ordering four and five of the most expensive appetizers and entrées apiece in the restaurants at every meal, plus the room service bills were astronomical."

"Having been to the Parrot Room to collect Kevin and Adam last night, and knowing that the group hung out there every night, I'm guessing the bar bill alone would've been enough to send the honchos into orbit," Ty mused.

"And then they found out about all the charges at the

spa and the gift shop,'' added Shannen. ''I thought Uncle Clark was going to kill Miles right in front of us.''

''Well, Miles was the one encouraging everybody to get everything. Too bad they got greedy.''

''I was in the gift shop today. They charge five dollars for a pack of gum and two hundred dollars for a T-shirt with the resort logo,'' Shannen marveled.

''Everybody in the *Victorious* group had on one of those last night at the Parrot Room. We're talking a few thousand in T-shirts right there.'' Ty laughed. ''No wonder Uncle Clark—''

''Had homicide in his heart,'' Shannen put in slyly. ''And before you can ask, no, I didn't buy anything in the gift shop, and I was there before the ban was imposed. The five dollars for gum struck me as high-end robbery. Gramma sells gum for fifty cents a pack at the diner.''

''The prices at the resort are inflated, all right.'' Ty thought of the overpriced box of condoms he'd purchased there. Not that they weren't worth it, of course.

A sudden gust of wind sent Shannen's skirt billowing, and she quickly pushed it down—but not before he'd caught a glimpse of her shapely tanned thigh. Last night he'd seen so much more....

He stared at Shannen, his gaze intimate, possessive. Thinking back on last night, would it really have been the end of the world if he had made her pregnant? He must've thought so when he plunked down twenty bucks for the box of condoms.

But today he reconsidered. Making her pregnant would be the end of the world as he knew it, but suddenly that didn't strike him as a bad thing. Perhaps he should've bought four packs of the overpriced gum instead, because the concept of Shannen carrying his child enticed him.

''Anyway, Clark issued the official network decree,'' Shannen continued, oblivious of Ty's startling yet irresistible daydream. ''Starting this afternoon, the network will pay only for the rooms, plus twenty-five dollars a day per person for food. No room service, no drinks at the bar, no spa or gift-shop charges. Nothing extra."

"Twenty-five dollars a day for food at those hotel prices isn't very much," Ty observed.

"True, considering a cheeseburger is one of the cheapest things on the menu and costs twelve dollars. A cola is six dollars. That's what I had for lunch before the boom was lowered. Guess I should've gone for the lobster and imported white asparagus instead, huh?"

"I understand why they've made restrictions, but their food allowance is pretty draconian, considering there's no alternative place to eat on that island." Ty frowned. "After your nonnutritional sojourn here, you should be eating three decent meals a day, and you can't do that over there on twenty-five dollars a day."

"I'll manage." Shannen dismissed his concern and waved to Lauren, who couldn't seem to summon the energy to wave back.

Shannen turned worriedly to Ty. "How much longer do you think they'll last out there?"

"That's anybody's guess, but I think Konrad will win. Lauren and Rico are definitely showing signs of weakening, but Konrad looks the same as when this madness began."

"Hey, everybody! Break's over, start filming again," called the assistant director.

Ty and the others retrieved their cameras. Reggie focused on Cortnee, who was feasting on an avocado salad and barbecued chicken; Ty turned his camera on the three stalwart contestants who remained in the competition.

Shannen continued to stand beside him, and nobody commented on it. Nobody even glanced their way.

"I like the freedom of being a reject," she decided. "It's like being invisible. And it sure beats standing on a beam out there. Poor Lauren! Besides being tired and thirsty, I can't imagine how bored she must be."

"I can. I was as bored as they are. Until you showed up, that is."

He shifted, moving imperceptibly until his hip grazed hers. The contact would look accidental if anybody were watching. He waited for Shannen's reaction. Would she move away or stay where she was, their bodies discreetly touching?

Ty was elated when she remained there, although she didn't acknowledge their proximity. She put her sunglasses back on and continued to look straight ahead at the contest in the sea.

Ty kept one eye on his subjects and one on Shannen. It felt so right to have her here with him. And they were on the same side of the camera at last! She was adorable, she was feisty, she was passionate and funny and down-to-earth. He yearned to tell her so—if only they were alone.

But they weren't, and he knew this was neither the time nor the place for a truly private conversation. Someone could join them at any minute and undoubtedly would. So he would stick to impersonal topics.

"I'm curious how you managed to nab a ride over here with Clark and the network bosses, Shannen," he said conversationally. "Considering their outrage over the bills, I can't seeing them eager to grant any favors to the *Victorious* cast."

"They aren't mad at me," Shannen said succinctly. "Since I was the newest to arrive on the island, I didn't have a chance to run up a big bill. I put all the food from the room fridge back in it, so I didn't get charged for that, and my only room service meal was the turkey sandwich. I slept through breakfast and had the cheeseburger for lunch. And I had no gift shop purchases."

She flashed a mischievous smile. "Ed—he's the one in the pale-peach shirt talking to Bobby—was ready to canonize me when he saw my expenses. Or lack of them."

"And what made you decide to join them on a visit over

to the old camp?'' Ty parried lightly. ''Didn't like the idea of lounging around a cushy resort, huh?''

''The other contestants thought I was suffering from separation anxiety because Lauren and I weren't together.'' Shannen matched the breeziness of his tone. ''I wanted to come here, so I decided to pretend to be the pathetic misfit they already thought I was.''

''The have-the-name-might-as-well-play-the-game strategy. A classic. Been in use since biblical times, I believe.''

''Maybe even earlier.'' Shannen laughed a little. ''I told Clark I had to see my sister because I was having twin vibes that something was wrong. He assured me Lauren was fine, but he invited me to come along and see for myself.''

''Is there any truth to the twin separation anxiety, Shannen?'' Ty asked quietly. ''You're not a pathetic misfit for worrying about your sister, you know.''

''I thought about Lauren, of course, especially with that snake Jed spreading those rumors.'' She scowled her disapproval. ''But Lauren and I have been apart before. Not often, but it's happened. We don't collapse when we're out of each other's sight.''

''Let me see if I have the facts straight, Shannen. You wanted to come here, but you weren't pining away for a glimpse of your twin, even though you let Clark think so. Interesting.''

''Isn't it?'' Shannen gave his foot a slight nudge with her own.

''Is this the part where I'm supposed to guess why you're really here?'' Ty asked huskily.

She nodded, flushing from head to toe, knowing the sudden rush of heat was unrelated to the tropical sun. Ty's dark eyes seemed to look inside of her. She felt exposed and vulnerable and was grateful that her sunglasses prevented him from reading her emotions in her eyes.

Had she made a major tactical error in showing up here

on the island today? Ty had looked very pleased to see her, but maybe any man would get an ego boost at the sight of his previous night's conquest.

She'd acted on impulse today, but when it came to her behavior with Ty, that was par for the course. He seemed to activate impulsivity in her…along with many other feelings.

"Here's my first guess, Shannen. Maybe you'd like to hear me admit that your appearance here is most timely?" Ty paraphrased himself from last night, his voice wry.

Shannen felt as if fireworks were going off in her head. Besieged with uncertainty, she knew if he'd made some cocky sexual comeback about his prowess and her craving for him, she would have gone as nuclear as the network executives facing the expense tally.

And then she would've had to grapple with being wounded by his insensitivity and arrogance. Been there, done that, nine years ago, even though he'd thought he was being noble. And nine years ago there had been no sexual intimacy between them to make the pain ever sharper. This time around…

Thank heavens they were more in sync this time around! His gently humorous reply validated her instincts for coming here.

"Your first guess is right," she said softly.

A broad grin creased his face. "I admit it, your appearance here is most timely, Shannen."

"Wow! That's the truth!" Heidi joined them just in time to catch the end of his remark. "You really must have that twin ESP going on strong! You *knew* your sister needed you!"

Heidi pointed to Lauren, who was swaying perilously, gripping the pole with both arms. Moments later she slipped off the post into the water.

Before anyone on the beach could react, Rico jumped in after her and pulled her to her feet.

"Just keep filming!" shouted Clark. "Nobody go in the water! The girl's okay, and we don't want to ruin the drama by cluttering up the scene with the crew."

Shannen ignored him and ran into the water, sandals and all. Within a split second, Heidi caught up to her and grabbed her arm, following another order from Clark.

Shannen began to struggle. "Get away from me!"

"You're not even supposed to be here," exclaimed Heidi, trying harder to hold her back. "Tell her, Ty," she pleaded to Ty, who'd followed them both.

"Tell her not to go to her sister who practically fainted in the water?" snarled Ty. "Forget it." He handed the camera to Kevin, who had raced in, too. "I'm not filming this."

Shannen successfully broke free from Heidi and ran toward Lauren and Rico. The pair were approaching the shore, hanging on to each other. Both looked fatigued and sunburned, and it was hard to tell who was supporting whom.

Shannen threw her arms around them both. "Oh, Lauren, you poor thing! And, Rico, you're a hero for jumping in after her like that, without even thinking twice."

"We got that part on film," Reggie called.

"Thank God! The rest we'll have to edit out," announced Clark. "Pan to Cortnee and to Konrad."

Cortnee held her hands to her cheeks and looked tearful.

Konrad was smiling. "I'm the last one standing, so I win immunity."

Shannen barely heard him as she prepared to tell Clark Garrett exactly what she thought of him.

Nine

The network executives wanted to watch the tribal council in person, so Shannen would stay on the island until they all returned to the resort by boat later in the evening. The contestant who was voted off would go with them.

"Keep that crazy twin out of camera range," Clark said to Ty. "Put her on a leash if you have to, just don't let her get filmed by mistake. Editing can only fix so much."

Clark wiped sweat from his brow with his already-damp handkerchief. He was looking haggard after an encounter with the enraged Shannen. Brimming with white-hot rage, she had reviled him, quite effectively, in front of everybody.

Ty, who had witnessed many a verbal annihilation directed at the Howes, recognized her as a true master of the art.

Silence had descended, and not even Bobby Dixon tried to deliver one of his annoying platitudes. Nobody cared to risk incurring the wrath of Shannen.

When she'd proclaimed, "Somebody better get my sister and Rico something to eat and drink right now!" even the network executives hurried to fetch food and water.

"Ty, I want you to know I appreciate you going into the water to try to stop that demented bitch from ruining the terrific scene of the two losers staggering in together," continued Clark. "*Twins!* Who knew they'd go psycho? We won't be casting twins in *Victorious Two,* I can promise you that."

Ty shook his head. He was disgusted with Clark's callousness toward Lauren's fall into the water, and to make matters worse, the obtuse executive producer had misinterpreted his lunge into the water after Shannen.

Ty had gone in to help her with Lauren, to show his support for her, not to restrain her, as that blockhead Garrett believed.

But Shannen hadn't needed Ty's intervention and refused it when he offered.

"We're fine. Go back and get your camera," she told him, slipping her arm around Lauren. "You'll get in trouble. Clark is throwing a tantrum as it is and—"

"Screw Clark Garrett!" cursed Ty.

Shannen flashed a sardonic smile. "I'd rather not."

Ty arched his brows. "You'd better not!"

Rico and Lauren laughed weakly.

And then the production assistants hauled away the two contestants, leaving Shannen and Ty to wade ashore together.

"Ty, seriously, you have to do your job," said Shannen. "You have to start filming or else—"

"I could be fired? I'm so worried." Ty was sarcastic.

"We all have these take-this-job-and-shove-it moments, Tynan," Shannen explained patiently. "And everybody has had at least one boss who's a jerk, but—"

"Shannen, I'll get my camera and film the contestants, but please dispense with the pep talk," growled Ty.

It was bad enough he was trapped in his own stupid deception. Hearing her try to console him about it made him queasy with guilt. He had too many deceptions going on in his life—his name, his career and his past relationship with Shannen.

Only she knew most of the truth, but he'd kept a vital fact from her too: his wealth.

How to tell her? *When* to tell her? Because he knew now that he wanted her to know the full truth.

Shannen, unaware of his dilemma, thought he was still mired in a take-this-job-and-shove-it moment.

She gave him a bolstering thumbs-up and headed toward Lauren and Rico, who were guzzling bottles of water.

Now it was time for the voting, and as the Final Four sat in the tribal council area, Bobby delivered a ponderous homily about four being narrowed to three.

Konrad clutched the immunity totem as if it were a priceless antiquity. Lauren, Rico and Cortnee looked tense and eyed each other warily.

Shannen stood next to Ty as he filmed. "It's kind of sad," she whispered to him. "I remember when those four were a solid alliance, maybe even friends. Well, sort of. But now they don't trust each other."

"It was inevitable, Shannen. They're each playing for themselves now."

"I know, I know." She sighed. "It's all in the game."

She saw Clark Garrett and the production assistants stealing nervous glances at her. And she noticed for the first time that the entire crew had taken positions well away from her and Ty.

"I see you've been chosen to be the human sacrifice and rein me in, should I suddenly go berserk," Shannen mocked, her eyes locking with Clark Garrett's.

It gave her a naughty thrill to see him brace himself, as

if expecting her to suddenly fly at him like a rabid vampire bat.

"Stop terrorizing Clark, Shannen," Ty admonished dryly. "You've already carved him up with that sharp little tongue of yours once today, and he's dreading another attack."

"My verbal skills have advanced beyond trite kid stuff like 'condescending, self-righteous jerk,' haven't they?" Shannen was pleased.

"Well beyond, honey. Remind me not to cross you."

"I will," she replied playfully. "Every chance I get."

"It's time to vote," Bobby's voice boomed, drowning out even their muffled whispers.

"Uh-oh!" Shannen's lighthearted mood evaporated. She met Lauren's eyes and held up her hand, her two fingers crossed for good luck.

Lauren bit her lip and looked away.

As always, the votes against each contestant were announced by Bobby with melodramatic flair.

"Cortnee." He held up a card and read the name.

From her position behind the camera, Shannen saw the voting cards for the first time. She recognized Lauren's handwriting immediately.

"Lauren," read Bobby, and Shannen thought the penmanship on that card looked girlishly embellished. The way Cortnee might write?

"I think the two girls just canceled out each other's votes," she whispered to Ty, who made no comment. "They should've stuck together."

"Rico," Bobby's voice boomed, and he held up a card with printing so atrocious, Shannen guessed it to be Konrad's. He'd often boasted of his school failures, and perhaps printing was one of them.

"Three votes for three different people." Bobby stated the obvious.

Shannen resisted the urge to rush him and snatch the remaining card from his hand.

"This is the last vote, and the name I read will be the person who will extinguish their flashlight and leave the island," Bobby intoned solemnly.

Dragging out the moment with agonizing slowness, he studied the card. Finally, *finally* he read it: "Lauren."

Shannen and Lauren each drew in a short, sharp breath, then simultaneously schooled their expressions into smiles of acceptance.

Ty watched, his eyes darting from sister to sister, fascinated by their identical responses.

One camera lingered an extra few moments on Lauren, but her smile didn't falter. Ty filmed Cortnee hugging Rico and then Konrad in turn.

"I'm sorry, sweetie," Ty whispered to Shannen.

She shrugged. "We were lucky to make it this far. And Lauren will win five thousand dollars for being the fourth of the Final Four. That's great!"

She gave him such a sunny smile, he felt perversely glum. Would five thousand dollars after taxes be enough to even fix their grandmother's roof, let alone cover the diner's expenses?

"Anyway, Jordan can keep on buying those powerball tickets," Shannen said, even more brightly.

"Shannen, it's okay to express disappointment," Ty murmured. "You don't have to put on a front with me."

The camera recorded Lauren extinguishing her flashlight and then turned to focus on the others. Immediately afterward, Lauren rushed over to Shannen and began to cry.

"Oh, Shan, I'm so sorry! I should've given you the immunity thing instead of keeping it for myself. You never would've fallen off the post. And nobody would've voted against you, either. I'm such a flop!"

"Lauren, no! You are not!" Shannen hugged her sister and rocked her in her arms. "You played a good game.

We both did. It was even fun, in a hellish kind of way, wasn't it?''

"It was horrible!'' Lauren wept. "I wish we'd never come here, I wish I hadn't dragged you to the audition. Oh, Shannen, I just want to go home!''

Heidi approached, giving Ty an apprehensive look. "It's time to get Lauren's things and for both of them to leave the island.'' Heidi addressed Ty instead of the twins.

"I'll take them,'' offered Ty and stepped between the sisters, holding a twin with each arm. "Let's go.''

Everyone's eyes were upon them.

"The crew is looking at you like you singlehandedly tamed the shrew,'' Shannen said as they walked along the path to the camp. "Was I *that* scary when I yelled at Clark Garrett? The heartless boor could run the ice concession in hell,'' she added fiercely.

"You made an impressive show of fury unbound,'' Ty allowed, his eyes gleaming. "But you didn't scare me. It takes a lot to scare me, Shannen.''

"I'll keep that in mind, Tynan.''

"Are you two ever going to tell me how you know each other?'' Lauren had stopped crying and was watching them.

Shannen and Ty exchanged glances.

"We'll get back to you on that one,'' said Ty, speaking for them both.

The network executives were impatient to leave the island for the resort and insisted that Clark Garrett hurry the twins along. He did, but with obvious trepidation.

"All of a sudden I feel like we're moving at warp speed,'' complained Ty as he walked with Shannen to the boat.

Lauren, clutching her few possessions, was a few feet ahead of them with Clark. The network bosses and the driver were already in the boat.

"While we were filming the immunity contest, time crawled by,'' Ty continued to gripe. "Why do some hours have sixty thousand minutes in them and other hours are only sixty seconds long?''

"If you don't mind me quoting Gramma again, 'Time flies when you're having fun,'" said Shannen. "Although I'm not sure if it applies here. Watching Lauren collapse into the water and then get voted off the island wasn't fun.''

"No, but being with you is," Ty countered huskily. "Even under these less-than-ideal circumstances."

"I'm glad I came today," she said.

Her words, her tone, were almost perfunctory. Ty sensed her withdrawal increasing in direct proportion to their nearness to the boat.

The frustration within him soared to this morning's high, before Shannen's appearance on the island. Maybe even higher, because he knew there would be no surprise visit by her tomorrow. She couldn't play the twin separation card because Lauren would be with her.

When was he going to see her again? Not knowing was intolerable!

"Come onboard, young lady!" Ed, the network executive in the pale-peach shirt, shouted from the boat.

Clark Garrett and Lauren had just boarded, and the driver revved up the engine.

"I'll get the crew boat and come to your room tonight," Ty said quickly.

"Ty, you can't." Shannen gazed up at him, her blue eyes wide. "You won't be allowed to go—there's no film to take to the network bosses. They've been here all day."

"I won't be marooned on this stupid island simply because I don't have an official okay to leave."

"But, Ty, if you don't have permission to take the boat, you—"

"Permission?" Ty repeated scornfully. "I'm taking the boat, with or without *permission.*"

"That's Tynan Howe talking, not Ty Hale," reproved

Shannen. "You might've been able to do as you pleased when you were rich, but now you have to…"

"…take orders from idiots like Clark Garrett and those network stooges?" Ty was incensed. "I could buy and sell all three, many times over!"

"Not any longer." Shannen laid her hand on his arm. "That was then, Ty. This is now," she reminded him gently. "Now you work for them and—"

"Shannen, they're ready to go," called Lauren.

Ty exhaled sharply. "Shannen—"

"Ty, even if you did manage to come to the resort tonight, I wouldn't let you in my room," Shannen's voice was low and urgent. "Because—"

"Oh, of course, there's Lauren," Ty said. "We'll get her a room of her own. Don't worry, I'll pay for it myself."

"It's not because Lauren will be sharing my room, Ty. I've done a lot of thinking since last night and I…I decided that I can't go to bed with you again." She expelled her declaration in a breathless rush.

"What?" Ty felt as though he'd been clubbed over the head.

Maybe he had been. Maybe Konrad had sneaked up and whacked him with the immunity totem.

He must've sustained a substantial blow, because he seemingly had lost the powers of comprehension. Shannen couldn't have said what he'd just heard.

"Last night we went too far too fast, Ty." She sounded tense and edgy. "We have to slow down, to back up and…and get to know each other."

"Shannen, one thing we can't be accused of is rushing things. We've known each other for nine years!"

"When you put it like that—"

"It sounds ridiculous? That's because it is, Shannen!"

"No, it sounds like a twisted argument. We *knew* each other nine years ago, Ty. That's a big difference from *knowing* each other for that long. We parted on bad terms and we certainly didn't keep in touch. When we remet here on the island, it was like two strangers meeting for the first time.''

"Keep in touch?'' echoed Ty. "Is this retaliation for not calling you on your twenty-first birthday? I explained why I thought you wouldn't want to hear from me at that time. Or any time after. As for being strangers to each other—''

The boat horn blasted, sounding as loud as the start at the Indy 500, drowning him out.

"The very fact you assumed I wouldn't want to hear from you simply proves my point about not knowing each other very well,'' Shannen said urgently. "Not then or now. And I have to go before they break the sound barrier again with that awful horn.''

Ty gripped her shoulders. "Shannen, we can't leave things this way.'' He wondered if he sounded as desperate as he felt. "I won't let you end it and just walk away.''

"Ty—''

"Which is what I did nine years ago,'' he admitted grimly. "And even knowing that I took the high moral ground back then is no consolation now, Shannen. If you wanted revenge, baby, you've got it.''

"Will you stop jumping to stupid conclusions and just shut up and listen to me for a minute?'' Shannen's temper flared. "I'm not out for revenge, and if you actually believe that, you've once again proved that you don't know me.'' Her voice softened. "But I want you to, Ty. Let me put it into TV terms you'll understand. I'm putting sex on hiatus, not canceling our relationship. If you can't accept that…''

The ear-splitting boat horn blared again. Shannen pulled away from him and ran to the boat.

"It's about time,'' grumbled the other network executive, the one who wasn't Ed. "What was going on, anyway?''

"I was thanking Mr. Hale for being kind to me today,'' Shannen replied demurely. "I'm most appreciative, especially after Clark Garrett's attitude toward my sister's fall. His lack of concern bordered on negligence!''

''I wasn't—'' Clark started, but Shannen cut him right off.

''Just thinking about it made me furious all over again, and Mr. Hale was trying to persuade me not to commandeer this boat on the way back and kick Clark Garrett overboard.''

''Oh,'' both network execs chorused. They glanced uneasily at the driver, who paid no attention to the conversation going on.

''Don't worry, Mr. Hale convinced me not to do it.'' Shannen was all smiles and reassurance. ''You really ought to think about giving him a raise, if you value Clark Garrett. Because Ty Hale saved him from being shark food.''

''What were you and Ty really talking about back on the beach, Shannen?'' Lauren asked as the twins entered the hotel lobby. Clark and the bosses were far ahead of them. ''And don't give me that lunatic story that he convinced you not to hijack the boat and throw Clark Garrett to the sharks.''

''Actually, he told me to go ahead and do it. That I'd be making the world a better place. And then we could toss Slick Bobby overboard tomorrow night,'' Shannen said flippantly.

''Shannen!''

''Lauren!''

The twins held one of their familiar face-offs, then grinned at each other.

''I'm so glad you're here, Lauren.'' Shannen gave her sister a small squeeze. ''You'll like our room. It's pure heaven to take a long, hot shower, and the bed is king-size and like sleeping on a cloud. Tomorrow we'll go to the pool and—''

''Shannen, look, there's Jed!'' Lauren exclaimed. ''He's

over there with the others by the entrance to that hallway. Let's go say hello."

Shannen saw the nervous excitement light Lauren's face, and gulped back an exclamation of dismay. "Why not wait till tomorrow, Lauren? After you've had a shower and a good night's sleep."

And I've had a chance to try and talk some sense into you, she added silently.

Jed was standing among the other ousted *Victorious* contestants and hadn't seen them yet, but Lauren was quick to change that. She bolted across the lobby.

Shannen felt she had no choice but to go after her. "Lauren, just play it cool," she whispered as they approached the group.

Lauren made no reply.

Shannen watched her sister closely and proceeded to duplicate her every move and every nuance of expression. It was a skill they'd perfected back when they were kids, and confusing people was a fun game.

Right now it was a necessity, Shannen decided grimly. If Jed couldn't tell who was who, she doubted he would risk making a play for Lauren. The rat would be too afraid he might be hitting on the Scary Twin, the one who'd had "homicide in her heart" last night.

"Hi, Jed," Lauren said, slightly breathless.

"Hi Jed," Shannen imitated her twin right down to the appealing head tilt. She wanted to laugh out loud at the look of sheer panic that crossed Jed's face as his eyes darted from one sister to the other.

And then he smiled directly, confidently at Lauren.

"Well, hello there, Lauren. And welcome! Can I help you with this?" Jed offered to take Lauren's things, which she'd almost dropped while hurrying across the lobby.

"Thanks, Jed." Lauren gave him a dreamy smile.

For a moment Shannen was too stunned to react at all. How had Jed known which one of them was Lauren? He certainly couldn't tell last night when he'd drunkenly barged into her room.

She looked at her sister, who was handing her bundle of belongings to Jed. And realized how he'd suddenly acquired the ability to differentiate between them.

Lauren was wearing the shorts and triangle top she'd worn during much of the *Victorious* filming, Shannen was in a sundress. Nobody wore dresses at camp on the island.

And while Shannen had enjoyed the luxury of a leisurely shower and shampoo in her private bathroom this morning, Lauren had to make do with the meager spring on the island.

A moment later Miles joined the group, no longer the effervescent lad who had greeted Shannen yesterday. He was subdued and sullen, the result of a scathing lecture from his uncle Clark and the network bosses, Shannen assumed.

"I'll take you to your room," Miles said flatly, making none of yesterday's grandiose offers. "You're sharing it with your sister. You can order something from the room service menu as long as it costs under twenty-five dollars, tip included."

"I know where the room is. I can take her there," Shannen volunteered.

"I have a better idea," said Jed. He turned to Shannen and dumped Lauren's things in her arms. "You take these to the room, and I'll go with Lauren to the coffee shop where she can order something—under twenty-five dollars, Miles." He winked at the production assistant. "Then I'll show you around the hotel, Lauren."

"That sounds wonderful!" Lauren beamed up at him.

"No, it doesn't!" Shannen snapped. "Lauren, you—"

"It's okay, I'll come up later, Shan. Don't worry, I'll find my way." Lauren took another small step closer to Jed. "Oh, and thanks for taking my stuff to the room, Shannen."

Jed slipped his arm around Lauren's waist and whisked her off. "She'll see you later, sis," he called, shooting Shannen a look over his shoulder.

A you-lose look, Shannen thought furiously. A triumphant ha-ha look.

Lauren didn't look back at all.

What should she do? Shannen wondered. Would Lauren be terribly upset if Shannen chased after them? Shannen was torn. She glanced up and saw Lucy eyeing her with sympathy.

"Hey, hon, why don't you join us in the Tikki Lounge?" Lucy asked. "Ron—you remember him, don't you? We voted him off right after the tribes merged—has a credit card and is buying everybody a round of drinks."

A pity invitation! They thought she couldn't bear to be away from her twin. Never mind that she'd played along to get to the island today. Shannen was humiliated.

"No, thanks," she murmured. "I, uh, don't really remember Ron. Sorry."

"I'm Ron, and it's okay." Ron stepped forward. "Nobody remembered me. I'd love to get better acquainted with you, though. Let me buy you a drink."

Shannen thought how much she didn't want to get better acquainted with Ron or any of the other guys in the group. There was only one man she wanted to become better acquainted with, and that was Ty.

She wondered if she'd made a major mistake by telling him that she wanted to put sex on hiatus. Not that the hiatus was a mistake—she was certain she was right about that— but saying so the moment before she had to leave him might not have been the best timing.

Maybe she should've said a simple good-night and left it at that.

Shannen trudged to her room carrying Lauren's things.

Timing. A crucial element in any game. The timing had been wrong for her and Ty nine years ago, but now...

Timing Is Everything, the saying went. Was it wrong for them all over again?

Ten

Shannen put on her one-size-fits-all West Falls University nightshirt and studied the list of movies available for viewing in the rooms of the resort. For a fee, of course. If she ordered Russell Crowe, would the cost be deducted from her food allowance?

She wasn't tired, and though she wouldn't have minded something to eat, she wasn't about to call room service. After the network decree, there was probably a block on the phones of all *Victorious* guests, anyway. Raiding the little fridge in the room wasn't worth it, either. There was nothing in it she wanted.

All she really wanted was Ty.

And to have Lauren come to their room saying she hated Jed's womanizing guts, that she hadn't slept with him and had never wanted to.

If she were given a choice, whom did she want more, Ty or a Jed-hating Lauren, to appear at her door? Shannen debated her hypothetical options. At least it was something to do.

Ty was her first choice every time.

When she heard a light knock, she opened the door without bothering to look through the peephole. She was sure it was Lauren, of course. Shannen could only hope it wasn't the under-Jed's-spell version of her twin.

Instead, Ty stood in the doorway, holding a bag.

"Room service. This is the alternate version provided by me and the coffee shop. I have sandwiches, fruit and cake. And wine from the infamous Parrot Room," he added, deadpan. "Not to get you drunk, of course, since that might lead to sex, which you've put on hiatus."

Shannen's heart beat very fast and very hard. "What...how..." She couldn't seem to find the words to ask the obvious questions.

"What am I doing here and how did I get here?" Ty supplied them for her, and she nodded mutely.

"I drove the boat over. I simply told the crew I was taking it to the resort. Nobody tried to stop me." His eyes gleamed. "It helped that Clark Garrett is already here and everyone probably assumed he'd asked me to bring something over. But nobody bothered to ask."

Shannen felt an absurd attack of shyness, definitely a first for her. Shy she'd never been. But standing here with Ty, who was looking so virile and gorgeous and oh, so dear, evoked feelings so powerful that she could do nothing but gaze at him.

"Now we get to the 'why I'm here' part." Ty handed her the bag of food. "I came for dinner. We can eat out on the balcony, like last night."

"Ty..." She was warm all over. From blushing from head to toe? "Last night—"

"Don't worry, I'm not expecting tonight to end like last night's little al fresco picnic. Though I'm certainly not objecting if it should."

Ty put his hands on her waist and carefully moved her aside so he could enter the room. "I respect the limits you've set, Shannen." He shut the door, closing them both in the room. "Stupid and unnecessary though they may be."

His arms encircled her, and he smoothed his hands over the length of her back. Just when she thought he would move his hands lower, just as she anticipated him doing so, he released her.

"You're as safe as you want to be with me, Shannen. Always." He kissed the top of her head. "Now let's eat."

Shannen watched him walk toward the balcony. She gulped for air as a sharp stab of desire pierced her to the core. It would be so easy to suspend her new rule, to lie down on the bed with Ty and make love with him. He was here, she was in love with him, and he wanted her.

After all, they had known each other for nine years. Never mind that she'd had no contact with him from age seventeen to twenty-six and that technically they weren't strangers. Especially not after last night.

She walked to the balcony and stood nervously on the threshold. "I'm in my nightshirt," she murmured, glancing down at the blue-and-white shapeless bag she wore. Wishing it were an eye-popping little number from Victoria's Secret.

"I ought to get dressed."

"Don't bother on my account." Ty grinned wickedly, then added, "Why not just stay comfortable in that? Keep in mind I've seen you in far less every day on the island. Those skimpy little tops and shorts you wore, that sexy bikini of yours... My brain short-circuited every time I looked at you—which was all the time. It was all I could do to remember to keep my camera rolling."

"Cortnee's bikini was much scantier than mine," Shannen protested weakly.

"I never noticed. You were the only one who interested me, Shannen. You still are. Now come out here and eat."

Trembling, Shannen went to him.

Two hours later, they were still out on the balcony, the food completely consumed, the second bottle of wine down to the last drop.

A light breeze from the sea broke the tropical night heat, a full moon lit a pathway in the ocean, but Shannen was oblivious to their physical surroundings. She could've been in a dank cave and she wouldn't have minded, as long as Ty was with her.

They talked and laughed, conversing as comfortably as old friends one minute, then switching to the intoxicating seductive manner of new lovers. Shannen felt an ease she'd never felt with anyone but Lauren, combined with an excitement she'd never experienced with any man. And a desire for him stronger than anything she'd ever known.

It was an irresistible blend, and she wondered if Ty felt the same way.

She should ask him, Shannen decided giddily. Why not? She trusted him enough to ask the question and to hear the answer.

"Ty?" She stood up, and the balcony suddenly took a precarious lurch. She grabbed onto the back of a chair for support.

Ty quickly supplied support of his own. "Uh-oh." He wrapped his arms around her waist, bringing her back against his chest. "Maybe we shouldn't have knocked off that second bottle of wine."

"I'm fine. Just a little light-headed." She looked up at the stars, which seemed to have turned into fireworks, exploding before her eyes. "Maybe very light-headed."

"Into bed you go, Ms. Cullen." Ty scooped her up and carried her inside.

"Ty, I have something to tell you." Shannen linked her

arms around his neck and snuggled against him. "I'll suspend the hiatus for this one night."

Laughing softly, Ty put her on the bed. "You're going to sleep, Shannen. And I'm heading back to camp." He started to tuck the sheet around her. "Good night, baby."

Shannen's fingers fastened around his wrists. "I decided I don't mind if you call me 'baby' every now and then. But only when we're alone."

"Duly noted," agreed Ty. He attempted to disentangle his wrists from her grip, but she held on fast.

"Don't you want me, Ty?" The thought suddenly struck her, and she lacked the control to keep from blurting it out. At this moment she also lacked the inhibition to be horrified by it.

"You know I do, Shannen."

He leaned down to kiss her hungrily, letting her know how much he wanted her. His hands cupped her face, holding her mouth firmly under his as he slanted his lips over hers, drinking deeply from the moist warmth within. His tongue moved provocatively against hers in an erotic, arousing simulation.

Pure liquid pleasure flooded her. She was aware only of Ty and the thrilling mastery of his lips and his hands. Lost in the head-spinning world of sensation, Shannen was completely unprepared for him to lift his mouth from hers.

She watched in confusion as he slowly straightened.

"I didn't come here to get you drunk and take you to bed, Shannen." His voice was husky, his smile roguishly sexy. "I don't *need* to get you drunk to get you into bed. But I do want you to be sure that we know each other well enough, so making love is officially on hiatus until then."

Shannen felt a fierce yearning swelling inside her, so intense she could hardly breathe.

"We know each other well enough, Ty," she whimpered urgently.

Ty walked to the door as if she hadn't spoken at all. He

opened it and paused in the doorway. "When you're stone-cold sober and say those words, we'll make love, Shannen. But you're not, so we won't. Good night, my love."

Sunlight poured into the room through the open curtains, making it literally bright as day.

Automatically, Shannen put her hands over her eyes to block out the light. Closing the drapes after Ty had put her to bed last night hadn't even crossed her mind.

She heard a hoarse moan from the other side of the bed.

"What time is it?" Lauren asked groggily, putting a pillow over her face to shut out the sunlight.

Shannen sat up and looked at the clock. "Five to six. That's a.m.," she added gingerly.

"Is that all?" Lauren wailed. "No wonder I feel so wrecked! I *have* to get some more sleep." She flopped over onto her stomach and buried her face in the pillow.

"I didn't hear you come in last night, Lauren," Shannen said. Or if she had, she didn't remember it.

Shannen vividly recalled her last memory of the night. It was of Ty kissing her senseless and then leaving her, her blood roaring in her ears, her body taut and wet.

His words sounded in her head as a narrative for the visual pictures playing in her mind. *I don't need to get you drunk to get you into bed.* No, she'd proved that beyond all doubt.

When you're stone-cold sober and say those words, we'll make love, Shannen. But you're not, so we won't. He had been noble again. Shannen clenched her teeth in frustration.

Noble and outrageously confident. Of course, why shouldn't he be, when she'd practically pleaded with him to go to bed with her? When she'd rescinded her ban on sex less than three hours after making it!

"Ohhhh!" Shannen groaned.

"My thoughts exactly," Lauren replied through gritted teeth.

* * *

"I don't think we're the type for living luxurious lives of leisure, Lauren." Shannen closed her book. "Having all this time on my hands with nothing to do is driving me crazy. At least when we were back on the island, we were always foraging for food. It kept us busy."

"We're doing something, we're reading," said Lauren, not looking up from her book. The cover was a frightening pair of eyes staring demonically at the silhouette of a cowering victim. Knives and droplets of bright blood completed the picture.

The sisters had gone to the gift shop earlier to buy paperbacks to read. Lauren remembered the thousand dollars they'd gained by not eating in the reward contest, money Shannen had completely forgotten about.

Shannen chose a historical romance and expected Lauren to select one in a similar vein. Those were their favorites, but Lauren had bluntly declared she wanted a page-turning thriller, grisly and gory, with a high body count. She'd read every book jacket until finally finding the most horrific. Shannen hated having it in the room with them; it seemed to emit bad vibes.

Or maybe that was Lauren emitting those vibes, because she'd been uncharacteristically difficult since they'd been awakened too early by the morning sun.

Lauren refused to walk on the beach or go to the pool. She wouldn't leave their room for breakfast, lunch or dinner, either. Shannen brought her food from the coffee shop, staying within the daily allowance, and the sisters ate together on the balcony.

Worst of all, Lauren completely clammed up when Shannen asked why she didn't want to leave the room except to buy her gruesome tome of terror. When Shannen casually mentioned Jed's name, Lauren exploded, insisting she never wanted to hear it again. Or the names of any of the other *Victorious* contestants. In fact, she never wanted to talk about the game and the time they'd spent on the island for as long as they lived.

Which ruled out speculating on who would get voted off the island today and who would be the Final Two. Shannen pictured Ty filming it all and silently speculated with herself.

Then she went back to her book, reading until she was stiff from sitting. She stood up and leaned against the balcony railing, gazing at the white sand on the beach and the vast expanse of ocean. The water looked aqua in the sunset. At noon it had been a deeper blue.

Shannen tried to guess which direction the *Victorious* island was. And she thought of Ty again. She'd relived last night in her head over and over, remembering how much she enjoyed being with him. The talking, the laughing, the kissing…

She swallowed hard. She missed him, she wanted to be with him. It was too much to hope that he would come back to the hotel again tonight after the day's filming was through. He simply couldn't keep taking the crew boat to go where he pleased; she knew that, too.

Resignedly she sat back down and picked up her book. The heroine was at that stage of holding off the advances of the hero, whom she claimed to loathe but subconsciously lusted for.

"Stop giving the poor guy such a hard time, Jacinda," Shannen muttered to the girl in the book. "You know you're going to surrender in the end." She gave up and laid it aside. "How's your book, Lauren?"

"Excellent! Another clueless jerk just got offed," exclaimed Lauren ruthlessly.

Now Lauren was rooting for the killer. Shannen walked inside the room to check the clock. How could it only be a few minutes past seven o'clock? This day had gone on for years! And the evening loomed endlessly ahead.

When a knock sounded an hour later, Shannen made a

quick stop at the mirror before answering the door. She pulled her hair out of the ponytail and fluffed it with her fingers. Her striped tank top and navy shorts were a definite improvement over the shapeless nightshirt she'd worn last night.

She admitted to herself that though she'd tried all day to pretend otherwise, she was expecting Ty. After all, he'd shown up unannounced twice before. Still, just in case, she warned herself to be braced for disappointment as she peered through the peephole.

And was not disappointed. She flung open the door.

"Surprise," said Ty. "Or not."

"You're three for three!" Shannen exclaimed, throwing her arms around him and hugging him tight.

Conveniently he had no food or wine tonight and his arms were free to pick her up. She wrapped her legs around his waist and their lips met in passionate fusion.

This was no tentative, preliminary kiss. His tongue entered her mouth and probed intimately, and she responded with an urgency and need that matched his. Instantaneously they were swept into fiery passion, their emotional connection so strong and so natural there could be no denying it.

However, they were not alone.

"To think I thought today couldn't get any worse." Lauren's voice, sardonic and cross, made her presence known. "Ha! The laugh is on me, because it just did. I landed the dreaded role of unwanted third wheel."

Shannen stiffened and Ty tensed. Their private little interlude had come to an abrupt end. She wriggled to be free, and he let her go, though he held her tightly against him, turning the release into a long, slow body caress. Both reluctantly stepped apart.

"Hello, Lauren," he said with commendable geniality. "How are you?"

"Not overjoyed to be playing chaperon," she replied baldly. "If you two want to be alone, you'll have to go

somewhere else. I'm not being driven out of my room."
She purposefully stretched across the bed on her stomach,
her book in front of her face.

"Let's take a walk, Shannen," suggested Ty. "Unless
you'd rather stay here?"

"A walk sounds good." Shannen grabbed his hand and
fairly dragged him from the room. "We've been cooped
up in there most of the day," she confided as they strolled
along the long corridor. "Lauren's…in kind of a mood."

"Tactfully stated." Ty grinned. "Want to know who
was voted off the island?"

"That's how you got the boat again. You offered to bring
the loser over!"

"I didn't offer, I said I was going to do it. Rico is checking into his room right now."

"Rico!" exclaimed Shannen. "How did that happen?"

"Whoever caught the first fish would win the immunity
contest. Konrad had a tug on his pole and immediately
handed it to Cortnee. Sure enough, there was a fish on the
line, which made her the first to catch one."

"So she won immunity. That is, Konrad gave it to her,"
Shannen amended, surprised. "That's unexpected, isn't
it?"

"Nobody saw it coming. Cortnee and Konrad cut their
little deal out of camera range. They both voted Rico off,
but he took it like a good sport."

"And Konrad and Cortnee are the two finalists." Shannen didn't care. She and Ty were together, headed toward
the beach on a beautiful tropical night. Whoever won the
Victorious game, she felt like the *truly* victorious one.

They held hands and walked along the beach together.

"I'm guessing that things didn't go well for Lauren and
Jed?" Ty asked. "She didn't look or sound like someone
who'd spent the day in romantic paradise."

Shannen appreciated the opening. She guessed that Ty
couldn't care less about the alleged Lauren-Jed relationship,

but he knew *she* did. And he was willing and ready to let her confide in him.

They walked and talked for a long time. After exhausting the topic of Lauren and Jed, they moved on to others. Sometimes they paused to discreetly steal a kiss; they were never not touching, either holding hands or wrapping their arms around each other's waists. It was a blissful idyll that neither wanted to end.

But after running into some of the *Victorious* contestants well past midnight, Shannen and Ty recognized it was time to call it a night. They declined the invitation to "join the gang," and Ty walked Shannen back to her room.

"This is kind of like an old-fashioned courtship," he said dryly. "Leaving you at your door with a chaste good-night kiss, my whole body aching with frustration."

"Who said the good-night kiss has to be chaste?" teased Shannen, and initiated a kiss that was anything but.

"Now I'm not only aching with frustration, I'm burning up with it." Ty held her tight, waiting, hoping for the tension to drain from his body. "Shannen, I wanted to tell you—I'm thinking of using the name Howe again."

His tone was deliberately casual, but she was too attuned to him not to know his family name was something he could never be casual about.

"I think it's a good idea, Ty. You're not the one who disgraced it. I think you're going to be the one to make it a name to be proud of again."

"Thanks for the vote of confidence. I hope so. But it won't be as a cameraman, Shannen." He leaned back and gazed down into her warm blue eyes. "If I resumed my law career, I'd take clients who needed me as an advocate but couldn't afford to pay exorbitant attorney fees. I don't want to practice law to become rich and famous."

"Good!" Shannen said succinctly. "There are already too many lawyers like that."

"Anyway, if I opened a law office, it could be anywhere

I wanted to live. That's an option a network cameraman doesn't have.''

Shannen nodded, shaky with excitement. Was he trying to say something she hadn't dared dream of?

If so, he never got the chance. Unexpectedly Lauren opened the door. Shannen and Ty, partially leaning against it, were thrown off balance and nearly fell into the room.

''Shannen, I feel like Gramma flashing the front light on and off when we stayed out on the porch too long back in high school,'' scolded Lauren. ''She wanted to go to bed and couldn't, as long as we were out there. Well, I can really relate to that now. Say good-night already and come inside.''

Shannen grimaced. ''You even sound just like Gramma, Lauren.''

''Good night already,'' Ty quoted lightly and touched Shannen's cheek with his fingertips. ''Tomorrow, sweetheart.''

The ten contestants who'd been previously ousted filed into the tribal council area, which was lit by hundreds of candles and tall flaming torches placed strategically to ensure the best camera lighting.

Ty waited for Shannen, who was one of the last to come in. She was followed by Lauren and last of all Rico.

Surprisingly, both twins were dressed alike in pale-pink sundresses. Their hair was styled exactly the same way, too, pulled back into a neat thick French braid. They looked like duplicates of each other, though Ty still knew which was Shannen. He just knew.

He also knew that the twins hadn't dressed alike during the entire Victorious shoot. Shannen had confided they'd stopped wearing identical clothing in elementary school unless they were plotting a switch.

Ty was curious and kept his eyes fixed on Shannen, willing her to look at him, to provide even a hint of a clue.

But she never made eye contact with him. Was she avoiding doing so?

It was as if they were back in the early days of *Victorious,* when Shannen had pretended she didn't know who he was, when she'd resolutely followed the game's guidelines "to treat the cameras and crew as if they weren't there."

"Can you believe it? This is our last night of filming!" Heidi whispered to him.

Ty brightened, drawing an odd look from Heidi, who was visibly saddened that the shoot was over. Now she would have to find another job on another show, the fate of production assistants when production wrapped.

Of cameramen, too. But he was an ex-cameraman after tonight. A kind of bittersweet relief surged through Ty. He felt like a refugee who'd decided to return to his native country after a self-imposed exile.

The jury was seated on a three-tiered riser with four of the ex-contestants on each bench. Shannen, Lauren, Rico and Jed sat on the lowest one. Ty noted that Shannen was seated next to Jed, which he knew wouldn't please her. But she'd made the sacrifice to spare Lauren from sitting there.

He wondered if he and Shannen would ever know what, if anything, had transpired between Lauren and Jed, and conceded that basically he didn't care.

Both twins tried to extend the coverage of the very short skirts of their pink dresses over their thighs, the struggle faithfully filmed by Reggie. Despite a valiant attempt, a major expanse of their slim, tanned legs remained exposed.

Ty drew in a deep breath. This was going to be a long night.

Konrad and Cortnee entered next, with Bobby Dixon between them. He motioned the two finalists toward two high-backed chairs. The pair took possession of their jungle thrones, and Bobby began to talk.

"As you know, this is our last night here on the island,

and the winner of *Victorious* will be crowned tonight. We have assembled a jury along with the surviving two contestants in the game." Bobby varied his inflections, perhaps in an attempt to create suspense?

If so, he was not succeeding. Ty was bored. He commiserated with the viewing audience who would have to endure the speech.

"Konrad, Cortnee, it's time for each of you to address the jury and tell us why you should be the one voted Victorious. Who wants to go first?" challenged Bobby.

If he was trying to start a conflict, it didn't work.

"She can go first," said Konrad.

"Really? 'Cause I don't mind if you do, Konrad," replied Cortnee.

Bobby looked vexed. "All right, all right, go ahead, Cortnee."

Cortnee jumped to her feet and gave a perky little speech about the fun she'd had and how much she'd learned during the game. She ended by saying she would like to win, but if her good friend Konrad was the winner, that would be okay with her.

It was Konrad's turn and he remained seated, holding a piece of paper in front of him. He began to read the same speech Cortnee had given, though there was nothing remotely perky in his delivery. He read in a monotone and replaced his name with hers in the appropriate place, but otherwise it was verbatim. Clearly a collaborative effort, with the actual writing undoubtedly done by Cortnee.

Bobby heaved a sigh, displeased by the lack of both drama and suspense. Ty saw the beleaguered announcer glance at Clark Garrett, who stood a few feet away from him. He saw Clark nod his head twice. Two emphatic nods.

Some sort of code? Ty was pondering that when Bobby started talking again.

"I guess everybody remembers that in the past, certain reality shows followed a format from beginning to end.

After the two finalists in the game told us why they should be voted for, each member of the jury would ask a question to be answered by the Final Two.''

Ty panned to the jury members, who were listening intently...or at least giving the impression they were.

"Those questions usually were versions of 'What have you learned about people as a result of being on this show?' or 'What is the most important quality a winner of this game should have?' Am I right?'' Bobby whirled around to face the jury, a move so unexpected a few of them gasped.

"Expect the unexpected!'' Bobby proclaimed. "Because from now on, we're blazing our own trail. After the questioning on those other shows, everybody on the jury would then vote on who they thought should get the money. The votes were read and the winner crowned. But here on *Victorious,* it's going to be different. Because we're different. We are no blatant rip-off of any other show. We're *original!*''

"Bobby's a better actor than I ever thought,'' Heidi murmured to Ty. "He sounds like he actually believes *Victorious* isn't a blatant rip-off.''

There were guffaws among the crew, including Ty.

"We're going to have one final contest to determine the winner,'' Bobby announced, sounding more and more like a carnival huckster. "In the unlikely event of a tie, we'll use the standard method of tiebreaking—that is, the contestant who's already accrued the most votes against them will lose.''

The jury members were talking among themselves. Some appeared annoyed, probably because there would be no TV camera time for them in light of Bobby's declaration.

Ty was a bit perplexed himself. Until this moment the crew had been told the game would be played out in the exact way Bobby had outlined just before repudiating the plan.

"Will our twins, Shannen and Lauren Cullen, please come over here?" Bobby asked, but it was really an order.

The twins exchanged confused glances, which Ty filmed while Reggie captured Konrad's and Cortnee's reactions. The two finalists appeared equally baffled.

"Come on, girls," urged Bobby when neither twin moved. "You see, *you're* the final contest! To win this game, Cortnee and Konrad are going to have to tell you apart. Not unreasonable, since you spent so much time together, true?"

The twins looked appalled. Shannen finally looked directly at Ty, sending him a "Did you know this was coming?" glare. He was glad to be able to honestly shrug his shoulders and shake his head no.

Bobby walked over to the twins, clearly ready to pull them from the risers if they didn't get up of their own accord. Perhaps sensing his determination, Shannen and Lauren rose together and reluctantly followed Bobby to stand in front of Cortnee and Konrad.

Shannen opened her mouth to speak, but before she could say a word, Bobby jumped in with, "No talking, girls. Just stand there and stare into space."

"It's not enough we're the freak show, but we're supposed to stand here like a pair of dummies, too?" complained Lauren, sounding so like Shannen that even Ty had to look twice to make sure it wasn't.

No, it was definitely Lauren who'd spoken.

Bobby frowned his displeasure at the display of disobedience. "Cortnee, Konrad, here are your pens and cards. Write down which twin is standing on the left. For one million dollars, is it Lauren or Shannen?"

Ty was surprised to actually feel suspense build. Winning a million dollars for telling a set of twins apart was definitely a departure from the formula. A rather stupid departure, in his opinion, but if Clark and Bobby wanted the game to end differently from those past shows, they'd succeeded in that regard.

It was too bad both Shannen and Lauren looked ready to commit mayhem for having their identities turned into a contest.

"Time's up!" cried Bobby. "Konrad, what is your answer? Who is the twin on the left? Hold up your card."

Konrad held up the card on which he'd printed "Shannen." "She's the one who mouths off," he said admiringly.

It was Cortnee's turn. She held up her card, which read "Lauren." "Just a guess," she said hopefully.

Bobby paused for heightened dramatic effect. And then: "Cortnee, you are victorious!"

Cortnee screamed and jumped up and down and hugged Konrad and the twins and even Bobby.

"It's like she won Miss Teenage America or something," Jed said disparagingly.

Ty recorded it. He also filmed Konrad saying, "I'm glad for Cortnee. She deserved to win. I got the second prize, and a hundred grand is nothing to whine about."

Finally, Ty recorded the twins' reaction when Bobby asked if they really minded being turned into a guess-their-identities contest.

"Yes," they said together, and glowered at him.

"We're happy Cortnee won, though," Shannen added. "She is so cute and she's going to be a big star."

The filming was through, and the production assistants set to work dismantling the tribal council area. Ty had to push his way through the throng of contestants and crew to finally reach Shannen.

Before he could say a word, Cortnee joined them. "Cute dress, Shannen!" she exclaimed enthusiastically. "Silk, too, huh?"

"We should've known Clark Garrett was up to something when he insisted that Lauren and I buy new dresses—at network expense—in the hotel shop. Then he practically begged us to dress exactly alike.'' Shannen rolled her eyes. ''He said it would be 'good television.' We said no until that snake Jed slithered over and said he agreed with us and we shouldn't listen to Clark.''

''That took care of that,'' Ty interjected wryly. ''Lucky for Clark, you and Lauren wouldn't go along with anything Jed suggested.''

''We were duped.'' Shannen was disgusted. ''Clark also said the network was buying everybody new clothes to wear tonight, and that turned out to be a lie. It was just Lauren and me for his dumb plan to use us. Sorry, Cortnee. Though I really am glad that you won,'' she added.

''As soon as Bobby said what the contest was, I knew I'd win,'' Cortnee said happily. ''I learned to tell you and your sister apart after Lauren started hating me. She'd shoot me these drop-dead looks, but you never did, Shannen.''

Cortnee glanced from Ty to Shannen. ''Now that the game is over, care to tell me what's going on between you two?''

''Us?'' Shannen and Ty said at the same time.

''Konrad told me about that day in the ocean when the camera was turned off and it was more than obvious you two knew each other well. He asked if we should use it against you, but I said no.'' Cortnee smiled shrewdly. ''We'd gotten Jed kicked off, and we might come across as mean and nasty if it looked like we were plotting against someone else—especially a twin. I told Konrad we had to think of our images for potential product endorsements. He saw my point.''

''Cortnee, you have the instincts of a marketing genius, packaged in a Britney Spears body. I predict you'll go far.'' Ty laughed.

''I hope so,'' said Cortnee. ''Clark just told me there's a list of agents waiting to contact me. I'll make sure Konrad and Rico get some good deals, too. They're kinda like the brothers I never had, even though I never *wanted* brothers.''

"You're sweet, Cortnee," said Shannen. "And whatever your reasons, thanks for—for keeping our secret."

"Which you're not going to tell me, not even now?" Cortnee looked disappointed.

"We'll send you an invitation to our wedding," said Ty. He caught Shannen's hand. "Think we can find a private place where I can propose?"

"I...I think you just did. Indirectly. You...you invited Cortnee to our wedding!"

Shannen was dazed as he pulled her along after him, away from the cast and crew, through the jungle path to the place where they'd first kissed what seemed like eons ago.

"Cortnee said that Konrad told her it was more than obvious that we knew each other well," Ty said, taking Shannen in his arms. "Do you agree that we *do* know each other well?"

"If we don't now, I expect we'll know each other very well by the time of our wedding." Shannen smiled up at him, her blue eyes shining with laughter and love.

"So you're accepting my proposal?"

"Actually you haven't officially made one yet, Ty."

"I'll correct that oversight immediately." Ty got down on bended knee and took her hand. "Shannen, will you marry me?"

"Yes, I will, Ty." She knelt down beside him. "I love you, Ty. I love you so much."

"And I love you, Shannen. I fell in love with you nine years ago and I'm still in love with you." He took her mouth in a long, lingering kiss filled with love and passion and commitment.

The emotional intensity shook them both.

"I wish we could be together tonight." Shannen sighed wistfully. "All night, in our own room. But Clark said the crew is staying here in the camp tonight."

"They are. But I'm going to the hotel with you—and we're definitely getting our own room," promised Ty.

"But, Ty—"

"My time with *Victorious* is over. The editors have the footage, and there is nothing more for me to film. I meant what I said about opening my own law practice, Shannen. I thought it could be in West Falls, if you'd like."

"Where my job and my family are." Shannen was thrilled. "I'd love that, Ty. But we'd better start economizing right away, because it'll take a while to get a law practice established in West Falls. Luckily my job at the hospital will provide us with health benefits, but I really don't think we can afford the five hundred dollars a night for a room at the resort. Maybe we can—"

"There's something else I've been meaning to tell you, Shannen," Ty cut in. "Five hundred dollars for a room is chump change to me. You see, uh, I didn't lose my money. My personal wealth wasn't touched by any of the lawsuits against the other Howes. It can't and never will be."

"You-you're saying that...that—"

"I'm rich. Very rich. Are you angry?" He challenged.

"I'm stunned! Why did you tell me that you'd lost everything?"

"You were the one who said I had money issues, Shannen. And you were right. But now—thanks to you—I no longer have them. At least as far as you're concerned."

He kissed her deeply. And kept a firm hold on her, locking his eyes with hers.

"You're not even going to let me get mad because you didn't trust me enough to tell me the truth, are you?" she asked in the testy tone familiar to *Victorious* viewers.

"That's the plan." He kissed her again. "I do trust *you*, Shannen. And I fully intend to use my money to buy your goodwill. You couldn't stay too mad at a guy who pays for the repairs to the family diner and Gramma's roof and sets

Jordan and Josh up in the landscaping business of their dreams, could you?''

"You remembered all that, even Josh's and Jordan's names," Shannen marveled.

"I also know the names of their two kids, if you care to quiz me. Everything you told me about you and your family is worth remembering, Shannen. What's important to you is important to me, too.''

"How could I ever stay mad at a guy like that?" Shannen murmured in a warm, tender tone familiar only to those she loved.

"How could you?" agreed Ty.

And holding hands, they went to find the boat that was leaving the island.

* * * * *

DO YOU TAKE THIS ENEMY?

by
Sara Orwig

Silhouette Books proudly presents
an exciting trilogy by

SARA ORWIG

Stallion Pass

Meet three of the most rugged, sexy
bachelors in Stallion Pass...

They're looking for love—
who can resist?

September 2003
Do You Take This Enemy?
Silhouette Desire

October 2003
One Tough Cowboy
Silhouette Sensation

November 2003
The Rancher, the Baby
& the Nanny
Silhouette Desire

With many thanks to my editors,
Joan Marlow Golan and Stephanie Maurer

SARA ORWIG

lives with her husband and children in Oklahoma. She has a patient husband who will take her on research trips anywhere, from big cities to old forts. She is an avid collector of Western history books. With a master's degree in English, Sara writes historical romance, mainstream fiction and contemporary romance. Books are beloved treasures that take Sara to magical worlds, and she loves both reading and writing them.

FOREWORD

Stallion Pass, Texas—so named according to the ancient legend in which an Apache warrior fell in love with a US Cavalry captain's daughter. When the captain learned about their love, he intended to force her to wed a Cavalry officer. The warrior and the maiden planned to run away and marry. The night the warrior came to get her, the cavalry killed him. His ghost became a white stallion, forever searching for the woman he loved. Heartbroken, the maiden ran away to a convent, where on moonlit nights she could see the white stallion running wild, but she didn't know it was the ghost of her warrior. The white stallion still roams the area and, according to legend, will bring love to the person who tames him. Not far from Stallion Pass, in Piedras and Lago counties, there is a wild white stallion, running across the land owned by three Texas bachelors, Gabriel Brant, Josh Kellogg and Wyatt Sawyer. Is the white stallion of legend about to bring love into their lives?

One

Gabriel Brant's stomach knotted as he drove along the hard-packed dirt road. He was tempted to make a U-turn and head home, but then he rounded a bend in the road and saw a sprawling house, two long stables, a corral, a guest house, a bunkhouse and several outbuildings. As his knowledgeable eye ran over the structures, his qualms vanished.

To his right was a fenced pasture filled with fine-looking horses. A sleek bay and a graceful sorrel, their ears cocked forward, paused to look at his pickup. Land spread out in all directions and his pulse jumped as he imagined all that prime land belonging to him. Still, as he drove, he was aware how much his father would have hated what he was doing. Father, grandfather, great-grandfather and great-great-grandfather. He wasn't too happy about aspects of it himself. The Ryders and the Brants had been feuding since the first generations of each family had settled in Texas.

Gabe was convinced that his relatives would understand

his actions once they knew what the Brants would gain. "Keep telling yourself that," he added aloud.

The possibilities—vastly more land, more water resources and a mother for his son—reassured him that he was doing the right thing. He crossed a narrow wooden bridge, speeding over Cotton Creek. The Creek was the reason the Brants and the Ryders had originally settled in this area. It was also the source of the old feud—water rights and border disputes. Gabe glanced at the winding narrow ribbon of murky water that gave life to both ranches. Today it was only inches wide, but Gabe knew it could go from a trickle to a flood.

As he approached the house and stables, a woman stepped from the porch into the May sunlight and strode down the wide graveled drive toward him, her cascade of midnight hair startling him. He hadn't seen Ashley Ryder since she was a kid. Back then she had been skinny, gangling and had worn braces. He'd occasionally heard news about her—going to the University of Southern California, working in the advertising business in Chicago. Then, three months ago, she had suddenly moved home, and rumors had started flying around town.

She waited, facing his pickup as he slowed. His gaze ran over her swiftly. Tall for a woman, Ashley Ryder was wearing cutoffs and a blue cotton T-shirt that she filled out nicely. He noticed the bulge of her stomach and saw for himself that the rumors were true. Since she had returned home, she had stayed in seclusion on the Ryder ranch.

Aware that he was not only breaking the tradition of generations of Brants, but that he had tricked her into this meeting, Gabe climbed out and closed the pickup door, going to meet her and offering his hand. "Ashley, I'm Gabe Brant."

Ashley's blue eyes blazed with fire. For an instant, Gabe forgot family histories, his grief over his losses, his mission, the rumors, the future, everything. The world vanished, and he was swallowed in blue. It shocked him to discover that

Ashley was a beautiful woman. All he could remember was that skinny kid with pigtails, years younger, all awkward arms and legs.

"Mr. Brant, get off my ranch," she said, not bothering to hide the fury in her voice. "I have an appointment with a lawyer, one Prentice Bolton. Did you put him up to calling me so you could get on our land?"

"As a matter of fact, I did."

"It's a wonder lightning isn't striking," she snapped.

"Yeah, it's a wonder it isn't," Gabe replied for a far different reason. He was doubly shocked at himself and his reactions because it was the first time since losing Ella three years ago that he could remember even noticing a female beyond the most cursory awareness.

"You can get right back in your truck and go."

"Hear me out, and I think you'll let me stay. Give me ten minutes."

"No! I don't want to spend ten seconds with a Brant! Get off our property!"

"Look. I have a deal I want to make, and it'll benefit you as much as me. You can't be so closed-minded and bullheaded that you won't give me ten minutes," he said patiently.

Her eyes narrowed as she considered what he said. Still in shock, Gabe waited. He hadn't thought of her as a person, just a nebulous nonentity—the only image that had ever come to mind was that scrawny teen she used to be. He was facing a beautiful woman who was poised and determined. And she was going to be trouble.

"Ten minutes is all you have." Ashley stood in the driveway with her arms crossed.

He looked past her across thick, green grass to a porch with clay pots of bright yellow bougainvillea and planters of ivy hanging from the rafters. Chairs, rockers, lounges and a swing stood along the shady, inviting porch. He took a deep breath. "We're just going to stand here and talk and not sit on the porch?"

"That's right. I don't want a Brant on my porch now or anytime."

"Where's your dad?" Gabe inquired.

"You're lucky he isn't home or he would be out here with a shotgun. I would have been myself if I'd known it was you coming up our road."

"Frankly, I'm glad he's not here. I can't imagine telling mine that I'm here—but I won't have to. He died almost two years ago."

"You've already wasted the first minute. What's on your mind?"

She was prickly as cactus, Gabe reflected, but easy to look at. Her skin was flawless. Ashley Ryder was probably half a foot shorter than he was. That made her almost six feet tall. As his gaze ran over her, he speculated that she must be about five months along.

He leaned against the front of his pickup and crossed his long legs.

"Your ranch is nice. Looked like I passed some fine horses when I drove in."

"The finest. We both know that," she said, sounding calmer and slightly pleased by his compliment. "Now what do you want?"

"You believe in getting right to the point, don't you?" Usually he got along with pretty women, although he knew why she was acting so prickly.

"I certainly do when I want to get rid of someone. I think this is the first time in my life I've ever talked to a Brant and I don't particularly like it."

"You don't know me," he reminded her.

"I don't have to know you. You're a Brant. That's enough," she retorted.

Her legs were bare, smooth and shapely and it was an effort to keep his eyes away from them. Of all females to notice, this one was not only a generations-old enemy, but pregnant.

"There are a lot of rumors going around town about why you're back home on the ranch."

"I'm sure there are," she said, looking away, but not before he glimpsed a glacial chill in her blue eyes. "That's no deep secret, though, because there's no hiding the reason." She met his gaze with a lift of her chin. "I'm pregnant, single and I came home to take care of my dad and have my baby."

"That's what I've heard. I also heard you were very successful in Chicago, and you left a thriving advertising business behind."

She nodded. "That's right, but life changes. My values changed. Now the advertising world doesn't seem as important as family. Do you ever get to the point, Mr. Brant?"

"I'm getting to it," Gabe said, trying to keep the purpose of his visit firmly in mind, because Ashley was becoming more interesting than his proposition. Crossing his arms over his chest, he took a deep breath. "I'm building up our ranch and I want more land and more cattle. I can get the cattle, but I can't get land in this neck of the woods."

Her brows arched. "If you think we would ever sell you one inch of this land, you're dead wrong. Never! Now—"

"I know you don't want to sell. I didn't come to buy."

Her eyes narrowed. He realized he could gaze into her blue eyes indefinitely. Why did the woman have to be so damned pretty? He hadn't considered that possibility.

"What *do* you want Mr. Brant?" she asked.

"First thing I want is for you to call me Gabe," he said.

"Your time is running out."

"All right. I've heard your father's health isn't as good as it used to be. And I've heard that before you came home from Chicago, your ranch had slipped into debt."

"Maybe it has, but none of that has anything to do with you."

"Maybe it does. You need help and your dad needs help. You can't afford to go out and hire the help."

"We'll manage," she said with a frosty tone and a lift

of her chin that he had to admire. "That's strictly a family problem."

"I came to offer you a marriage of convenience. It would join our ranches and benefit both of us."

"Marriage!" Her jaw dropped and her brows arched. She placed her hands on her hips and then to Gabe's surprise she threw back her head and laughed. It was a peal of merry laughter that held no rancor and piqued his interest even more. She shook her head. "You're loco! Get in your truck and go home, Mr. Brant. Thanks, but no thanks."

She had been gorgeous with sparks in her eyes. Now, with laughter, she was irresistible. "Forget it," she said, turning to walk away.

"Just listen to me," he ordered, catching her lightly by the arm to turn her around. The moment he touched her an electric current rippled through him. "You're being stubborn."

"Stubborn!" she said, spinning around to glare at him, yet her tone of voice softened.

"Yeah. I feel like I'm talking to my grandma when she's in one of her moods. You may be cutting yourself, your baby and your dad out of a deal here. Just listen a moment," he commanded, assured that he had a viable proposition for her.

Ashley was breathing as hard as if she had run a race, but she was silent. He was as aware of his hand on her arm as if he had touched a burning brand, and he stood close enough to catch a tempting, flowery scent. As their gazes locked, he could feel the sparks snapping between them and suddenly, he wondered if her ragged breathing was for a reason other than anger. Was the lady responding to him when he looked into her eyes? Fascinated by what was happening between them, he let the silence lengthen.

He had come over here to give her a good business offer, but his interest had shifted from her ranch to her. How long had it been since a woman had made him feel anything? Since the loss of Ella, and then both of his parents, he had been buried in grief. Yet here was this wild, volatile chemistry that had broken through grief—a chemistry that had ignited the moment he looked into Ashley's eyes. He suspected she was feeling it, too.

"Listen to me," he repeated in a husky voice, and she merely nodded. "I can rebuild this ranch. It'll help your dad, yet he'll still be a big part of it because he knows horses and I don't. My money will be backing you and with both ranches joined, we'll have one of the most successful spreads in the Southwest."

"Mr. Brant, you're plenty good-looking. Find yourself another woman. I'm sure you can," she said, yanking her arm out of his grasp.

"It isn't your body I want."

"You're not getting your hands on this land."

"Just remember, mine would be yours, too. I want to join them. Running something this large has to be hard on your dad and on you as well."

As she looked away, a flush brought pink to her cheeks. When he saw her fists were clenched, he realized that he had struck a nerve.

"Look, we can help each other," he insisted. "You have room for me to run cattle."

"I've always heard that you're driven with ambition," she said, looking him in the eye again.

"Damn straight, I'm ambitious."

She tapped her toe on the ground and crossed her arms in front of herself, shaking her finger in the direction of his truck. "Get in your pickup and get off our land. Your ten minutes are up. I'm not marrying a Brant. No way in hell. And you're not getting your hands on our ranch."

They stared at each other, and he knew he was running out of time.

"I can end all of the Triple R's debt and with no demands on you—" he began.

She tossed her head and a curtain of silky black hair

swung across her shoulders. "Get off our land. You're trespassing."

"I'll go, but you think about it. For both of us, it would be a means to an end."

He moved toward the door of his pickup. "You could protect yourself with a prenuptial agreement. You have lawyers." He opened the door of his pickup and paused, his gaze raking over her again.

"How far along are you? Five months?"

"Seven months."

"Seven! Then, Ashley, you better think about my offer," he said, liking the way it felt to call her by her first name. "You don't have much time left to make choices. You'll be so busy when your baby comes, you won't have time for this ranch. A paper marriage would take a huge burden from your father. Life and family are more important than land or money," he added harshly. "I can promise you that."

While her eyes narrowed, he climbed into his pickup and started the motor, backing and turning, driving slowly so he wouldn't stir a cloud of dust in her face. He looked into his rearview mirror. Ashley Ryder stood with her hands on her hips, still watching him. Even pregnant, she was one good-looking woman.

Mule-stubborn, she was trouble, yet she still had him attracted. She was gutsy, quick-witted and he suspected she was tough, willing to give up her plans and successful career in advertising to come home to help her father—all admirable enough qualities to offset stubbornness.

The Ryders were trouble, but they'd never been dumb. They were smart people, and he knew she had heard what he'd said, and she would think about it. For a first visit, it could have gone much worse.

If they joined their ranches, he could buy more cattle and expand. He knew for a fact that the Ryders' horses weren't taking up all the land they owned. Their ranch was as big as his, and it had been talk around the county for some

time now about how Quinn Ryder had cut back and was
in poor health, and the ranch was failing. The old man
needed help desperately, yet couldn't afford to hire it, and
Ashley was going to be too busy to take charge completely.
Quinn Ryder's brothers had their own problems that kept
them from stepping in. Ashley was seven months along.
That didn't leave a lot of time if they wanted to be married
before the baby was born.

Gabe was lost in thought about Ashley and the future
until he rounded a bend on his Circle B ranch and saw the
two ranch houses ahead. The main road led to the old family home, a sprawling house that had been added to through
generations. A branch of the road led to the house he had
built for Ella.

Grief swamped him, and he gripped the steering wheel
tighter, his throat closing up. He and his son Julian now
lived in the family house. Memories tore him up in his
home, so he had moved, but it made little difference because the memories still hurt. First he'd lost Ella, then two
years ago, both his parents. Too many losses too close
together.

He took a deep breath and tried to think about the Ryders
and what he had just done in proposing to Ashley.

He had calculated how much land he would gain down
to the last acre and he had flown his own plane over the
Triple R, studying it carefully. It was the only way he could
expand. Each of his neighbors was a descendant of settlers
who had acquired the land at statehood or earlier, and no
one around here was willing to sell. As far as he could see,
Ashley was his best hope. She and her dad needed what he
was offering. Gabe hoped she was mulling over his offer
right now.

Ashley stood watching the dust hang in the road behind
Gabriel Brant's red pickup. She shook with anger. There
would be a next time. The Brants didn't give up on anything they set their mind to. The two families were still

fighting over Cotton Creek, only now the battles were in lawyers' offices instead of with fists.

Marry him! Paper marriage, sham marriage, it wouldn't matter. Anything that tied a Ryder to a Brant was impossible. For four generations—five counting hers and Gabe's—the Ryders and the Brants had fought over water rights. They had fought over damming up Cotton Creek, over the boundaries of their two ranches where Cotton Creek angled between the two and was the boundary line— a boundary line that kept shifting as the creek had shifted and changed. Now this miserable Brant wanted to break all traditions.

She thought of the generations of hate, years of silence. Even in her childhood, she could remember her father's rage at finding dead horses and overhearing him talk to Gus, their foreman, about killing cattle. When old Thomas, Gabriel Brant's father, had run for the Texas senate, her dad had done everything he could to defeat him, including making very generous donations to Thomas's opponent. Yet, in spite of her father's efforts, Thomas Brant had won, giving the Brants even more power.

Ashley had always heard that Thomas Brant was ruthlessly ambitious. The son obviously took after his father.

She was furious that Gabriel Brant had tricked her into meeting with him and angry with herself because the moment she had laid eyes on him her pulse had jumped wildly. When she was younger, she had always thought he was the most handsome boy in Piedras and Lago counties—a deep secret she had never admitted to anyone except Becky Conners, her best friend growing up. Ashley shook her head. She didn't want to discover that Gabriel Brant had turned into a sexy, handsome hunk who could make her short of breath. She should have outgrown all that when she got braces off her teeth and went away to college.

But in all of Chicago, she had never met a man who made her breathing alter and her pulse jump like that. Not even Lars Moffet, and she had been ready to marry him.

She was still seeing Gabriel Brant—tall, long-legged, dressed in a tight-fitting T-shirt that revealed abundant muscles. His dark-brown, thickly lashed bedroom eyes were sinful. His ruggedly handsome features were devilish. And his ambition was pure Brant.

Frustrated, Ashley picked up a pebble and threw it down the road as hard as she could, wishing it was a big rock and she could lob it through the back window of Gabriel Brant's pickup.

She turned to walk to the house, but she knew she had to get control over her emotions before she returned indoors. Mrs. Farrin, their cook, had been with them since Ashley was three years old. She wasn't ready to discuss Gabe's proposition with Mrs. Farrin.

Gabriel Brant had called her stubborn. "You're a greedy snake, Gabriel Brant!"

What angered and hurt the most, though, was the truth in what he said. Her dad had had a heart attack. He took medication for his blood pressure. They had had a run of sick horses and she knew that her dad wasn't able to handle the ranch the way he used to. She had come home to help, but she couldn't do all that needed to be done. She wasn't a horse trainer, either. She was spending sleepless nights trying to figure out what to do because every month they were running deeper into debt and every month her father was working too hard.

Constantly she ran through possibilities, but never came up with a good solution. She had two uncles who ranched, but Uncle Dusty's health was worse than her father's and he had his hands full trying to keep his ranch going. Her other ranching uncle, Colin, had had a run of bad luck: his barn and house had burnt and he'd carried no insurance. Cal, the youngest brother, a dentist in San Antonio, had helped all of his older brothers, but there was just so much he could do and it wasn't enough when there were three who needed help.

She inhaled and rubbed her hand across her brow. Gabe Brant's words hurt because she knew they were true.

Life and family *were* more important than land. Her father's life meant more than the ranch. She kicked a clod of dirt, hating that she had to give Gabe's words some serious thought.

She shook her head. It was simply a ploy by a Brant to get the Ryder ranch. Forget it and forget Gabe Brant. But she had never been able to do that in her life. She thought she had, giving him little thought when she'd lived in Chicago. Yet the moment he had stepped out of his pickup, her pulse had jumped. And when he had touched her, every nerve had quivered. She could still hear exactly how his voice had sounded when he had spoken her name.

"What's the matter with me?" she snapped, speaking aloud. She lifted her hair off her neck. Even though it was only May, it was hot outside. On the porch she turned to look at the rolling land that was the Triple R. Tall live oaks sent long, graceful limbs out over the yard, giving much-needed shade in the hot afternoon. Beyond the barn and outbuildings were green pastures dotted by more tall oaks. The land was good. It was home to her, and she would fight to her last breath for it, but her dad's life was more important. Then the memory of sexy dark-brown eyes mocked her and she took a deep breath. Why did she still respond to him? How could he turn her insides to jelly with just a look?

She crossed the porch and went into the kitchen that smelled of baking bread. A ceiling fan turned slowly above glass-fronted cabinets. A pitcher of tea sat on the walnut pedestal table and preparations for supper were spread on the white counter.

A stout, gray-haired woman stood by the kitchen sink. She turned to look at Ashley. "Are you all right?" she asked, her blue eyes filled with concern.

"Yes, it's just hot out," Ashley replied, hurrying across the kitchen. "I'll be in my room."

"You didn't let that lawyer fellow get very far. I fixed a pitcher of tea because I thought you'd at least let him come sit on the porch to talk. You didn't let him come near the house."

"Nope. I didn't want him wasting my time." Ashley hurried out of the room. She'd tell Mrs. Farrin soon enough, but she had to tell her father first. And if Gabe Brant had come closer to the house, Mrs. Farrin would have recognized him.

Ashley thought about the blood-pressure medication her father took. She didn't want to get him all worked up, but she knew she had to tell him about Gabe's proposal, and when she did, he was going to raise hell.

That night, after Ashley and her father had finished supper and retired to the family room, her father sat reading a magazine. Seated near him on a leather sofa, she glanced around the room with its throw rugs and polished plank floor, Western art and shelves of books lining the walls. The quiet they were enjoying was about to be shattered—it was time to tell her father the news.

"Dad, I got a call yesterday from Prentice Bolton, a lawyer in San Antonio."

Quinn Ryder lowered his magazine and looked at her over his half glasses. Brown-eyed and tall, Quinn was rawboned, with thick black hair streaked with gray. He removed his glasses.

"That outfit represents the Brants." Her father frowned. "Why would he call you?"

"He said he wanted to come out and talk to me about a business proposition. If I tell you, will you keep calm?"

"Why don't you think I'll keep calm?" her father demanded.

"I have to tell you something you're not going to like. I don't want your blood pressure going up," she said. His shirt hung on his frame because of the weight he had lost.

It hurt to see her father ailing; he had always been robust, a strapping giant to her when she had been a child.

"I'm going to have high blood pressure if you don't go ahead and tell me."

"The lawyer wasn't the one who came out here. He was just a decoy, calling for someone else." Quinn's eyes narrowed and he waited. "Dad, it was Gabriel Brant," she said.

Her father's ruddy face drained of color and he stood. "Gabriel Brant was on our land?"

"Yes, he was. Now sit down, or I won't tell you another word. I don't want your blood pressure jumping."

"Dammit, Ashley, he knows better than to set foot on our place. That son of a bitch on our land!"

"Dad, just keep calm. You don't want to have a stroke because of a Brant."

"I'm not going to have a stroke. What in blazes did he want? I know he wanted something and it must be a dilly." Quinn told his daughter.

"He wants me to marry him."

The explosion she expected came; Quinn stormed around the room, swearing and waving his hands. She let him rant for a moment and then stepped in front of him.

"Now listen to the rest. You know a Brant is not in love with a Ryder, much less a woman he's never talked to before."

"He wants the ranch. He wants this ranch, dammit!"

"He wants a paper marriage—a marriage in name only," she explained. "He can run cattle on our ranch and expand a little because he knows we don't use all our land."

"The only way he can know that is if he's been on our property. I will shoot that greedy son of a bitch if I catch him trespassing!"

"He could know that without getting on our property," she said calmly, trying to stay calm herself to quiet her father. "Everyone in town knows you've had health problems."

"Why in thunderation did he ever think you'd agree? Damn, he's ruthless and greedy. There's nothing we'd get out of it." Quinn grumbled.

"According to him there is. We'd get his help running this ranch and his money backing it."

Her father clenched his fists, his face growing more red. "Dammit. He just wants our land."

"But his would be ours as much as ours would be his," she argued.

Quinn shot her a searching look. Shutting his mouth, he went to the mantel to prop his elbow on it, and she saw that he was actually thinking about Gabriel Brant's proposition. Her spirits sank a little because she had had to think about it herself.

"There have to be a dozen other guys around here who would marry you and work with me on the ranch."

"No one has called and asked me out," she answered dryly. "At least going out with Gabriel Brant might be interesting."

"How do you know that? You don't know the guy at all."

"Of course, I do. I've been around him when we were growing up. I saw him at parties and football games. He was older, but he was always in the middle of things and sort of the life-of-the-party type," she said. Back then she had thought he was incredibly sexy and handsome and wished he would notice her; wished that he was anything except a Brant.

Quinn turned to study her. "You're not actually considering this, are you?"

"I have to think about it. It holds possibilities."

"Hellfire. The guy's a shark like his dad. He owns ranches all over Texas. He's land-hungry and you can't trust a Brant."

"Maybe, but the marriage would still give us the same rights with his ranch that he would have with ours." She gazed into the distance and frowned. "I thought he *was* married."

"He was, but she died about three years ago. He's really thrown himself into ranching since then. If I remember right, I think he has a little boy." Quinn ran his hand over his head.

"A son?"

"Now don't go getting soft because he has a motherless child. I know what a pushover you are about kids. Honey, if you're thinking about his proposal, you're doing it for me. Don't."

"I'm doing it for you, for me, for the baby, for the ranch. It's for all of us," she said, walking over to give her father a hug. He wrapped his arms around her to hug her in return. She could feel his shoulder bones and thought again about the weight he had lost.

"I love you, Ashley. I don't know what I'd do without you."

"I love you, too," she replied, giving him a squeeze and moving away. She sat on the sofa. "Dad, Gabe's offer has possibilities."

Quinn shook his head. "I can't imagine—a Ryder marrying a Brant." Quinn rested an elbow on the mantel and stared into space. "You just think you'll always have your health and then one day you don't."

"Please don't worry. I promise that I won't do anything I don't really want to," she said, leaning back and wondering if she was trying to convince herself.

Ashley discussed it until he announced that he was going to bed. After he was gone, she paced the room. Her father was frail and the burden of the ranch was stress in his life that he didn't need. The ranch was losing money daily— something that hadn't ever happened in her lifetime.

Was what Gabriel Brant proposed absolutely unthinkable? It would be a paper arrangement. She ran her hand across her head. She couldn't trust a Brant. Old hurts plagued her as she remembered how she had trusted Lars, a man she had thought she had known and loved. He had broken her trust and she had learned a bitter lesson.

An hour later, Ashley went to bed, but she tossed and turned and didn't sleep well. She kept seeing Gabriel Brant, legs crossed, leaning back against his pickup. And she kept remembering how, when she had met his dark eyes, her pulse had raced.

Finally she fell asleep but overslept the next morning. When she went to the kitchen, her father had already gone. Ashley fixed her breakfast and got out paint samples to pick colors for the nursery.

Fifteen minutes later, she realized her mind wasn't on colors. She was thinking about Gabriel Brant's proposition. He had a child. A son. She wondered about the little boy who had lost his mother when he was so young. Yet the marriage would be a business arrangement and nothing more. Gabe wouldn't make any demands on her. No emotions would be involved. Lawyers could protect her. She threw up her hands. How could such an arrangement work?

The phone rang and she crossed the room to pick it up.

"Ashley?" came a deep, masculine voice. "This is Gabe Brant. I'd like to see you again."

Two

"I'd like to see you right away. I'll drive to your place. How's an hour from now?" Gabe asked.

Ashley closed her eyes and ran her fingers across her brow.

"Good. I'll be there," he announced before she'd had time to answer. He hung up, and she was left with a dial tone.

"You don't believe in saying goodbye, do you?" She hadn't said much·more than hello. She slammed down the receiver, glanced at her watch and went to her room to change her clothes. Then she became annoyed with herself for changing just because Gabriel Brant was coming.

Yesterday she'd had an intense, prickly awareness of him. She ran her fingers through her hair, and studied herself in the mirror. She was in a T-shirt, a denim jumper and sneakers. So be it. She combed her hair into a ponytail and went downstairs. Forty minutes later, she left the house and climbed into one of the ranch pickups and headed toward the road.

Alongside the county road in the shade of a tall cottonwood, she parked by the mailbox, retrieved their mail and climbed onto a fender to sit and wait for him.

Right on time she saw his red pickup coming up the highway. Sliding off the fender, she watched as he slowed. To her surprise, she could see a small boy in the back seat. Gabe parked and climbed out. He wore a T-shirt and jeans. His thick, slightly wavy brown hair was neatly trimmed. Her pulse jumped at the sight of him. Brant or not, the man was good-looking. Her gaze slid past him and she watched the little boy and jump out of the truck to take his dad's hand. The child stopped in his tracks and studied her with large, dark-brown eyes that were as thickly lashed as his father's.

"Ashley, meet my son Julian."

Julian held out his small hand, and Ashley was instantly won over. The child was adorable, and she took his hand lightly. "I'm glad to meet you. How old are you, Julian?"

"Four," he answered promptly, holding up four fingers.

"You're a very big boy," she said, and he grinned.

"I wanted you two to meet," Gabe said quietly. "Kiddo," Gabe continued, picking Julian up. "You've got your cars in the back of the truck. Will you play with them a few minutes while I talk to Miss Ryder?"

Julian nodded.

Ashley waited while Gabe set his son in the back of the pickup and Julian seemed to lose interest in the adults and began to play with his toys. Gabe walked back to talk to her.

As he neared, his brown eyes held her. What caused all this electricity when she was within four feet of him? It surely wasn't from the schoolgirl crush she'd once had.

He stopped only a few feet away and hooked his hands into his pockets.

"You cheated," she said, too aware that her voice was breathless.

"How's that?" he asked while his brows arched with curiosity.

"Bringing your son. He's adorable."

Something sparked in Gabe's eyes, and he inhaled deeply. "You don't know that. You only said hello. He could be a little terror."

"Little children aren't terrors," she replied promptly.

"When have you been around any?"

"My younger cousins. I volunteered to teach Sunday school and to coach soccer when I was in Chicago. I like kids."

"You're making me like my proposition even more," he said, moving closer and reaching out to touch her arm lightly. "If you're seven months along, do you know what you're having?"

"Yes. A girl."

"Ahh. That's nice. Boy or girl—it's great. Except I know a little more about boys. But I can learn," he said, smiling at her, and she shook her head.

"You're irrepressible," she said.

"I'm surprised that you wanted to meet here, where any neighbor who passes will see a Brant talking to a Ryder and start all kinds of rumors."

Electrified by his touch, she stepped back slightly.

His brow arched, and he gave her a look that made her whole body tingle. "It bothers you to stand close to me?"

"I'm not accustomed to being around Brants," she said, knowing it was a ridiculous answer, but she didn't want to admit how much he disturbed her.

He reached out again to stroke her arm lightly with his finger. "This is an interesting surprise, Ashley," he said softly, his voice growing husky. "We have some kind of chemistry between us."

His dark eyes were full of curiosity, and she flushed. "It

doesn't outweigh all our family history of feuding," she replied.

A faint smile curved one corner of his mouth and his long-lashed, bedroom eyes snapped with interest. "I disagree. I think it snuffs out any idea of feuding with you. No, when I get around you, feuding is not what I want to do," he drawled in a sexy tone that made her pulse jump another notch.

She leaned closer to him. "You know what I think? I think you're trying to sweet-talk me into this marriage you're proposing. *You* may forget about the Brant-Ryder history, but I can't."

"Now I find that a real challenge—to see if I can make you forget about the feud," he said softly.

She knew he was flirting, and, while it was exciting, at the same time she was suspicious of his motives. There was too much at stake, and in five generations, no Ryder had ever trusted a Brant.

"It's absolutely impossible for me to forget."

"We'll see," he said with amusement dancing in his eyes. "Did you think about what I said?"

"I'm thinking about it." She would never admit that she couldn't put him or his proposal out of her thoughts.

"Good." His gaze swept over her. "You sure have changed since high school."

"You didn't know me in high school," she said. "You'd already gone off to college."

"I was home at a couple of parties—I saw you around town. We just didn't speak. You were a skinny kid with braces—you've grown up into a beautiful woman."

"Thank you, but you can save the compliments."

"Did you tell your dad about my proposal?"

She was looking into dark eyes that nailed her with their forcefulness. He was too close, too masculine, too sinfully handsome. She could detect his aftershave, and facing him at this range was more disturbing than ever.

"Yes, I did. He was furious and appalled."

"But you know I have a proposition that's worth considering, don't you? Admit the truth now."

"Yes, I do," she snapped.

"Go to dinner with me tomorrow night so we can discuss marriage."

"I don't want to go out to dinner and start all kinds of wild rumors. This whole thing is impossible," she replied, feeling butterflies at the thought of a date with him. She clamped her lips closed, turning to reach for her pickup door.

His hand shot out and held the door closed. "Now just calm down and let's talk a minute." His breath blew against her nape and he stood so close behind her that she could feel the heat of his body. As she looked at the tanned wrist and hand that held her door closed, her pulse skittered.

She turned around. "Move away."

He studied her, and her heart drummed. When his gaze dropped to her mouth, she couldn't even breathe. "Move back and give me room," she said, placing her hand on his chest to push lightly. It was a tactical error because the instant she touched his muscled chest, tingles raced through her and the curiosity in his eyes shifted to blatant desire. She yanked her hand away.

"My, oh my, this is a surprise," he drawled softly. "You and I have some wild attraction going here."

"It's purely physical," she said, but all force had gone out of her voice. He still stood too close to her, and she hoped he couldn't hear her thudding heart.

"Might be purely physical, but it's damned powerful. Too powerful to ignore, I can tell you that." He touched her hair, pulling free the ribbon that held it behind her neck. "You grew up to be a real beauty."

"Thank you, but I don't believe your compliments are sincere."

Again, she saw that flash of amusement in his expression.

To her relief he stepped to one side, leaning a shoulder against her pickup, looking relaxed, sexy and curious.

"Let's go to dinner and talk about my proposal," he suggested. "We can go to San Antonio. It's a big enough city that we can find a spot where no one will know us."

"This is so absurd. I don't know why I'm listening to you."

"Because you're intelligent and you know I'm making a good offer. You're listening because when we get near each other, both of us almost go up in flames. Which surprises me as much as it does you."

"Will you stop!"

One corner of his mouth lifted in a crooked grin. "I have all sorts of reasons why this would benefit you. I just want a chance to present my case. And don't tell me a Ryder can't exist in proximity to a Brant. What do you think goes on at rodeos and cattle sales? I've rubbed elbows with your kin, including your dad. We don't like it, but we do it. We can talk without bringing down the wrath of our kinfolk. Now, how about tomorrow night?"

She debated only a few seconds because she was intrigued and she knew there was a possibility of solving a lot of problems for her father. "Yes, I'll go with you to dinner."

"Good. I'll pick you up around seven. Will your father let me set foot on the place?"

"Yes, if I want you to."

"So I don't have to wear my gun?"

"Don't you dare be packing!" she gasped.

"Sorry. I couldn't keep from teasing you," he said, touching her cheek while his dark eyes twinkled. "I'll be there in my best suit at seven, and we'll go to San Antonio so we won't see anyone we know. That suits me fine, too."

"Have you ever not gotten your way?"

"Yes," he replied. She heard the harsh note in his voice while his expression became solemn.

"Well, what happened? That must have been a dilly."

"When my wife got pneumonia and died. When my folks died."

"Your wife *and* your parents?" She could hear the pain in his voice. "I'm sorry," she said.

"Yeah. See you at seven at your house." He turned away and in long strides went around his pickup.

"Gabe," she said, hurrying after him, too aware of using his first name. "Let me tell Julian goodbye." She moved past Gabe, going to the back of the pickup.

"Wow, you have a lot of cars," she said, leaning over the side of the pickup. "Which one is your favorite?"

Julian held up a blue one. As she talked to him about his cars, she felt Gabe standing nearby, watching and listening to her. After a few minutes, she smiled at Julian.

"I have to go now, Julian. It was nice to meet you."

"Thank you. It was nice to meet you," he said politely and she turned to look at Gabe.

"You've taught him well," she told him.

"I try. See you tomorrow night."

"Who takes care of Julian?"

"I have a nanny," he replied.

She nodded and walked away, hearing him talk to his son. When she climbed into her pickup, Julian was buckled in again and Gabe had started the engine. Making a sweeping turn, he drove away while she watched. She was still surprised—tomorrow night she had a dinner date with Gabe Brant.

The man ran roughshod over all her arguments. Marry him—it would be like getting a dictator in her life. They were strangers and already he was getting his way. And his flirting struck nerves. There *was* a chemistry between them. She was surprised he felt it, but she had felt it around him all her life.

She threw up her hands. She had to tell Mrs. Farrin, which would be bad, but telling her father about her dinner date would be much worse.

*   *   *

That night as they ate thick steaks, Ashley set down her fork and braced for a storm. "Dad, I'm going out tomorrow night with Gabe Brant."

"Dammit, Ashley," Quinn snapped, dropping his fork and frowning. "Why? You can't consider a sham marriage or any kind of marriage to that man."

"I think I should hear his arguments," she said quietly, torn between agreeing with her father and trying to do what was best for everyone.

"You're a grown woman now and a smart one, but you shouldn't be going out with a Brant."

"It's just a dinner date."

"I've heard talk from Gus and the men. He lost his wife last year and he lost both his parents the year before that. Now all he has on his mind is expanding his ranch—with our land!"

"What happened to his parents?" Ashley asked, curious, yet wanting to avoid asking Gabe.

"Old Thomas died of a heart attack, probably because he was meaner than sin. Brant's mother had cancer, I think. But don't go feeling sorry for the man. They say he's hard as granite. I'm sure he's like his dad." Her father's eyes narrowed. "Where's he taking you? How do you know you'll even be safe with him?"

"I'll be safe," Ashley answered, smiling. "I have my cell phone and besides, he doesn't want my body. Like you said, he just wants my land."

"Don't do this, Ashley. I hate the thought of you going out with him," Quinn grumbled. "I can take care of myself and this ranch. We've just had a little setback. Marry him! The man has nerve. I'd like to take my shotgun and run him off the place and forget it."

"I don't think that would be good for your blood pressure," Ashley responded dryly. "I wish you wouldn't even think about it."

"I think it would make me feel immensely better to run him off our ranch. I don't want you to go out with him."

"And I don't want to go, but I think I should hear him

out. His offer may hold possibilities,'' she reminded him, feeling as if she were arguing with herself instead of her father.

"Ashley, to be caught up in a marriage—any marriage— would still be hellish. That means dealing every day with someone you can't stand to be around."

"I might manage to stand to be around him," she answered quietly, thinking how sparks flew between them when they were together.

Her father swore softly and she felt torn between conflicting needs. "I can't stop you," he admitted.

"It's just a dinner. Only a few hours and I'll be back home."

Her father stared beyond her and shook his head. He tossed down his napkin. "I have to get outside and walk around while I think about this."

"Please don't worry. Forty-eight hours from now the time with him will be history."

As Quinn left the room, Ashley rubbed her pounding head. She was half tempted to cancel the dinner date, but then she thought about her dad's health, the debt that was accumulating, and she knew she had to go out with Gabe.

After breakfast the next morning she went to her room and looked at her clothes. She waded through her dresses and finally decided on a dark blue, high-waisted sheath dress. Something simple and dark. She wanted to wear a hood over her head. The world grew smaller daily and the chances of running into someone they knew loomed large to her.

She was on edge most of the day, and her nerves still jangled when she finally went to her bedroom to get ready for her date. Closing the door behind her, she looked at the room where she had grown up. It still held her maple four-poster bed, maple furniture with a rocker covered in blue cushions. An oriental rug covered the floor. As a girl, how many nights had she slept in that bed and dreamed of Gabe

Brant, fantasizing about a date with him? Well, she finally was going on that date.

He had lost his parents and wife all within the past few years. She knew he had to hurt over those losses. Whether he grieved or not, Gabe was tough and ruthless.

She kept thinking about Julian. The little boy was adorable. Marry the father and she would have a son. She drew a deep breath. She shouldn't marry him because of his little boy.

Was she setting herself up, too, for another heartache like Lars? Trusting a man again when she shouldn't?

She bathed and pulled on the simple, dark-blue sleeveless cotton dress. With care she pinned her hair behind her head. She put on her diamond stud earrings and watch. She studied herself in the mirror, turning first one way and then another. She was seven months pregnant and that was that. She couldn't change her shape.

With one last glance at the mirror, she prayed to herself that her father didn't come home until after she was gone. He had argued with her about the dinner date, but had finally accepted that she wanted to go.

To her dismay, when she entered the family room, her father sat in his leather recliner, reading a magazine. She saw he had cleaned up for the occasion. He wore a fresh blue shirt and jeans. His hair was damp and recently combed and he scowled slightly as he read. When she stepped into the room, he looked up.

"Don't you look nice," he said.

"I look big."

"Well, that's the way you should be and you really aren't very big to be ready to deliver in two months," he said reassuringly. "Sure you don't want to change your mind about tonight? I can go out and run Brant off when he gets here."

"I want to hear what he has to say. You know I'm not going to do anything to hurt the ranch or you."

"That's what's worrying me. I think you're doing this for me and for the ranch. All the wrong reasons."

The doorbell interrupted their conversation. "He's at the front door," she said. "I'll bring him in and introduce you."

"We've met. I'd still like to get my shotgun and run him off."

"Just hang on to your temper." She headed to the door, feeling butterflies in her stomach that didn't have a thing to do with her pregnancy or her father's anger.

She swung open the door to face Gabe Brant.

Three

Gabe looked handsome in his dark-blue suit, a white shirt and dark-blue tie. "I'm here," he said, his gaze sweeping over her, sending tingles racing over her nerves.

"Great. I told Dad I'd bring you back to say hello. He isn't looking forward to it, and I'm sure neither are you."

Gabe entered and closed the door behind him. "Maybe it's time for the Brants and the Ryders to bury the hatchet."

"I rather agree, but when it's a more-than-a-hundred-year-old family history, you can't switch feelings off like turning off a light," she said.

"I don't know," he drawled. "You're going to make it easy for me to forget the feud."

Ashley looked up at him and was caught in another intense, solemn gaze that made her heart skip a beat. "I don't know how *I'm* going to make it easy for you to do that."

"Oh, yes, you do, but we'll pursue that later. Let me see your dad."

She led the way to the family room. "Dad, you know Gabe Brant."

"Evening, sir," Gabe said, extending his hand. Both men looked as if they were ready to fight, and she wanted to hurry things along and get out of the house.

"This is a bunch of damn foolishness, Mr. Brant," her father snapped, refusing to shake hands. Gabe's eyes narrowed, and she could feel the animosity sizzling between them.

"I hope not. I have a proposition, actually a business offer. If you want to meet with me and let me talk to you about it, too, I'll be glad to anytime."

"No, I don't. I don't know why Ashley is going with you now. It's by the grace of her arguments that I'm not running you off our property."

Gabriel Brant was withstanding her father's wrath without a flinch. She just wanted to get the two separated.

"Can we go now and get this over with?" she asked.

"Fine," Gabe replied. "We'll be back early."

"You better be. My daughter is seven months pregnant."

"I know that, sir. I'll take good care of her."

Ashley wanted to shake her fist at him. "You don't have to take care of me," she snapped under her breath.

He shot her a glance before he nodded to her father. "Good night, Mr. Ryder. I appreciate the time Ashley is giving me."

As they went out the front door, she knew her father was trailing after them. He stood in the doorway watching them as they drove away in Gabe's black car.

Gabe glanced at her. "Well, we got through that without anyone being any worse for the exchange. Your dad held his temper mighty well. And I held mine."

"You'll hold your temper because you're the one after something."

"True." He glanced at her. "You look pretty."

"Thank you, but you can skip the compliments," she replied coolly.

"Don't sound so huffy. I'm still amazed how much you've changed since you were a kid."

"You told me how you remember me—skinny, braces," she remarked dryly.

"I'll bet you remember me the same way."

She cocked her head. "No, actually, I had a crush on you for a few years there. Does that surprise you?"

"Yes, it does," he answered.

"It was a long time ago. Just figure—you were exciting because you were forbidden. And you were older."

"Don't rub it in. I'm thirty-three. How much younger are you?"

"I'm twenty-eight. Plus, you were captain of the football team—you and Wyatt Sawyer were chosen by the girls in my class as the best-looking guys in Stallion Pass High School."

"Maybe tonight won't be so bad after all."

"Don't get your hopes up," she said, laughing. "I grew up. I've dated and my values have changed, and you're no longer forbidden."

"For a minute there my hopes were soaring."

"We've got a long drive into town. Why don't you start telling me your plans now?" she suggested.

"Relax, Ashley," he said. "I won't bite. Let's get to know each other. Tell me about your job in Chicago."

"Well, if you really want to know, it was just typical ad agency stuff. I was involved with thinking up ideas and dealing with clients."

"Do you miss it?"

"Terribly sometimes, but I'm needed here."

"Do you plan to go back to it?" he asked, half thinking about their conversation and what she had just told him. She had had a teenage crush on him. That meant she hadn't always hated him. And she thought he was good-looking. Sparks danced in the air when he was around her, and he was drawn to her in a way he hadn't been for a long time. Maybe there really was some hope for his proposal. And yesterday morning with Julian...Ashley and Julian had taken to each other instantly. That was a bonus that made this union far more important to him.

"Ashley, I was thinking about that crush you had—"

"Don't let that go to your head. I was a kid."

"Well, I wish I'd paid more attention then—"

"No, you don't. Remember, skinny, braces, five years younger. I don't think so."

He shrugged a shoulder. "You're right. You were a scrawny little squirt. But you aren't now."

"Thanks for that bulletin," she snapped with sarcasm. "Seven months pregnant is far from scrawny."

"I meant that in a nice way."

"Then thank you," she answered quietly, wondering whether she could really trust his answer, yet liking his compliment.

"So are you going to take over running your ranch now?" he asked.

"I've taken over the books—but I don't know the things my Dad does about breeding or training."

Gabe studied her intently. "I'm surprised you're not dating."

"No, I'm definitely not interested in anyone around here."

"Are you still in love with some guy in Chicago?"

"No, I'm not," she answered in a frosty tone. He was surprised to find her so self-possessed and cool. He shot another glance her way, looking at her profile. He had started this to acquire land, but now he was more intrigued with the woman sitting beside him, a turn of events that stunned him because he was still in love with Ella. He didn't want to be caught up in a situation where Ashley expected love. Whenever he thought of Ella, he hurt and he knew that wasn't going to change. Gabe realized Ashley had been speaking to him.

"I'm sorry," he said. "What did you say?"

"Where are we going to eat?" she asked. "We could still run into someone we know in San Antonio."

"I've thought about that. It seems to me that the least likely place is a sort of generic hotel. It might not be the best dinner you've ever eaten, but it will be private. Not many locals will eat in the hotels and it's unlikely we'll know the out-of-towners."

"You're probably right."

"Now if you want real seclusion, I can rent a room in the hotel and have dinner sent—"

"Not in the next two lifetimes will I go to a hotel room with you! Nice try."

He shrugged. "Fine with me. You're the one who's more worried about who will see us." He glanced at her. "Are you scared to go to a hotel room with me?"

"Hardly."

"I swear I won't make a pass."

"I'm sure you won't," she snapped, and he could hear the annoyance in her voice. Gabe knew he needed to quit teasing her, but when he could get such a passionate reaction out of her, he couldn't resist. He wondered how passionate she would get over long, steamy kisses. He drew a deep breath and knew he'd better stop following that line of thought.

"I do not, now or ever, want to go to a hotel room with you."

"Why does that come out as another inviting challenge?"

"I was thinking more as a threat. You're not helping your case."

"Okay. Back to a neutral subject. Where would you like to eat?"

"A hotel dining room sounds fine."

Thirty minutes later they were seated in a beige-and-green dining room of a hotel half a mile from the Riverwalk. The room was quiet except for piped-in music that played softly in the background. They were in a corner.

She prayed they would not see anyone from Piedras or Lago counties.

Gabriel ordered wine for himself and water for her. Shortly after their drinks came, they ordered dinner. As soon as the waiter left, Gabe sipped his red wine and studied her. "Ashley, you have the bluest eyes I've ever seen. They're very pretty."

"Thank you, but that isn't why you asked me out tonight. Get to the point."

He was amused at her dogged insistence on keeping the evening impersonal. "You know that kind of reaction from you just makes me all the more interested."

Surprising her, he leaned forward suddenly and took her hand. She tried to pull away, but he held her firmly, his thumb on her wrist. She was acutely aware of his touch and of his dark-brown eyes boring into her.

"Your pulse is racing. I think we should pursue getting to know each other for more reasons than saving your ranch and expanding mine."

"You're adept at smooth-talking to get what you want," she answered, realizing that he had admitted feeling an attraction to her and that he was still holding her hand. She was reacting to him in ways she didn't want to, and she found him exciting. Every time he fixed her with one of his piercing looks, his dark eyes took her breath away.

"I'm just observing what's happening here."

"All right, I'll admit my pulse is racing," she said, "but I chalk that up to not dating in a long time, my crush on you as a kid, and your sexy looks. We're not friends, and I barely know you, so whatever I feel when I'm with you is not significant."

"I don't agree. Does it happen with every guy you go out with?" he asked with great innocence.

"That's none of your business! You can cause my pulse to pound, but you also can cause my temper to rise. Now stop flirting with me."

"You don't like it?"

She took a deep breath, and he grinned.

"Let's talk about getting married," he said softly.

He made everything sound sexy. There was nothing about his offer that made Ashley feel she was considering an impersonal business decision. "I don't see any way we can work out this marriage of convenience."

"Sure, we can," he said, releasing her hand and leaning back in his chair, pushing open his coat while he studied her. He looked dashing in his dark suit, his eyes not missing anything. "I think there are vastly more possibilities here than I imagined. A marriage between us would mean financial help for the Triple R. It would let me get started with expansion. I'll have to admit, it would give Julian a mother and I would be there for you when the baby comes."

She laughed. "I don't need you when the baby comes. You're not part of me and my baby."

"I could be." He paused infinitesimally, then said, "Your dad's health isn't good, is it?"

To hear Gabe say that about her father hurt, and she looked away. "Ashley," Gabe said in an incredibly gentle voice that surprised her so much it brought her attention back to him. "I don't mean to upset you about your dad. I've lost too many people I've loved, and it hurt to lose them."

"I'm sorry," she said, hearing the pain in his voice and seeing it cloud his eyes. A muscle worked in his jaw, and she realized he was still grieving his losses.

"You have to face the truth. Your dad has health problems and he may need more help as time goes by."

"We have our foreman, Gus," Ashley protested.

"I've heard that in two years he's going to retire and move to Wyoming where his son and grandkids live."

The waiter came with their salads, and for a moment they ate in silence.

"I know Dad needs help—that's why I'm sitting here listening to you, but marriage is just impossible," Ashley said, wondering if she was arguing with herself more than him as she had done with her father the night before.

"It isn't at all. I wouldn't make demands on you. There wouldn't be anything physical unless you wanted there to be."

She couldn't keep from raising an eyebrow and giving him a look. "So if I said let's hop in bed, you'd be ready and willing?"

Putting down his fork, he smiled, and she drew a swift breath because it made him even more attractive. "Ashley, you're a beautiful, appealing woman. I'm a guy. That's all it takes."

She shrugged. "Why should I have been surprised?"

Amusement flashed in his eyes again.

Their entrées came and they were silent a few minutes as they ate, yet her mind was seething with conflicting thoughts. Over it all was the replay of his velvety voice telling her that she was beautiful and appealing.

"Ashley," he said, lowering his fork, "for the next hour, why don't we just pretend that you're Ashley Smith and I'm Gabe Jones. You'd see me a whole new way."

"That's like trying to pretend the rattlesnake a foot away from you is a kitten. That's not possible."

He grinned again, and she wondered how many female hearts he had melted with that smile. The man was wickedly handsome. This whole affair would be easier if she didn't have this constant prickly awareness of how sexy he was.

"A rattlesnake?" he asked with another arch of his brow. He leaned across the table. "Isn't that a little harsh?"

"All right. Maybe not a rattlesnake, but I can't pretend you're not a Brant. I'm far too aware of who you are."

"And I'm incredibly aware of you."

"That wasn't what I meant," she protested with amusement. He was fun to flirt with, exciting to be with. Ashley knew she was on dangerous ground. She barely knew him.

She needed to keep things impersonal and keep her wits about her.

"Will you answer something truthfully?" he asked.

Surprised, she set down her water glass. "Sure, unless it's too personal."

"I don't think it's personal at all. If I were really Gabe Jones, would you consider my proposition?"

She had walked into that one. She wanted to say no to his question and all other similar questions, but she had promised to be truthful. "I haven't for one second considered that you're anything other than a Brant."

"Okay, while we eat, think about it that way. Just for the next hour, see me as Gabe Jones. If you were really Ashley Smith, I'll tell you, I'd be a whole lot happier about all this."

"I'd hate to see you want this any more than you already do," she said. "All right, I'll try to think of you as Gabe Jones, but that's a stretch."

"It shouldn't be. You don't know any Brants and never have. And if you think about it, this is an irresistible proposition."

"That's because it's your idea and it's been irresistible to you from the start," she retorted.

"*Au contraire.* I've had a difficult time getting around the Ryder factor."

"You hide it well."

He touched her cheek. Her skin was soft and smooth as silk. "I'm glad you have a sense of humor."

"I think it falls more under sarcasm than humor. You're rather thick-skinned, aren't you?"

"When I'm after something," he agreed, and his dark eyes riveted her with a look that, under other circumstances, could have implied much more. "Now, remember, think Gabe Jones."

Ashley sighed and looked around the almost empty dining room. To her relief, the only people she saw were strangers. A popular old ballad played softly, what her father called his "elevator music", yet music he liked, and she wondered if every time she heard it played, she would always remember this evening.

While she took another bite of salmon, Gabe cut another bite of his juicy steak. The dinner was good, and the man across from her was exciting. She still couldn't believe she was here with him. She glanced swiftly at him and then away. Why couldn't she see him as an ordinary man instead of someone extraordinarily handsome and dashing?

Her gaze ran over planters of artificial greenery that served as dividers for part of the dining area. It was a hotel she had never been in before and would never be in again after this one unusual night that might set her on a course to changing her life.

"You aren't using all your land, are you?" Gabe asked, breaking into her thoughts while he took a sip of his water.

"Not all," she answered.

"There, you see? You aren't using the land—I could expand on a quarter of your ranch and it wouldn't interfere with your family or your horses. In exchange, you would have—"

"I know, help for Dad. And a hubby in name only. That is about as useful as a heater in July," she replied.

"Let's just talk—try the Jones-Smith approach. Tell me more about your life."

"It's pretty simple. I went to California to college and then got a job in advertising in Chicago." Silence stretched between them.

"Want to tell me about the guy you left behind?" he asked.

"No." She took a sip of water and considered Gabe's life. "You seem to have a good relationship with your son."

"I think I do. And don't worry, if we marry I won't let Julian be a burden to you."

"I told you, I like children."

"Julian is a good kid. He's too quiet," Gabe said solemnly. "The pediatrician tells me that she thinks he'll out-grow it."

"He wasn't quiet yesterday," Ashley said.

"He liked you. You have a way with kids, evidently."

"He might not want you to remarry," she said.

"He's too little to have many ideas on the subject."

They ate in silence for a few minutes and then Gabe said, "For all we know the old legend of Stallion Pass could come true. I've seen that white stallion on my land and on yours."

"Well, the legend of the white stallion is foolishness," Ashley snapped.

Gabe chuckled. "I agree, according to the legend, love comes where the white stallion lives," he said. "It started way back with the first settlers battling the Apaches. A warrior fell in love with a cavalry captain's daughter. The captain learned about it and was going to force her to marry another soldier. The warrior and his love planned to run away and marry. The night the warrior came to get her, he was killed by the cavalry. His ghost became the white stallion, forever searching for the woman he loved."

"And she ran away to Sacred Heart Convent that's just outside Stallion Pass—I think the convent was an old mission originally. From the convent, on moonlit nights, she could see the white stallion, yet she didn't know it was the ghost of her warrior," Ashley finished.

"What's fueled the legend is the number of wild white stallions seen in this area off and on through all the years. I heard my grandfather talk about one," Gabe said. "Who-ever captures the white stallion is supposed to find true love. Right now there's one running on your place, so Ashley, maybe I'm bringing true love."

She laughed. "You're thirteen years too late. There was a white stallion in these parts when I was growing up and had that crush on you, and I knew the legend and took that stallion for a sign of love coming, but alas, what a disap-pointment. You never noticed me."

"I'm sure as hell noticing you now."

She smiled and shrugged. "Too late. Now I know the legend is just a silly story. And right now, that white stallion that's running on our land, and yours, is upsetting my dad. That stallion had bred on some of our fine mares— something Dad never intended to have happen, so we'd be glad to be rid of him."

"I'll see if I can catch him and give him to someone who can use him. I'm not about to be stopped by the old legend," Gabe replied.

They had both finished eating, and he sat back to watch her, sipping his water as he talked. "I've given you excellent reasons why we'd make a good match. The fact that our families have fought for generations doesn't hold much weight against all these reasons to go ahead and marry."

"At this point in my life, I don't want a relationship, much less some kind of paper marriage. And you won't want a paper marriage. You're healthy and virile and you'll want sex."

He almost choked on his water and he put down his glass.

"Right to the point as always. So, okay," he said. "If we have a marriage of convenience, I won't make any physical demands on you. You can put that in a prenuptial agreement. Now if you want sex—I told you before, you're pretty and I'm a man."

"Gee, thanks. I'm not interested. It's not strictly a physical thing for me. Never has been, never will be. Besides, sex with a Brant is sort of like contemplating climbing into bed with an alligator," she said with a smile.

"That's something I haven't ever been told before." He leaned close to touch her, drawing his fingers lightly along her cheek down to her mouth. He traced her lips with his forefinger, and she couldn't get her breath. She was drowning in his brown eyes, unable to stop her reaction to him.

"See what we do to each other," he said softly. "I'm getting more curious by the moment about you. And more interested in pursuing you than in pursuing this paper marriage.''

"Intense physical attraction isn't love," Ashley said, wishing her voice was more firm, wanting to look away and break the eye contact with him, yet unable to do so.

"But it'd be interesting to see where it leads."

Thunder rattled the windows and lightning flashed. The lights in the restaurant went off and they were left in candlelight.

"C'mon, Ashley, think about my proposition. It might be a lot more fun than staying single. Better for everyone. You're making decisions that will affect your baby as well as your father and yourself.''

Candlelight flickered, reflecting in her blue eyes. She was beautiful, and Gabe meant every word he said to her. He was fascinated with this feisty lady.

The lights came back on, and she leaned back in her chair. "I've heard what you had to say, so it's time to go home," she said abruptly.

"Don't you think it's workable?"

"Yes, it is, but I still don't want to do it."

"I'm making progress if you'll admit it's workable," he said, standing and coming around to hold her chair.

As Ashley stood and turned to walk out, he remained where he was, beside her chair, blocking her way. She looked up with wide eyes.

"It's been a fun evening," he said, and she tilted her head, studying him solemnly. His gaze drifted down to her full lips, and he wondered what it would be like to kiss her.

She smiled, a wonderful, happy smile that made him draw a sharp breath. "Yes, it has been, but it doesn't make me want to accept your proposal. It's only a few hours together.''

"It's a good start." He was close enough to catch the scent of her perfume. Her hair was sleek and thick and he itched to tangle his fingers in it.

Knowing this wasn't the time or place, he took her arm and they left. They stepped outside beneath a canopy and waited for a valet to bring the car. Rain was coming down steadily.

A car drove up, slowed and stopped. A valet ran around the car to take the keys from the tall, handsome, brown-haired cowboy in jeans, boots and a sport shirt who climbed out.

"Looks like our dinner isn't going to stay a secret," Gabe said.

Four

———

"That's Josh Kellogg," Ashley said, touching Gabe's arm.

At that moment Josh turned, saw Gabe and grinned. As he looked at Ashley, his brows shot up.

When he walked over to them, Ashley realized they couldn't have selected a worse scenario for someone to discover them. Josh had found them coming out of a hotel together. Once word got around, that would stir rumors beyond her wildest imagination.

"Are you both real or is this just a figment of my imagination?"

"We're real," Gabe said. "Josh, this is Ashley—"

"I know Ashley," Josh answered easily. Curiosity filled his eyes as he looked back and forth between them. "Hi, Ashley."

"It's not what it looks like," she said.

"Not at all," Gabe added, reaching out to shake hands with his friend. "If we had to run into someone, I'm glad it's you. I have a business deal I'm trying to interest the Ryders in and I talked Ashley into going to dinner to listen to me."

"Did you now?" Josh asked, his eyes twinkling, and Ashley realized he didn't believe a word of what Gabe had just told him.

"Josh," she said firmly, "Gabe's telling the truth."

"Sure, Ashley," Josh said solemnly, but she knew he didn't believe her either. "I'll forget that I ever saw y'all. What you two do is your business. I'm meeting Trixie and I'm late because of the rain. See you." He turned to enter the hotel.

"He didn't believe either of us," Ashley said.

"Nope, he didn't. But he won't tell anyone."

"You sound really certain."

"I am. Josh is one of the best friends I've ever had. I would trust Josh with my life."

In the car, Gabe headed out of town. "Who's Trixie?" Ashley asked, trying to remember if she knew anyone from Piedras or Lago counties with that name. "His girlfriend?"

"Josh? Josh doesn't date. He spends every waking minute just trying to hang on to his ranch. Trixie is one of his multitude of stepmothers."

"I'd forgotten. His dad bought horses from us, and I've known Josh forever, but he's older, so I never knew him well."

"He's my age," Gabe said dryly. "We went all the way from kindergarten through high school together in Stallion Pass."

Ashley settled in the seat. It was comfortable in the car, and Gabe had driven carefully going into town. Until they had run into Josh Kellogg, she had actually enjoyed the evening. For too many nights on the ranch she had been lonesome and bored. Long before dawn her father left to take care of his horses. By nine o'clock at night, he was usually in bed, so she ended up spending a lot of time by herself. She hadn't been out on a dinner date in a long time.

Would it be so bad to be in a paper marriage to him? He had some valid arguments. She turned to stare at the rain sliding over the window.

"Has the doctor told your dad to cut back on his work?" Gabe asked.

"Yes, he has," she replied.

"And does your dad work less?"

"No. Perhaps an hour or two less in the evening sometimes. Gabe, your proposition is enticing in some ways, but it's totally impossible."

"What's impossible?" I'm trying to join the two ranches. *Join,* not take."

"It's you and I locked into a loveless relationship," Ashley told him.

"That doesn't mean we can't work out a viable way of living that would be mutually beneficial," he said quietly.

"You sound like a commercial," she said.

Gabe smiled. "You have some of the finest quarter horses in the world. Your dad is one of the best horse trainers ever. I don't want to change that. I'd leave your horses alone."

A huge bolt of lightning streaked the sky, making everything silvery for an instant, followed by thunder that banged like a cannon shot.

"Watch what you say. The heavens may open up and lightning strike you for such prevarication."

"I don't think I've ever known anyone as stubborn as you."

"Careful," she cautioned. "Your Brant fangs are showing."

They rode in silence for a time. When they reached Cotton Creek, Gabe switched on the brights and she stared out at the creek in concern. "We must have had a lot more rain out here than in town," she commented. Water was almost high enough to cover the wooden bridge and had spread out on both sides of the creek.

"You might not be able to get back across after taking me home. Of course, you could stay in the guest house."

"And you could fumigate it the next day."

Surprised, she looked at him and laughed. "It hasn't been that bad getting to know you," she said, touching his arm lightly. The moment she touched him, Ashley was intensely conscious of the contact.

"I'll get back across," he said. She watched the dark waters lapping at the bridge, splashing over the wooden edge as he drove slowly across.

"You don't scare easily, do you?" Ashley inquired.

"Maybe not. I'll bet your bridge has been there a long time without sweeping into the creek."

"You're right. It's the original bridge—as old as the ranch."

Rain began to pour in great driving sheets that blinded them to everything. Gabe cut the motor. "We'll wait this one out. It's comfortable in the car. You're not expecting anyone else to come along here, are you?"

"No. Everyone with any sense is somewhere out of this storm."

"So now to add to my list of sins, I don't have any sense," Gabe said with a sigh.

"Unfortunately, you're plenty smart. Too smart. That makes you all the more dangerous," Ashley told him.

He unbuckled his seat belt, turned to face her and scooted closer. She was aware of being closed in such a small space with him, of the drumming rain that shut them off even more from the world. Now she could detect the faint scent of his aftershave, and she felt his intense gaze on her.

"I find it interesting that you consider me dangerous."

"How many times do I have to tell you that any Brant is dangerous to any Ryder?"

"I thought maybe it was just you and me you were talking about," Gabe said softly.

He traced his finger along her cheekbone to her hair, lifting a tendril to let it curl in his hand. Tingles always followed his touch. "I don't think your baby's father made the decision about whether to get married or not. I think you did."

"Well, he did make the decision," Ashley replied stiffly. "And he's not the father of my baby. If you really want to know, I went the sperm-bank route."

"Now I'm surprised."

"I suppose I should tell you," she said, hating to open her private life to him, especially with him sitting so close, with his fingers still toying with her hair. In the next few minutes Gabe Brant might be as repelled as Lars had been. "I have endometriosis. My Chicago doctor told me that if I wait much longer, I might not be able to have a baby. I want a baby. I meant it when I said that I love children. Hence, the sperm bank."

"Wow. Are you in pain with the endometriosis?"

"No, thank goodness."

"There was a man involved somewhere here—you said it was his choice to part."

"That's right. Lars Moffet. We were practically engaged. But when Lars found out I had endometriosis, he wanted out of the relationship. He didn't think I could have the family he'd want."

"You talk about the Brants being bad! This guy sounds like a first-class jerk."

"I thought that he was very nice until my...crisis," Ashley admitted, the pain of Lars's rejection still haunting her. "I'm wary of trusting a man again."

"I'll keep my word." Gabe promised.

"Coming from a Brant, that doesn't reassure me." Ashley stared at the rain hitting the windshield. "You'll have to stay in our guest house tonight," she said.

"No, I don't have to. I can make it across your bridge."

"In spite of the feud, I'd hate for a Brant to get washed into the creek because of me."

"Ashley," Gabe said softly, and she turned to look at him. Lightning flashed and the desire she saw in his dark eyes made her grow warmer. "I think we can at least break the ice here," he said in a husky voice. Her heart pounded louder than the rain on the roof and words failed her.

Gabe put his hand behind her head, slid his arm around her and leaned closer, his lips brushing hers so lightly.

His soft kiss played havoc with Ashley's insides. She melted as his lips pressed against hers and his tongue slipped into her mouth. Her hands flew up against Gabe's rock hard chest. Ashley shook, lost in a spiraling kiss, then suddenly she was returning it, sliding her arms around his neck, thrusting her tongue over his, remembering how she had dreamed of this kiss a thousand times in her girlhood. And it was better than all the wildest imaginings she had ever had. Hotter, sexier, far more devastating.

And then thought was gone, taken away on a wild escalation of desire that made her want more. She wanted him never to stop.

Ashley ran her hands through Gabe's hair, kissing him fiercely until she realized just who she was kissing. Startled, she pushed away. Gabe looked as surprised as she felt.

"Damnation, we've been wasting a lot of time," he whispered and leaned toward her again.

Ashley placed her hand on his chest and he paused, his brow arching as he met her gaze.

"You're just going to complicate everything," she whispered. Her heart was pounding and she was breathless and his kiss had turned her world upside down.

"All right, I won't rush you," he replied solemnly, sliding his arm across her shoulders and holding his other hand against her back. "But I want to get to know you. I want this marriage, and I'm thinking there can be a lot more to it."

"Has it ever occurred to you to wait and take things as they come?" she demanded.

"No. I don't like waiting and you can't tell me that your dad doesn't need help now. From what I've heard, every day your ranch goes deeper into debt. That has to stress your father badly.''

She drew a deep breath, thinking of the long hours her father tried to work and how exhausted he looked at night when he came home. "You're right," she whispered.

"Ashley, marriage could be a good thing," Gabe said quietly. "Heaven knows that kiss was," he added.

"It was a kiss, nothing more. That doesn't change anything between us or our families."

"If we do marry, they'll have to accept it. And if it helps your father, do you really care what the others think?"

She ran her fingers across her brow. "*Our marriage.* I can't believe I'm seriously considering this."

"You are because it's a good offer."

"And you would get our ranch in the bargain," she said. "You're taking advantage of a bad situation."

"Not advantage of it. I would be helping to alleviate it." He waved his hands. "Look at me some other way than as a Brant whom you've been taught to hate. You managed to forget about a feud for a few minutes there when we kissed."

"So did you."

"Damn straight I did." He caught her chin and looked into her eyes. "It was fine and good, wasn't it?"

Her pulse jumped again. "All right, it was, but don't let it go to your head. A sexy kiss can't change everything else."

"It changed things for me. Let's go to dinner tomorrow night."

"You're rushing me," she protested.

"Go out with me tomorrow night," he repeated softly. "Seven o'clock, all right?"

"All right," Ashley answered, wondering if she was doing the right thing or if her brain had turned to mush with his kiss. "I'd better go in now. It's just a sprint to the house," she said.

"No running over wet ground," Gabe said, starting the

car and driving as close as possible to her back door. He leaped out and dashed around to open her door before she could react. Dropping his coat around her, he put his arm across her shoulders. "Let's go."

They hurried to the porch and she laughed, shaking her head. Before she could shrug off his coat, he caught the lapels with both hands, pulling her close. Her heart missed a beat and her insides fluttered.

"We can both think about tonight," he said solemnly.

He stood close enough to kiss her, his hands and arms rested lightly against her, although her clothing and his coat were between them.

"It's not any solution at all," she said, but the force had gone out of her voice.

"Think about it and you'll see. You're an interesting woman, Ashley. From that first moment, you've surprised me. I had a good time tonight."

"Actually, I'll have to admit, I've enjoyed the evening."

"Son of a gun, I'm making progress. Let's celebrate," he said and leaned down to kiss her again, his arms sliding around her waist. He held her lightly, while his mouth covered hers.

She opened her mouth, her tongue touching his as he held her and kissed her long and soundly. Her heart thudded, and thought was gone in a dizzying spiral. The man could kiss beyond her wildest dreams.

She didn't know how much time passed before she pushed against his chest and stepped back. All her senses were heightened and she was aware of the drumming rain—the fresh, wet smell mixed with a faint scent of Gabe's aftershave—of touching his chest and feeling his drumming heartbeat, of his gaze enveloping her.

"We need to call it a night," Ashley told him.

"Sure," he said, stepping back and taking his coat. "Thanks for going to dinner and listening. You think over my offer."

"I have thought about it, and every time I come up with the same answer—no. It's impossible."

"Don't decide yet. Give it more time," Gabe said and then he was sprinting through the rain back to his car.

"Impossible man!" she called, knowing he couldn't hear her above the rain. She watched his long stride eat up the ground. He was filled with energy which made him sexier. She touched her fingers to lips that still tingled. She had finally had some of that girlhood dream come true, and it had been fantastic.

Marry him, a small voice inside her said. She shook her head and knew she had to get a better grip on reality. The reality of everyday life, the reality of the Brants and the Ryders who hadn't mixed for five generations.

The best kisser ever or not, Gabe's proposal was ridiculous, and she couldn't consider it.

In her room, dressed for bed, she sat in her rocking chair and placed her hand on her stomach as she felt her baby move.

She could marry Gabe, have help for her father, someone to help run the ranch, a father for her baby and a sexy man for a husband. And she would have two children—her own and Gabe's little boy, Julian.

His proposition was tempting until she considered her family. Her relatives would disown her. Her father would be upset. And Gabe might have another side to him she hadn't seen. She didn't really know him.

Ashley remembered Lars and the pain he'd inflicted only too well. After working together and dating for two years, she had thought she had known Lars. Yet, he had betrayed her trust completely.

She sighed. Tonight's dinner date had been fun, but she had no illusions about Gabe Brant. He was attracted to her land, *not* to her. She needed to turn down his wild proposal and get on with her life. And she needed to find some way to get more help for her father. Tomorrow night she would

give Gabe his answer. He wouldn't like her decision, but
he was going to have to live with it.

The next day, her father left for a horse sale. Ashley
spent the day working on the nursery, getting it ready for
the baby. She spent an hour trying to decide what she
would wear to go out with Gabe that night.

At half past four, she heard a motor and glanced out to
see a pickup she didn't recognize coming up the road.

She went downstairs and outside into the sunshine,
shielding her eyes with her hand. As the pickup slowed and
neared the back gate, she was startled to see it was Josh
Kellogg driving, and her father was riding beside him.

She stared in surprise, then she rushed to meet them.
Something had to have happened for Josh to be bringing
her father home.

With her heart pounding, she ran through the gate and
waited. Her fears were confirmed when Josh jumped out
and came around the pickup, giving her a solemn, worried
look.

"Your dad isn't feeling well, Ashley," he said. "He
wouldn't let me take him to the hospital."

When Josh opened the door and helped Quinn out, fear
chilled her. She knew something terrible must have happened for her dad to lean on Josh. Quinn's face was ashen.

"Dad, why didn't you go to the hospital?" she cried.
"I'm going to call Dr. Bradley right now."

"Calm down, Ashley," her father said. "I've taken my
heart medicine and I don't want to go to a damned hospital.
I just wanted to come home."

"I'm calling Dr. Bradley," Ashley repeated. She dashed
ahead to the house and phoned, her fingers shaking as she
punched numbers. She talked briefly to a physician she had
known all her life and then hung up.

"He's coming over," she said, when she entered the
family room. Quinn was stretched on the couch while Josh
was pulling off his boots. The contrast in the two men made

her aware how frail her father had become. Josh was tanned, muscled and fit. He moved with ease and his jeans and T-shirt revealed the flex of muscles. Her father on the other hand, was thin, pale, and appeared helpless.

"Now Karl doesn't need to come over here," Quinn said with his eyes closed. "I just got woozy. I feel better already. You're making a mountain out of this when it's nothing."

"Karl said he'd be here in about twenty minutes," she said.

"Josh, thanks," Quinn said. "You want to sit down a while? Ashley can get you iced tea or pop."

"Thanks, sir," Josh replied, "but I'll get on back." He stood at the foot of the couch with his hands on his hips, a frown creasing his forehead while the worry in his green eyes frightened Ashley even more. Josh was tough just like her father and the other men who were ranchers. Whatever had happened had to be terrible for Josh to look so worried. "I'll get your truck and bring it to you, sir," Josh added.

"Don't bother," Quinn replied without opening his eyes. "We can send someone for it. Ashley will take care of it."

"I don't mind at all and I'm going back there anyway," Josh insisted. "You take care now."

"Thanks," Quinn replied with his eyes still closed. He looked ashen and frail on the big sofa and Ashley wanted to throw herself down and hug him, but she suspected that wouldn't help anything.

"I'll see Josh out, Dad. Call if you want me."

She left the room with Josh, both silent, but once they were away from the family room, she said, "Thanks for bringing Dad home."

"Sure. It was no trouble."

When they went outside, she paused and turned to face Josh. "Now please tell me what happened."

"Your dad collapsed, but he didn't lose consciousness. Otherwise we would have called an ambulance. And probably should have. Ashley, he isn't well."

"I know that," she said softly, fighting back tears.

Josh gazed at her solemnly while wind caught locks of his brown hair. "I'm glad the doctor is coming. I wanted to take your dad to the hospital, but he wouldn't hear of it and he wouldn't let anyone call an ambulance. Even when he's sick, your dad can be pretty forceful."

"I know that, too. Thank you so much for taking care of him."

"I was glad to, but he needs to see someone. He could hardly breathe for a while there. He just crumpled. Sorry to worry you, but you better know what happened."

"I'm glad to know." They paused beside Josh's green pickup. "He works harder than he should," Ashley added, lost in thought about her father.

"Yeah, I can understand. This size ranch takes a heap of attention."

She tilted her head to study Josh. "I want to ask you something. You've known Gabe Brant all your life, haven't you?"

"Yep."

"Well, he's proposed to me."

Josh's dark brows arched, otherwise, he didn't look surprised. "A Brant and a Ryder getting married?"

"It would be a paper marriage. But I have to give it thought."

"Why in blue blazes would Gabe want to do that?"

"He wants more land."

"Of course," Josh said. "That sounds like Gabe. Since he lost Ella, he's eaten up with ambition. I work hard because I have to. Gabe works hard because he's driven by grief."

"I'm sorry if that's why, although Dad thinks he was always that way."

Josh grinned. "No Ryder has kind thoughts about a Brant and vice versa." His grin faded. "You're considering Gabe's offer. What do you get out of it?"

"Someone to help run this ranch—and the Ryder money."

Josh looked beyond her. "A paper marriage is a damned weird thing, but he may have made you a good offer. Your dad probably needs help badly, and Gabe has the money and resources to get any ranch running smoothly. That's why y'all were out together last night?"

"Yes, it is."

"I should have guessed. Gabe has told me he'll never love anyone again after Ella. I've never seen a man grieve like he has. 'Course, losing his parents too was another big blow." Josh looked over his shoulder, his gaze taking stock of the ranch. "Why doesn't Gus just take over?"

"Dad won't let him. Gus has always worked for Dad, and Dad just doesn't know how to step down and turn it over to Gus, and Gus isn't going to take charge until Dad tells him to."

"I can see that. Well, I can tell you one thing, Ashley, Gabe will live up to his promises. He's my best friend, and he'll keep his word."

"You feel sure about that?"

"I'd trust him with my life. You can count on him to do what he promises. On the other hand, if there's something he's not telling you, that's another matter. I'd get everything straight and clear going into it because he *is* ambitious and right now, he's trying to drive his grief away with work."

"Thanks for your opinion. I was going to tell him no tonight," she said, glancing back at the house, "but seeing my dad like this, I think I just changed my mind. Dad's more important than the ranch."

"I would say a marriage of convenience to Gabe might be the lesser of two evils unless you don't think you can stand to have him around. There are sure no guarantees with love—look at my dad and his six marriages." Josh climbed into his truck and looked at her through the open window.

"I'd offer to come over here and help your dad, but I'm spread so thin, I can just barely keep my place going."

"Don't worry," she said, touched by his concern. "We each have our problems to work out. Even my uncles can't do anything to help because of their own problems. And dad isn't able to help them."

"Yeah, we've all got problems. Well, if you decide to marry Gabe, I don't envy you or Gabe when it comes to telling your relatives. That'll stir up the next three counties like nothing has in this century."

"I can't worry about my relatives. It's Dad that I'm concerned for."

"I'll bring your truck home in a little while."

"Thanks, Josh. Thanks for bringing Dad home. And I better get back to him now."

She turned to hurry inside, checking on Quinn and then going to call Gabe on the kitchen phone and cancel their date that night. She didn't want to leave her father alone. Ashley went in to sit with him and found him asleep. As she watched the slow rise and fall of his chest, she mulled over the future and knew what she had to do.

All day at the Triple R, Gabe was kept busy by problems caused by the storm—a downed fence, a truck mired in mud, a windmill broken by wind gusts. When he got in, as soon as he had greeted Julian, Gabe listened to the message from Ashley and wondered if her father's collapse would push her closer to accepting his offer.

He picked up the phone to call her, changing their dinner date to the following night. When he hung up the receiver, he gazed into space, recalling their kiss that had started his pulse racing. Sparks flew when he was with her, and her kiss had been magic, heating him like wildfire.

Even if she turned down his proposal, he wanted to date her. Ashley Ryder was sexy and appealing even when she was seven months pregnant. A sperm-bank baby. He admired her for setting the course for her own life. It took courage to decide to have a baby by herself. Ashley looked like she could be good for Julian.

Gabe closed his eyes and thought about her kisses again. Finally, he got up, knowing he'd better get Ashley out of his thoughts if he wanted to get any sleep tonight. He shook his head, amused at himself. For three years he hadn't been able to sleep because of grief and memories that hurt. Now Ashley was taking him out of his grief, but now he couldn't sleep because he was so stirred up over her.

It wasn't until Julian was tucked into bed and asleep that night that Gabe's thoughts turned back to Ashley. Ashley had told him that Josh had brought Quinn home today.

For a few minutes Gabe thought about Josh. He had as many problems as the Ryders. Josh's old man had died a year ago, but not before gambling and drinking away every cent the Kelloggs had, running the ranch into the red, going through six wives. Now Josh was trying to save the Kellogg ranch. Gabe had offered to loan him money or help however he could, but Josh was determined to do it on his own. On his own, and with his bank's cooperation. It amazed Gabe how Josh had stayed friends with all his father's ex-wives. Josh didn't date, was as solitary as an owl, but he was good friends with each one of his stepmothers.

He, Josh and Wyatt Sawyer had been best friends since they were little kids in school in Stallion Pass. Wyatt had gotten himself into trouble with a local girl and had disappeared. Not even Josh or Gabe knew where he had gone. Wyatt's old man was still alive, making money like crazy, one of the most successful cattlemen around, but he was meaner than a snake, and Gabe hated him for all the terrible things he had done to Wyatt. Wyatt may have been wild and always getting in trouble, but a lot of that was because of his old man.

Gabe remembered Ashley telling him that the girls thought he and Wyatt were the best-looking guys in Stallion Pass High. Gabe smiled. And all that time, Ashley Ryder had had a crush on him. How he wished she still had that crush. She might feel something when he was close, but he suspected that was nature and hormones and the fact that the beautiful lady had been stuck out alone on her ranch with her father for months now.

Those blue eyes of hers sent him off into erotic daydreams. Her kisses all but melted him. For long periods with Ashley, he didn't hurt as much or grieve over his losses. He knew he could never love anyone except Ella, but at least his pain and grief were diminishing.

He would just have to wait now to see what she decided. He had given it his best pitch. How much would this latest flare-up of her father's heart condition influence her?

The following day Quinn was back on his feet, but he stayed around the house and didn't go out to work. Ashley had sat in the family room with him while Karl Bradley had checked him over and heard the physician tell her dad that if he wanted to live, he'd have to cut back on his work. And she had heard her father's noncommittal grunt of annoyance which meant he wasn't going to pay any attention to what his doctor was telling him.

As soon as breakfast was over, she called Gabe and left a message.

Within thirty minutes he returned her call. "You called?"

"Yes," she said, "I want to talk to you."

"I can come over right now," he offered.

"Thanks, that would be nice."

She replaced the receiver, took a deep breath and went to her room to comb her hair. She wore a green cotton jumper and a white cotton shirt. As she pulled her hair into a ponytail, her thoughts churned over her situation, her dad, their future.

Finally she went downstairs and thrust her head into the family room. "I'll be outside if you want me. I have a pager if I go to the barn."

Quinn waved his hand. "I'm fine. You don't need to hover."

Ashley smiled and left, going outside to sit on the porch in the shade and wait for Gabe.

It was thirty minutes later when she heard his pickup. He parked in the shade by the gate and climbed out. She hurried to meet him and walked around the pickup. Facing her, Gabe stood with his hands on his hips. He wore a T-shirt with the sleeves ripped out, and he looked fit and handsome and strong. He tossed his wide-brimmed black hat into his pickup and raked his fingers through his hair.

"How's your dad?"

"He's better today. His coloring is back to normal. The doctor told him to take it easy."

"I'm sorry."

She shrugged. "I spent all last night thinking. We can't go on like we are, and Dad won't let Gus take charge."

Gabe's pulse jumped as he talked to her. She looked worried, her blue eyes were filled with concern, and his hope grew.

"Marry me, Ashley," he said. "That would solve some of your problems."

"It would make new ones."

"Might at that, but we can work through them. Do you want to marry me?"

The question hung in the air; suddenly he couldn't breathe. He wanted her to say yes, and it wasn't just to acquire her ranch.

She bit her lip and looked past him as if deep in thought, yet he had a feeling she had already made a decision.

Five

Squaring her shoulders, Ashley raised her chin.

"Don't look as if I asked you to throw yourself into a cage of lions." He stepped closer and touched her cheek.

"It's scary to go into marriage when there isn't love."

"We're doing pretty well together, I'd say," he said softly.

"Maybe, but it's too soon to tell."

"Just take it a day at a time." His hand rested on her shoulder, and his pulse still raced. Gabe knew what he wanted. At the same time, he ignored the qualms that assailed him, the memories of a marriage filled with love and happiness, a stark contrast to what he was proposing here.

"What'll it be, Ashley? Will you marry me?"

Her blue eyes focused on him. "Yes, I will," she answered. "I have to do something, and your offer looks like the best solution."

He couldn't resist. His pulse jumped, and eagerness

flashed through him like lightning. He stepped closer, wrapping his arms gently around her to lean forward to kiss her.

Startled, Ashley's hands flew up to rest on his forearms. And then his mouth covered hers and she forgot all her worries and fears. She was surprised by his reaction, amazed that he seemed happy because she had seen the look that had momentarily clouded his expression, and she could guess why. She gave herself to his kiss, returning it, letting go of questions and cautions. Heat filled her, desire stirring, a longing to have a real union and not a paper one. Could she let go and trust what he said, or was she being taken in by a land-hungry, madly ambitious rancher who was still wrapped in grief over the loss of his loved ones?

Then she didn't care. She was swept away in his stormy kiss that turned her knees to jelly and made her heart pound. She wound her arm around his neck, curling her fingers in his thick hair. She placed her other hand on his chest, rock-hard with muscles.

She forgot time or place or circumstances as their kiss deepened, awakening a depth of responses. Finally she pushed against him, and he leaned away slightly to look down at her.

"It'll be good between us," he said in a husky voice

"You can't know that," she said, wondering at his optimism and confidence.

"I'll try, Ashley. I swear I'll try to make it good."

"There are a million questions and things to work out."

Gabe framed her face with his hands. "Ashley, I'm happy. This is good."

Her surprise at the enthusiasm in his reaction was tempered by the realization that, after all, he was getting what he wanted. She rubbed her brow. "I've got to do something. I don't want another incident with Dad like yesterday."

"Stop worrying," Gabe said gently. "I'll help, and our marriage will relieve your dad."

She studied him intently. "You want a quarter of our ranch for your cattle—that's all?"

"Right. Unless you want to give me more. That'll allow me to expand a lot. I'd like to keep horses here, but I don't have many horses."

"We've got a million things to iron out before we can marry," she said. "Where'll we live?"

"Come to dinner tonight at my house. Your dad is invited, too. We can make our plans. Does your dad know yet?"

"No, he doesn't. I wanted to tell you first in case you had changed your mind."

"Never," Gabe stated, his dark eyes hard as he looked at her. "Want to go tell him together?"

"I better break the news first."

"Let me come in with you. Unless it will really upset him, I'd like to talk to him," Gabe said. He was elated, his mind racing over their future together. And he would see her tonight. She might come with her father, so he wouldn't get to be alone with her, but they would be alone soon enough. Her kisses set him on fire, and he wanted her in his arms. To his surprise, he realized he wanted her in his bed. He also couldn't resist imagining the two ranches joined—a sprawling ranch that he'd dreamed about for years now.

They walked to the house, and he knew he'd better think about what he would say to Julian, as well as to Quinn Ryder. When he draped an arm across Ashley's shoulders, she gave him a sharp look.

"Mind?"

"No, I'm just surprised. You're far more interested in me than I thought you would be since my ranch is really the object of your affections."

"We might as well try to make the most of this arrangement we're agreeing to."

"It's a marriage of convenience, nothing more, nothing

less," she said. Blocking her path, he faced her and placed his fingers lightly on her throat.

"Your pulse is racing," he said softly.

"You know you do that to me, but that doesn't mean a whole lot."

"It means something to me," he replied solemnly.

"Well, you told me that's nature."

"Don't twist my words around. Ashley, the sooner we do this, the better off everyone will be."

Gabe held the door for her and she went inside, still in shock over promising to marry him, just as much in shock over his reaction. Had he really meant what he'd said?

She turned to Gabe, placing her hand lightly on his arm. "If you'll just wait in the living room, I'll talk to him and then you can see him. I don't want you to be the one to tell him. It's not like we've been dating."

"No, it's not, but I wish it were."

"You say things like that—I find them a little difficult to believe."

"Time will tell."

"Yes, it will," she answered, scared to trust his words, scared to trust a man again. She left him and went to the family room. She dreaded breaking the news to her father, yet this seemed like a solution to all sorts of problems.

"Dad?"

He put down a magazine and smiled at her while she closed the doors to the hallway. His brows arched. "What's happening?"

"Gabe Brant is in the living room and he wants to talk to you after I do."

"Why?" Quinn asked, frowning.

"Dad, I've accepted Gabe's offer of marriage," she said, letting out her breath.

"Aw, Ashley, don't do that! Hell, it's just because of me and yesterday. Now don't go flying off and do something you'll regret forever."

"I don't think I will regret it. I think it might be very good."

"How in blue blazes do you think that? You don't know each other or even like each other."

"We're getting to know each other, and we do like each other. Dad, I'm doing what I want to do. I wouldn't do this if I really didn't want to."

"Yes, you would. You're doing it purely for my sake and I don't want you to! Ashley, the man is after this ranch."

"We've got lawyers to protect the ranch. We'll have a prenuptial agreement drawn up that will safeguard the place. I want your blessing."

"You don't love him and he doesn't love you."

"We both think there is a chance for love," she said, knowing that was a real stretch, but desperate to get her father's agreement.

He clenched his fists, and she hurt for him, but something had to be done. "Dad, I want to marry him. I had a wonderful time with him the other night. Will you let him come talk to you? Please?"

Quinn inhaled and unclenched his fists. "All right."

She crossed the room to hug her father and kiss his cheek, closing her eyes and saying a silent prayer that she was doing the best possible thing.

As soon as she entered the living room, Gabe stood.

"You can talk to him now," she announced.

"He's okay with our marriage?"

The words sounded strange to her. *Our marriage.* Was she really going to marry this stranger, this Brant, a member of the family that her own hadn't spoken to or dealt with in generations? This man who excited her more than any other man she had ever known, even though he was still a stranger to her? This man she was going to have to trust?

"Not very okay, but he'll talk to you. And he'll go along with what I want to do," she replied.

"Good." Walking over to her, Gabe placed his hand on her shoulder. "Stop worrying. We'll work things out."

Leaving the room, they walked down the hall together. He draped his arm across her shoulders. She was aware of the energy he exuded. Her father was ill, she was seven months pregnant. Gabe was filled with vitality that showed in every step he took and every move he made. They could use some of that energy on this ranch, and she knew it too well.

At the door of the family room, Gabe turned to wink at her and then disappeared inside, closing the door behind him.

She paced the hall, touching picture frames, looking into empty rooms, wondering what was happening with the two men. Finally after twenty minutes, Gabe opened the door.

"Ashley, come join us," he said, sounding cheerful and looking relaxed and happy.

Her hopes jumped that her father would accept this bargain she was making because life would be easier for all of them if he did.

Gabe put his arm around her shoulders as she entered the room. Quinn looked less upset and angry, so Gabe must have settled him down, which was good.

"Your dad has given us his blessing."

"I hope you two know what you're doing," Quinn said, looking back and forth between them.

"We do, as much as anyone who gets married," Gabe said cheerfully, and Ashley wondered how badly he wanted this union.

"We'll put off drinking a toast until another day," Gabe continued. "Even so, this is a day to celebrate. I wanted you both for supper tonight, but your dad has other plans."

She didn't know about any other plans and looked at Quinn.

"This afternoon Dusty called and said he would pick me up and take me to his place for supper. He'll bring me home later or if I want, I can stay there tonight."

"You can come to my house another time," Gabe said to Quinn. "We'll make our plans tonight," he told Ashley, looking down at her. For the moment she wished with all her heart that this was going to be a real marriage with love and hope, but then she knew she was getting help for her dad and the ranch, and she would have to be satisfied with that.

"Sir, thank you," Gabe said, shaking hands with Quinn as he stood.

"You keep your word, you hear?"

"Yes, sir," Gabe said brightly. "I promise."

"Promises are leaves tossed in the wind. Time will tell, but heaven help you if you hurt Ashley."

Ashley felt the cold threat from her father, and for an instant, all Quinn's old strength seemed to return to his demeanor and his voice.

"I don't want ever to hurt either one of you," Gabe answered solemnly, tightening his arm around her slightly to pull her closer against him. "Come to the door with me, Ashley," he said, keeping his arm around her shoulders as they left the room.

"I think he's accepting this even though it's reluctantly," she said, looking up at Gabe.

"It'll be better with a little time." On the porch, Gabe turned to face her. "I'll pick you up tonight about half-past six."

"I can drive over."

"Nope. I'll pick you up. Start letting me take care of you."

She laughed. "I'm pregnant, not feeble."

"I know you're not feeble, but I want to do things for you."

"Stop it! Two weeks ago you would barely have spoken to me."

"Two weeks ago I hadn't kissed you."

"That hasn't changed the world or you," she said, but her pulse had jumped.

"Oh, yes, it did," he answered softly, leaning closer to her and brushing her cheek with his fingers. "I keep telling you that it changed the whole world." His fingers slid down to tilt her chin up and he kissed her a long, lingering kiss that had her heart pounding.

When he leaned away, she opened her eyes.

"See, nothing's like it was before," he said solemnly, his expression changing. "For three years I've lived constantly with grief. From that first day I met you, something broke through and for a little while grief vanished. And it's diminishing, Ashley. I have you to thank for that. Hurt still comes, but not like it was. Not that terrible sense of loss that took my breath and made everything ache."

"I'm glad, Gabe," Ashley said quietly, touched and surprised.

"I'll pick you up," he said, his voice growing lighter as he started to walk away. She caught his arm.

"Gabe, let's wait until after tonight to tell our families. Let's have the details worked out when we break the news to them. I want to call our family lawyer first, too. I'll get Dad to wait to tell Uncle Dusty."

"Sounds like a good plan to me. The minute one of us talks, word will be all over the county within the hour."

"I'd give it twenty minutes," she remarked, and he laughed.

"You're right. Okay, for now, only the three of us will know our plans. But the first person I tell is Julian." He stepped back. "See you this evening."

She watched him stride to his pickup, climb inside and wave before he drove away.

It wasn't until she was alone in her room that doubts loomed large. She thought of how Lars had smashed her trust. Was she doing something incredibly foolish? Yet, how else could she get immediate help for her father? And a lot of help—both physical and financial.

Just before seven that evening she opened the door to face Gabe, who looked as handsome as ever in jeans and a blue, long-sleeved shirt. As his gaze went over her appreciatively, she became aware of her size again. She had dressed in a plain navy jumper and simple white blouse, a silver bangle her only jewelry.

"You look pretty," he murmured.

"Thank you. I just feel huge," she replied.

"Well, you're not, and you're beautiful pregnant."

"You're very nice." She felt herself blush.

"No, I think you do look beautiful," he said, touching her hair. "Very expectant."

"I'm that, all right," she said, closing and locking the door behind her. Gabe took her arm.

When they drove up to Gabe's house, she saw that it bore a resemblance to her own. It was rambling, added to through the years, a hodgepodge of wood and stone and glass. A wraparound porch held chairs and gliders and a swing. Just the same as hers, the yard was fenced and the grass well-watered. The road divided and the other branch led to a low, rambling brick-and-wood house that looked much newer.

"Who lives there?" she asked.

"I built that house for Ella," Gabe replied gruffly. "After Mom and Dad died, one house was going to stand empty so I decided to move here into the old house. The memories aren't quite as painful."

"Sorry, Gabe."

"Yeah." He parked near the back door and came around to open the door for her. "Welcome to the Circle B," he said.

"I can tell you right now that I don't want to move into your house," she said as she stepped out. "I can't leave Dad and I don't want to uproot him."

"That's fine. I have a lot of memories here that hurt. I have to know, will your dad be good to Julian? If we live in your house, those two will be together often."

She smiled. "You don't know my dad. He'll love Julian. You'll see."

Gabe touched the corner of her mouth. "I love it when you laugh or smile. You're a beautiful woman."

She could feel her cheeks burn. At the same time, his compliment warmed her and made her feel as if she glowed. "Thank you."

He took her arm and walked beside her. "Come on and I'll give you a tour of my home."

As they stepped onto the porch, the back door opened and Julian ran out. He was followed by an attractive blonde in cutoffs and a yellow T-shirt. She smiled at Ashley. Julian stopped and gazed at Ashley with big brown eyes as he said hello.

"Hi, Julian," Ashley replied.

"Ashley, meet Lou Conrad," Gabe said. "Lou is our nanny. Lou, this is Ashley Ryder," Gabe said easily.

Ashley greeted Lou Conrad and then turned back to Julian. "Are you going outside to play?"

"I get to ride Popcorn," he answered with a big grin.

"Popcorn's the horse we save for Julian to ride," Gabe explained. "Lou promised Julian a ride on a horse, so they're going to the corral."

Ashley suspected the ride had been arranged to keep Julian from interfering in any conversation Gabe wanted to have with her. As Lou and Julian walked away, Gabe took Ashley's arm to cross the porch and go through a small entryway.

"Too bad Lou doesn't own a neighboring ranch," Ashley commented. "She's very pretty."

"She's also very engaged and pretty doesn't figure into the equation, although you certainly are."

"So if I had been incredibly homely, you'd still have made your offer?"

"Your looks have nothing to do with what I want," he said quietly, but with an underlying force that surprised her.

"I better remember at all times—you're after our land."

She met his solemn, dark-eyed gaze and wondered about
Josh's declarations that she could trust Gabe. There were
moments when he looked unfathomable and determined.

"Will I get to see Julian later?"

"Of course. I want you two to get to know each other,"
Gabe answered as he ushered her into a kitchen with new,
shiny appliances, dark oak cabinets and an oak cabinet for
the refrigerator. A large, well-lit alcove held the table and
eight chairs.

"Let's go this way first," he said, taking her arm and
leading her into an adjoining room. While she looked at a
huge room with a vaulted ceiling and rough beams, floor-
to-ceiling windows along the south giving a glorious view
of ranch land, she was more aware of his hand on her arm
than of his house. No matter what she told herself or him,
that schoolgirl crush had a residual effect, because she still
felt something anytime she was around him. Or was there
an attraction now that was completely adult and went way
beyond a crush?

"We had the wall taken out and put the family room and
the living room together."

"For a minute there I was beginning to think our houses
might be a lot alike, but this is entirely different from
ours."

"Over here is the dining room," he said, taking her arm
lightly again and they moved to another large room with a
spectacular view to the west. "This was all remodeled
about eight years ago."

"It's beautiful. I wouldn't think you'd want to leave this
at all."

"I don't. But one of us ought to live in the other's
house."

"My father hates the thought of our marriage. There's
no way I'm asking him to move and no way I'm leaving
him. That was the whole purpose of my coming home in
the first place." They stood in the doorway of the dining
room. Gabe rested a hand on the doorjamb above her head

and his other hand on his hip, leaning a little closer, and she had to catch her breath as she looked into his riveting brown eyes.

"But there's more here than either one of us expected." He touched her hair lightly.

Her heart thudded. Was she being taken in by a smooth-talking man who was accustomed to getting what he wanted out of life?

"You and I barely know each other." She reached up and caught his chin with her hand. "Are you falling in love? she demanded. "And don't ever lie to me, Gabe."

As he drew a deep breath, his gaze went beyond her, and she had her answer before he spoke.

"No, you're not," she continued solemnly. "Let's just stay realistic."

"I promised I wouldn't rush you or make physical demands. I'll keep my promise."

"You may be locking yourself into a situation you won't like later," she warned.

He shook his head, his gaze going over her with an intensity that made her tingle all over. "I'm happy with our agreement and I'll stay happy with it."

"You want our land!" she snapped impatiently. "Show me the rest of your house."

His gaze held hers a moment longer before he turned, taking her arm to lead her down the hall. They looked at bedrooms, his office, a playroom adjoining Julian's bedroom, Lou's sitting room and bedroom.

"Does she live here?"

"Nope. This is just to have a place available if she sleeps over or is out here and I bring Julian with me. She's engaged and going to college. She commutes and isn't here on Tuesdays and Thursdays. I have a housekeeper, she cooks and cleans, and watches Julian on those days if I don't take him out with me. Here's my bedroom," he said, leading her to a room that adjoined Julian's.

The moment Ashley entered, she seemed surrounded by

Gabe. His bedroom reflected his presence and revealed the man. She looked at pictures of his wife, Ella, his king-sized bed covered in a navy comforter, Navajo rugs, several bronze statues of cowboys and cattle. She turned to face him.

"Sure you want to move to my house?"

"Yep. I've been damned lonely here. Get your lawyer to draw up whatever kind of deal you want. We can work out a feasible bargain."

He moved closer and placed his hands on her shoulders, sending a tremor through her.

"Let's get married soon. If for no other reason, your dad needs help as quickly as possible."

"Gabe," she said, "I don't want to tell anyone except Dad that it's a paper marriage. I don't want to tell my uncles. I think I would have even more of a hassle."

"I agree," he replied quietly. "It's no one else's business. Let's sit in the family room where it's comfortable and we can talk," he said.

In another half hour Lou returned to leave Julian with them and to tell them goodbye because she was leaving for the evening. Gabe went to the back door with her and left Julian with Ashley.

As Julian leaned against a chair, Ashley smiled at him. "While we wait for your dad to come back, do you want me to read a story to you? Do you have books in here?"

He was gone in a flash, darting to a bookshelf to rummage around and return with an armload of books.

Ashley moved to the sofa and patted it as Julian brought the books to her. When he climbed up beside her, she asked him, "Which one shall we read first?"

Julian pulled out a large, colorful book about bears and as Ashley began to read, Julian scooted close to her. He turned the pages for her, and she realized he had the book memorized. As soon as she finished the book, she laid it aside on the coffee table. "Now which one shall we read, Julian?"

"I want this one," he said, fishing out a book about a dragon.

Ashley put her arm around him and began to read, suspecting that the minute her father met Julian, all his protests about this marriage would vanish.

When Gabe returned, he paused in the doorway while he watched Ashley read to his son. A lump came in his throat because he knew Julian had been a lonely little boy without a mother to care for him. Lou was a good nanny and full of life, helping Julian, but Lou wasn't around a lot of the time. He hoped that Ashley would be a good mother for him.

Julian touched the bracelet on her arm. "What's that?"

"My bracelet," she said. "Do you want to see it?" She shook it off her arm and handed it to him and Julian turned it in his small hands and handed it back.

"You smell pretty," he said.

"Thank you, Julian," she said, brushing locks of hair off his forehead.

He tapped the book. "Read."

As she continued reading about the dragon, Gabe saw that Julian was enthralled. Gabe entered the room quietly and sat down near them. Ashley gave him a look, but continued reading. He didn't think Julian even noticed him.

When he had started this, Gabe had expected a business arrangement, but now he wanted more. Ashley had been hurt in Chicago—was she ready to love again? Could *he* love again? He thought about their kisses and knew there was a magic chemistry between them that made him want her desperately. Now he saw that she might be a mother to Julian. And he knew he could be a daddy for her baby.

She glanced up and met his gaze and it was as if she had touched him. Without a word being said he felt tension snap between them. How could she be sexy at seven months pregnant? But she was. With a look, she could get his heart pounding.

He crossed the room to shove books away and sit down

beside his son. After a few minutes, as Gabe watched, Julian reached up to touch her hair. She smiled at him and continued reading. After the fifth book, Gabe reached over and closed the book.

"That's enough for right now," he said to his son. "Ashley gets a break, and we're going to eat dinner." He looked over Julian's head at her. "Come into the kitchen while I toss some steaks on the grill."

Julian hopped down and went to get more toys to show Ashley.

"You've won over father *and* son," Gabe informed her.

"My ranch has won over the father and my reading the son. Neither one really means a lot in the long term."

"You'll see," he said.

Gabe tried to entertain her through supper and let her get to know Julian. Afterwards they went outside to play with Julian and after Gabe had put his son to bed, he sat making plans with Ashley.

She paused to look at him solemnly. "I can't believe this is happening."

"It's happening," he said quietly, reaching over to squeeze her hand. "Let's announce it and tell the relatives and stand our corner of the world on its ear."

She laughed. "I'm game!"

"Good!" He pulled her into his arms to kiss her hungrily, and Ashley returned it, winding her arms around his neck. Gabe's pulse pounded while he gloried in her soft mouth and her hot kisses that caused him to break out in a sweat. She finally pushed away and he released her instantly.

"I should go home now. You should have let me drive myself over here because now you have to get Julian up to take me home."

"Watch—Julian will sleep through the whole thing."

An hour later Ashley closed the door in her bedroom and stood with her eyes closed, remembering Gabe's kisses, his words, his flirting through dinner, remembering his prediction that their marriage would be good and so much more than either expected. Could she trust him? Was he being sincere? Was he really more interested in her than in her ranch? Only time would tell. She thought about the moment when he had said that her looks hadn't entered into his plans. She knew he had a side to him that was ambitious and unyielding.

She had to keep her wits about her with the lawyer. She'd better keep her wits about her through everything. And Julian—Gabe's son was adorable. Julian made Gabe's proposition even more appealing. A little boy in her life and a new baby girl. A husband who might fall in love with her. Was she being a fool again to trust him?

The next cloud was telling her relatives. How was she going to break the news to a family who hated Brants?

Six

On Saturday, Ashley, her father, her aunts and uncles and three teenage cousins were gathered in the dining room for lunch.

Ashley looked around the table at her relatives, thinking about each one.

Dark-skinned with black hair streaked with gray, Dusty Ryder was the second-oldest brother and owned a large ranch in the neighboring county. In spite of being younger, Dusty's health wasn't any better than her father's, and he had had to cut back on his work and hire more men.

Colin Ryder was next in line and had a ranch adjoining Dusty's. Colin had had his run of bad luck with a devastating fire and no insurance.

Cal Ryder, a dentist who lived in San Antonio, was the youngest. Although the four brothers resembled each other more as they aged, Cal was the least like the others, with his blond curly hair that didn't hold a hint of their Apache heritage. All four men were over six feet; Dusty was six feet and eight inches. Other than Cal, the brothers had straight, jet-black hair and all of them had dark-brown eyes, along with the brown skin of their father.

Dusty's wife, Kate, smiled at Ashley and Ashley returned her smile. Her Aunt Kate had always been fun to be around, and Ashley had a close bond with her. Colin's wife, brown-haired Cordelia, was wrapped up in her own children and her hobbies. Two of her children, Brett and Ginger, both teens, were present. With diamonds glittering on her fingers, Lucy, Cal's wife, and Jed, their sixteen-year-old son, were present.

Ashley knew that with the wives and children present to keep a lid on the uncles' tempers, this was the best moment she would ever have to give her news. Even though her father had planned to make an announcement about her engagement after the family finished eating, she wanted to take responsibility for breaking the news. She clinked her spoon against her glass and stood.

"I want to make an announcement."

"Ashley," Quinn said swiftly, standing. "Let me tell everyone. They're my brothers. Sit down, honey."

Faces filled with curious expressions swivelled back and forth between Quinn and Ashley. Wanting to avoid further argument, she sat down.

"Now first," Quinn said, "I want you to remember Ashley is only two months from the due date for her baby. I don't want anyone upsetting her. Is that clear, Dusty? Cal? Colin?"

"We're not going to upset Ashley," Dusty said. "Since when have we ever done that?" he asked, looking at Ashley.

"Not ever, Uncle Dusty," she answered and smiled at him, knowing there might be a first in their lives soon.

"All right, here's the news. Ashley is marrying Gabriel Brant."

There was silence until Dusty exploded. "You can't! Dammit, you can't marry a Brant!"

Then all the uncles were talking at once, Kate trying to get Dusty to stop, Lucy and Cordelia talking, too. The din was loud and the three teen cousins stared round-eyed and openmouthed at Ashley.

"Cool!" Ginger exclaimed. "Gabe Brant is good-looking—" The rest of her words were drowned out.

The air was blue with foul language and shouting. Dusty had shoved back his chair so suddenly that it overturned. All three uncles were on their feet and then her father was in a confrontation with Dusty. Ashley hurried to step between them.

Her Uncle Colin caught her arm and pulled her back. Kate put her arms around Ashley and Ginger moved beside her and they hurried Ashley out of the room.

"I don't need to run out of here, Aunt Kate. I don't want to leave Dad. You know what a bad week he's had."

"Your father doesn't let his younger brothers get him too worked up. Let them rant and rave and get it out of their systems. You don't have to listen to them."

"Way to go, Ashley!" Ginger exclaimed. "Gabe Brant's a hunk."

"Ginger, you're man-crazy," Aunt Kate said. "Can't you think of something besides hunks?"

"Oooh, this is awesome! Wow, Ashley, I didn't know I had such an exciting cousin." She wriggled all over. "Now Gabe Brant will be at family things, and I'll get to see him. Can I call my friends and tell them?"

"Yes, you can," Ashley said, knowing Gabe was telling his relatives now, so the word would be out instantly.

"Aunt Kate, I'm afraid of what this will do to Dad's blood pressure."

"You can't shield your daddy from his brothers. He's the oldest, and he can handle them. He always has."

As they went into the formal living room, Ginger fled to call friends. Ashley knew that the two male cousins had probably gone to play pool. Lucy and Cordelia came into the living room and sat down facing Ashley.

"Ashley, I don't know how you can do this," Lucy said. "It will hurt all of us for you to marry one of those horrible Brants. They're disreputable people."

"Lucy, you know that's not so!" Kate snapped. "The Brants move in the same social circles we do, for heaven's sake. You make them sound like thugs."

"They are," Cordelia said. "They're certainly beneath the Ryders and you shouldn't even want to associate with one, much less marry him."

"I'm going to marry him," Ashley said, feeling more certain about her decision, annoyed by all her relatives' stepping in and trying to run her life. "Maybe it's time for the old feud to stop."

"We're going home right now," Lucy snapped, her face turning red. She hurried from the room, and Cordelia left behind her.

"Let them go. They'll accept him someday, but it may take a while," Kate said.

"I just don't want to lose your love," Ashley stated, and Kate hugged her.

"You couldn't ever do that. When your little girl is born, all your aunts and uncles will be right back showering her with love, and you know I'm right."

"I hope so."

"I know you're smart enough to make a sound decision. Just ignore a bunch of silly old uncles. They'll cool down. Anytime you need a substitute mama, give me a call. And I'm going to be an honorary granny to your baby."

"Ashley." She looked up to see Dusty standing in the doorway. "I'd like to talk to you for a minute."

"Of course," she said. Kate stood and hurried from the room, pausing in the doorway to look up at her tall husband.

"Don't you dare cause her any grief."

"I'm not going to," he said, scowling fiercely. Kate nodded and left, and he closed the door behind her.

"Are you really in love with Brant?" Dusty asked bluntly, scowling as he faced her.

"I have strong enough feelings for him to marry him," she replied evenly.

Dusty's brown eyes narrowed. "There are other very nice men around here who would marry you in a minute."

"I'm not interested in others," she answered patiently.

"So it's like that with you and Gabe." He shook his head. "Your father's not well and he's not thinking as sharply as he used to. Two years ago I don't think he would have willingly gone along with this."

"Maybe not, but he is now."

"Yep. I can't help but feel like your dad's situation is causing you to do this. Are you going to move away and leave Quinn here alone?"

"No, we're not. Gabe will live here."

Dusty's eyes narrowed. "Dammit Ashley, at one time I could have just stepped in and bailed Quinn out, but you know I'm trying to keep myself afloat now."

"Uncle Dusty, I *want* to marry Gabe. You don't need to step in."

"Well, I think if you're not careful that Brant is going to take this ranch from you. This is the original spread, and I hate to see it go. I damn well hate to see it go to a Brant."

"Both ranches will merge."

"The hell they will. You don't know the Brant men like I do. His dad was cutthroat ambitious, buying up land around him whenever he could. Gabe Brant is after this land. Your dad is one of the finest horsemen in the world. Brant is a cattleman. He'll get rid of these fine horses, and he'll turn it into a cattle ranch."

"I don't think that's what Gabe intends," she said, trying to be patient.

"You can't see the truth." Dusty frowned, and she knew he was exasperated with her and trying to hold his temper in check. "I can't help what you do, Ashley, but I hate like hell to see my brother destroyed when he's getting up in years and not well.''

"Gabe isn't going to destroy Dad."

"That's what you think now." Dusty placed his hands on his hips and stared at her. "You're wrong about Gabriel Brant. The Brants have always been ruthlessly ambitious, and the young one is no different from his old man. You're going to regret this."

"I don't think I will, Uncle Dusty," she said quietly. "But I appreciate your concern. I won't let him hurt Dad."

"You won't be able to stop him. He's a fast-talking hustler who could sell refrigerators to Eskimos." Dusty crossed the room to put his hands on her shoulders. "You're smart and pretty and you've been successful in your career. I just hate to see you blinded by a fast-talking scoundrel who's going to hurt you and your daddy and your baby."

She looked into his eyes and said, "I've thought about this a lot."

He dropped his hands and walked away. "Think about it a lot more."

Over the next few days Ashley did think about her approaching marriage. She and her father spent hours with their lawyer. Then the lawyers got together. Tuesday, a week after their announcement to their relatives, Gabe called her.

"Ashley, we better rethink this wedding. If you want to go through with this—and I still do—we need to marry soon. I'm talking elopement."

"We can't do that. Look at all our relatives—we can't leave them out."

"Ashley," he said, sounding grim and angry, "someone tore up two miles of my fences last night."

"No!" she said, sitting down and staring into space. "You're blaming a Ryder."

"Well, I think so," he snapped. "Who else? Let's get

together with our lawyers, get this agreement finalized, and then let's elope. Frankly, I'm worried about your place because one of my uncles was with me when I discovered the damage, and he's madder than hell.''

"My relatives wouldn't tear down your fences. They're not vandals," she said, growing angry with him for his snap judgment.

"I think it was a warning to stay away from you. I just don't want to wake up one night to see my barn burning."

"Aren't you overreacting? Maybe it was kids tearing up property."

"One of my men saw someone and chased them. He lost the guy, but it was a green pickup, and he saw the license. I don't think you want me to tell you who owns that pickup."

"Oh, heavens!" she exclaimed, knowing her Uncle Colin had a green pickup. Silence stretched between them again until she spoke. "I guess we should elope, but, if he will, I want Dad to be a witness."

"Fine with me. I've already asked Josh to be my best man, so I'll just ask him to be a witness. He can bring Julian and then take him home afterwards."

"Afterwards? We're not going on a honeymoon?"

"No, we won't, but I thought we could spend the night away from here—in separate rooms. It'll give us a chance to get to know each other a little better. How's that sound?"

She ran her hand across her forehead again. "It's all right."

"Ashley, you sound as if you're being forced to marry Attila the Hun."

"It's just all that's going on and the anger of my relatives, and, after all, Gabe, we're not starry-eyed in love."

There was a long moment of silence. "I want to marry you," he said quietly, and her heart thudded.

"Don't tell me you love me when you don't. If you ever say those words, I want them to be true."

"If I say them, I'll mean them. And I did mean it just now when I said I want to marry you. I miss seeing you and want to be with you, and I'm looking forward to our date tonight."

Her pulse raced at his words, and she clung to the phone. "Thanks, Gabe. And I'm sorry about your fence."

"I've talked with my lawyer, and he can see us at two o'clock today. He's going to call your attorney. Can you and your dad go on such short notice?"

"Yes, we can," she said, her spirits sinking over her uncle's destruction of Gabe's property.

"And then what about flying to San Angelo and getting married Friday? We have to get the license and blood test and a notice will go out in the paper. Do you know anyone who lives in San Angelo? Any of the Ryders?"

"No, I don't know anyone there. That would be fine," she said, taken aback now that the actual wedding was going to happen.

"I'll pick you up about a quarter before one o'clock."

"Fine."

The line clicked and he was gone. She stared at the phone.

"Goodbye, Gabe," she said to no one. She looked out the window and saw her father in the corral with one of his horses. As she went out to tell him the news, all she could think was that she was marrying Gabe Brant within the week.

Friday morning of the first week of June came faster than she thought possible. Her stomach had butterflies along with kicks from a very active baby.

Dressed in a knee-length, two-piece pale-blue silk dress with tiny pearl trim along the border of the overblouse and along the skirt hem, Ashley was conscious of how large her body had gotten. Her hair was looped and pinned on top of her head and Gabe had had a bouquet of white and pale-pink roses delivered to the courthouse, waiting for her.

Now she stood in the courtroom of the San Angelo City Hall, facing a judge who was about to read their wedding vows. Ashley glanced over her shoulder at her father who stood in his seldom-worn navy suit. His hair was parted and combed and he had a slight scowl on his face, but he smiled when she looked at him. She turned back around and looked at Josh Kellogg who was there in a black suit, black boots and a white shirt with a dark tie. He looked handsome and as relaxed as Julian.

Julian was adorable with a little boy's insatiable curiosity about everything around him.

But it was Gabe who took most of her attention and kept her pulse racing. In a navy suit, white shirt, navy tie and black boots, Gabe looked incredibly handsome. She was uniting Ryders' lives with his. Time would tell if her trust was misplaced, she reminded herself. She was committed now.

Was he having second thoughts? Was he happy with this? Or was he working toward a sly takeover of the Triple R? When she gazed into his dark eyes, she could find nothing to reassure her because their dark depths were unfathomable.

When her father placed her cold hand in Gabe's warm one, she turned to face Gabe. His dark gaze seemed to devour her, yet at the same time, she found reassurance there. His brown eyes didn't hold the cool gaze of a businessman about to consummate a deal. Instead, she found warmth and desire. He placed his other hand over her hand.

Her surroundings vanished and she was alone with Gabe, uniting with him in an arrangement that could change so many lives forever.

She and Gabe repeated their vows, vows that held a promise and at the same time scared her without the glow of love. When it came time to exchange rings, she thought of the plain golden bands that Gabe had purchased for both of them. He took her hand and looked into her eyes.

"With this ring, I thee wed," he said with a solemn conviction that made her draw a deep breath.

She looked at the large, tanned fingers in her hand, felt the electric tingle of touching him as she placed a gold band on his finger. Finally, the judge pronounced them man and wife. "You may kiss the bride now," he said.

When Gabe leaned down to kiss her, his lips were warm, lightly brushing hers. Her heart thudded, and her lips parted beneath his. As he raised his head, his dark, searching gaze made her heart beat even faster.

For an instant there was only silence as if they were all caught in a freeze-frame movie still. And then Gabe turned to thank the judge and the moment was gone, Julian began talking and Josh and her dad got into a conversation.

All through lunch she was filled with a bubbling anticipation for the evening ahead of them.

They told Julian, Josh and her father goodbye at the restaurant where the three took a cab back to the airport, leaving Gabe and Ashley standing on the curb, waving as they drove away.

She turned to look at him. "Well, we did it. Now we'll have to see if we can live with it."

"Let's go to the hotel and start planning our wedding reception. I want a real reception—a big, fancy bash that makes all our relatives realize they are now kinfolks."

"It might be a big task."

"We'll have such a party, they'll forget some of the old animosities," Gabe said, smiling at her. He took her hand in his as they strolled toward their hotel.

It was a hot afternoon with a deep blue sky and thick, white clouds. Ashley was conscious only of the tall man at her side and the new ring on her finger.

Gabe had taken two adjoining suites on the top floor of an eight-story hotel. "Get into something comfortable and come to my suite."

She changed to a sundress and sandals, leaving her hair

still fastened on top of her head, then went to his suite and knocked on the door.

It swung open and he stood there barefoot and in jeans, a T-shirt in hand, his belt still unbuckled. ''Well, you do surprise me, Mrs. Brant, a woman who can change clothes faster than I can. Come in.''

Seven

—

Dimly she heard him say, *Mrs. Brant,* but she was mesmerized by the sight of his bare chest. He was tan, muscled, and extremely fit. When she realized how she was staring, she blinked, blushed and looked up to meet a curious gaze. "Come in," he said in a husky voice that ignited desire.

When she stepped inside, he closed the door and put his hand on it over her head, blocking her and standing entirely too close.

The man could still befuddle her as much as he had when they were kids. Her pulse was racing, and she couldn't breathe and that marvelous male chest was inches in front of her. And she was aware of her size, too.

"I seem to remember," he drawled in a sexy, husky voice that sent tingles rippling along her nerves, "that you said something to the effect that never in the next two lifetimes would you be alone in a hotel room with me."

"I was wrong. You've turned my life upside-down."

He traced his finger along her cheek to her ear and then

down across her throat. "I think I'm the one whose life is topsy-turvy. I expected one thing and here I have another. I want to know you, Ashley, to know everything about you— what you like to eat, what you like to read, what you do for fun. I want to kiss and touch you and feel the electricity that sizzles between us."

He caressed her throat in the barest of touches, yet it made her pulse jump. "I'll tell you what," he said softly. "I don't know whether my new wife can cook. I don't know whether you can sew. But I know you can kiss a man into spontaneous combustion."

"Can I?" she asked, slanting him a look. She stepped closer and wrapped her arms around his neck. "Let's see how long it takes me, Gabe." She closed her eyes and kissed him. For one brief second, she realized she had taken him by surprise. Then his arm banded her, and he held her and kissed her passionately.

Her heart pounded and all her qualms and fears fell away. She wanted this tall, sexy cowboy who could set her heart pounding, who was decisive and thrilling and handsome.

In seconds their breathing was ragged, and then she leaned back. "Slow down. We rushed into marriage. We're not rushing into anything else."

He smiled at her and ran his finger along her jaw. "Whatever you want," he said in a husky voice and stepped away.

She walked across the sitting room of his suite. Looking around, she saw that the room was very much like hers with cherrywood furniture, a large television, a bar, an adjoining bed and bath. Floor-to-ceiling windows ran around two sides of the corner room, giving a view on one side of the patio and pool area and on the other of tennis courts and a putting green. She turned around as he buckled his belt and then yanked his T-shirt over his head, his muscles rippling.

He had a marvelous body that made her pulse jump. His stomach was flat, with solid muscles. Her mouth went dry, and she knew that all too easily she could walk right back into his arms. Realizing how she was staring at his body, she looked up and met his curious gaze. His brow arched and she turned her back to him, moving to the window, both embarrassed and annoyed with herself.

"I've got cold beer and wine and I know you can't drink either, so I ordered up a pitcher of lemonade and I have pop and ice water. What can I get you to drink?"

"Lemonade, but if you don't mind, I'm worn out. I'd like a nap and then we can plan a party."

"Sure. I'd like to go for a swim. You can sleep here."

She smiled at him. "I'm not getting into your bed," she said, laughing.

One brow arched wickedly. "And I think I just got another one of those challenges from you. Sort of an 'I double-dare you.'"

"It certainly wasn't!" She smiled at him, "I'm going to have to learn when you're teasing."

"I'm not teasing right now. I'm in earnest."

"We'll see," she answered coolly. "I'll go take a nap and you go swim, and then we'll make our plans."

She knew he was watching her as she walked out of the room. Before she closed the door, she turned to look at him and his smoldering gaze took her breath. In her room she leaned against the door. He could set her heart racing more now than when she had been a teenager, and it wasn't fair.

Sheer curtains were pulled back on either side of the floor-to-ceiling windows. She crossed the room to look below. The pool and patio area was filled with black wrought-iron tables, palm trees and pots of flowers. As she watched, Gabe came into sight. He dropped a towel on a chaise lounge and headed toward the deep end of the pool, which had few people in it. She drew another deep breath at the sight of his fit body. He was tanned, all muscles and wore a narrow, black swimsuit.

He had said he was willing to forgo a physical relationship. Josh had told her that Gabe was wrapped in grief, but she suspected he was coming out of his grief. While he had promised no physical demands, after the kiss they had just shared, she knew that when he decided to, he would probably seduce her. The thought made her hot and tingly.

"I hope I have sense enough to halfway resist you until we have some kind of real relationship," she whispered. She went to the king-size bed and stretched out, replaying in her mind their wedding that seemed like a dream.

It was two hours later when she stirred. She showered, changed again into a full blue shirt and denim jumper. As she combed her hair and secured it behind her head, she walked to the windows. Still at poolside, Gabe sat on the foot of a chaise on the shady side of the pool. He had a newspaper spread before him and a white towel draped across his shoulders.

She didn't care to sit alone in an empty hotel room, so she pocketed her key and went downstairs.

"Hi," she said, as she walked up behind him.

He glanced over his shoulder and then stood and at close range, the bare body that had looked so fit from her hotel window was sexy perfection up close. She couldn't keep from letting her gaze drift over him. The black swimsuit covered little and she realized she had just married a man who had an extremely sexy body.

"I've had my nap and I didn't want to sit in a hotel room by myself."

"Don't blame you." He folded the paper. "Let's go to my room. I'll change, and we can have those drinks now."

He took her arm and she was overwhelmingly conscious of him walking beside her, that tiny strip of black and the white towel around his shoulders the only coverings he had. At his hotel door, he stepped forward to unlock it and she gave him another swift, raking glance, looking at his muscled back tapering to a tiny waist, narrow hips and butt. His legs were sprinkled with short, dark-brown hair. She looked up as he opened the door and strolled inside, pulling off his towel.

"I'll get your lemonade and then I want to shower."

As she watched him pour the lemonade, his gaze swept over her, and she felt bigger than ever.

"You looked beautiful today."

"Thank you. I feel as big as a barn. I was envying your flat stomach."

Just then her shirt rippled on her stomach, and she felt the baby kick. She put her hand on her stomach. "My baby." She took Gabe's hand and looked at him questioningly. "Want to feel her kick?"

"Yes," he answered and she placed his hand against her stomach while she and Gabe locked gazes. It was a terribly personal moment, and she wondered if he sincerely was interested in her baby.

"Have you picked out a name?"

"Actually, when I've gone over lists, the name I liked best and the one I had in mind was Ella, the same name as your first wife. I can find another one if you'd rather."

"No," he said, his gaze still boring into her. "Ella would be very nice. I'd like that. Aah!" he exclaimed, a surprised and happy expression coming to his features. "I felt her. Ashley, I'm going to think of her as *our* baby, yours and mine. I'll be the only daddy she'll ever know."

"You will if things work out between us," Ashley whispered breathlessly, trying to resist his words that tempted her to let go of all caution and trust him completely.

He slipped his hand behind her head to kiss her, finally leaning away. "It's going to be good between us."

"I hope so," she said, knowing it was far too soon to know what their future together would be.

"Make yourself comfortable. I'm going to shower and then I'll be right back."

Wondering about him, she watched him disappear into the bedroom. She sat in a comfortable chair and put her feet up on an ottoman, looking at the new ring on her finger, filled with wonder about it. Julian had wanted to sit beside her at lunch which made her feel good. She didn't have to guard her heart around him and knew she was going to love him.

She intended to tell Gabe she would keep Julian some of the time. Even after the baby came, with Mrs. Farrin and her father always around, she would be able to manage.

"Sorry to keep you waiting," Gabe said, crossing the room. He carried a T-shirt and had his wet hair slicked back from his face and her pulse jumped at the sight of him. Her new husband was incredibly handsome, and she just hoped she wasn't being taken in by a handsome, charming man as she had been taken in so easily once before in her life.

Gabe dropped his shirt on the chair and threaded his belt through the loops on his jeans, buckling it and then pulling on his T-shirt. "I'll get you more lemonade," he said, picking up her half-full glass.

He returned with her lemonade and his cold beer and sat down across from her to try to plan a wedding reception.

"I want a real reception," he said. "Let's have food and music that each of our families can't resist so they'll have a good time in spite of their animosity."

"Too bad we can't have Vince Gill. He's Uncle Dusty's and Uncle Colin's favorite singer."

"He's my aunt's favorite. I'll see what I can do."

"No way! You can't get a celebrity!" she protested.

"You don't know until you try," Gabe replied.

She stared at him. "Nothing daunts you, does it? Except death," she added, remembering when she had asked if he had ever failed to get what he wanted. She covered his hand with hers. "I'm sorry—I've reminded you of something that hurts."

"You're helping me through the hurt," he replied, shifting his hand to hold hers. He rubbed her knuckles with his thumb while she smiled at him.

"Vince Gill. There's no way my family could resist. But I still think it's impossible."

Gabe winked at her. "Another challenge that I can't resist."

He released her hand to write notes while they planned

and she knew whether they had a star to sing or not, it was going to be a grand party.

Later, Gabe ordered dinner sent to their room and they sat and talked until shortly after eleven o'clock when she stood.

"As much fun as the evening has been, I have to go to my room. I'm not accustomed to staying up late any longer."

"I'll walk you to your door," he said, draping his arm across her shoulders.

She laughed when he said he would walk her to her door which, since they had adjoining suites, was only yards away. When she opened her door, she looked into her room. "It locks from either side."

"You can lock me out. I hadn't planned on trying to sneak in during the night." He framed her face with his hands. "When we finally make love, I want it to be very special. And that time will come, Ashley," he said in a husky voice that made her heart thud as much as his kisses did.

"That would be good," she whispered. "And today was good, and I hope love comes to us, Gabe." She slid her hand behind his head and leaned forward to kiss him. He held her lightly, returning her kiss until she stopped him.

"For now, good night."

"Good night, Mrs. Brant. Someday, Ashley, we won't say good night like this. I'll carry you to my bed with me."

She inhaled swiftly, looking into his dark eyes that confirmed his words. "'Night," she repeated, stepped into her room and closed the door. She took deep breaths and wondered how long before her pulse calmed and her heartbeat returned to normal. She was going to fall in love with her handsome husband. She just prayed it wasn't a mistake.

In the middle of June they had a spectacular reception at the hotel in San Antonio that did include a celebrity singer and caused the Ryders and the Brants to lose their hostility for one grand evening. Friends from several counties poured into the large ballroom and adjoining dining hall to join the festivities.

Ashley wore her blue silk wedding dress and had her hair secured behind her head with a clasp covered in blue silk and pearls.

Darcy Vickers, petite, blond and her closest friend from Chicago, had come for the party along with five other Chicago friends. Gabe's friends arrived along with the Brants and Ryders. The Brants congregated on one side of the room while the Ryders sat on the other.

As Ashley looked at Gabe, she barely thought about her relatives. In a navy suit he looked dashing, handsome, dangerous. Gabe's dark eyes were inscrutable and she wondered what he really felt.

At least Julian and her father, both cooks and the foremen from both ranches seemed happy for them even if the relatives weren't.

When the band began with a waltz, Gabe took Ashley's hand to lead her to the middle of the dance floor where she stepped easily into his arms.

"Well, we've done it, and lightning hasn't struck us, although your relatives look as if they would like to get out their trusty forty-fives and get rid of me," he said.

"No more than your relatives would like to get rid of me," she replied, glancing beyond Gabe at the ring of onlookers. More than half of them looked enraged, while blatant curiosity filled the expressions of the others. As all three of her uncles stood watching her, she could feel the invisible waves of anger. "I'm making some of my family very unhappy. They've given me dire predictions about your motives."

"Have they now?"

"Goodness only knows what your relatives have said about me—only don't tell me. I don't even want to know."

"Don't worry, I'm not going to tell you. What I will tell you is that you look gorgeous, and the males in six counties are turning green with envy."

She smiled. "Thank you, and I think you exaggerate. I'm

very pregnant,'' she replied, yet she warmed to his compliment.

Ignoring the looks of angry relatives, she tossed away her
worries, not caring at the moment what the guests thought.
It was heaven to dance again, to move around the floor in
Gabe's arms, and there was something settling and reassuring about him that lowered her guard. And something very
appealing. She still remembered her reaction to his brief kiss
at their wedding, a kiss that meant nothing to him and should
have meant nothing to her. Instead, her heart had fluttered
and her breath had caught.

"Your Chicago friends are nice. Good looking women,
too."

"So you notice a few things."

"Sure, I notice. I just haven't had much physical reaction
to it."

"They want to meet cowboys," Ashley said.

"Well, they came to the right place, although Josh is
about as reclusive as a bear in winter, but there are plenty
of others around."

"I frankly hope no one else, except Dad and my uncles,
wants to dance with me."

"You're safe with Josh. I doubt if he'll dance, and my
uncles won't ask you to dance," Gabe replied. "Look at all
of them now. The Ryders on one side of the yard, the Brants
on the other, and they're not mixing. They're the Hatfields
and the McCoys all over again."

"They can keep on feuding. I think we're doing the right
thing." She was aware that she moved easily with Gabe, as
if they had danced together many times. And she was aware
of how handsome he looked, wondering if she was going to
lose that hurt caused by Lars and fall in love with her new
husband. He was gazing beyond her, lost in his thoughts,
and she wondered whether he was remembering his first
wedding when he had been wildly in love. The thought saddened her, both for him and for the moment, but she knew

that his grief was part of him and would be part of her life, too.

She noticed Josh Kellogg standing on the sidelines talking with her father.

"I've heard the Kellogg ranch is in trouble. That might be one you could have bought."

"Josh's busting himself trying to salvage what his old man wrecked. If he ever has to sell any land, I told him to come to me first, but knowing Josh and knowing how hard he's working to make a go of it, I'd never take advantage of his situation. I'd loan him the money he needs." Gabe looked down at her. "I guess now, *we* would be loaning him the money and we'd have to discuss it. You might not approve."

"You could probably do it without disturbing anything that's mine."

"Yep. I can, but we need to work together as much as possible."

"I'm glad you feel that way," she admitted. "That's reassuring if you really mean it."

"I mean it. I'll always level with you, Ashley," he said. His dark eyes were wide and clear and he looked as if he meant what he said.

"I hope so."

The dance ended and her father came to claim the next one. She danced with each of her uncles before she was back in Gabe's arms again for a fast two-step that had him shedding his coat and getting rid of his tie. He had relaxed and was a good dancer. She wondered about his past and if life was empty and tedious for him now and that's why he had thrown himself into work so much. She hurt for his loss again and was sorry for the turn of fate, hoping she could help bring some kind of warmth and fun back into his life, knowing that Julian helped immeasurably because Gabe brightened whenever he was around his son.

Gabe danced easily, relaxed, too satisfied with his new marriage to worry about the wrath of his relatives. They would adjust in time, and before long they would be talking about his big ranch. Gabe's thoughts shifted from the ranch to Ashley. She was beautiful, and she was smiling at him as she danced. He let his gaze wander down to her mouth that looked sensual and was so soft.

This awareness of her still startled him. He expected it to pass and dwindle away, not increase. She was very pregnant, yet she moved easily and seemed tireless. There was a sparkle in her eyes he hadn't seen before, so he hoped she was happy with this union, too. A little girl. He didn't know one thing about little girls. The prospect of having a daughter put butterflies in his stomach. It would be one more thing he would deal with when the time came.

The party grew livelier and the people who were the most angry left early until finally it was only Ashley's dad, Julian and their closest friends. Then they all adjourned for the Ryder ranch where Ashley and Gabe brought out drinks and their friends stayed for another hour.

Darcy told them goodbye, leaving with one of the local ranchers, Ed Rebman. Quinn Ryder went to bed, and Gabe had long ago put Julian to bed. Now Gabe sat on the porch, his feet propped on the rail, his shirt unbuttoned to the waist, sipping a cold beer while he talked to his friend Josh about cattle.

Ashley sat beside Gabe, content, knowing that now her baby would be Ella Brant with a large family, including an older brother, to love her. As Gabe talked, he reached over to take Ashley's hand, lacing his fingers through hers.

Surprised, she glanced at him. He was turned away talking to Josh, and she wondered whether he even realized he had taken her hand. He was relaxed about casually touching her. She knew it didn't mean anything to him beyond a friendly gesture.

When Josh came to his feet, Gabe stood. "I need to get going and leave you folks alone," Josh said. "I wish you both the best," he added, shaking hands with Gabe and turning to her. "'Night, Ashley. You got a good man." He tapped Gabe's chest. "And you, *amigo,* got a very wonderful woman."

"I'm finding that out," Gabe answered.

"Thank you," she told Josh, surprised by his compliment because she didn't think they knew each other that well. She watched Gabe's friend walk down the porch steps. Josh Kellogg was over six feet tall, maybe an inch shorter than Gabe, with dark brown hair. She knew his father had married a half-dozen times and none of the wives lasted long, although Josh seemed to have stayed friends with all his stepmothers. Quiet and solemn, Josh was as tough as Gabe. She had seen both of them ride in rodeos and had seen both of them at feedlots. She knew Gabe considered Josh his closest friend.

As they watched Josh drive away, Gabe slipped his arm across her shoulders. "And a good time was had by all. Or at least by half of us," he added lightly. "All the disgruntled, battling Ryders and Brants went home early."

"That they did. Josh's nice."

"He's great. We've been friends since we were too little to remember. It used to be Josh and Wyatt Sawyer and me, but Wyatt's as wild as Josh's dad—maybe wilder. Years ago when we were in high school, he ran away from home. He's the reason I hope to hell I can be a good dad for Julian, and it scared me to go it alone."

"Why?"

"Wyatt's mother died when he was only three. His dad was a lousy father. Damn fine businessman—he's one of the wealthiest men in Texas."

"I barely know him, but he was there tonight."

"Yeah, but you invited him. I wouldn't have. I guess he remembers what close friends Wyatt and I were. He's a bastard. He was terrible to Wyatt. I would have run away sooner than Wyatt did if I'd had an abusive father like Duke Sawyer. I don't think he's heard from Wyatt in years. I don't think anyone around here has."

"I remember Wyatt vaguely because all the girls thought he was the best looking cowboy in Texas."

Gabe laughed. "That's Wyatt."

"I think you came in second."

"No kidding!" Gabe said, grinning at her. He turned to face her, squeezing her shoulder. "We did it, Ashley, and it was a fun party. I'll have to admit, in a lot of ways I dreaded tonight because of my first reception, but the evening was all right. Thanks for a good time. I haven't had many in too long a time."

His arm was warm across her shoulders, and she felt good about his praise. "I'm glad. It was a fun party for me, too," she replied.

"You're getting cheated in some ways because if you'd waited, you could have fallen in love and married for real, darlin'."

She knew the endearment was as casual as his hugs, but it pleased her.

"Let's go to bed," he said. "You're probably tired. You and the baby. Our baby now." As they entered the kitchen, she glanced at him.

"Want anything to drink?" she asked.

"I might get one more beer and sit on the porch a few minutes longer," he said, yanking off his shirt and tossing it over a chair as he opened the fridge and leaned down to search for a beer.

As he peeled away his shirt, Ashley stood transfixed. His tanned chest was solid muscles. Her mouth went dry and she was riveted, unable to look away. He moved to the fridge to look inside and she watched muscles ripple in his back with his movements. He was incredibly sexy and appealing and to her surprise, she was reacting to that sexiness.

He turned. "You want anything?" His eyebrows arched, otherwise, he didn't show any sign of noticing her reaction, but she was flustered, embarrassed how she had reacted and how he had caught her staring at him.

"Good night, Gabe," she said, hurrying out of the room

and feeling ridiculous, but it had been an awkward moment. She went down the hall to her room and closed the door. She crossed the room to look at herself in the mirror. With her dark skin, blushes rarely showed, but she could feel the heat in her face. Surprised by her own reaction, she pictured Gabe whipping off his shirt. She had married an incredibly appealing man who seemed to barely know she existed, treating her almost in the same manner he did her dad. What kind of bargain had she made?

After the party, through the rest of June and into July, their lives became routine. Gabe and Julian had adjoining bedrooms across the hall from Ashley's bedroom and the nursery. Immediately, Quinn occupied the large master bedroom at the opposite end of the hall. Gabe immersed himself into helping her father and taking charge of the Ryder ranch so Ashley saw little of him most of the week.

When Lou was off duty, Ashley kept Julian and found she enjoyed the little boy whose dark eyes were so much like his father's. It came as no surprise to Ashley when Julian and her father bonded swiftly. Quinn accepted Julian as much as if he were his full grandson and Julian was soon tagging along behind Quinn whenever he was home.

Living under the same roof with Gabe, even though he was gone most of the day, Ashley realized she was becoming more and more aware of him. When he touched her now, she was more disturbed than before, something she hadn't thought possible. Where his light hugs had been comforting, they were now stimulating. Both Gabe and her father were solicitous of her well-being, and she thought she should be satisfied and happy, but her sensitivity to Gabe's presence was becoming more acute all the time. Then it seemed to fade away and she relaxed, most of her focus shifting to Julian and getting ready for the baby.

On Thursday evening Gabe entered the kitchen. He was dusty, had a scratch on the back of his hand and his shirt sleeve was ripped, but his dark eyes sparkled.

Ashley was watching Quinn peel and cut up an orange

for Julian. Now Gabe had everyone's attention. Julian ran to throw himself into his father's arms. In spite of Gabe's disheveled appearance, Ashley's heartbeat quickened at the sight of him.

"I've got your horse, Quinn."

Quinn raised his shaggy eyebrows in curiosity. "What horse?"

"We caught that wild, white stallion today," Gabe said, grinning, and Ashley realized he was proud of his catch.

"Son of a gun!" Quinn exclaimed. "You actually caught that hellion. Every inch of him is wild. I've tangled with him, but I never could bring him in. Let's go look at him. Where is he?"

"I've got him in the pasture by the barn. Let's go."

"Can I go?" Julian asked.

"Sure can," Gabe said, swinging his son up to ride on his shoulders. Gabe looked at Ashley. "Want to come see this legendary horse?"

"Of course, I do," she replied. "He's going to bring you true love now," she said, teasing Gabe, and he grinned.

"If he does, he'll bring true love to you, too. He's your horse now, too. Maybe Quinn's going to fall in love. Which widow is it going to be, Quinn?" Gabe asked, teasing his father-in-law who had widows occasionally calling him.

"I think I remember hearing you say that you'd get rid of the rascal if you caught him. So the person who gets him will find love, not those left behind."

"I'm taking a picture of this," Ashley said. "Wait a moment while I get my camera."

As soon as she returned, they poured out of the house and both men slowed their step so Ashley could keep up with them.

As they neared the fence, she saw the stallion. He was white and as spotless as if he had just been given a bath. He raised his head, snorted and pawed the ground, his ears standing up.

"He is pretty," Ashley said.

"Pretty as sin," Quinn remarked. "He isn't going to like being cooped up."

"Might not, but he isn't getting over this fence," Gabe said. This pasture held high, pipe fencing and the horse ran nervously along a stretch of ground beside the fence.

"Dad, you know he's pretty. You have to be impressed."

"I'm impressed as hell that Gabe caught him," Quinn replied. "He's pretty, but he doesn't have the pure blood-lines of our horses and I don't want him anywhere near my mares."

"Stand by the fence, Gabe, and let me get a picture," Ashley urged. She snapped one and then Quinn took the camera from her.

"Get over there with him and I'll take one of both of you."

"I didn't have anything to do with capturing the horse," she said, but Gabe extended his hand and she took his hand in hers and stepped beside him. Quinn snapped their picture and then Gabe took one of Ashley, Quinn and Julian with the stallion in the background.

"Are you going to ride him?" Julian asked in a high voice, and Gabe laughed.

"No, I'm definitely not. He and I agree on that one. I think I'll call Josh and see if he'd like to take the stallion off our hands. If Josh says no, I've got several people in mind. You have anyone you know, Quinn, who would want him?"

"I don't. He's a hellion. I'll never know how you caught him."

"It took seven of us to get him boxed in and then we backed a trailer up and ran him into it. He kicked the day-lights out of the trailer, but it's an old one of mine. I thought we might lose him before we got here and could turn him loose, but we didn't."

"Well, cowboy, did you work up an appetite?" Ashley asked him. "Supper's almost ready."

"I could eat that horse, I'm so hungry."

They all turned back toward the house. "I just can't believe you've got him. Damn good, Gabe," Quinn said.

"Thanks," Gabe replied easily.

Two nights later, Josh agreed that he would come over soon and try to move the white stallion to his ranch, but the time was postponed, and the stallion remained at the Triple R, a spectacle that friends and townspeople came out to the ranch to view.

As Ashley's due date, the thirteenth of July, approached, she forgot about the stallion.

By the sixteenth, she began having twinges and mild contractions. Gabe rushed her to the hospital twice, only to be sent home because of false labor.

On the twenty-fourth of July, a Monday afternoon, Ashley drove back to the ranch from Stallion Pass where she had had her hair cut and stopped at the grocery. While her hair was being cut, contractions had started again. After two false labors, she didn't think this would be the real thing either, so she finished her haircut and went to the grocery store.

Even though she was in her thirty-ninth week, she wasn't going to the hospital for a third time until she knew that she was really going to have this baby.

When she was halfway home, the first hard contraction came. In another five miles she had a contraction that almost doubled her over.

Gripping the wheel, she slowed and pulled off the road. "Not now," she said aloud to herself.

She yanked up the cell phone and called her father, first paging him and then, when he didn't answer his pager, trying his cellular phone. She knew Julian was with Gabe out on the ranch somewhere.

Feeling panic, she turned the ignition on and tried to drive, hoping to get home, but with the next contraction, she couldn't. Gritting her teeth, she pulled off the road beneath a shady cottonwood and tried home again, getting the answering machine. She rummaged in her purse, found a slip of paper with Gabe's cellular number and called him.

"Yep?" she heard his deep voice, but she was in the throes of a hard contraction and didn't want to talk.

"Gabe—"

"What's wrong?"

"I'm on the road," she paused to pant, "about twenty minutes from the entrance to our ranch. I can't find Dad. I'm in labor. I think it's real this time."

"I'll be right there. I'll call nine-one-one now. Keep your phone on, and I'll call you back."

She opened both doors to get a breeze and stretched out across the seat. "Not here and not now, please," she whispered, wiping her brow.

In minutes the phone rang. She answered and heard Gabe on the other end. "I'm on my way."

"Where's Julian? Is he with you?"

"He's with my foreman, and he's fine. I've called your doctor and he'll be available if you have the baby in the pickup."

"Gabe, I don't want to deliver this baby myself," she said, gasping.

"When did all this start?"

"A long time ago," she said, not wanting to tell him that she had experienced twinges and contractions off and on since the first false labor. "But it really started this morning in Stallion Pass."

"Ashley, why the hell didn't you go to the hospital? Why were you even in Stallion Pass in the first place?"

"I've been to the hospital twice and it was false labor!" she snapped. "Now stop yelling at me and start being a help."

"I'm not yelling and I'm on my way. You won't have to deliver by yourself. You keep talking to me."

"I don't think—" Her sentence was forgotten as another contraction came.

"Ashley! Ashley? Are you all right?"

"No! I'm in labor and I don't feel like talking!" She

turned off her phone and dropped it on the floor beside her. "Just get here," she whispered.

Time blurred in a haze of heat and pain and relief between contractions. Twice she turned on her phone and tried to find her father, leaving messages everywhere she called.

Occasionally, cars raced past and every time, she wondered if it would be Gabe. And then he was there, his pickup door slamming.

"Ashley!" he called and appeared at her feet. She raised her head to look at him, thankful to see him arrive.

"I'm here and help is on the way," he said, leaning into the pickup to touch her cheek. "I'm in contact with the doctor, so just relax. You're not alone," he said calmly, smoothing her hair from her face, and some of her panic receded.

"When will that ambulance get here?"

"They're on their way, but the Stallion Pass ambulance had gone to a wreck on the highway, so we had to get one from San Antonio."

"That's going to be too late, Gabe. My contractions are less than two minutes apart now."

"The ambulance will get here fast. If the baby isn't ready to deliver and if you can ride, I can drive you to meet the ambulance."

"Let's try that," she said.

"All right. Let me get things from my pickup."

In minutes they were driving toward the city. Gabe had the air conditioner on again, and she was cooler.

"Gabe!" she gasped as another hard contraction came. "Gabe, I don't know how long—"

He took her hand and held it, driving with one hand on the straight road that had little traffic. She was barely aware of his presence other than knowing that she was no longer alone.

Fifteen minutes later, she gasped. "Gabe, this baby is coming now!"

Eight

Pulling off the road, Gabe cut the motor, and she heard the rumble of his voice as he talked to someone on his cellular phone. They were parked beneath a spreading oak, and a slight breeze played through the leaves.

Gabe stepped out of the pickup. "I'm going to get the back ready. Fortunately, I've got two blankets and part of a clean sheet. Just a few minutes and I'll move you."

"You can't deliver this baby!"

"Oh, yes, I can," he answered calmly. "Remember, I've been delivering animals for a long time now."

"A baby is different."

"Ashley, it's not that different." He leaned forward to squeeze her shoulder. "I have professionals on the phone. We'll be fine."

She relaxed. Gabe sounded confident and calm and she was willing to leave things up to him and let go of her fears.

She didn't know how much later it was that he came

around to open the other door. "Ashley, can you sit up where I can reach you and carry you to the back of the pickup?"

She panted as a contraction stopped. "I'll try," she said. "I want something to put over me."

"I've got part of a clean sheet. You're between contractions. I'm moving you."

With great care he lifted her into his arms. She wrapped her arm around his neck, feeling his solid strength, thankful he was with her. Gently, he placed her on a blanket in the back of the truck. She had more space and it was cooler than the cramped front seat.

"You and little Ella will be fine," Gabe said soothingly. He poured ice water from a thermos onto a bandanna and sponged her forehead. "I talked to Gus and he's on his way. He'll find your dad and get him here. Your dad and your uncles have gone to a horse sale."

"This isn't what I expected," she whispered.

"Gabe, if anyone stops to help, you keep strangers away. I want some degree of privacy," she said.

"Don't worry, Ashley. Leave it all up to me. You just breathe and relax between contractions," he said, smiling at her and stroking her hair away from her face.

She looked at him as he moved around her. They had developed a friendly relationship, but she knew if he delivered her baby, she would have to give her body over to him in the most intimate way, and she would have to trust him completely.

He poured more water on the bandanna, placing it on her forehead. "Babies have their own agendas about when they'll come into the world. For such tiny little people, they have a way of taking charge of your life."

She smiled, and Gabe's hand slipped down to cup her cheek tenderly. "That's my girl. We'll get this baby here, Ashley."

A contraction gripped her in a wave of pain that wiped

out all other considerations. When she cried out, Gabe held her hand. "You're doing fine," he said quietly.

He moved between her legs, spreading the half sheet over her stomach. As the wave passed, she looked at him between her legs. Before she could think, another contraction came, and she had to push.

"Gabe, I'm going to have this baby. I should be in the hospital—" she gasped, some of her panic returning.

"You're doing great," he said calmly.

"Suppose the baby needs something special—"

"Right now everything is as normal as blueberry pie."

"Oh!" Through the haze of pain, her panic subsided as Gabe talked in a steady, calm voice. His confidence was catching and she concentrated on contractions, no longer thinking about the doctor or ambulance or hospital.

She lost all sense of time as more contractions came.

"Push, Ashley. Bear down and push." Gabe held her hand and she was aware of squeezing his hand tightly.

"That's it! Good going!" he said, calling encouragement. His voice was a steady reassurance and she was calm, feeling secure, now excited to have her baby.

"I can see the head, Ashley! That's the way. Push. We're going to have a baby here."

Dimly she could hear Gabe's encouragement, but she was lost in pain and a force that she seemed to have no control over. Yet through it all, she was aware of his eager voice, telling her what a great job she was doing.

"Gabe—" she cried out, feeling wracked by a contraction. And then she felt the baby being born and she heard Gabe's exultant voice.

"Push! That's it, Ashley! That's great. Here's our girl, Ashley! Here's our beautiful girl!"

Gabe placed the baby on her bare stomach. "There she is," he said, looking at Ashley and bending down to kiss her forehead. "You did great, and we have a beautiful baby girl."

With Gabe's words and the tone of his voice. Ashley felt

something inside her clutch and warm. She squeezed his hand and he brushed another kiss on her cheek.

Gabe moved back between Ashley's legs, working and listening to directions from the doctor on the phone. She pulled the baby close, looking at the little girl in her arms and tears of joy streamed unheeded.

Finally, Gabe took his T-shirt to wrap around the baby as best he could.

"Gabe, thank you. I wasn't very cooperative—"

"You were great," he said, bending down to kiss her forehead again. He touched the baby's cheek. "Even if she needs to be cleaned up, she's beautiful, Ashley."

"Little Ella," she said.

"Our Ella," he echoed, his voice becoming hoarse. "I think it's a miracle, Ashley."

"You're certain naming the baby Ella will be all right?"

"I think it'll be the best possible name." With great care Gabe took the tiny baby into his arms, looking at her strands of black hair and wondering if she would look like her mother, knowing he would love her and be a father to her. "She's beautiful," he said, feeling as touched as if she were his own baby. "Little Ella," he repeated, his throat closing. Thank God she was healthy and normal and the birth had been routine! He gave the baby back to Ashley and stroked locks of Ashley's hair from her face.

"Thank you for all you did." It was then that she realized he was shaking. "Gabe?" She caught his hand. "You're trembling."

"Reaction."

"You were so cool and collected."

"I wasn't quite as calm as I sounded. You were right, there is a world of difference between a baby and a calf or a colt."

"Well, you could have fooled me. You sounded as if you had delivered dozens of babies." Impulsively, she pulled his hand up and brushed a kiss across his knuckles. They looked into each other's eyes, and she felt a bonding with him that ran deep. He wrapped his hand around hers and gave her a gentle squeeze.

"We did good together, honey."

Her heart thudded as she gazed into his eyes and then he leaned down to envelop both her and little Ella in a gentle embrace. "We did really good together," he whispered.

"I'm glad you were with me."

He straightened up and looked beyond her. "Hey, here comes the cavalry," he said, and she heard engines. "Here comes Gus and your dad leading the ambulance."

She covered herself with the sheet. "Gabe, this is bad enough with you and dad, but Gus—"

Gabe grinned. "I won't let Gus near you. Hang tight. I'll meet them." He swung over the side of the pickup and jumped down. Doors slammed and she heard the wail of a siren.

"They're too late," she said, smiling at the tiny baby who had stirred up such a storm with her arrival.

Two hours later in a San Antonio hospital, Ashley was propped up in bed with Ella nearby in a bassinet. Gabe had stepped out and bought a new shirt and jeans and had showered in her adjoining bathroom. He looked as fresh as if he had just gotten up on the ranch in the morning. He had brought her a huge bouquet of pink roses.

At a knock on the door, he stood and turned as Julian came into the room, his hand held by Quinn Ryder. Julian flew to Ashley's bedside to give her a hug.

Her dad held a bouquet of mixed flowers which he set down and crossed the room to give her a hug and a kiss. "When you came back from Chicago and said you wanted to have this baby at home, I didn't know you meant in a pickup out near the ranch."

She laughed. "I didn't."

"Let's see your new little sister," Quinn told Julian as he carefully picked up the tiny baby.

"Can I hold my little sister?" Julian asked.

"Yes, you may," Ashley said.

"You're sure?" Gabe asked, and she nodded.

Quinn motioned to the sofa. "You sit down, Julian, and I'll put her in your lap." Quinn carefully handed the baby to Julian and Gabe sat next to his son while Quinn settled on the other side of him.

"She's little," Julian said.

"Yes, she is. So were you at one time," Gabe said, smiling.

"She's perfect," Quinn said. "Delivering all those calves must have given you experience," he told Gabe.

"It wasn't quite the same, but it helped."

Ashley looked at the men in her life. Her marriage wasn't real yet, but she saw hope, and Gabe had been a tower of strength for her today. She felt a closeness to him now that ran deep. Gabe's dark head was bent over his son and the baby. She remembered his words clearly, *"Our baby..."* He acted very much the proud father, and she was relieved that he had completely accepted Ella from the first moment.

Bringing gifts, her aunts and uncles came to visit and Gabe discreetly took Julian and left, staying away for a couple of hours and returning after the Ryders had gone. Friends visited, and then finally only her father, Julian and Gabe were there. "I'll take everyone out to dinner," Gabe said. "Want me to bring you something?"

"No, thanks," she answered, feeling exhausted. The moment she waved goodbye to them, she fell asleep.

When she stirred, she opened her eyes to find Gabe relaxed in a chair, his long legs stretched out and his sock feet on the foot of her bed.

"How long have you been back? Where are Julian and Dad?"

"They've gone home. Your dad is keeping Julian tonight. I'll spend the night. That sofa makes into a bed."

"You don't have to do that," she said, surprised.

"I know I don't have to," he answered easily. "I didn't want to leave you two here by yourselves this first night."

"That's sweet, Gabe."

"This is an exciting moment in our lives, Ashley, and I've gotten to share every second of it with you. That's important."

"I'm glad you think so."

"It's been a big day," he said, stroking her hair from her face. He reached into his pocket. "I brought you something to remember the occasion." He handed her a box.

Surprised, she took the box from him, aware when their fingers brushed. She opened the box and looked at a sparkling diamond drop on a thin gold chain. "Gabe, it's beautiful! Thank you!" she exclaimed, touched by his thoughtfulness.

"You may want to wait until you get home to wear it."

"No. I'm wearing it tonight. You can take it home for me tomorrow morning when you go."

He smiled and took it from the box to lift her hair and fasten it behind her neck while she leaned forward. His warm fingers brushed her nape. She settled back against the pillows and took his hand. "Thank you. You were great today."

"I'm glad I was there. We have a beautiful daughter," he said quietly. "I want to be a daddy for her, Ashley."

"That would be good," she said, surprised and touched by all he was doing for her. "You're good to treat Ella as if she's yours."

"She will be mine. I'll raise her, and she'll know me as her daddy. You're already getting to be a mother to Julian." Ashley gazed into his dark eyes and knew they had forged a strong bond this day. While it wasn't love, it was a tie that bound them together.

"When I thought this deal up," he said, "I was thinking how we could each benefit, but I didn't know you. You were a dim blur and so was the baby. This is all so much better than I ever thought it could be. Today was special,

Ashley.'' He leaned forward, brushing her lips lightly as he had done on their wedding day. His arms went around her, and he hugged her gently. She knew he was hugging and kissing in a friendly manner and nothing more, but an ache for more blossomed within her. She closed her eyes, leaning against him and hugging him lightly in return, her face against the solid muscles of his chest.

"I trusted you completely today," she whispered. "I hope I can always trust you like that."

"You can," he said quietly.

She looked into his dark eyes and knew only time would tell.

"Want something cold to drink?" Gabe moved around waiting on her, getting things for her, giving Ella to her when the baby woke. He disappeared down the hall for a while and then returned to sit with her until she began to nod.

"I can't stay awake," she said. "Are you sure you can sleep on the sofa?"

"Absolutely." He stood.

"Call me if you want anything," he said. "I'm going to sleep. I'm bushed, too."

While he moved around in the darkness, she switched off the small light by the bed, leaving the only light in the adjoining bathroom. There was an intimacy in sharing a room with him even if he was sleeping on the sofa and she had just been through childbirth. She glanced at him and saw that his back was turned and he had stripped to the waist, was wearing only his jeans and boots. She watched the muscles ripple in his back as he spread covers on the sofa. Then she turned her head to look at her baby, and Ella filled her thoughts.

The next day they took Ella home, and Ashley's life revolved around the baby and Julian through the rest of summer and into fall. During that time, Gabe, Quinn and Josh moved the white stallion to Josh's ranch.

* * *

As the months passed, Ella began sleeping through the night and Ashley began to get her life back. Autumn leaves turned red and yellow and a chill was in the air now at night.

Most mornings when Julian and Ella were with Lou, Ashley worked out in the utility room where they had a treadmill and small weights.

The weeks passed swiftly, and there were moments when she realized she had a good life with Gabe. His energy astounded her; he threw himself into ranch work on the Triple R, yet she knew he wasn't neglecting his own ranch either. He was learning from her dad, taking over many of the responsibilities. Her dad was home long hours now, playing with Julian and Ella until Ashley realized Lou was hardly necessary and they wouldn't miss her when she quit after her graduation in December.

Gabe spent hours when he could with Julian and Ella. The only person seeing little of Gabe was Ashley. She knew he was busy and knew why, and it hadn't bothered her because she had been recovering from childbirth and caring for Ella. As she began to get time for herself, she became physically aware of Gabe again, as well as conscious of how little she saw him.

The last week of October, while fall leaves swirled in the air outside, Gabe came through the kitchen with Julian, both of them dressed in jeans and sweatshirts. As Julian ran outside to his swing, Gabe paused. "You haven't been out since Ella was born except for times the whole family goes somewhere. I've already talked to Lou about staying tonight. How about dinner and dancing? Nothing fancy, just fun."

"Sounds good to me," Ashley replied, her pulse jumping.

"Great. How about six?"

"Sure. I'll tell Dad he's on his own."

"He knows. I told him, and he's happy. I think he's going to Dusty's for dinner." Gabe left, closing the door behind him. Ashley immediately thought about what she might wear and went to look at her clothes.

At ten minutes before six, she studied herself again in the mirror, turning to stare at her stomach, now as flat as it had been before her pregnancy. Ella was three months old now and Ashley decided her morning workouts had paid off. She wore a red blouse tucked into her jeans and black boots. Her hair was caught in a red clasp at the back of her neck. Anticipation hummed in her because Gabe was exciting, and she remembered how much she had liked waltzing with him at their wedding party even when she had been pregnant. Eagerly, she switched off the light and went to the nursery to look at Ella.

Lou rocked the baby while Julian built a small fort of toy logs on the floor. "Ella's sleeping now. She's been content since you fed her," Lou said.

"I'll be home to feed her, but if you should need one, I have bottles in the refrigerator."

"Look at my fort, Mommy," Julian said, and she knelt down to look at his construction. One morning he had called her Mommy and she had answered, happy to have him call her that. When she'd asked Gabe whether he cared, he had smiled warmly.

"I think it's great if he wants to call you Mommy," Gabe said. "His own mother is going to be a dim memory. I know that, and I won't ever let him forget her or how much she loved him, but for all practical purposes, you're his mommy now."

She kissed Julian and then touched the sleeping baby's cheek. "You have my cellular phone number," she told Lou. "Don't hesitate to call if you need us. 'Night." Ashley left, going down the hall to the family room.

"I'm ready," she said, stopping inside the door. Gabe was across the room piling logs in the fireplace, ready to start a fire. He glanced over his shoulder at her. "Sure. I'm read—" He broke off, standing while his gaze drifted down over her and her pulse jumped.

"Wow," he said quietly. "You look great."

"Thank you."

"I'll be fighting guys off all night. I may have to rethink where I take you."

"I don't think you'll have to fight guys off. I'm married and a mother now. That's different."

"Yeah, sure," he said darkly, scowling. Gabe looked at her from head to toe and wondered why, even though he saw her daily, he hadn't really noticed the changes in her since childbirth. He knew she had lost weight, but she wore baggy T-shirts a lot and at first she'd still had some extra weight and a tummy. Lately he had been too busy to pay attention. Now he could hardly stop staring at her. The woman was gorgeous. His wife. Wife in name only.

Her figure was great, and that thick black hair shone with blue glints in its darkness. Her thickly-lashed, vivid blue eyes always fascinated him. She wore the diamond drop he had given her. It sparkled in the light and nestled against the open V of her blouse, bright against her dark skin. The room seemed hot and he knew he needed to stop staring at her, but Ashley was good to look at.

With an effort he tore his attention from her. He crossed to the hall closet to get their leather jackets, and in minutes she was seated beside him in his pickup as he drove to a local restaurant and bar that had good music and a good place to dance.

While his pulse drummed in eager anticipation, he slipped his arm around her waist to cross the parking lot. Stars twinkled in an inky sky, and the cool October air was invigorating. Gabe became conscious of everything with a heightened awareness, while that magic chemistry caused by Ashley tingled his nerves.

As they crossed a porch and he opened the door to enter the rustic nightspot, he tightened his arm around her. She was his woman and he didn't want anyone thinking differently. It had been a long time since the afternoon of their wedding and those few, hot kisses, yet she had steadily grown more important to him. Tonight he was going to discover more about her. He had thrown himself into ranch work, trying to relieve Quinn as swiftly as possible, but running two huge ranches and trying to pull one of them out of debt was a time-consuming task. He had kept time for Julian and Ella, but he hadn't given any time to Ashley. Now he vowed that would change.

He didn't want to share her for even one dance with anyone else.

They ate ribs, but his appetite for dinner had fled. As soon as he could, he took her hand. "Want to dance?"

"I thought you'd never ask," she replied.

He followed her to the dance floor, watching the sway of her hips in her tight jeans. When had she gotten her figure back and why hadn't he noticed before now?

On the dance floor she turned to face him, moving to a two-step. The next slow dance, he reached up and unfastened the barrette, stuffing it into his back pocket. "There, that's better."

She smiled and shook her head, her thick curtain of raven hair swirling across her shoulders. As they moved together, he caught the scent of her perfume.

Aware of her soft body, of her moving sensuously with him, her thighs touching his, he wanted her. Desire rocked him, an urgent, hungry need that consumed him.

He thought about Julian and how his son had bonded with Ashley, calling her Mommy easily and loving her as much as if she were really his own mother. Maybe if Julian could let go and love again, he, too, could, Gabe thought. And he knew Ashley had eased his grief. That terrible longing for Ella, as well as the pain for the loss of his folks, didn't swamp him daily the way it once had.

"When did you get back in such great shape?" he asked her.

"I suppose a day at a time. I exercise in the morning when Lou is with Julian and Ella."

Gabe's eyebrows arched in a surprised look. "I didn't know that."

"After you leave you don't know what goes on at home," she replied, smiling at him.

"I get a rundown from Julian," Gabe replied as his legs brushed against hers. How could he have missed the changes in her? he wondered. Had he been working that hard? Right now, she had his total attention.

"I can imagine the information you get from him. What pictures he colored and what books I read to him and what his favorite TV characters said and did."

"I guess you're right. Maybe I should stay home some day and see what goes on."

"You're not watching me work out," she said emphatically, and his curiosity was stirred.

"Why not?" he asked.

"No way. I'm not that good at it, and you'd laugh at the little weights I lift."

He was imagining her working out and it was getting another response from his body. It had been a very long time since he had been intimately involved with a woman, and all at once he was aware of the deprivation.

"I seriously doubt if I'd laugh. Try me."

"Nope. You stay far away, cowboy."

"I think I've been missing out on some things."

"Like what?"

"Like slow dancing and long wet kisses and a little flirting," he said.

"Oh my! Well, you're getting to do a little slow dancing and a little flirting, so that's two out of three."

"I always did like one hundred percent. All or nothing."

"You already have a lot more than nothing." She moved her hips sensuously against him and his temperature rose. His wife was flirting with him, sending him signals that she was okay with his flirting and dancing. She was his wife, yet in a lot of ways he hardly knew her. Sweat beaded his brow and he knew it wasn't from the room temperature or the dancing.

The music ended and a fast number came on. "Can you keep up with this one?" she challenged.

"I sure as hell can," he said, pulling her beside him to scoot around the floor with other couples, watching her as they danced because conversation was impossible during the fast number.

They danced for another hour and he was on fire. He wanted her, wanted to bury himself in her softness, wanted more than she could or would give him and more than he knew he should take. Reminding himself to go slowly with her, he stopped dancing.

"Let's go home." He knew he was cutting the evening short by about an hour, but he wanted to be alone with her.

Watching the slight sway of her hips, he followed her from the dance floor and then took her arm to go to his pickup. It was cool in the dimly lit parking lot and wind caught her hair, blowing it slightly. At the truck, he placed both hands on cither side of her, holding the door closed and hemming her in between himself and the pickup. Her eyes were wide, filled with curiosity as she looked up at him.

Nine

"**Y**ou said I had two out of three," he drawled, his voice becoming husky. "I told you, I like one hundred percent."

Ashley looked up at him. "Well, maybe you should do something about it, then," she said in a sultry voice, wanting his kisses.

"Damn straight, I will," he whispered and leaned down to kiss her.

She was breathless. Daily, moment upon moment, Ashley had become more intensely aware of Gabe, until tonight he had set every nerve in her body on edge. And tonight he seemed to see her as a man sees a desirable woman, in her own right with no ghosts of the past between them.

Beneath her leather jacket, his arms slipped around her and he stepped closer, pulling her against him. Her hands flew to his shoulders while her gaze locked with his. As her pulse speeded, his mouth covered hers.

Her insides clenched and then seemed to burst into flames while she opened her lips and his tongue touched hers. She moved her hips against him, feeling the thickness in his jeans, realizing he was aroused and wanted her. As she wrapped her arms around his neck and held him, her heart thudded.

When his arms tightened around her, she shook with pleasure. Moaning softly, she wound her fingers in his thick hair. His hand combed through her hair and then cradled her head, holding her while he kissed her. She was running the risk of losing her heart to a man she still didn't know completely, yet danger no longer mattered—except the delicious danger of more kisses. She wanted to taste, to know, to be touched.

Too long she had been with him now without succumbing to anything physical. With that first touch, her desire for him flashed like a windstorm.

With raw, hungry passion they kissed until she knew they needed to stop. The moment she wriggled and pushed against him, he leaned away to look at her.

"Gabe, we're in the parking lot," she said, breathlessly, her pulse pounding as his hand caressed her throat.

"Ashley—"

"Let's slow down a little."

His dark gaze was steady, holding hers. "Come on, we'll go home," he said.

When he opened the door of the pickup, she climbed inside, knowing that in the last few minutes, their relationship had changed forever. Was she ready for whatever he wanted? She wondered. How much of himself was he offering her? Was she willing to trust her heart to him?

Gabe walked around the pickup and slid behind the wheel. Shedding his leather jacket, he tossed it over the seat, flipped the locks on the doors and turned to her.

"All I want is you," he whispered, sliding his arm around her waist and pulling her to him.

"Things will never be the same between us," she whispered, her hands on his shoulders.

"It's too late now to go back to the platonic relationship

we had this morning,'' he murmured. ''That went out the window when we kissed.''

Gabe kissed her again, and desire flamed. He wanted her—here and now. She was his wife, legally. They were a team and had grown closer since Ella's birth. Their marriage could be a whole lot better. The lady set him on fire. Her kisses were irresistible.

''Ashley, you've made me whole again,'' he whispered against her lips.

Ashley's heart drummed, a roaring in her ears that almost drowned out his words. His hungry kisses consumed her. She was barely aware when he lifted her over the seat onto his lap, moving the seat back to give them room and shoving away her jacket. Cradled against his shoulder, she wound her arms around his neck, running her fingers through his thick hair. His hand caressed her throat, sliding so lightly over her breast, twisting free buttons to slide beneath her shirt.

Gasping with pleasure, she caught his wrist. She wriggled to sit up and then moved deftly back to the passenger side of the pickup and buttoned her blouse.

''We're still in the parking lot. Let's get out of here.''

He was breathing as hard as she was. He started the motor and they drove to the highway.

''I had the best time tonight that I've had in far too long to remember,'' he said quietly.

''Good. So did I.''

''I feel something holding you back. Am I right?'' He glanced quickly at her. ''What are you afraid of?''

''I don't want to rush into an intimate relationship and then discover that neither one of us was ready for it or that one of us expected too much from it,'' she answered truthfully.

''I don't think that we're in danger of either one of those things happening, but I can slow down.''

As the truck sped quietly through the night, she was acutely aware of him beside her.

They were quiet the entire ride home. As they crossed the yard, he draped his arm across her shoulders and pulled her close against his side. Tossing their jackets on a chair in the kitchen, he switched on a hall light. "Wait in the family room for me. I'll go tell Lou we're home. We're early enough, she may want to drive into town tonight."

Ashley nodded and left him, going into the family room to start the fire. In minutes, flames curled over logs, and she stood watching them until the scrape of Gabe's boots indicated he was in the hall. He entered, closing the door behind him and switching on the baby monitor.

"Lou left. I walked out to the car with her and she called her fiancé to tell him she was driving home." Gabe crossed the room to pick Ashley up easily, carrying her to the sofa to sit with her on his lap. He stroked her cheek lightly. "I want you, Ashley."

"I want you, too, and you want me, but right now this attraction is a physical thing."

"What I feel is more than lust," he said softly, trailing kisses along her temple, down over her ear to her throat and to her mouth. His lips brushed hers in featherlight kisses that were an exquisite torment, while his hand caressed her throat.

Ashley moaned, knowing she was lost to seductive arguments, hot kisses, Gabe's magnetism. "Uncle Dusty said you were a fast-talking hustler—" she whispered, winding her fingers in Gabe's thick hair and pulling his head down to her.

His mouth settled firmly on hers, his tongue thrusting over hers, as he leaned over her and kissed her hard and long. At the same time she unbuttoned and pushed away his shirt, his hand slid down to twist free the buttons of her shirt and shove it open. With a flick, the clasp of her bra was undone, and then his warm, calloused hand cupped her breast. His thumb drew delicate, lazy circles over her sensitive nipple and she moaned again, her hips shifting against him.

"You're a beautiful woman," he whispered and then leaned down to take her nipple into his mouth and draw circles around the tight bud with his warm tongue.

Ashley ached with a fiery need for all of him. She wanted him desperately, she had poured out her emotions and fears to him yet caution held her back.

While her thoughts raged a silent battle, his kisses were torment. He shifted and she was beneath him on the sofa as he moved between her legs, and his fingers were at the buttons of her jeans. Ashley shoved against his chest. "Wait, please," she whispered.

He paused instantly, moving back to hold her on his lap. Even though she had stopped him, she wanted him. While she straightened her clothes, she combed her fingers through his unruly hair. As she did, he watched her, and she wondered what was running through his mind.

"You think I'm being foolish," she said.

"I can slow down," he said in husky voice. "Tonight was great. I'm happy."

"Tonight was great for me, too. I'm over my hurt from Chicago because of you," she said, stroking his cheek and jaw and feeling the faint rough stubble of his beard. "It's like something that happened very long ago and is no longer significant in my life."

"Good. That's progress. You've healed my grief. There are moments I still hurt. I think of Ella and miss her, but the pain and loss are easing. I'll always remember, always miss her, but not on a hellish moment-by-moment sea of memories like I have had. Her loss along with the loss of my folks was overwhelming. Julian is better now because of you. He talks more now and he laughs more."

"I'm glad." She hesitated, then murmured, "Gabe, if I lost this ranch, I'd like to think you'd still want me," she said quietly, admitting the truth to him. It was hard to say it aloud, the words had a peculiar ring and caused a barrier to the closeness they had been achieving. He didn't withdraw, yet she ached for a denial.

He stroked her cheek and ran his fingers lightly through her hair, gentle touches that still invoked fire. "I'd still want you. I swear I would, Ashley. I haven't been very romantic, darlin', but maybe I can improve," he said, a light tone back in his voice.

"It goes a lot deeper than being romantic, Gabe," she said solemnly. A baby's faint cry could be heard, and Ashley slid off Gabe's lap. "I hear Ella. I'll go feed her."

"Sure." He stood, and she faced him, knowing her shirt was a thousand wrinkles from his hugs. His shirt was the same, unbuttoned now to his waist and his muscled chest showing. His mouth was red from their kisses and locks of brown hair fell across his forehead. She smoothed back the locks of his hair and then moved closer, standing on tiptoe to pull his head down and kiss him, putting all her feelings into it.

His arms banded her, holding her tight as he leaned over her and kissed her in return until they both were breathless and she knew she had to go. "I better run," she whispered, pushing against him. "It was a wonderful evening, Gabe," she said and left swiftly.

Gabe watched her go, looking at the sway of her hips, her long legs, mentally undressing her and wishing he had her in his bed.

Going to the kitchen, he stripped off his shirt and tossed it over a chair, then got a cold beer and carried it to the kitchen table. He thought about the evening, replaying it in his mind, thinking about her kisses that could heat him in a flash. He mulled over all she had told him; they had married in the coldest way possible, without one shred of romance in a bargain that, in truth, had been a business deal. No wonder she was disturbed about his feelings, he thought, mentally swearing at himself for his lack of finesse.

It had been a damned good business deal, but that's all it was. Prenuptial agreement, contracts, legal advice— they'd had all the business trappings. She had been treated

cruelly by the jerk in Chicago, had returned home to spec-
ulation and gossip about her baby, then had agreed to the
deal with him.

Well, the lady deserved better, Gabe decided he wanted
to court his new wife, wanted to please her. He thought
about his feelings for her. Gabe took another long drink,
feeling the cold beer go down his throat. He wanted her,
there was no question about that. He had a growing admiration and respect for her. He liked her company. Love?
He didn't know the depth of his own feelings for her, but
she was becoming essential to his life.

They needed more nights like tonight where they could
be together without the rest of the family. Moments that
were shared fun and companionship. He thought of all the
work he needed to get done, yet he could rearrange his
schedule slightly, take a little more time for his family. It
would give him more time with Julian and Ella, too.

His thoughts shifted back to the evening with Ashley
until he was hot and bothered again, wanting her and knowing sleep wasn't going to come easily. Maybe he was falling in love with his wife. Why not let go? Julian had, and
he loved Ashley without question.

Gabe knew that one thing he could do was court the lady
a bit. A courtship was something she was long overdue to
receive.

He decided to take a cold shower and to read a book he
had bought on cattle breeding.

Monday afternoon the refrigerator quit cooling, and
Quinn was on his knees on the kitchen floor working on it
while Mrs. Farrin worked at the sink peeling carrots for a
casserole. Holding Ella, Ashley sat at the table helping Julian with a model rocket ship he was building. Quinn swore
softly and stood.

"I need a smaller wrench to get in there," he said, glancing out the window. "Looks like we're going to have
company."

Standing to look out the window, Ashley saw a white panel truck coming up the road, a plume of dust rising behind it. The truck stopped at the back gate and a man emerged with a large bouquet of two dozen red roses.

Surprised, Ashley stared at the bouquet. "Looks like someone in this house is getting roses," Quinn remarked dryly, glancing at Ashley.

"Who're they for?" Julian's high voice piped up, joining them at the window.

"I think for your momma," Quinn replied, and all of them turned to look at Ashley. Her cheeks grew warm and she felt as dithery as a new bride.

Stepping outside, Quinn met the deliveryman and accepted the bouquet of roses. "Might pretty flowers," he said, setting them on the kitchen table.

"Mommy, will you help me?" Julian asked, returning to his rocket ship.

"I'll help you," Quinn said, "when I finish fixing the refrigerator. In the meantime, Julian, come with me to find a wrench."

"Sure," Julian said, always happy to tag along with Quinn. The two left, and Mrs. Farrin turned to take Ella.

"Put your flowers where you want them. I'll take care of the little one." She took Ella from Ashley and went down the hall, talking softly to the baby.

Turning to her flowers, Ashley inhaled their sweet scent and carried them to the family room. She placed them on a table and then opened the card.

Thanks for a special Saturday night. Let's try to have another one this weekend.

                                             Love, Gabe.

She ran her fingers over the card, then smelled the flowers again, feeling a rush of longing for him. Next Saturday night he wanted to go out again. Joy filled her. She read the note again, once more running her fingers over his signature. Love, Gabe. She knew it was a casual closing, yet it gave her a thrill to read the words. If only—she closed her eyes and thought about him, recalling their evening, knowing she was falling in love with him whether he was in love with her or not.

Tucking the card from Gabe into the pocket of her cut-offs, she went to get the baby from Mrs. Farrin.

Ashley cradled Ella in her arms, feeling a rush of love for her child. She was such a good baby. Ella was rosy and plump and slept most of the time. The only fussiness had been during the past few weeks when she wasn't getting enough milk, and after a trip to the pediatrician, Ashley had finally given up nursing. She held her baby close as she carried her to the changing table, talking softly to her while Ella's big blue eyes gazed up at her and she cooed.

At half past six Gabe called and told them to go ahead with supper because he was delayed by a sick cow and was waiting on a vet to come. After bathing and changing to jeans and a red shirt, Ashley ate with Julian and Quinn.

She was in the nursery when she heard the scrape of boots in the hall and knew Gabe was home. She put a sleeping Ella in her bed and hurried out of the room. Her pulse skipped a beat when she stepped into the hall and saw Gabe.

He had stripped off his shirt and his jeans were muddy. In his hands he carried his shirt, muddy boots and his hat. He had a smudge on his cheek and unruly locks of hair fell across his forehead, but he looked handsome and sexy to her.

Instantly, he smiled and her pulse accelerated another notch. "Thanks for the roses," she said quietly as he approached. "They're beautiful."

"And Saturday night? Want to go out again?"

"Sure. That would be nice," she answered eagerly, wanting to be alone with him now. "Your supper is ready."

"I need a shower before I eat," he said, waving his hand slightly.

"How's the sick cow?"

"All right. The pickup had a flat on the way here so that took even longer." He moved closer. "I can't touch you because I'm dirty, and you look a damn sight more scrumptious than any supper that's waiting."

Her heart fluttered with his words, and she trailed her fingers across his bare chest.

"I don't think I'd mind if you touched me even without a shower."

He inhaled and dropped his boots and shirt on the floor to slide his arm around her waist and pull her against him. She looked up and met his smoldering gaze; it took her breath. While her heart drummed, she slipped her hand behind his head to pull him down to her. His mouth covered hers in a hungry, passionate kiss that she returned fully.

Abruptly, he released her. The hot desire in his eyes made her tremble with eagerness to be back in his arms again. "Want to come shower with me?" he asked.

Startled, she blinked. "I don't think so," she answered, breathlessly, knowing if she said yes, they would both be in his shower in seconds. "I'll be waiting," she said, aware she needed to put some distance between them. "Now I need to change," she said, looking at smudges of mud on her blouse. She hurried to her room.

When Gabe reappeared, he was in a fresh T-shirt and jeans, and his wet hair was combed and slicked back from his face, giving him an entirely different appearance that she found also appealing. She sat across from him while he ate, hearing about his day and telling him about hers and what Julian had done. All the time they talked, she was intensely aware of him, remembering their kisses in the hall earlier. Once he reached across the table to stroke her cheek.

"You look pretty tonight."

"Thank you."

He reached behind her head and untied the ribbon that held her hair. "I like that better. Do you mind?"

"No, it's fine," she said, basking in the warmth of his gaze as he studied her. She looked forward to being alone with him later, feeling a steady tingle of excitement.

When he'd finished eating, they joined the others in the family room. Gabe read to Julian and helped him with a puzzle he was working on. Finally Gabe took his son to bed.

While he was in Julian's room, Ella awakened. Ashley fed the baby, changed her and carried her to the family room where Quinn rocked her until Gabe returned and took her for a few minutes before carrying the sleeping baby to her bed. Then the three adults sat talking until past ten o'clock when Quinn told them good-night.

"I didn't get to see Ella or any of you enough today. I'll try to get home early tomorrow night," Gabe told her when they were alone.

Ashley stood and crossed the room to him. For an instant his brows arched in surprise, and then he smiled and uncrossed his legs as she sat on his lap. "I haven't thanked you properly for the roses," she said in a soft voice, looking at his mouth.

Ten

Her heart thudded as she leaned forward to kiss him. His arms wrapped tightly around her and he returned her kiss, shifting her to cradle her head against his shoulder. She wasn't aware that he had reached out to turn off a lamp until the room grew darker. A small lamp still burned across the room.

"I'll have to send flowers every day if I get this kind of thank you," he said in a husky voice. He picked her up, moving to the sofa with her.

"They're beautiful, and it was a surprise."

"You're beautiful and I want to take you out again next Saturday. Will you go to dinner with me?"

"I'd love to," she whispered while he kissed her throat and she ran her fingers through his thick hair.

His fingers twisted free the buttons of her blue blouse and then he shoved it off her shoulders. With a groan, he cupped her full breasts, stroking her tender nipples so lightly, yet making her gasp with pleasure.

Ashley tugged up his T-shirt and he yanked it the rest of the way, pulling it over his head and tossing it aside and then she turned so she pressed against his bare chest while she kissed him. He stroked her back, then his fingers sought and found the buttons to her jeans. Deftly, he unfastened them and stripped them away. His hands caressed her back, moving over her bottom and to her bare thighs.

Gabe shifted, his hand sliding along her thigh, trailing between her legs, touching her so lightly, intimately while they kissed.

She shook with need, wanting him, torn between longing and caution.

It was Gabe who finally sat up and pulled her up on his lap, wrapping her blue blouse around her shoulders, yet bending to kiss her breast before doing so.

"What's this?"

"You didn't want to be rushed, so you won't be. I can show some kind of restraint," he said, kissing her throat and ear, his warm breath a sweet torment. "If you change your mind, all you have to do is let me know. You know what I want and how I feel."

"No, I don't know how you feel. I don't know what you think or how you feel, but your card and the flowers and your kisses make me feel good."

"Good," he said, still trailing kisses along her temple and nape, his hand stroking her leg. "I care, Ashley," he said, and she opened her eyes to look at him. His dark gaze was filled with desire, but beyond that she couldn't discern what he was thinking.

"I want you. I want you more each day," he said in a husky voice that played over her nerves as his fingers did on her body. "I want you to want me the way I do you."

"Gabe," she whispered, touched by his words, wanting to tell him that she wanted his love, but that was something that she knew would have to come from him. She turned his face up, brushing his hair back and then kissing him passionately.

Gabe was the one who stopped again and held her tightly. "I can wait, Ashley, but it's damned hard. *I'm* damned hard," he added.

She slid off his lap. "I better move away and go to bed. You've had a long day."

Slipping her arms into her blouse and yanking up her jeans, she turned to find him watching her with a hot gaze that indicated his desire as strongly as his words. Her heart missed a beat, and she turned away. "I'll see you tomorrow."

"Wait. I'll head that way with you. That way I get another kiss at your door."

She smiled at him, and he slid his arm around her waist, pulling her close against him while he switched off lights and walked through the silent, darkened house to her bedroom.

"Here we are," she whispered, turning to face him as she wrapped her arms around his narrow waist. He walked her backwards into her bedroom and closed the door quietly.

Leaning against the door, he spread his legs and pulled her up against him tightly to kiss her. She wound her arms around his neck and returned his kisses while time disappeared.

Finally she pushed against his chest, and he raised his head, his dark gaze devouring her. "I want you in my bed. I want you to really be my wife. Soon you will be," he said, kissing her throat and nuzzling her ear. His husky voice was as coaxing and as seductive as his kisses.

"Is this a proposal?"

He leaned back to study her, and she met his unfathomable gaze, still at a loss to know what he was thinking. "You'll know when you get a proposal." He kissed her long and hard and she clung to him, aching with longing and knowing that she was in love with the tall cowboy.

He caressed her throat, his fingers light and warm and then he was gone, closing the door behind him.

"I love you, Gabriel Brant," she said, thinking about the generations-old feud and the hate and anger that had spilled between the two families.

Later, after going over books for an hour, Gabe restlessly returned to his room. He crossed to his dresser to pick up a picture of Ella, looking at her smiling face and feeling a pang rip through him as painfully as ever. He would always love her. Nothing would change that, but she was gone and he had to go on with his life.

"I loved you so much," he whispered, as he looked at her smiling face. "I think you'd like Ashley and little Ella. Julian is a fine boy, and now we have Quinn and Ashley to help raise him and that's good. We have to do things we didn't want to do, but Ashley's good for me."

He opened the drawer and put away the picture, moving around the room to gather up the other pictures except one of Ella with Julian. He would move that one to Julian's room.

Saturday night couldn't come soon enough; he would have Ashley all to himself for hours, and he intended that soon they would have the wedding night that they had missed after their hasty marriage.

Wednesday, another floral delivery arrived, a huge basket of daisies, roses and carnations.

Gabe had said he would be home early and Ashley was eager to see him, even though each night was a torment at the same time it was a delight.

She moved to the new bouquet, smiling and pulling the card from the pocket of her denim skirt.

Can't wait until Saturday. I want you all to myself.
　　　　　　　　　　　　　　Love, Gabe.

She couldn't wait either. She ran her hands across the card as if by touching it, she could touch part of him.

"So you got the flowers," he said quietly from the doorway.

She whirled around to face him. "You surprised me!" she said, blushing to be caught running her hand across his card. "Thanks for the flowers, but you don't need to buy out all the flower shops in San Antonio."

"I'm not," he said, looking amused as he sauntered toward her and her pulse jumped. "You look great."

"Thank you," she said, watching him narrow the distance between them. She stepped forward to meet him. "I'm glad you're home," she said softly.

His arm went around her and he kissed her until she pushed against him. "Dad will come in—"

"So? Quinn knows we're married and I think he's happy to see you happy."

"Even so," she said, stepping away, "I'll be embarrassed."

With a twinkle in his eyes, Gabe slid his hand behind her head. "You're all prim and proper until you get in my arms," he said quietly.

"Maybe one of us *should* be prim and proper," she replied. "And it won't be you. You have a streak of bad boy, Gabe."

"And you love it," he answered.

"Maybe I do. Show me tonight and I'll tell you."

"That's a promise. Now I'm going to clean up, but that offer to join me in the shower still stands."

"You'd faint if I accepted."

"Not on your life would I faint," he replied, leaning closer. "I'd have you in my bedroom, into that shower so fast your head would spin. Try me."

Laughing, she stepped away from him. "Not yet. I'll see you at supper." She hurried toward the door, then turned back. "Gabe, Dad is going to Wyoming and Oregon next month with Uncle Dusty and Aunt Kate. He's going to ask you if he can take Julian along. Uncle Dusty has that big mobile home."

"I'll think about it," Gabe said, "but if Julian wants to go, seems like it's okay. I can't keep him shut away on the ranch forever, and between Quinn and your Aunt Kate, he'll be watched all the time."

"That's for certain. Dad is crazy about him."

"I'm glad. He's good for Julian. And so are you."

Smiling, she left the room, her pulse drumming. She was growing more anxious for Saturday and if he was telling the truth, he sounded as eager as she.

On Saturday evening Ashley took one last, long look at herself. Gabe had told her they were going to San Antonio to dinner at the country club where they had had their wedding reception. She gave herself another critical study, looking at the straight black sheath, sleeveless with spaghetti straps, and her black pumps. She wore the diamond drop he had given her, diamond studs in her ears and no other jewelry. Her hair was looped and twisted and pinned on top of her head.

Ella lay on a blanket in the middle of Ashley's bed. The baby kicked and cooed and waved her fists, playing with a bright plastic rattle.

"You're a good girl, Ella Brant. A real sweetie, did you know that?"

Ella cooed, her big blue eyes gazing up at her mother and Ashley scooped her up, holding her close. "I hope you don't spit up on me because I'm all ready to go out. Nanny Lou is going to take care of you and Julian. Pretty soon you should be ready to go night-night, sweetie."

She found Lou in the nursery. "Here she is, all ready for bed, but she doesn't act sleepy yet."

"I'll take her to the family room with your dad and Julian."

Ashley carried Ella to Lou and went to find Gabe. He stood at the end of the hall, talking to her dad, who held Julian in his arms. Gabe turned to watch her as she walked toward them. His gaze flickered over her, making her tingle.

While both men stood waiting, she thought how lucky she was to have them in her life and how lucky to have Julian who was already precious to her. How glad she was that she'd decided to come home from Chicago to have Ella. Dressed in a dark suit and tie, Gabe was as handsome as ever. Her racing pulse jumped another notch when she looked into his eyes.

"I'd say you're all ready to go," Gabe said.

"Yes, I am. When are you leaving for Dusty's?" she asked Quinn who glanced at Julian.

"In a few minutes. I told Julian I'd read two books to him before I go. You two have fun."

"We will," Gabe said, taking Ashley's arm. She brushed a kiss on Julian's cheek.

Gabe kissed his son and then took her arm and they left. As soon as they went out the back door, he glanced at her. "We'll drive to dinner in San Antonio, but if I had my way, we'd head down to the barn, close and lock the door and spend the evening in the loft."

"Not on your life, mister. This dress wasn't meant for hay."

"I wouldn't get one little straw on that dress. You'd never know it had been near a hayloft."

"This is one time you're not selling your idea."

"I really didn't expect to, and I'm not giving it my all. I'll take you out like I promised. I just wanted you to know what I'd prefer." He held open the door of his car and she slid inside. He closed the door and went around to sit behind the wheel, and in minutes they were speeding along the highway to San Antonio.

Ashley reached over to place her hand on his knee. He glanced at her and took her hand to brush kisses across her knuckles. She inhaled swiftly.

"I've thought about tonight all week," he said. "I've wanted to be with you."

His words gave her a thrill, and she ran her fingers across his nape. "Watch out, Gabe. I may make you fall in love with a Ryder."

He gave her another smoldering glance that sent tingles running over her nerves.

"Just try me, honey."

"Ah, a challenge! You're on, Gabriel Brant. Watch your heart!"

He inhaled deeply. "I wish I had you in my arms right now."

"Instead, you watch the road."

In the sprawling clubhouse, they were seated at a table near a large window that overlooked the first hole of the golf course.

Their table was covered in a white linen tablecloth centered with a pink rosebud in a crystal vase. Gabe ordered a steak and smoked salmon for Ashley. With glasses of wine, they talked about the day, the children and the ranch, yet all the time, Ashley felt sparks dancing between them, and she wanted to be in his arms far more than she wanted to eat.

"Dad said if you keep buying flowers at the rate you have this week, you should get your own greenhouse."

"I'm making up for things I didn't do back when."

"You've more than made up for them," she said. "You don't have to keep sending flowers."

"I know I don't. I wanted to."

Their dinners were only half eaten, the elegant dessert barely touched when the band began to play and lights dimmed. A waiter cleared their table and Gabe took Ashley's hand to dance.

She moved with him, glad to be in his arms, wanting to dance all night. It was a slow number and he wrapped his arms around her, holding her close as they moved together perfectly.

Gabe inhaled her perfume, dancing slowly with her, feeling on fire with longing, yet reminding himself to go slowly. She deserved this courtship, deserved to be taken out to dinner and dancing. This was a special time and Gabe wanted to make it as enjoyable as possible for her. They couldn't have done this when she was in the last month of her pregnancy or right after Ella was born even if both of them had wanted to.

The dance ended and a fast one followed and he watched her as she danced with him. She was willowy, graceful, tantalizing. He knew he was falling in love with his beautiful wife. Every hour they spent together, she was becoming more important to him, more exciting. She responded to him with an eagerness that made his control almost shatter.

He twirled her around and pulled her close. "Let's go, okay?"

"Sure," she answered, her blue eyes changing as she inhaled. It took all his willpower to keep from kissing her right then. He led her off the dance floor and waited while she picked up her purse, and then they walked silently out of the club. As soon as they drove away, he glanced at her.

"We can head right back to the ranch. What I'd rather do is get a hotel room—"

"A hotel room?" she asked with amusement. "We have a home."

"I want some time with you all to myself," he said in a husky voice. "Just a few hours. Lou is staying the night and I'd like to get out where we won't get interrupted for hours."

Her pulse drummed. "Whatever you want is fine with me."

He caught her hand to brush a kiss across her knuckles and turned the car to head into town. He wanted her with a need that made him feel he would explode into a million pieces if he didn't get her into his arms in the next few minutes.

He slowed, pulled over and parked on the side of the road. While she waited, Gabe retrieved his cell phone, called information and soon found a hotel with a vacancy. Twenty minutes later they entered a suite on the top floor of an elegant hotel on the river. Gabe shed his coat and tie, tossing them on a chair, unbuttoning his snowy shirt. While he opened and poured wine, Ashley stood looking at the view. Only a light from the bathroom was on in their suite, and she looked out at sparkling lights reflected in the rippling, dark river.

Then Gabe was standing in front of her, offering her a glass of wine. She took it and raised it. "Here's to our marriage. May it be long and oh, so happy, Gabe."

Without taking his gaze from her, he touched her glass with his and then sipped. He set down his glass and took hers to set it on a table beside his.

"I've waited forever," he whispered, pulling her to him to kiss her hard and long, bending over her until she was moaning softly, the sound caught in her throat. She returned his kisses wildly, letting her feelings for him show in her response. He was strong, so handsome, and she was in love with him, wanting him to want her and love her, hoping that was what was happening.

His hand combed through her hair, sending the pins flying until her black locks fell freely over her shoulders. Ashley pushed away his shirt, running her hands over his muscled shoulders and across his smooth, bare back.

Still kissing her, he picked her up and carried her to a sofa where he sat down with her on his lap, leaning over her and cradling her head against his shoulder. His hand caressed her, sliding down across her breasts, down to slide beneath her skirt and peel away her stockings and pumps.

Winding her fingers in his hair, she kissed him passionately, their tongues tangled, escalating her desire.

She didn't know how much later he stood, still kissing her. He trailed kisses from her mouth to her throat, turning her to lift her hair and kiss her nape while his fingers tugged the zipper of her dress down and it fell away.

Love for her tall, handsome husband made her tremble.

He was sexy, romantic and irresistible. Ashley turned to face him and he placed his hands on her hips, leaning away to look at her while he stroked her breasts lightly. She inhaled, quivering, wanting to reach for him, yet unable to move as his dark eyes devoured her. She stood in wisps of lace.

"Saints alive, you're beautiful," he said, his hands caressing her and then unfastening the clasp to her bra and slipping it off. His large, dark hands cupped her breasts, his thumbs stroking her nipples so lightly. She moaned with pleasure, closing her eyes and momentarily clinging to his arms. She ran her hands over his thick muscles, his hard chest, trailing her fingers to his waistband to unbuckle and remove his belt and then unfasten his slacks.

Yanking off his boots, he tossed them down and stepped out of his slacks.

She inhaled, trembling, reaching out to slide her hands over his narrow waist, slipping her fingers beneath the waistband of his briefs and sliding them down to free him.

Gabe shook as she knelt and stroked him, kissing him slowly. He groaned, pulling her to her feet while he kissed her hard. He knew that any control he had was fast vanishing. And he remembered the resolutions he had made during the week.

With another groan, he released her and stepped back, yanking up her dress from the floor and dropping it over her head. He scooped up his clothes and headed for the shower, thinking that he had to get distance between them.

"Gabe?"

"I made a promise to you," he said with his back to her. "Ashley, I intend to keep it. Tomorrow I don't want you to think I fast-talked you into something you didn't want—"

She was against him, pressing her softness against his backside, her arms sliding around him, touching him intimately. "Gabe, I know what I want," she said quietly. His heart thudded violently, and he clenched his fists, turning to her.

"I want you with every ounce of my being," he said, grinding out the words. "But a promise is a promise."

"Gabe, are you hearing me? I know what I want."

"You've told me you wanted to go slowly. I can do that." Why was he arguing with her? Yet the words *fast-talking hustler* kept resounding in his memory and that wasn't what he wanted her to think about him in the light of day. "If you still want to make love, we can tomorrow night or next Saturday night, but you didn't walk into this hotel room wanting that. It's called seduction, lady. I want you to like me in the morning."

He turned and hurried to the bathroom and closed the door, swearing and wondering if he had just been the biggest fool. "You're damned if you do and you're damned if you don't," he told himself. Had he hurt her or made her feel rejected? Or would she be glad in the morning? If they had made love would she hate him when the sun came over the horizon and reality set in? To himself, he had sworn that he would take time to court her. Tormented by questions that held no answers, he stepped into the shower and turned on the cold water full-force. The cold gave him a jolt, but it didn't cool his desire or his seething thoughts. Was she back there in the other room crying because he had said no?

Ashley stood in the dark, staring through the bedroom at the closed bathroom door while his questions and statements ran through her thoughts. Would she feel the same in the light of day?

She loved him and wanted him, and he obviously cared more about her every day. And tonight, whether he recognized it or not, he had acted like a man in love. He was trying to do what he had promised, and she admired him for that, but she knew her own feelings and she was ready to consummate this marriage that with every passing hour was becoming more real.

"Gabriel Brant, this is one decision that's going to be taken out of your hands," she whispered and stepped out of her dress as she hurried through the darkened bedroom. She heard the gushing shower before she opened the bathroom door.

Eleven

Through the almost opaque shower door she could see the blurred image of his naked body as he showered. She smiled and walked with determination to the shower, yanking open the door.

He looked around, his brows arching.

"I remember being invited to shower with you," she said, not caring that water was spilling out. Icy water splashed over her. "Turn on some warm water, Gabe!"

He stared at her, his eyes round with so much surprise, she almost laughed. Her gaze went over him and flew back to his. "Doesn't look as if that cold water is cooling you down one bit. Are you going to let me in with you or not?"

His surprise was gone. He inhaled and turned on warm water along with the cold as he stepped back and slipped his arm around her waist. "You had your chance. Don't ever say I didn't try to keep my promise."

"I won't," she said, running her hands across his chest,

leaning forward to kiss him, feeling his flesh, still cool from the freezing shower he had been taking.

"Damn, woman, my intentions were honorable," he said, hauling her tightly against him while he kissed her hungrily. As her heart thudded, she wrapped her arms around him, both of them getting drenched, yet all she could feel was his body, warming fast.

"Mine aren't," she said. "I want you, Gabe. I love you."

He kissed her long and hard, holding her close with one hand while the other slid over her wet, naked skin. Then he stepped back, cupping her breasts in each hand. He leaned forward to take a nipple in his mouth. His tongue was hot, teasing her and she closed her eyes, clinging to his strong shoulders.

Gabe couldn't believe she was here, in his arms. Never in his life had he been as surprised as when she had opened the shower door. Yet she always had seemed to know exactly what she wanted.

He had done what he should have. He had given her the chance to stop and go home. If this is what she wanted, then he could let go. *"I love you."* He heard her words and knew he should say them in return, yet he didn't.

Rational thought stopped as she closed her warm hand around his thick shaft, stroking him and causing him almost to lose control. He wanted to take her here in the shower, but he also wanted this first time to be slow and special. He turned off the water, stepped out of the shower and yanked a towel from the rack to hand it to her. Retrieving one for himself, he dried her, moving it lightly, slowly, teasing her with it until she tossed hers aside and hugged him.

He picked her up and carried her to the bedroom. Light spilled into the room from the bathroom, yet the room was still shadowy. He set her on her feet and grabbed the covers off the bed, yanking them down, and then he turned to her to cup her breasts again, leaning down to kiss her. "I want to love you all night long, to make this last until you're falling apart in my arms. I want to kiss every inch of you, know every inch of you."

Ashley closed her eyes, trembling, caressing him as he kissed her breasts, and then he lifted her to the bed and moved to her foot to do what he had said, taking her foot in his hand and kissing her ankle, moving higher, slowly trailing hot, wet kisses that made her writhe with longing. Reaching for him, she sat up, but he pushed her gently down. "Just let me love you."

She inhaled, watching him as he watched her, his kisses going higher, his hands a magic torment. He moved to the inside of her thighs, caressing her and then trailing slow kisses, gradually moving up to her breasts. She did come up off the bed then, winding her arms around him with a soft cry.

"I want you, and I want to kiss you like you're kissing me," she whispered, pushing him down. She caressed him, discovering the scar on his calf, another on his thigh, her hands sliding over him while she kissed him until he groaned and shifted, suddenly turning her onto her back and moving above her, his hand caressing her thighs and then moving between her legs.

His dark eyes blazed with passion as he leaned down to kiss her while he stroked her. She gasped before his mouth covered hers and then she clung to him, arching against his hand. She tore her mouth from his, trying to move. "Gabe, I want you!"

"Shh, let me love you. I want you to want me more than this."

"I couldn't," she ground out the words, knowing in a minute all arguments would be impossible. Then she was lost, rocking against him, kissing him wildly while her hands flew over him.

"Gabe!" she cried. She wanted them to be one. "Come here," she whispered. "Now—"

He moved between her legs. He was fully aroused, ready

for her, masculine, so handsome. She ached for him, wrapping her legs around him and pulling him to her.

Gabe eased down, and the velvet tip of his shaft touched her, moving lightly against her, an exquisite torment. She pulled him closer, her hands cupping his hard buttocks. "Gabe, please," she whispered.

Sweat poured off his body as he moved slowly, entering her and then withdrawing slightly while she gasped and arched beneath him again.

"I want you to want this more than anything," he whispered and then leaned over her to kiss her as he slowly entered her again. Driven to a mindless urgency, she moved beneath him.

He slowly filled her and they moved together and still Gabe tried to hold back, to last as long as possible for her—and then his control was gone.

"Gabe, love!"

"Ah, Ashley," he whispered.

Ashley was swept away in passion until release burst within her, and she felt his hard thrust and then he slowed. Their pounding hearts beat in unison and she held him tightly, feeling his weight on her and wishing she could hold him this way forever. She knew that tonight her life had changed totally. And she knew she was deeply in love with her husband.

His smooth back was damp with a sheen of sweat, and she stroked him as he showered light kisses on her face and then raised slightly to look down at her. Their gazes met and the warmth in his dark eyes made her breath catch. She tightened her arms around him as he leaned down to kiss her long and hard, a kiss that affirmed that what had happened between them was special.

"Ahh, darlin'," he said, and rolled over on his side, taking her with him as he lay facing her. He stroked damp locks of hair from her face. "You're beautiful and wonderful and I'm a very lucky man," he whispered.

Ashley thrilled to his words, her heart beating fast as her

hands trailed over him. She couldn't get enough of touching him. She ran her finger lightly over his lips. He caught her finger in his teeth gently, then took her hand to kiss her palm, his tongue stroking her sensitive skin.

"We're good together, aren't we?" he asked quietly.

"I think so, Gabe."

He lay on his back and pulled her close. "I never expected this, but then I never expected a lot of things that have happened in my life."

"To say the least, I didn't expect to marry when I came home. I'm still surprised constantly," she said, leaning over him, her dark hair spilling over his chest.

He played with locks of her hair. "It's so damned good," he said in a husky voice. "Come here and we'll get another shower."

She laughed as he stood and picked her up and in minutes they were soaping each other and then in a short time they were back in bed as Gabe made love to her again.

It was far into the early hours of the morning when she rolled on her side to study him as he lay sleeping. She shook him lightly, and he was instantly awake, wrapping his arm around her to pull her down to kiss her.

After a few minutes she pushed against his bare chest, moving her fingers lightly across him. "I hated to wake you, but we should go home."

Gazing back at her solemnly, he sat up. "I don't want to, but I will."

She slipped out of bed and began gathering her clothes. She glanced over her shoulder at him to find him still sitting in bed watching her.

"I could look at you forever, Ashley."

She could feel the heat flush her cheeks as she blushed. She turned to hold her dress in front of her. "I'm glad."

He slid off the bed and crossed to her, shoving away the dress. His hands were on her hips as he looked at her slowly and thoroughly. Her mouth went dry and she inhaled, trying to get her breath.

"Gabe—"

He pulled her into his arms to kiss her. She wound her arms around his neck and returned his kisses, wanting him as badly as she had in the night, but she knew they needed to get back to the ranch, so she pushed against his chest again. "Gabe, we have to go."

"Let's shower."

"No way. I'll shower by myself and you shower alone. We need to get back to the ranch."

She left him, and within the hour they were on the highway, headed home. Gabe pressed her hand on his thigh and she felt a closeness with him that she hadn't known before. At the same time, a shyness about him gripped her because she still didn't know what was in his heart.

They talked about the ranch, about Julian, about Ella, but Ashley kept wondering about them. How much would their lives change now?

When they moved down the hall, Gabe went into her bedroom with her and closed the door behind him. They stood in moonlight as he leaned against the door and pulled her to him.

"Gabe—"

"I'll just be here a minute. I wanted to ask you to come stay with me. Move into my bedroom, Ashley," he said.

She drew a deep breath. "I will," she answered, "but I think I'd like to break the news first that we'll be husband and wife and the business arrangement has changed. I'd like to tell Dad instead of just coming out of your room in a few hours."

"Whatever you want," Gabe said. "Only do it soon."

"After all the flowers you've sent and our dates, I don't think Dad will be surprised."

"Nope, he won't. 'Night, darlin'." Gabe kissed her long and hard, pulling her tightly against him, tugging up her dress to slide his hand over her bottom and against her bare back.

"Ashley, you can't imagine how much I want you," he

whispered. He left quietly, closing the door behind him and she leaned against it, wanting to go with him tonight, to spend the next hours in his arms, to love again.

She moved to the window to look at the ranch that had brought her this marriage. She loved Julian and she loved Gabe. And she thought Gabe was beginning to love her. She knew Julian did.

"I love you, Gabriel Brant," she whispered. "I want you to love me in return."

When she climbed into bed later, she lay in the dark, thinking about the night, about Gabe's lovemaking. She longed to be in his bed, in his arms. She hoped he was as awake as she was, wanting her there as much as she wanted to be with him.

Later, when Gabe stayed with the napping children, Ashley strolled toward the corral where she could see her father working with a horse.

She perched on the fence to watch him and when he was finished, she walked around with him to water and groom the horse.

"Dad, I wanted to tell you that I'm moving in with Gabe."

Her father looked around, his eyes narrowing as he studied her, and a blush heated her cheeks.

"Are you in love with him?"

She nodded. "Yes, I am."

Quinn nodded. "Then that's good." He put down the brush and turned to hug her lightly. He stepped back with his hands on her shoulders. "I hope both of you are very happy. A good marriage is a wonderful thing. I'm not surprised, honey."

"I didn't think you would be. The flowers are a giveaway."

"Yeah, that and Gabe is getting a little absentminded. His thoughts are elsewhere."

"Oh, my," she said, surprised.

Quinn smiled and turned back to grooming the sorrel.

She stood talking to her father for the next few minutes and then returned to the house, her thoughts on Gabe. She went to his room, stepping inside and looking around, moving idly around the room. Since he had moved in, bringing his own bedroom furniture, she had been in his room a couple of times, but not often. She had been in there enough to notice now that pictures of his former wife were no longer on display, and she wondered how long ago he had moved them.

"Like what you see?" he asked and she whirled around to see Gabe standing in the doorway.

"I thought you were working on the books."

"Nope. And your dad has Julian and Ella now."

Gabe wore a T-shirt, jeans and boots and he looked sexy, too appealing. Unable to resist, she flew across the room into his arms and he caught her up, kissing her hungrily.

"Darlin', I want you more than you can ever know," he said gruffly, holding her tightly, his gaze sweeping over her face before he kissed her again. His arms were strong and tight around her, and her pulse roared. She wanted him, wanted his kisses, wanted to kiss him in return.

"Gabe, I've told Dad I'm moving in here."

He looked up at her. "Good. You'll move in tonight, won't you?"

"Yes." She could feel the sparks jump between them and she longed to stay in his arms, but she knew she should go see about supper and the children. "I'd better go."

As soon as she left, he gathered up belongings that needed to be moved to make room for her and he mulled over how deep his feelings ran for her. Ranch or no ranch, he wanted her. He was in love with his wife.

His gaze shifted to the bed. She was moving in here tonight. His pulse jumped at the thought, but he wanted more, so much more. And she deserved more.

The following weeks were bliss for Ashley who felt incredibly fortunate.

Julian and her father left with her aunt and uncle for Wyoming, so at night she was there with only Ella and Gabe.

It was early December and Ashley was in a dreamworld, cherishing moments together with Gabe and enjoying having the house just to the three of them for a little while. They had given Lou and Mrs. Farrin the week off and Ashley found it easy to manage for just Gabe, Ella and herself.

One morning Ashley hummed as she worked chopping onions and green peppers. A few feet away Ella was in a swing that gently moved back and forth while she played with toys secured to the tray in front of her.

While Ashley chopped food, she glanced out the window and was startled to see Gus approaching the house. One look at the slump in his shoulders and the grim set of his jaw, and her heart missed a beat because something was terribly wrong.

Her first thought was her father, but instantly she knew he was traveling so it couldn't be him. Gabe! Something had happened to Gabe. Grabbing up Ella, Ashley flew out the back door as Gus came across the yard. It was an overcast, chilly December day, but the cold that gripped her wasn't from the weather.

"What's happened? Is Gabe hurt?"

"No one is hurt," he said, and she almost shook with relief. Pinpoints of fire were in Gus's eyes, and she realized he was angry along with his bad news.

"What is it, Gus?"

"Your dad is gone." He hitched his hand in his belt. "Your husband is running cattle on this ranch and he's taking a huge chunk of land to do it. Far more than the quarter you said he'd agreed to. He's had me move the horses—"

For a moment she didn't hear what else Gus was saying because of the buzzing in her head. She became lightheaded while pain stabbed through her.

Gabe had broken his promises. He was taking over the

ranch and changing it without telling her or discussing it. Betrayal ripped through her, hurting so badly, she almost doubled over.

"How long ago did he start doing this?" she asked, still not hearing what Gus was telling her.

"Ashley, I'm sure as hell sorry. Do you want to go inside where it's warmer and you can sit down?"

"Come in," she said, thinking she should offer him a cup of coffee. "Come have coffee."

They walked in silence to the kitchen. By this time Ella was dozing. "Pour yourself a cup, Gus, while I put the baby down for her morning nap."

While she carried Ella to bed, fury and hurt battled in her. *How could he?* The question ran through her mind over and over as she placed Ella in her crib and left the room. She went to the bedroom she shared with Gabe, looking at the bed and thinking of all the hours of lovemaking and talk they shared at night. She was so close to him, so in love with him. And all the time he had gone behind her back and broken his promises to use only a quarter of their land. His word was worthless.

She was furious and hurt, beyond any hurt she had had in Chicago. He had betrayed her trust. Gabe was after the Triple R. Uncle Dusty had been right.

She thought of Julian, traveling with her dad. How could Gabe do this? Their lives were so entwined, but maybe that's what he had counted on. She was in his bed, loving him while he was getting everything he wanted, including the Triple R.

She ran her fingers across her forehead, remembering she had left Gus waiting in the kitchen.

Hurrying back to the kitchen, she found Gus seated at the kitchen table with a cup of steaming black coffee in front of him. She got cookies from the cookie jar, placing them on a plate in front of him. Then she pulled out a chair and sat facing him.

"Where are the cattle?" she asked.

She listened as he told her that they were in sections all along the ranch border spreading out toward the center of the ranch. Far enough away that her father would not be likely to see them.

"He did this while Dad was gone," she said woodenly.

"He started before that, but your dad isn't all over the ranch as often since Gabe stepped in. He hasn't needed to be and that's been better for your dad."

"Better for Gabe. What's he said to you about the cattle?"

A muscle worked in Gus's jaw. "He said it was okay with you and Quinn."

She rubbed her forehead again. "How could Gabe do that behind our backs?"

"Ashley, I'm sorry. Now when Quinn gets home, I have an obligation to tell him."

"I'll tell him," she said, looking into Gus's angry face. "You'll have to talk to him, too, but I'll tell him. And before he gets home, I'll tell Gabe to get his cattle off of our land," she said angrily.

"He may and he may not. I don't think you have much recourse if he doesn't want to."

"I want to take care of this, Gus, before Dad gets home Sunday."

"Ashley, anything you want me to do, I will. If you want me to get those cattle off this land, I'll do it, but if Gabe wants to get the sheriff out here, then there's little any of us can do. You're married now and this ranch is his, too."

"He'll get those cattle off our land, Gus," she said harshly, thinking of the old feud that might burst into existence before sundown.

Gus stood, crossing to the sink to rinse his cup. "I'll get back to work. You want me, you know I have my pager."

She went to the door to see him out. She watched him stride away and her gaze slid past him to the sprawling land beyond him. Gabe was out there somewhere. He usually called her several times during the day, but now she didn't want to talk to him over the phone.

"How could you do this?" she asked the empty kitchen, seeing Gabe as if he were present.

Her fists were clenched. Had he known all along that's exactly what he intended to do? That thought hurt the most.

The day passed in a fog. In the afternoon she put Ella into her carrier, buckled it into the pickup and drove out to see for herself, her thoughts seething all the time. She had walked into this paper marriage and then into his arms and bed willingly, so gullible and trusting.

She hurt all over as if she were bruised everywhere, yet it was only her heart that was bruised.

On a high hill she parked beneath a tall oak and climbed out, taking binoculars with her. She stood looking over a vast spread of their land and her hurt intensified. She couldn't guess how many head of cattle she was viewing. It looked like all the cattle Gabe owned had been moved to her ranch. As her gaze swept the area, she saw men on horses, separating some of the cattle.

Gabe was easy to spot. Although she could see him, she raised the binoculars, brought him into focus so he looked only yards away.

He sat tall in the saddle, his black Stetson squarely on his head as he rode in the mingling herd. She was unaware of the hot tears that rolled down her cheeks or the angry trembling that shook her. Nothing had ever hurt her as this did. Nor had anything ever made her as angry.

What a fool she had been! Yet even the sight of him now made her pulse jump and her breath catch. He had seduced her and tricked her and deceived her. And she loved him with all her heart, yet she couldn't live with this because it would hurt her father. Her stomach churned and she lost what food she had eaten earlier that morning.

That evening, after getting Ella to bed, Ashley sat in the kitchen, her thoughts seething, waiting for Gabe to get home.

Losing Gabe hurt incredibly. Losing Julian added to the terrible pain, but she wasn't going to accept what Gabe had done and let him take the ranch and hurt her father.

She heard Gabe's footsteps on the porch. He was late, which was just as well.

The back door swung opened and he strode into the room and stopped as he closed the door behind him. His eyes narrowed.

"What's wrong, Ashley? Where's Ella? Are Julian and Quinn all right?"

Twelve

"**A**ll of them are fine," she answered evenly.

"Well, something sure as hell is wrong," he said, hanging his hat on a hook and tossing his denim jacket over a chair. He wore a long-sleeved blue plaid Western shirt beneath the jacket. "What's the matter?" Switching on a light, he stood facing her with his hands on his hips.

She came to her feet, her fury mushrooming. "What's the matter is you've broken your promise to me. You're running cattle all over this ranch."

"Is that all?"

"All?" She shook, clenching her fists at her sides. "You promised me that you would use only a quarter of the Triple R."

"It's just cattle, Ashley. I was going to tell you and I'm sorry I didn't."

"You're taking the Triple R from us!"

"I'm not taking anything! Ashley, you're overreacting.

I should have told you, but I thought we were sharing all this.''

"Dammit! You don't mean sharing. You mean you thought you could step in and grab everything. You've talked me into your bed and now you've got everything you wanted.''

"Look, I think you were willing to get into my bed. And I didn't think I was taking anything from you.''

"You promised me you wouldn't make changes without telling me.''

"I said I was sorry, but cattle have been the last thing on my mind when I got home the past few weeks.''

"If that isn't a fast-talking hustler, I don't know what is! I'm not having my dad come home to this. Get those animals off this land tomorrow!''

Gabe's eyes narrowed. "That's ridiculous.''

"No, it's not. This is my land, and I want your cows off it.''

"Can I wash up and then can we sit down and discuss this like rational people? Where's Ella?''

"She's down for the night. And no, there really isn't much to discuss. Gabe, I want every Brant animal off our land by this time tomorrow night.''

"Look, I've bought a lot more cattle and I need more room and I thought that was understood and part of the deal.''

"No. It wasn't understood. Don't tell me now that I'm supposed to *understand* the changes you're making to our ranch. It definitely wasn't any part of the deal. Just the opposite. You weren't supposed to do this.''

"Well, how about giving me a little longer than twenty-four hours? Don't you think that's unreasonable?''

"No more unreasonable than you breaking your promise. I trusted you!''

"Well, hell. I don't think I've broken any promise except to tell you about the cattle and I explained why I didn't do that. You're overreacting and you're being unreasonable.''

"No. I'm protecting my family's land and rights. Today you have cattle on our ranch. Tomorrow you'll get rid of a lot of the horses. You'll bring more cattle and suddenly, you're running this ranch and horses are gone."

"That isn't what I intend at all."

"I can't believe you. I was foolish to trust you, so gullible, believing everything you said, falling in love with you—"

"If you were really in love with me, I don't think you'd act so unreasonably now, and I don't think you can turn love off in less than a few hours."

"Don't talk to me about love or trust or reason," she cried, furious with him and wanting to pound on his chest. Yet she stood still, trembling slightly as she glared at him. "You get those cattle out of here and you get yourself out of here."

He inhaled swiftly. "Just like that, Ashley? After all we had—"

"All we had was an illusion! I trusted you and you know how important that was to me. The most important thing. And you destroyed that trust." She shook with anger. She kept her voice even and kept her control, but she wanted to scream at him and throw things.

"All I've done is bring some cattle over on this ranch. You're ending our marriage and throwing me out over that?"

"You're damned right I am," she snapped.

"All right. You want me out of here—I'm out. I'll get the cattle as fast as I can."

"You get them completely off this land before my father gets home."

"If you think he's going to be happy with what you've done, you're dead wrong."

"I know my father better than you do."

"Maybe you don't. I'm working with him daily and he tells me things he doesn't want to worry you with."

"Don't you dare tell me that he said you could bring all those herds on our ranch."

"No, he didn't because I didn't ask him. I didn't think it was necessary to ask either one of you."

"Just try to answer me honestly—have you gotten rid of any of the horses? You promised to leave them alone."

He glared at her. "That's not fair, Ashley. There was a reason to get rid of the ones I did. Your dad has bought and sold horses all his life. He didn't expect me to keep the status quo and never sell a horse."

"How many have you bought since we got married?"

"I haven't bought any, but that doesn't mean I won't sometime."

"How many have you sold?"

"Look, that isn't fair."

"Answer me."

"I've sold eight. They needed to be sold. Your father doesn't want to work with them like he once did."

"Save your excuses. I don't believe them, either. Uncle Dusty was oh, so right."

"I wondered how long before you'd throw that at me," he said. His dark eyes were filled with fire. "It looks to me like where I made a mistake was in thinking we had a real marriage. I trusted you about that, Ashley."

"Get out, Gabe. Just get out. When you want to move your things, you let me know. I'll make arrangements so I won't have to be here."

"Fine," he snapped and jammed his hat on his head, yanked up his jacket and slammed out of the house. In minutes she heard his pickup roar to life and then it faded away. Sitting down, she folded her arms on the table and put her head down to cry, still suffering both hurt and anger, knowing that her marriage had just ended and she had lost Gabe and Julian.

Yet she knew she was right. If she had let him talk her into accepting what he had done, it was a step toward tak-

ing over completely and she couldn't imagine how that
would hurt her father.

She went upstairs to her old room, avoiding the room
she had shared with Gabe, trying to stop the memories that
plagued her and hearing his arguments swirl in her
thoughts. Most of all, she wanted to protect her father. At
this point in his life, he didn't need to fight to keep his
horse ranch.

She sat by the window thinking that if it weren't for her
father, she might feel differently. That, and the fact that
Gabe had broken his promise to tell her if he made changes.
Yet, how earnest he had sounded. But then he always did
when he was trying to talk her into something.

"Gabe," she whispered, "why?"

Gabe sat at a bar at a roadside honky-tonk twenty miles
from his ranch. He nursed his third beer morosely, running
off anyone who tried to talk to him; no one had attempted
that for over an hour now. He didn't want to go home to
an empty house that held sad memories. He didn't want to
be alone. He wanted Ashley. No matter how unreasonable
she was being, he loved her and he wanted her.

A Western tune played on the jukebox, and several men
played pool in one corner. Only one other person sat at the
bar, and he was at the far end from Gabe.

"Cowboy, it's time to go home."

Gabe looked around to see Josh Kellogg sit down beside
him.

"What are you doing here at this hour?" Gabe asked.
"I didn't think you hit the bars much."

"Don't. I heard you were here."

"Tank? He was in here earlier and saw me."

"Yep and he's worried about you, so he called me."

"I don't need a nanny, Josh. Go home."

"Where's your wife?" Josh asked.

"She threw me out." Gabe took a long drink of beer

and set the bottle down, glancing at Josh. "Just like that, it's over."

"Come on. I'll go home with you, and you can tell me about it," Josh said.

"I don't want to talk to anyone, and I can get myself home."

"You always were as stubborn as a mule. You can tell me, and it'll help. Maybe you need some marriage counseling."

Gabe couldn't keep from smiling. "You would be the last person on earth to be a marriage counselor. What you know about women would fit in this bottle and leave a lot of room for beer."

"Is that right?"

"Yes."

"Well, what I know about someone hurting is plenty, so let's get going. Do I have to drag you out, or are you coming on your own steam?"

"It isn't worth fighting you for." Gabe said, sliding off the barstool and walking out with Josh, knowing he had to go home sometime, so he might as well do it and get it over with. Better get used to it before Julian got home.

At Gabe's pickup he turned to his friend. "Thanks, buddy. Your intentions are good, even if unwanted and annoying."

"Give me your keys."

"I'm cold sober."

"Yeah, and I'm ten feet tall. Give me the keys."

"Here," Gabe said in disgust, handing over his keys, not wanting to fight his best friend. And he knew Josh well enough to know he would fight. Josh slid behind the wheel of Gabe's pickup and they drove in silence halfway to the ranch.

"She threw me out over a bunch of cows. She thinks I'm taking her ranch from her."

"Are you?"

"I thought since we were married, that we were sharing all of it."

"How important are those cows?"

Gabe was silent, staring at the dark night and missing Ashley. "I love her," he said, looking out the window and forgetting he was talking to Josh.

"Did you tell her that?" Josh asked.

"She knows I love her."

"That's not like telling someone."

"Are you going to do this all the way home?"

"Nope. I'll shut up, but I hate to see you hurt again."

Gabe rode in silence and to his relief, Josh stayed silent. At the ranch Josh came in with him.

"No one has been in this house for awhile. I'll light a fire, and it'll get the musty smell out."

"You'll set yourself on fire. I'll light it. Want me to get some guys and help you move your cows?"

"Nope. We can do it."

"You know, I almost want to punch you myself," Josh said, glaring at Gabe. "What hacks me about this is I swore to Ashley that she could trust you to keep your word. Now it sounds to me like you didn't do that. Did you make a liar out of me?"

Gabe shot him a look. "Go to hell, Josh. Or at least go home."

"So you did. Well, dammit. That takes the cake. Now I owe her a big apology."

Gabe remained silent, staring at the flames roaring in the fireplace and still seeing Ashley, knowing that all day long he had expected to come home to dinner with her and love her into the early hours. Instead, his marriage had crashed and burned.

"I do love her, Josh," he said almost an hour later. He glanced at his friend to see Josh stretched on the sofa, boots pulled off, hands folded on his chest as he slept.

"I love her a hell of a lot," he said softly, sinking lower in his chair. "More than a bunch of stinking cows." He wanted her. He glanced at the phone, but knew calling her wouldn't do him any good. He had to get his cattle off her land and then make some decisions.

Four nights later, Saturday, Gabe ate at the bunkhouse with his men. Josh and two of his men had helped and they ate with them. Afterwards, Josh walked up to the house with him. At Josh's pickup, Gabe turned to shake hands with him. "Thanks for helping me. We got it done, and my cows are home. Now I've got to move my things and Julian's home."

"Try to talk to her again, Gabe."

"I don't think it will do any good."

"Never know until you try. Let me know if you need more help."

As Josh drove off, Gabe went into the empty house. Tomorrow Julian would be home.

Gabe hurt, missing Ashley and wanting her. Ashley had been unreasonable, furious and lashing out at him, and he had been angry in turn. He raked his fingers through his hair and moved restlessly.

He missed Ashley and he missed Ella. He wanted to see his baby, and he wanted to be with his wife.

He should have told Ashley what he was doing, but it had never occurred to him that she would feel threatened by it. He had simply assumed that they would share both ranches. And Quinn had made it clear that he couldn't continue working as much as he had before.

Gabe hadn't slept last night and he didn't see much hope for tonight. He missed his wife, and didn't want it to end this way.

Ashley fed Ella and put her to bed. She had talked on the phone each night to Julian and Quinn. She didn't want to tell her father about Gabe until he was home. She didn't want to upset his trip, because it sounded as if they were all having a wonderful time. And she wasn't ready to hear a lot of "I told you so's" from her uncle.

Sunday evening, when Quinn and Julian arrived home, Gabe came over to get his son. The moment Gabe stepped out of his pickup, Ashley's heart lurched. In his jeans and a navy sweater, he looked incredibly handsome, and she longed for what they'd had. Yet beneath her longing was a hot thread of anger. He looked purposeful, just as he had looked the first few times he had come to the ranch, yet even so, she had to fight the urge to run and throw herself into his arms.

His dark gaze met hers. While she drew a swift breath, her insides clutched and she hurt badly. Her father and Julian were too busy to notice. Julian ran to Gabe's arms and then Gabe and Quinn were shaking hands.

When Julian ran to her and she picked him up, her head swam. *Her son.* That's how she thought of Julian now. Hot tears stung her eyes, and she squeezed Julian. She didn't want to lose him, and she knew he needed her. Pain enveloped her, and she opened her eyes to meet Gabe's hard stare.

Setting down Julian, she turned. Everyone went into the house. Kate wanted to hold Ella, and it was an hour before her aunt and uncle drove away.

Gabe took Ella from her father and Ashley saw him hug the little baby and then cradle her in his arms, Ashley busied herself with Julian.

Gabe asked Quinn to come with him and she knew he was going to tell Quinn about the cattle before she had a chance.

Gabe handed Ella to Ashley, and she looked into dark, unreadable eyes. A muscle worked in his jaw, and she hurt, watching him turn away to join her father. They left, heading toward the stables.

When they returned, Gabe explained to his son that they were going back to their old house. Julian mildly protested, but at a look from Gabe he quieted and kissed Quinn and Ashley goodbye, unaware it would be longer than for just an evening. Standing in the kitchen to watch them drive away, Ashley fought back tears. She wanted Gabe and Julian back. Their marriage had been wonderful, and it had held such glittering prospects. She hugged herself and turned around to face her father.

"Ashley, let's talk," her dad said, pulling out a kitchen chair to sit down.

"I know Gabe has already told you that when I found out about the cattle, I told him to get them and himself off our land," she said, turning to look at her father.

"Yes, he did tell me. And he got his cattle home. Ashley, I have the feeling that you think you're protecting me. I don't care if Gabe keeps some of his cattle on our land."

"You don't care?" Stunned and upset, she stared at him.

"No, I don't. I'm tired of taking care of this great big ranch and he can do a fine job. He's a fine rancher and he's a good daddy for Ella."

"When I started seeing him, you were so angry and worried that he would steal the ranch from us."

"I know I was, because of the old feud, but he's become one of us. He's Ella's daddy in every way except blood kin. He's taken so much of the load off of my shoulders, and frankly, I don't miss it. And I love Julian. I don't want to lose that little boy. He's my grandson now."

She sat down on the edge of a chair. "You don't care?"

"No, I don't. I'm glad for him to take charge of some of this. Do you want to do it?"

"No, not by myself."

"I don't either any longer. Ashley, I've worked hard all my life. I was beginning to enjoy Julian and Ella and I had this nice trip. I never could do that before. Gabe is going to make this place turn a profit again."

"I had no idea—"

"Honey, Gabe's suffering."

She brought her attention back to her father and then thought about Gabe. "So am I," she said, still adjusting to what her father had said.

"Then why don't you get them back here?" he asked

gently. "Julian is going to be one unhappy little boy tonight. He's losing another mama."

"Oh, Dad—" She flew to the bedroom she had shared with Gabe to close the door and yank up the phone.

When he didn't answer, she called his cellular number. As soon as Gabe answered, she clutched the phone tightly and closed her eyes.

"Can I come see you?"

"Yes," he answered solemnly. "I'll be home in another ten minutes."

"Don't tell Julian about us until we can talk, please."

"Julian's asleep. I think he's exhausted."

"I'll be right there," she said. She ran to the back door. "Dad, I'm going to see Gabe. I'll be at his place, and if I leave to come home, I'll call you."

Quinn was finishing a glass of milk. "Honey, you get Gabe to check on your whereabouts. In ten minutes, I'm going to be asleep for the night. I won't hear the phone."

"Okay," she said, blowing him a kiss. She raced out the door to their pickup and climbed in, still thinking about what her father had said.

The drive to Gabe's house seemed interminable, but finally she was there and knocking on his door. It swung open, and he leaned a shoulder against a doorjamb. "Want to come in?"

When she nodded, he stepped back, and she hurried past him, shedding her jacket as she crossed the room. She turned to look at him.

"Gabe, I was wrong."

His brows arched and he drew a deep breath. "Ashley, the damn cows don't matter to me. I'll keep them on the Circle B land. All I want is you and Ella back."

Relief and joy flooded her, and she ran to throw herself into his arms. He caught her up, crushing her against his chest to kiss her long and hard.

She kissed him back wildly, wanting him, and then all

the joy over being together again burned into flames of passion. Gabe picked her up to carry her to his room.

Clothes were tossed aside, and then Gabe laid her on his bed. His hands were everywhere, his tongue setting her on fire while she couldn't get enough of touching him.

He moved between her legs, gazing down at her before coming down and entering her swiftly.

They moved together and she was lost in sensation that built as her roaring pulse drowned out the world until she heard him cry her name.

"Ashley, my love!"

She held him tightly, her heart pounding with joy.

Later, she lay in his arms, stroking him lightly while he held her.

Gabe shifted away from her and stood. "I have a surprise for you. I got it last week." He came back to bed and handed her a large flat package.

Tucking the sheet beneath her arms, she looked at him. "What on earth?"

"Open it and see."

Ashley ripped away wrapping paper to hold up a picture. It was the one Quinn had taken of Gabe and Ashley standing in front of the wild, white stallion the evening Gabe had caught the horse.

"Gabe, I love it!"

He grinned. "Well, we brought some credibility to the old legend, didn't we, darlin'?"

She smiled, set down the picture and turned to wrap her arms around him. "We surely did."

She pulled his head down, kissing him, knowing she would remember this night forever. In minutes, she leaned away.

"Gabe, come back. And you can bring your cattle back. Dad and I had a talk. I didn't know he liked what you were doing and was glad to have you take charge."

"Yeah, I talked to him tonight. I just didn't think, darlin'. I should have told you. I knew your dad was happy and I thought you were."

"I was, Gabe. Happy beyond all I dreamed about."

"I want you. I don't care what we do with the cattle."

She ran her fingertips over his muscled shoulder. "We ought to change the name of the two ranches so it's just one."

"It's fine with me, but all our relatives will howl."

"Let them howl. They'll adjust, just like they did to our marriage. You know what else I'd like someday?"

"What?" he asked.

She ran her fingers through his thick hair. "A long time ago you said two children would be enough for you."

Gabe's eyes darkened and his brows arched. "And?"

"I told you I might not be able to have another baby, but during this next year, I'd like to try."

Gabe leaned down to kiss her. "I think that's a grand idea," he said, pausing to look at her. "I love you, darlin', with all my heart."

"Oh, Gabe," Ashley whispered, pulling him to her and knowing her family was the most important thing in her life. "I love you more than you can ever know."

While he wrapped her in his strong arms, Ashley sighed with contentment, certain that her trust had been well placed and she was with the love of her life.

* * * * *

Don't miss Josh's story,

One Tough Cowboy
by Sara Orwig,

the second book in her new series

STALLION PASS

*Coming to Silhouette Sensation
in October 2003.
And now, for a sneak preview of this
exciting story, turn the page.*

One Tough Cowboy

by

Sara Orwig

The sound began as a distant rumble. On the wooded hill-side that was part of his Texas ranch, Josh Kellogg's hands stilled while he raised his head to listen. The damp, foggy February afternoon had been quiet, but now the sound in the distance was growing in volume. Deciding it was just an approaching car, Josh bent over his barbed wire fence and continued to repair what had been ripped up in a storm during the night.

He raised his head again, listening to the approaching whine until it had become a roar that sounded like a car accelerating to an incredibly high speed.

Someone was in a hell of a hurry, he decided. Fog limited visibility, and he knew that a quarter of a mile to the west the road curved, so even on a clear day, he wouldn't be able to see much farther. Something was wrong about this noise. It wasn't the usual engine rumble made by cars and pickups that traveled past his ranch.

The county road was lightly traveled, mostly by neigh-

bors and people he knew, and Josh was certain this would
be neither. He knew his guess was right when a gray sedan
came around the curve, tires squealing, going off the road
slightly to spew mud and gravel into the air. Immediately
behind the gray car was a black one—two cars, each pushing powerful engines to dangerous speeds. The black four-
door sedan gained on the gray car, almost touching its
bumper.

"Damnation!" Josh said under his breath while he
watched the cars flash past as if they were on a raceway
and not a curvy country road.

He knew every foot of road in this county, particularly
the stretch of asphalt in front of his ranch, and he knew the
next curve was too sharp for such high speeds. Concerned
they wouldn't make the turn safely, he dashed up the
incline.

As Josh reached the road, the lead car swung into the
curve. Stunned, he watched as the second car pulled alongside to sideswipe the first car.

"Hey!" he yelled in angry protest as he raced toward
them.

Above the roar of engines, metal clanged against metal.
The first driver lost control. The gray car tore off the road
and plowed down the ravine churning up weeds and mud,
smashing brush.

Metal scraping against bushes and branches, the car ran
through the creek, hit a tree, rolled a little farther and
smashed into another tree. The crumple of metal mixed
with the tinkle of breaking glass and the hiss of steam from
the radiator. An ominous silence settled. The black car disappeared around the bend and into the fog.

Fearing the worst, Josh rushed toward the wreck. As he
neared, Josh could see that the metal was crumpled and
crushed, the windows shattered. A spiral of smoke came
from the wreck as he approached. He smelled gasoline.

The closer he came, the stronger the stench of gasoline.
If someone were still alive, Josh knew he had to get them

out of the car in a hurry. A red curl of flame licked up from the crumpled hood.

Stopping beside the car, Josh looked inside. A woman was flung face down across the front seat with her long brown hair hiding her face and shoulders. The buckled roof narrowed the space above her. Shards and jagged pieces of glass covered her and the seat. One of her hands bled with cuts from the broken glass.

When he tried to open the door, he couldn't. The roof of the car was smashed too low, so he went around to the passenger side. He reached through the broken window to check her throat for a pulse.

To his relief, she felt warm to the touch and had a strong pulse. When he pushed her hair away from her face, he saw that she had a deep cut across her temple. She groaned and stirred.

He bent down to talk to her through the open window that now held only shards of jagged glass. "Lady, I have to get you away from this wreck."

Suddenly, Josh found himself face to face with enormous brown eyes that momentarily stunned him. For a frozen instant they stared at each other, and in that instant he forgot the wreck and the danger.

Then, she scrambled wildly away from him, twisting around and trying frantically to open the door on the driver's side.

She bent almost double to push the door in a futile effort to escape.

Josh leaned in and caught her jacket, yanking her toward him. His hands grasped her beneath her arms, pulling her to the passenger side. "Let me get you out."

To his surprise, the woman fought him. She jerked away from him and twisted around to strike at him.

"I want to help you," he told her forcefully, and he caught her tightly beneath her arms, hauling her across the seat and through the broken window. He hoped her clothes were protecting her from the jagged glass. He swung her into his arms.

She fought wildly, and he tightened his grip. "Be still!" he snapped. "I'm trying to help you." She quieted, wrapping her arms around his neck.

She stared, wide-eyed, at him, her lips slightly parted while her arms tightened around his neck. He inhaled, catching the smell of gasoline that stabbed him with an awareness of their increasing danger.

"We've got to get away from the car," he muttered.

"My things!" she cried.

"The hell with them," he said, holding her tightly and running across the creek, heading west and angling up the ravine.

She was light in his arms, easy to carry, and he was intensely aware of her body pressed against him. He dodged behind a thick oak and sat down with the woman on his lap, trying to cover her and bracing for a blast that he was certain would happen.

As soon as he sat down, she struggled to break free.

"Let go of me!" she cried.

He tightened his grip, enveloping her and holding her tightly against him. This was one stubborn woman. "Stop fighting me! You'll hurt yourself. The car is going—"

There was a whumpf as the flames found the gasoline and a loud blast ended his conversation. Josh leaned around the tree to look.

A fireball shot into the air, yellow and orange flames twisting high through dark green leaves and brown branches. A column of black smoke followed. The ground shook with the blast, and Josh ducked back behind the tree. After a few long seconds, he leaned around again.

Bits and pieces of metal, chrome, clothing and money rained down. He stared at the money. Some fell back into the fire, but other bills tumbled through the trees, drifting to earth.

He released her slightly, and she raised her head to again stare at him wide-eyed in obvious shock.

"I have to go!" she cried, fighting his hold.

"Where do you have to go?" he demanded.

She gave him another startled look and went still.

"You're in shock and you're bleeding badly. Just sit still and let me get some pressure on that cut," he ordered, his patience gone. "You're safe. Don't worry," he said.

She merely stared at him in silence, but she was sitting still and doing what he told her to do. Even though her leg was bleeding with a dark stain spreading along the jeans covering her thigh, her head wound needed attention first. He retrieved the brown blanket, shook it out and covered her with it, tucking it around her, and received a trusting look that made his insides tighten.

Josh opened the first-aid kit and pulled out the gauze, taking out his knife to cut it. He picked up a bottle of antiseptic, glanced at her to find her watching him in silence. While the sedan crackled and burned, Josh heard the noise of an approaching car, then the slam of a car door.

Josh froze and placed his finger on the woman's lips to silence her. In seconds he spotted a dark figure emerge from the fog and hurry down the ravine toward the crash. Whoever had run her off the road had come back. Hot anger flashed through Josh—the man had attempted murder.

Josh leaned forward to put his mouth near her ear. "Don't move or make a sound," he commanded. "I'll be back."

Josh stood, running as quietly as he could. He had only a few seconds before the man's head whipped around in Josh's direction.

Instantly, the man reversed his course, turning to run back up the incline for the road.

Josh stretched out his legs, racing after him and gaining. The man spun around and raised a gun.

Josh threw himself behind a tree, a blast shattered the quiet. Then he was out, racing after the man again.

Furious and determined, Josh rushed forward again, seeing the shooter race up the incline, reach the road and dash for his black car.

Lunging for the car, Josh landed on the trunk, but he couldn't get a grip anywhere. He slid across the smooth metal, and fell.

Swearing in pain as he hit the ground, Josh rolled over and stared at the license plate, memorizing the number as the car sped away.

Staring at the empty roadway, angry and frustrated that the man had escaped, Josh got to his feet.

He headed back to the woman. On his way, he found his hat and jammed it back on his head.

She, as well as the blanket, was gone.

* * *

Don't forget One Tough Cowboy *by Sara Orwig will be on the shelves in October 2003 from Silhouette Sensation.*

0903/51a

SILHOUETTE®
DESIRE™ 2-IN-1
AVAILABLE FROM 19TH SEPTEMBER 2003

RIDE THE THUNDER Lindsay McKenna

Morgan's Mercenaries

Beautiful Lieutenant Rhona McGregor was *dangerous*, but from their first death-defying flight together, Lieutenant Nolan Galway realised they shared something more powerful than passion...

PLAIN JANE MacALLISTER Joan Elliott Pickart

The Baby Bet: MacAllister's Gifts

Emily MacAllister thought she had no chance with her childhood sweetheart, gorgeous Dr Mark Maxwell—until he melted her doubts with kisses. But how would he react when he discovered her secret?

THE SECRET BABY BOND Cindy Gerard

Dynasties: The Connellys

For two years Michael Paige had been missing, presumed dead. But now his memory had returned—could he convince his wife Tara to give their love another chance?

CINDERELLA'S CONVENIENT HUSBAND
Katherine Garbera

Dynasties: The Connellys

Wealthy lawyer Seth Connelly told himself he'd only married Lynn McCoy to help save her home—but then he kissed her...

THE SECRET PRINCE Kathryn Jensen

Elly Anderson turned Dan Eastwood's orderly existence upside down when she told him he was the son of a king. But the unlikely prince had more important things on his mind—like a certain hazel-eyed siren...

THE RAVEN'S ASSIGNMENT Kasey Michaels

The Coltons

Samantha wished someone had warned her that the Special Agent who would be posing as her boyfriend was handsome Jesse Colton. For his 'pretend' kisses were inflaming very real desires...

AVAILABLE FROM 19TH SEPTEMBER 2003

 SILHOUETTE®

Sensation™

Passionate, dramatic, thrilling romances

THE PRINCESS'S BODYGUARD Beverly Barton
SARAH'S KNIGHT Mary McBride
ONE TOUGH COWBOY Sara Orwig
TAKING COVER Catherine Mann
HER GALAHAD Melissa James
ANYTHING FOR HER MARRIAGE Karen Templeton

Special Edition™

Vivid, satisfying romances full of family, life and love

MERCURY RISING Christine Rimmer
HIS MARRIAGE BONUS Cathy Gillen Thacker
THE CUPCAKE QUEEN Patricia Coughlin
WILLOW IN BLOOM Victoria Pade
MY VERY OWN MILLIONAIRE Pat Warren
THE WOMAN FOR DUSTY CONRAD Tori Carrington

Superromance™

*Enjoy the drama, explore the emotions,
experience the relationship*

EXPECTING THE BEST Lynnette Kent
FULL RECOVERY Bobby Hutchinson
WIFE BY DECEPTION Donna Sterling
AN OFFICER AND A HERO Elizabeth Ashtree

Intrigue™

Danger, deception and suspense

ROYAL TARGET Susan Kearney
NAVAJO JUSTICE Aimée Thurlo
McQUEEN'S HEAT Harper Allen
THE BRIDE'S RESCUER Charlotte Douglas

0903/51b

With a Southern Touch

Heather Graham
Diana Palmer
Jennifer Blake

Three new stories from international bestselling authors

On sale 19th September 2003

*Available at most branches of WHSmith,
Tesco, Martins, Borders, Eason, Sainsbury's
and all good paperback bookshops.*

1003/009/SH61

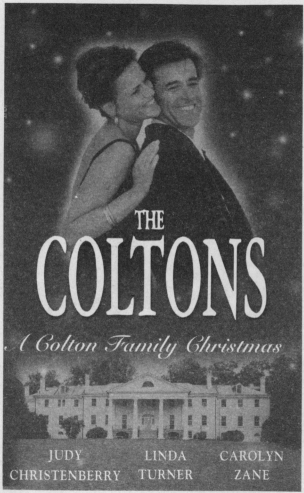

THE
COLTONS

A Colton Family Christmas

JUDY
CHRISTENBERRY

LINDA
TURNER

CAROLYN
ZANE

Maitland Maternity

Where the luckiest babies are born!

The Detective's Dilemma
by Arlene James

A murder charge… A Maitland suspect!
A detective's temptation…

Beth Maitland is not sure she will be able to trust a
man again. After all, her ex-fiancé is trying to frame
her for murder!

Ty Redstone knows his chief
suspect is one of the Maitland
clan. But Beth is nothing like
the pampered princess he
expects…

Vincent Eckart: Why does
this angry stranger accuse
Jake Maitland of stealing
his wife?

Maitland Maternity

Where the luckiest babies are born!

Formula: Father
by Karen Hughes

A long-ago teenage crush… An unexpected reunion… A baby on the way?

Mitchell Maitland: Since his wife died, Mitch has concentrated solely on his career. So it's a good thing the woman of his dreams walks right into his office...

Darcy Taylor: She's got the looks, the fame and the fortune; the one thing she wants is a child—with or without a husband!

Harrison Smith: Another stranger arrives at the clinic, but why is he asking so many questions about the Maitlands?

Karen Hughes
Formula: Father

❤ SILHOUETTE®
DESIRE™

is proud to introduce

DYNASTIES:
THE CONNELLYS

*Meet the royal Connellys—wealthy,
powerful and rocked by scandal,
betrayal...and passion!*

TWELVE GLAMOROUS STORIES IN SIX 2-IN-1 VOLUMES:

February 2003
TALL, DARK & ROYAL by Leanne Banks
MATERNALLY YOURS by Kathie DeNosky

April 2003
THE SHEIKH TAKES A BRIDE by Caroline Cross
THE SEAL'S SURRENDER by Maureen Child

June 2003
PLAIN JANE & DOCTOR DAD by Kate Little
AND THE WINNER GETS...MARRIED! by Metsy Hingle

August 2003
THE ROYAL & THE RUNAWAY BRIDE by Kathryn Jensen
HIS E-MAIL ORDER WIFE by Kristi Gold

October 2003
THE SECRET BABY BOND by Cindy Gerard
CINDERELLA'S CONVENIENT HUSBAND by Katherine Garbera

December 2003
EXPECTING...AND IN DANGER by Eileen Wilks
CHEROKEE MARRIAGE DARE by Sheri WhiteFeather

NORA ROBERTS

Nora Roberts shows readers the lighter side of love in the Big Apple in this fun and romantic volume.

Truly Madly
MANHATTAN

Two fabulous stories about the city that never sleeps...
Local Hero & Dual Image

Available from 17th October 2003

*Available at most branches of WHSmith,
Tesco, Martins, Borders, Eason, Sainsbury's
and most good paperback bookshops.*

SILHOUETTE® SUPERROMANCE™

is pleased to present

Girlfriends

by
Judith Bowen

*Three women who've been best friends for
ten years decide to look up their first
loves. Find out what happens in...*

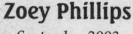

Zoey Phillips
September 2003

Charlotte Moore
November 2003

Lydia Lane
January 2004

0903/SH/LC70

INTRIGUE™

Danger, deception and suspense.

Breathtaking romantic suspense,
full of mystery, deception and
dangerous desires…

SILHOUETTE®

FREE

2 BOOKS
AND A SURPRISE GIFT!

We would like to take this opportunity to thank you for reading this Silhouette® book by offering you the chance to take two more specially selected titles from the Desire™ series absolutely FREE! We're also making this offer to introduce you to the benefits of the Reader Service™—

★ FREE home delivery
★ FREE monthly Newsletter
★ FREE gifts and competitions
★ Exclusive Reader Service discount
★ Books available before they're in the shops

Accepting this FREE book and gift places you under no obligation to buy; you may cancel at any time, even after receiving your free shipment. Simply complete your details below and return the entire page to the address below. ***You don't even need a stamp!***

YES! Please send me 2 free Desire books and a surprise gift. I understand that unless you hear from me, I will receive 3 superb new titles every month for just £4.99 each, postage and packing free. I am under no obligation to purchase any books and may cancel my subscription at any time. The free books and gift will be mine to keep in any case.

D3ZED

Ms/Mrs/Miss/Mr ....Initials..
BLOCK CAPITALS PLEASE

Surname..

Address..

....

....Postcode ....

Send this whole page to:
UK: FREEPOST CN81, Croydon, CR9 3WZ
EIRE: PO Box 4546, Kilcock, County Kildare (stamp required)

Offer valid in UK and Eire only and not available to current Reader Service subscribers to this series. We reserve the right to refuse an application and applicants must be aged 18 years or over. Only one application per household. Terms and prices subject to change without notice. Offer expires 31st December 2003. As a result of this application, you may receive offers from Harlequin Mills & Boon and other carefully selected companies. If you would prefer not to share in this opportunity please write to The Data Manager at the address above.

Silhouette® is a registered trademark used under licence.
Desire™ is being used as a trademark.